THE BEAUTY
OF
THE FALL

THE BEAUTY

OF

THE FALL

RICH MARCELLO

Langdon Street Press, Minneapolis

Langdon Street Press
322 First Avenue N, 5th floor
Minneapolis, MN 55401
612.455.2293
www.langdonstreetpress.com

ISBN-13: 978-1-63505-402-6
LCCN: 2016913226

Distributed by Itasca Books

Edited by Donna Anctil

Cover Design by Emily Keenan
Typeset by Robert Harmon

Printed in the United States of America

Praise for Rich Marcello

"Few novels are as intelligent and relevant as *The Beauty of the Fall*. Almost none is as eloquent, compelling, heartbreaking, and, ultimately, uplifting."

— **MARK SPENCER,**
FAULKNER AWARD WINNER AND AUTHOR OF *GHOSTWALKING*

"Rich Marcello's *The Beauty of the Fall* takes the reader on two intriguing journeys: the exciting coffee-fueled rise of a high-tech start-up and the emotional near-collapse of the man behind the revolutionary company, his personal journey through grief and healing."

— **JESSAMYN HOPE,**
AUTHOR OF *SAFEKEEPING*

"Rich Marcello's third novel, *The Beauty of the Fall*, intermixes poetry and prose fluidly throughout the manuscript, and in fact, incorporates poetry as one of its major themes. As a practicing poet, I was swept away by the lyrical language, the characters, and the unexpected twists and turns in the plot. Overall, a great and inspiring read!"

— **REBECCA GIVENS ROLLAND,**
AUTHOR OF *THE WRECK OF BIRDS*

"*The Color of Home* sings an achingly joyful blues tune. It's the song of lives stripping away the hardened scars until all that's left is the possibility of each other. It's a tune we've all sung, but seldom with such poetry and depth. Read this and weep . . . and laugh, and sing, and sing some more."

— **MYRON ROGERS**,
   CO-AUTHOR OF *A SIMPLER WAY*

"A distinct and original narrative voice and protagonist. Just as there is significance in Holden Caulfied's catch phrases, reviewers and serious readers will find significance in Paige's persistent use of 'you know.' This common and simple phrase resonates in the context of this highly philosophical work . . . Overall, *The Big Wide Calm* is a fabulous novel."

— **MARK SPENCER**,
   AUTHOR OF *TRESPASSERS*

"Weeks after reading *The Color of Home*, I am still reeling. The lyrical prose is captivating, attention-grabbing, but it's the characters who really pull you in. The main characters, Nick and Sassa, are real, relevant, wounded, and their story is one of hope and passion. I found myself rooting for them, even when they made me angry at times. I found myself sucked into their lives, wanting to learn more. Why are they hurting? What's their story? But it seems to me that the story was never actually about them, after all. The story was about me, about you. About all of us. And the journey doesn't end when the reading stops, so be ready to dig way down. Bravo, Rich Marcello! You've done quite a thing."

— **MICHELLE JOSETTE**,
   AUTHOR OF *AFTER HENRY*

"Marcello's novel (*The Big Wide Calm*) has a lot going for it. Well-written, thought-provoking, and filled with flawed characters, it meets all the basic requirements for best-of-show in the literary fiction category."

— THE US REVIEW OF BOOKS

"We all have our own list of what-ifs when it comes to relationships, and often for a lot of us, we tend to play some of it over and over in our heads. Personally, one of my relationship what-ifs is: What if we are absolutely, no-holds-barred, downright honest about everything with our significant other? How different will our relationship be? *The Color of Home* by Rich Marcello explores this standpoint and creates a narrative that is both liberating and heartbreaking."

— BOOK BEAST

"The story of Nick and Sassa was so engrossing for me, but the prose of *The Color of Home* really drew me in as it was written beautifully and yet in a way that wasn't distracting. The characters also weaved in several philosophical thoughts that I enjoyed pondering."

— BUILDABOOKSHELF.COM

"*The Big Wide Calm* is a must read for any fan of music and the struggle to succeed. It's perfect for those who love the idea of chasing down a dream with all your heart and learning life lessons along the way. It will be one of those books that stays with you long after you have read it."

— BOOKINFORM

"The whole songwriting and production processes were very interesting with the intimacy and emotional involvement between songwriters, which made it cool to experience. The preparation (full carafe of coffee), the position (legs crossed on the floor), and even the writing methods (cursive, landscape not portrait) were intriguing relating to the whole creative process. The drive, the ambition, and the paths a determined musician must take to achieve her dream was also very inspirational (getting everything handed to you wouldn't make for an interesting story now would it?)"

— BINDBLOTTYANDCAJOLE.COM ON *THE BIG WIDE CALM*

"This story is also about what happens to your life when you realize you've been living someone else's dream—when you've spent much of your life trying to get to the bottom of a phrase that's stayed with you and hasn't let go, 'the big wide calm.' It's about a relationship between Paige and producer John Bustin, and while it's not traditional (neither of our lead characters are, though, so that's just fine with me), it's engrossing."

— MOONBIRD BOOK REVIEWS

"The fact that Marcello was able to weave some profound stuff together with a good story and a great character is what sets the novel apart. Finally, while *The Big Wide Calm* is a millennial coming-of-age story, it's at its core about truly and deeply learning to love in a troubled world. When I read the last page, and especially the last paragraph, I thought this novel would have made John Lennon proud. I highly recommend this novel to lovers of music, of strong female characters, of bigger existential ideas. It was a heartfelt journey of self-discovery, of forming chosen families, and of finding life-altering love. Go check it out. You won't regret it."

— VIDEOMUSICSTARS.COM

"I didn't want to stop reading this book. It has a great empowering message that fits in with this blog's theme of individual empowerment. One telling trait of a great book is reaching the last page and craving more, which is what happened at the end of *The Big Wide Calm*. This alluring story is full of surprises, making it difficult to put down. You may think you know how things will end, but the twists and turns are not predictable; you will be surprised at how each one plays out."

**— IMPOWERYOU.ORG
(AN INDIVIDUAL EMPOWERMENT BLOG)**

"Lyrics, music, and love come together in this wonderful novel, *The Big Wide Calm*, exploring human relations and development. It will keep you wanting more up to the final page."

— PURPLE BIRCH PUBLISHING BOOK REVIEW

"In *The Big Wide Calm*, Rich Marcello captures a unique voice in the character of Paige Plant, who is intriguingly attractive in the most bizarre way possible. Named after Led Zeppelin members, twenty-something Paige is the kind of YA protagonist that puts others to shame. She is reminiscent of some of the most memorable protagonists in other bildungsroman novels—Alaska Young from Green's *Looking for Alaska*, Holden Caulfield from Salinger's *The Catcher in the Rye*, Hazel Grace Lancaster from Green's *The Fault in Our Stars*, Josephine March from Alcott's *Little Women*. You will root for her from the very beginning, get excited with her in her journey, hope with her that the recording goes well, and share the butterflies in her stomach as she realizes that she's getting closer to her dreams."

— BOOK BEAST

Also by **Rich Marcello**:

THE BIG WIDE CALM

and

THE COLOR OF HOME

For my family

"The problem with the world is that
we draw the circle of our family too small"

–Mother Teresa

PART I—*Fall*

So It Spins

"Dan, Olivia would like to see you now."

Summoned, I hang up the phone, lift off my chair, and exit my corner office. A year in the making, it's about to happen, and even though I had a hunch it was coming, nothing has prepared me for the end walk. As I'm heading to Olivia's office, the last months flash in Technicolor until the credits, the epitaph rolls—*He put his head down, tried to rekindle the wildfire he helped birth years ago, tried to daydream down a riven path. Didn't work, but hey.* Midway, my legs go wobbly, so I restroom to regroup. After I wash my hands and face and adjust my tie, I stare at my regrouped selves in the mirror and recite Willow. She sent me one of her poems the other day after we chatted about my current predicament: *When sudden loss dances / When the inexplicable fogs / When you're about to lose what you love most / Remember this: You're fucked.* Well, that's not exactly the poem. Her last line made some poignant point about all the "Whens" being gifts, but I like my version better.

When I arrive, Olivia, who's waiting for me at her door, blank-faces me into her glass-walled corner office. The place reeks of new paint, new rugs, new leather, power. She sits, calm, hands folded on her mahogany desk, dyed chestnut hair expertly styled, wearing one of her many black bespoke suits. Gold and diamonds adorn her hands, her ears, her neck. Directly over her heart, pinned perfectly, is a pendant shaped like a sickle. I touch down across from her in the seat I've frequented countless times over the years. At least she

1

didn't swap that out. Awards and photos line the wall behind her—RadioRadio Software named one of the best companies to work for in America, opening bell on the day of our IPO, CEO of the Year back in 2008, she and the Dalai Lama at a leadership retreat, the anniversary she gave me a Martin guitar. I'm in one of the awards ceremony photos with her, wearing a black tuxedo with my hair slicked back. When was that one? I had much less gray.

Another picture of the two of us in jeans and T-shirts, during our first year when we still worked out of her house, is still my favorite. I had long hair then; Olivia did too, all the way to the middle of her back. That day, we ate Chinese take-out and background-marathoned Pearl Jam and Nirvana for sixteen hours straight as we worked well into the night. Sometimes I shake my head at how far we've come since those early years in the nineties. I reach down and stroke my plastic employee badge, number 2, securely fastened to my belt. It feels like skin.

The room is unnaturally quiet until Olivia clears her throat and says, "This is going to be a difficult conversation, Dan." Instantly, I zone out. Why listen in the middle of an avalanche when I already know my fate? "Blah. Blah. Blah. We're no longer simpatico. Blah. Blah. Blah. HR will contact you with your package. Blah. Blah. Blah. We'll spin a positive message about your departure."

Right.

I push off my chair, make my way over to one of the glass walls, and stare out into a sea of color. New England in fall. What beauty. Barely touching the glass with my index finger, I cursive R, R, R, R. Sixteen years in this place. Why so long? Well, until recently Olivia touched me. Honestly, if she were a man, she would have been a priest. She rocketed RadioRadio Software from nothing to greatness in a decade, a decade in which we grew triple-digit fast, a decade in which she had the team, the Street, our customers, me, fully bought in. Her sermon—we will change the world; we will do work faster, cheaper, better; we will give the power back to the people. It was the same pitch all hi-tech CEOs used, but nobody delivered it better than Liv. During the ascent, she golden-girled through, well, everything, and I was her right-hand man, helping her craft and implement the vision. Our vision. For fifteen of the sixteen years, she trusted me, respected me, believed in me, valued my advice. Until she didn't.

Olivia joins me at the window and places a hand on my shoulder. "We've been through a lot of autumns, but I don't recall one this vivid."

"I love the fall."

"If there were any other way, Dan."

When growth stopped a year ago, for the first time, big-league adversity loomed over RadioRadio, over Olivia. The stock fell to fifty percent of its fifty-two-week high. We lost two hundred million in a quarter. Many called for her resignation, but somehow she held on. Still, the spotlight judge rocked her, made her second-guess long-standing goals and values, made her hire consultants. Like cancer, they spread through the company; like brain cancer, they crowded me out.

At first, I coped. Olivia had to have her reasons for not inviting me to the consultant meetings, for not wandering into my office every day, for no longer asking my opinion. The board, the Street, had put her under a lot of pressure, and she needed space to search for an answer. I got that. Sometimes, like during our Friday lunches, I convinced myself that we were going through a rough patch, that we were still best friends, that everything was going to be okay, that I would weather the storm of consultants. But most of the time I buried the abundant signs under the now-replaced carpet.

Then, about a month ago, in their full Ivy League, overpriced splendor, after eleven months with little impact, the consultants designed a new narrative. We owe it to our shareholders to reduce spending. Lean and mean is the name of the game. Cut the deadweight. Their goal: rationalize the harm Olivia was about to do to her employees, to the very people who had dedicated their lives to helping her build the twenty-second largest software company in the world. One day, shortly after the new narrative had taken hold, I asked Olivia: "How exactly are living, breathing human beings who built this place deadweight?" That was probably a mistake.

I turn my back to the fall foliage and lean against the window, hands behind my back as a cushion. Olivia takes a step away from me, readies herself for the last barrage.

"We could still pull this thing out together," I say.

"It's too late for that, Dan. I have a board-approved plan."

"But the company is in a death spiral."

"That's why I need to make these changes."

"Thirty percent of the workforce?"

"If there was any other way."

"But there is."

"No, Dan, there isn't."

Olivia folds her arms across her chest. Her face is blank, except that her eyes keep wandering off trying to hide something. But what? Does she agree with me, but believe her hands are tied? Does she believe Wall Street screwed us? Does she believe that I failed her in some way? Or maybe there's nothing hidden underneath. It wouldn't be the first time this year I couldn't read the woman.

My black loafers, normally grounding, threaten to levitate and whisk me out of the room before she can say another safe, canned, board-approved thing. Couldn't she at least have had a real conversation after sixteen years? I manage a fake smile, though my eyes, filled to the brim, betray me. Did she really just fire me? After everything we've been through, how could she walk away? In twenty-five years weren't we going to be the last two standing at this place? Wasn't what we had stronger than any marriage?

As I leave the corner office for the last time, Olivia says, "We'll stay in touch, Dan. Our relationship transcends work." She hugs me. The same perfume she's worn for years, Tom Ford, induces a dry heave. I can't ditto her hug. Billions of prickling needles freeze my arms at my sides. Am I bleeding? Don't look down, the pinpricks have spouted and are covering the new carpet in blood.

Moments later, somehow magically transported back to my office, I have a brief conversation with a friend, Sally, the HR VP, who hands me the severance document that apparently details what Olivia overviewed. I phone my lawyer, fax the document, and after I talk him through the details, manage the strength to scribble a signature on the voluntary severance package: Daniel Underlight. By taking the high road to a golden parachute, one that is fully extended and generous, I'm agreeing to never publicly say anything negative about the company or Olivia. At least one will be easy. My secretary, Annette, who's been with me since the start, who will be assigned to someone new tomorrow, helps me clean out my office. The keepers: my infinite number of management books, a few early awards, a bursting-with-color glass paperweight my wife gave me years ago, a picture of my son playing soccer, a stone arrowhead. Everything else we throw away.

I slowly drift out of the office building, stopping often to shake hands or say good-bye to boatloads of friends and colleagues, most of whom seem genuinely sympathetic. You'll be missed. RadioRadio won't be the same without you. Let us know where you land. Forty years old, divorced, with a dead son who paid a heavy price for my long work hours, I've come untethered. What was that line in the poem? *When the inexplicable fogs.*

As I pull out of the parking lot in Gordon Bell, a name I've given my 1972 Triumph TR6 convertible, and race onto Route 128 away from corporate headquarters, toward my oversized Concord home, the wind washes my face. Even at seventy miles an hour, the air is warm and embryonic, temporarily warding off the vast blackness of non-RadioRadio closing in. But oblivion won't wait for long. Yes, I could easily get another job, but there is no other RadioRadio. Yes, I have enough money, but there is no other RadioRadio. Yes, there are other strong CEOs, but none like Olivia. Do people wear firings like a missing wedding band, like an old soccer jersey, like a medical bracelet after an unwanted surgery? I survived my firing and had my heart removed and replaced with an artificial one. It's as good as new. I'll see you at the health club tomorrow.

A short time later, I pull into my driveway. The crunching sound of rubber against gravel causes me to stop midway up and run my fingers through my hair until the rearview mirror reveals Einstein-hair in the making. How to net out my time with Liv? That was always my strength. Analyze. Strategize. Synthesize. Net Out. ASSNO. I even had it added to the RadioRadio list of corporate acronyms. After a few rationalizations, which are surprisingly easy to do when unemployed, I zero in on the truth, the main takeaway, the sixteen-year NO—I got all caught up.

So it spins.

#

In the living room, I take my guitar from its stand and study it. The best gift Olivia ever gave me, given at my five-year RR anniversary party. Even though I'm a novice, I relish the particulars. A Martin OM28, built using East Indian rosewood for the back and sides and solid Sitka spruce for the top. The body has scalloped braces, a bound ebony fretboard adorned with abalone rosette and top trim, a tortoise pickguard, and a gold open geared tuning machine with butterbean knobs. Custom pearl inlays of old-fashioned radios are on the first, third, and fifth frets, added at Olivia's request. I've loved this instrument for a long time.

Guitar in hand, I make my way out to a spot behind my garage and place the guitar across the truck-size tire that I've been sledgehammering for the last week since I got fired. Each day I wallop the tire hundreds of times until I'm completely exhausted or too depressed to continue. Each day, after surviving the onslaught, the tire resumes its shape, regains its strength, confirms its readiness for another go in the near future.

For today's round, the air is thick with fall, and dead leaves color the ground. The twenty-five-pound sledgehammer stands waiting next to me, the heaviest one Home Depot had to offer. Led Zeppelin blasts through the garage speakers, one of a few artists on my pommeling playlist. Like most aspiring guitarists, one of the first songs I learned was "Stairway to Heaven," though I could never master the rhythm of the fast part. Even then I guess I knew the Martin was more of an object to admire than an instrument to play. I've destroyed other Olivia gifts this last week, but nothing this big, this valuable. A framed picture of the two of us during our first product launch. A gold paperweight shaped like a radio with the inscription, *Thank you, Dan. Olivia. January 30th, 2002.* A leather briefcase monogrammed D.Z.U. They were all buildup to this moment, to the big one.

I raise the sledgehammer over my head and hold it there in perfect form, one hand near the hammerhead and the other at the bottom of the wooden handle, mimicking the how-to Internet video. In no time, my arm starts to shake. Am I going to do this? Am I really going to destroy a work of art? I take a deep breath and strike the guitar at the sound hole again and again in a groove much better than I was ever able to achieve while strumming the thing. Over countless blows, I pulverize the guitar. Wood becomes sawdust; metal strings snap; tuning knobs pop and degear; pearl radios shatter. When I'm done, I rest the hammer on its head and lie down on the ground faceup. Some of the guitar dust settles on my skin, invades my nostrils, and smells like new construction.

Later, I roll out a Shop-Vac close to the mess, vacuum until there's no visible sign of my no-longer prized possession. I empty the Shop-Vac into a black trash bag and immediately drive the bag to the town dump. I toss the bag in the compactor, and watch as it's slowly crushed with the other local garbage until indistinguishable.

Galaxy Mist

Nessa opens her door and smiles me in. She's especially tall today, the result of multicolored alligator pumps, and is wearing black slacks, a cream-colored silk blouse, and a black, brown, and white shawl that matches her shoes. Her straight, almost blonde hair falls within an inch of the shawl and frames her face, which, even though she's my age, doesn't look a day over twenty-five. Sometimes during our sessions, I wonder if her smile would be enough. No words. No past. No loss.

Rabbits inhabit her office. All kinds. Little ceramic ones in different poses cover the table next to her chair. A stuffed wool one on the top row of her bookshelf watches over us. Abstract metal ones next to the music player stand ready to dance with the push of a button. During my first session fifteen months ago, after my son, Zack, died, I counted nine of them. Why so many? I have no idea, and I don't plan to ask. Do I like them? Maybe. I angle a dark-brown leather chair, my chair, toward her an inch or two and collapse down.

"How are you?" Nessa asks.

"Still angry."

She tilts her head slightly, and her eyes widen. All therapists apparently have perfected this move during their training. It means, I'm not going to say anything now because it's better if you figure things out on your own; please continue. The rabbits acquiesce, and who am I to argue with rabbits?

"I thought Olivia and I were in sync."

"It's hard to stay in sync forever."

"The things I've called that woman these last couple of weeks."

"You mean like . . ." She mouths the C-word and the B-word.

The big C and the big B. I had those words socialized out of me a long time ago, like many men, but these last three weeks I've logged enough for more than a few lifetimes. Mostly they came in my house in the middle of the night or in my car during a long drive; they always came when I was alone, when I couldn't stand another minute without one. Together with the things I destroyed these last weeks they at least, in fits and starts, uncapped the rage.

"Your sledgehammer recommendation also helped," I say.

"The anger has to go somewhere."

"Do you think there's any way back?"

"Do you want to go back?"

"I don't know. I love that company. I think I still love her, though I hate her too."

"Anger is such an underrated emotion. It's transformative."

"So you said last week."

Nessa looks calmly at me. In therapy much of the conversation is nonverbal. The look means she can hold as much anger as I have—or at least as much as I want to show—so I anger-her-up on my week. The hammering. The hating. The often-overlooked benefits of plotting out revenge. Throughout, the Cs and Bs and the Fuck Olivia's punctuate at shorter and shorter intervals. Throughout, Nessa's face remains supportive: an understanding nod, lips that curl upward, eyes that soften. She's not like therapists I've gone to in the past who pretty much say and show nothing, then take your money after fifty minutes. She's a relational therapist, and although I'm not exactly sure what that means, I like it better than the traditional Freudian guy I saw after Hannah and I split. Those sessions didn't last long. I mean, not everything wrong in a marriage boils down to what you lost from your mother or father long ago. Sometimes you get fucked in the present.

When I'm done, hollowed out, when I've passed my anger to her for safe holding, I shift gears and tell her about going fetal in bed. Until Zack died, my bed was a place for sleep, for sex, for recharging. After his death that all changed. I rarely slept well, all but gave up sex, and, well, how does one recharge while frozen? When I did sleep, it wasn't in bed; I slept on sofas, in movie theaters, at the office, almost anywhere but. When I did have sex, it happened in cars, parks, and public places, and was more about numbing than pleasure, more about obliteration than recharging. Strangely, this last week I found my bed again, and for the first time it cradled loss. Invisible loss-bugs leached pain out of me slowly, steadily, from what I'm now sure is a never-ending pool. Loss-bugs; Nessa likes that one. Maybe, like Visa, she should offer points, but not for purchases—for good lines. At this rate, I'll earn enough to buy my own rabbits soon.

Nessa glances over at a case of Play-Doh stored in her bookcase. Last week, we molded it into different shapes: a car, a beetle, my son, a radio. I had a blast, and she did too, I think. My favorite part was smashing the Play-Doh shapes back into the containers at the end, where they belonged. Well, not Zack. Statuesque, he's still on Nessa's bookshelf, done in blue.

"I don't think Doh will help this time," I say.

"What would you like to do instead?"

"Quit coming here."

"I see."

"I mean, I lost my job. You can't help with that. I just want to cocoon, live off the money I made, eat junk food, and drink scotch.

I don't need your help for that. I've tried therapy for fifteen months and look where it's gotten me."

Nessa folds her hands across her lap, makes firm eye contact, and smiles, remaining silent for a good minute. "I remember when you first came after Zack died. You were pale as a ghost, you'd lost weight, and you had started drinking scotch like water. You've moved from that place."

"I don't know. I guess." I fold my arms across my chest and cross one leg over the other, repeatedly bouncing it off my knee. Maybe there's something to what she's saying. I do feel better talking with her for the hour I'm here each week, and I have moved away from Ghost Place. But there's nowhere left to go now, except to my house where I can be alone, where I can catch up on sixteen years of HBO series, where the bar is full of eighteen-year-old scotch I made sure to restock right after the firing. Now that it's all over, where else would I go? There's no redemption, no forgiveness for what I did to Zack. There's no desire for new love after Hannah. There's no desire for a new company after Olivia and RR. There's just weight. Relentless weight.

"I have an idea." Nessa stands up, walks over to a small cabinet, and pulls out a large box filled with Dove milk chocolate, dark chocolate, and chocolate with almond pieces. At the end of my first session all those months ago, she asked me if I wanted a piece of chocolate, opened it for me when I said sure, and read a pithy slogan from the wrapper, something like, "Drive all blames into one." Ever since, each week while holding the box in front of me, she's made the same offer, though this time she hands me the whole box.

I study the pieces. There must be a hundred of them. The dark chocolate ones are wrapped in blue, the milk chocolate in red, the almond in lavender. I pick up a red piece. I like the wrapper's texture, which is soft and sharp at the same time. I bet I'd need to open most of the chocolates to find a single piece of truth, but I don't open any.

Instead, while grinning at Nessa, I dump the box. The chocolates spread out on the floor as though they're galaxies in the universe, like they're desperately trying to move away from each other, like a no-longer-relevant strange attractor holds them together.

Nessa smiles, takes the empty box from my hand, walks over to her desk, and puts it down. She grabs a chalice of colored pencils and offers them to me. Chalice in hand, I sprinkle pencils on the floor, where they mesh with the chocolates, morph into wormholes connecting the galaxies. Ever since I was a boy, I've loved clutter and color—a bunch of bright things in proximity to each other is generative. How Nessa knows this too is beyond me.

She next gets a box of colorful, giant pipe cleaners and a Buddha Board. With a Buddha Board, a person can paint kanji-like symbols with water on a whiteboard coated with a chemical that turns black when it comes in contact with water. One can dip a brush in the water well at the bottom of the board, which doubles as a stand, and presto, in no time she's creating black art on the whiteboard. But not yet. She places the board on the floor between us and turns her attention to the pipe cleaners.

She hands me a bunch and keeps one for herself. Without saying a word, we shape. With yellow, green, and orange ones, I weave together a crown and place it on my head. With every color in her bunch, Nessa loops together pipe cleaners into a necklace that she slips over her head. It complements her shawl. I shape hanger earrings, one purple, one red, and hook them on my ears. She fashions a braided bracelet that matches the colors in my crown.

Fully jeweled in pipe cleaners, we turn back to the Buddha Board. I dip first and draw horizontal squiggly lines until I've created a squiggly square. I do the same thing with vertical lines. In no time the entire board is covered with squares except for the center. There I draw a circle. One of the downsides about painting with a water brush is that sometimes the water runs. My horizontal and vertical squares are doing that now, streaming into the circle.

"It'll take a minute or two for the water to dry. Then you can paint," I say.

"I love your squares and circle."

"Even the streams?"

"Especially."

We watch the board evaporate to white. Ephemeral art is deep-rooted; something about the lack of permanency heightens the viewing experience. When it's Nessa's turn, she sketches a stick figure of a girl and adds a think bubble with a heart in it. She hands the Buddha Board back to me. In the corner of the board, I draw a stick figure of a boy holding a radio walking away from the girl. I hand the board back to Nessa. She sketches a circle around both stick figures and a bunch of squiggly lines connecting the two. She puts the board down on the floor between us. The girl starts to fade first, followed shortly after by the boy.

I stand and go over to one end of the chocolate-and-pencil universe, opposite the sofa. For a moment I study the layout of the galaxies, the wormholes. When I'm confident, I hopscotch through. Two feet. One foot. Two feet. One foot. I make it all the way to the safe zone, the sofa, where I fall into a sitting position on the left cushion. I lost an earring along the way that's become a gaseous cloud in the center of the universe. That's cool. I always liked those.

Nessa pops up from her chair, makes her calculations on the opposite side of the universe, and hopscotches through with grace and skill onto the right cushion, where she slouches down and crosses one leg over the other to match me. On closer examination, her jewelry weathered the trip much better than mine, though she didn't get all rug on her jumps.

"You crushed an almond galaxy," I say.

"I know. Isn't it cool that I have that much power?"

"I want that much power."

"You already have it."

"I lost it all."

Nessa considers the galaxies and wormholes on the floor, smiles, and kicks a few. She does it again, and I join in. A moment later we've made over the universe, moved it away from the safe zone, reversed a long-standing scientific theory that it's ever expanding, and validated the possibility of an implosion.

"Will that get me my power back?"

"Are you ready to take it back?"

"How do I do that?"

"That's for you to answer."

I stand and walk around our creation, taking it in from all angles. How can I extract meaning from the universe when loss and betrayal have corroded and burnt my cherished memories? How can I reconstitute after being charred and dissolved? "You know, RadioRadio was my life, even more so after Zack died. So much of who I am was caught up in that company. Maybe it's time to build something better, something for myself."

"Maybe."

"Have I told you lately you're great at your job?"

"Thank you. Will I see you next week?"

"I guess I'll stick it out a little longer."

"I'm glad. Mist?" she asks.

Nessa gets up and brings over a box loaded with dozens of cobalt-blue spray bottles, each filled with a different mist. Each week, right before I leave, I pick one, and then she sprays some a few times above my head. Apparently, misting will help me move forward into my better, currently undefined future. How? I have no idea, but why not? Eyes closed, I guide my fingers over each bottle until I find one I like, lift it out of the box, and hand it to her.

"Eighth Chakra Awakening Mist. That's a rare choice."
She mists.

Wash Over Me

Fall, two years ago, Zack, in soccer cleats, clomped into the house. He was ten, the spitting image of me at that age—tall with the same curly brown hair, the same brown eyes, the same smile, the same nervous energy. A moment later, he plopped himself on the sofa beside me, put his feet on the coffee table, and folded his arms across his chest. A college football game, Harvard versus a lesser opponent, backgrounded on the flat screen TV, and a heavily highlighted paper on the future of big data, opened to a middle page, rested on my lap. The room, with all the windows open, hinted of fall.

In the front hallway, Zack's mother stood witness before waving and smiling good-bye. Hannah and I had come a long way in the years since the breakup. She had remarried a decent guy, a surgeon, and we all got along fine, to the point where if asked, I would have professed friendship. We both lived in Concord, only a few miles apart, she in a Victorian near the center of town and me in the home we previously shared together. Proximity and an increasingly accepting relationship made spontaneous visits like the one that day easy to pull off.

Zack didn't sit still for long. He launched a tickle war, slow at first, with one hand weaving up and down my arm like a drunken centipede. Soon after, he swiped the paper off my lap and jumped me, tickling with both hands in the spots where I failed to protect myself. "No more work, Dad." "No more football." "Let's play soccer." At some point, I had no choice but to tickle back. So I did. Under his arms. On his stomach. Behind his ears. Later, the tickling morphed into wrestling, the kind fathers and sons often engage in, the kind that subsides later in life when sons become men, often replaced with talk of sports or technology. As he wrapped me up in a first-rate headlock, all I could do was smile.

We wrestled until Zack declared himself the winner, jumped to his feet, and with both hands, pulled me to my feet demanding we go to the field. I agreed, but first we had to prepare. I slipped into my Patriots jersey, found my almost-new cleats, filled a couple of Patriots squeeze bottles with water, and cut and bagged a half-dozen oranges. Zack grabbed a couple of soccer balls, a boom box, and the Pearl Jam CDs I'd introduced him to that year. *Ten. Yield.* Packed, we headed out to the car.

Then my phone rang.

"Zack, I need to take this. I'll only be a minute. Why don't you wait for me in the car?"

"Hurry, Dad."

Olivia wanted to talk about our upcoming enterprise software release, the one focused on enterprise resource planning. Did I think it was ready? Was I willing to bet my badge that it would disrupt the market? Was the launch plan solid? Even though I quickly answered yes, yes, and yes to her questions, even though the conversation could have waited until the next day, even though I mentioned I had plans, she kept me on the phone more than an hour as I paced up and down the driveway. Repeat questions. More and more detail. Frequent sidetracks about industry trends and futures. When I finally reached the car, Zack was buckled into the front seat and playing *Jetpack Joyride* on his phone. He glanced up and appeared a little surprised, as if he didn't expect me so soon.

"I'm sorry, Zack, you know how work is."

"I know, Dad."

Fifteen minutes later, Zack and I dribbled two balls onto the soccer pitch. Indian summer flexed its muscle, and the heat smeared the distant view as we began our one-on-one game. Facing each other at the eighteen-yard line, separated by a foot in height, a hundred pounds, and twenty-eight years in standard time, we crouched into athletic positions and smiled. "Even Flow" blasted from the boom box.

Zack had started his soccer career a couple of years earlier right after Hannah and I had broken up, and over time, had earned the starting striker position on the Concord town A-team and the FC Concord club team. I'd missed only a few games that year, but before that, I would have given myself a D, had I graded my attendance. Until that year, Olivia had held Saturday morning operational meetings, and well, attending them had been my priority. That year after the meetings mysteriously stopped, my D became a B. That year, in addition to attending Zack's matches, I squeezed in one-on-one soccer games whenever time permitted.

The score seesawed. 2-1, Zack. 6-5, Dad. 8-7, Zack. When he dribbled, the ball seemed glued to his feet, and I sometimes found myself admiring his skillful moves instead of defending him. Between goals, we talked about the best players in the world. Messi. Ronaldo. Beckham. Donovan in the US. I agreed to build Zack a compilation video of all of their best goals before Christmas. I told him one day he would be featured in one just like it.

Even though I was thin for my age, even though I'd once been athletic, I found myself winded after most of my goals. That's because I didn't have any real foot skills and relied instead on sprinting. My strategy was simple: kick the ball far away from us, sprint to it faster than Zack, shoot. Sometimes it worked; sometimes not so well. If we'd kept playing that year, if I had kept up my one-trick pony approach, I would have been forced to get back in shape; otherwise, Zack would have beaten me before it ended. Though fitness was easier goaled than achieved while I was at RR. A few years into my tenure there, I gave up physical exercise with full support from Olivia, and with the exception of those games, never returned. Here's an early Olivia-ism that stuck—mental exercise is better for you than physical exercise and better for the company, too.

Halfway through our match, sweating profusely, with Zack's face covered with dirt muddied from his sweat, we stopped for a water break. We gulped our squeeze bottles until we both drank our fill, and we ate all the orange wedges. Then I poured half of my remaining water over my head and the other half over Zack's. He screamed, "Dad!" and we both burst out laughing. He then emptied the remainder of his bottle on me. Until that year, we'd rarely goofed around that way. Instead, in the rare times when we had played, it was always with structure: robotics sets, Legos, K'nex, whatever, as long as it had an end goal, as long as it would help him eventually Ivy League.

After our break, Zack geared up. He'd held back until then so he could finish strong and smart. At first, his strategy worked well and he took a few-point lead, but just when he thought he had me, I amped up and closed the gap. Soon after, we were seesawing again, laughing, talking trash. "It must be hard finishing second." "You're done, old man." "Maybe you'll beat me when you're twenty." "How does it feel to be crushed by your son?"

With the score 20-20, we both quieted down for the last goal, as we'd done in our previous matches. Zack nodded. I nodded back. Then I kicked the ball about ten yards in front of us and sprinted toward it. Stride for stride, Zack stayed with me. As I was about to shoot, he slid, tackled the ball, and cleared it away from my feet. Within seconds, he was on his feet again, but instead of racing toward the loose ball, he let me regroup outside the eighteen. With a classic Underlight look on his face, one of determination, of I-can-do-anything-I-put-my-mind-to, he waved his index finger back and forth.

Out of breath, my foot resting on top of the ball, I smiled and began again. This time, instead of my normal kick-and-sprint tactic, I tried one of Zack's moves: I faked one way, and then went the other. That caught him and I gained a crack of separation, enough to strike the ball, which with little momentum made its way toward the corner of the net. Zack sprinted toward the ball, hoping to clear it before it crossed the goal line, but he arrived a nanosecond late. With my hands raised over my head, I started dancing and singing, "I win. What a grin. I win. Time to spin," in a little rhyme of a song I made up.

Zack wasn't amused. He kicked dirt and then the goalpost before punting the ball all the way to the centerline. Then he silently jogged off to retrieve it. After he had secured the ball, he dribbled back toward me, head down. When he was near, I could see he was close to tears. Part of me wanted to comfort him. Part of me was proud of him for being so competitive, for hating to lose. It would have served him well in this world of technology and globalization. But most of me was thankful that, win or lose, we'd found the time to play.

Some of us who get caught up in work sacrifice our loved ones on the altar of big business. It's not as though we intend a sacrifice from the start. At first, we fully plan to do it all, fully believe in the possibility of spending quality time with our families as we build killer technology. But then, surprise, surprise, we discover that there's only so much time each day. We discover having it all is something the work gods let you believe is possible until you're hooked, until they're sure you'll sacrifice your family when the inevitable choice points arrive. That year, I'd done a little better.

A few feet away, one foot resting on top of the ball, Zack wiped his face.

"What's the matter?"

"Sad."

"How come?" I asked.

He shrugged.

"Did you enjoy our game?"

"Didn't suck."

We sat on the grass at the top of the box. The crying mounted. Then he said, "I miss Grandpa." That was his go-to line when he was upset about anything. Trouble with a bully from school. "I miss Grandpa." Upset about a new rule that Mom or Dad put in place. "I miss Grandpa." Angry about a loss to FC Concord's archrival, FC Harton. "I miss Grandpa." I put my hand on his shoulder and patted it gently, as my father had with me when I was young and had missed a winning basket. I didn't know until that moment that a child could inherit loss, generalize it beyond the specific. I didn't know I'd passed loss along to Zack.

Back then, every single day I missed Dad—his laugh, his love of family, his advice. From the start, he'd never understood why I was so obsessed with RadioRadio. *Dan, why don't you spend more time at home? Dan, take a family vacation or one alone with Hannah. Dan, why don't we plant a vegetable garden together? Dan, life at its best is a delicate balance of work and family.* Why hadn't I listened to him? Dad had died five years earlier. To this day, I'm thankful he hadn't witnessed Zack's death or my divorce. They would have destroyed him. On my divorce, he would have said, "Son, sometimes things are better after a divorce, but mostly not." The jury's no longer out on that one. On Zack's death, we would have talked little and drunk often.

The promise of sports is resiliency within a structured environment. When you lose, as everyone does, you can work harder and smarter and grow in some way. The rules will still be the same next time around, and if you do your work, you'll win. There's a beauty, a fairness to it that's often lost later in life. That's why we Underlights loved the NFL. But if you pass loss on to your child, losing can darken a game until it's no longer capable of teaching resiliency. How, as a parent, do you avoid passing on? Is it even possible? I remember thinking all I could do was wish that any pain Zack experienced down the road was his own, that he would learn and grow from it, that it would help him lead a productive life. But I couldn't speak of resiliency to a ten-year-old, so instead I said, "I love you."

"I love you, too, Dad."

"Do you think I'll love you less if you don't win at soccer?"

He shrugged again.

"You don't have to be good at soccer."

"I am good at soccer, Dad. And a bunch of other things too."

Zack reached out for another hug. We both started to cry, him openly, me quietly. What would the news helicopters have seen had they been hovering? Father and son, drenched in sweat, hugging, crying. The evening news headline—*Hi-tech workaholic dad beats his son at soccer to show he still has it.*

"When can we do this again, Dad?" Zack asked.

"How about tomorrow?"

Near the goalpost next to my water bottle, my phone started to play the ringtone I had set up for Olivia, the theme to her favorite TV show, *The Powers.* I jumped up and started the eighteen-yard jog toward the phone, but stopped halfway. I thought, let Olivia go to voicemail; she can wait. I thought, let Olivia go. I turned back to Zack, who was expertly juggling the ball between his feet, his knees, his head, and his back. I slid my hands into the large center pocket of my Patriots sweatshirt and interlaced my fingers. A gentle fall breeze washed over me.

Spring in the Garden of Return

When I need to think, I drive. Even though it's spring, the TR6 will remain garaged until the temperature breaks sixty, so today I'm heading north in my second-generation Prius. To be clear, the Prius is the ugliest car ever made. Some days I'm sure that I'll never drive it again, but it gets great mileage, and something can be said for using fewer fossil fuels. Normally, I do these drives alone, but Willow Kaye is buckled into the passenger seat next to me, staring out the window, running her finger back and forth along the door handle, off in some distant Willow-only place. She's the only person I know who doesn't mind my long stretches of silence, of think time, who parallel-thinks with me. I have to give her points for that.

"Want to go any place in particular?" I ask.

"What?"

"Want to go any place?"

"Oh. No. Anywhere north."

"A lot on your mind?"

"Not really."

Willow runs a nonprofit in Boston for battered women, and she's a poet, a seeker, a repaired spirit. Her big, brown, round eyes see potential, and she wears her long brown hair in a reverse central braid that rivers into a hair delta of sorts, with dozens of spiked hair rivulets shooting off in random directions. Like creation, it's stunningly wild and singularly expressive. I once asked her where she learned to sculpt her hair, but she shrugged me off and said she didn't know. She's as tall as I am, taller with her rivulets, so that during an occasional hug, our eyes level. When she's happy, which is often, her pace is a half step faster. It makes me smile.

We met a year ago on an unusually warm spring day when I was driving Gordon Bell downtown. She glided right up to the car at a red light, tapped on the front window, announced she was a Triumph fan, and asked me for a ride. I was so surprised that of course I said yes, and we've been friends ever since. A short time afterward, I remember asking her if she'd ever done something like that before. "I haven't, but for some reason I knew it would be okay with you." That's when I first accepted there are people you meet in life that, early on, you know you can love. You don't know what form it will take, and often fear gets in the way and keeps the love shapeless, but when it doesn't, well, you may end up with a lifelong friend. These last six months, after the firing, after the crash, she visited me once a week to check in and see if I was okay. Toward the end of those months, when I came out of my funk, the weekly meetings continued, and now I couldn't imagine a week passing where I didn't see Willow. I'm still not sure if our current shape is our final one, but I hope not.

On back roads, we pass through a covered bridge, by a homemade ice-cream shop, by pick-your-own blueberry and strawberry farms, and cross the border into New Hampshire. I'm heading toward this place in Hollis, Lullwyle Farm, for the apple blossom festival. For years, Hannah and I played and laughed at the farm with Zack each fall. We filled bushel baskets, ate Honey Crisps, drank freshly pressed apple cider, and went on hayrides, but I haven't been since the split. At first, it was too painful. And later, who was going to eat all of those apples? When Zack died, the probability of ever returning to apple land dropped to when hell freezes over, which now is only moments away. Should I go through with it, go to one of my sacred Zack places with someone new? What would he say? Probably that it's okay, that I've never been here in the spring.

The Lullwyle Farm parking lot is full, so we're directed to overflow parking across the street. For a second, I'm tempted to skip the whole thing and find a local coffee shop. But Willow has never been to an apple blossom festival, so we park and lock, cross the street, and enter. A large store is on the right, and a portable wood-fired pizza oven with a long line on the left. Our first stop is the store. Greenhouse fruits, vegetables, and homemade baked goods fill rows of shelves, and the place smells like my mom's warm apple pie. On the way out, we buy a freshly made caramel apple covered with crushed nuts and share it as we stroll toward the orchard.

A long walk later, we're in the middle of the orchard admiring a magnificent tree in full bloom with hundreds of showy, white, five-petaled blossoms, tinged with pink, confirming my view that in a few areas science or technology will never outperform nature. I pick up a snapped-off flowered branch and hand it to Willow.

"Thank you. It's beautiful," she says.

"As it should be."

"You were deep in thought on the way up."

"You, too."

"The shelter."

"Ah. Trying to figure out next steps."

"You've had a lot of offers."

"True, but they're more of the same," I say.

For a time, we tour the orchard, holding hands, something we've taken to doing more lately. Sunny, zero clouds, fifty degrees, it's a perfect spring day, red cheek air and all. Because the morning sun in New Hampshire tints the landscape gold and because the orchard is large with the trees barely above our heads, it seems more like we're in Big Sky country than in New England. In moments when the sunlight touches Willow's face at a certain aura-inducing angle, she takes my breath away, makes me believe that she was raised on a farm instead of in Brooklyn, that she knows some secret about this place that will make everything okay, that I should pull her closer and learn from her. Instead, despite my best efforts, a wave of emotion overcomes me, and I turn away.

"Are you okay?" she asks.

"Yeah. It's nothing."

"What?"

"I didn't think I'd ever come back here."

Willow lets go of my hand, wraps her arm around me, and tugs me into a walk. Slowly, arm-in-arm, we resume the orchard tour, stopping to take in views from different perspectives. The rowed apple trees are about the same age, yet there's enough variety across them that each view adds to their story, which seems never ending and inexhaustible. Couples pass by, smile, assume we're lovers rather than friends. The orchard is full of them, some with children, some without. One boy, dressed in soccer gear and running, reminds me of Zack. Zack loved sprinting up and down the long rows between the apple-laden trees, uncatchable, protected by their order.

Part of me wants to run the rows, to feel the wind against my face and the rush of blood to the head. I stop walking, turn toward Willow, and smile. "Bet you can't catch me." I take off, and after a short sprint, turn around and backpedal. Willow's chasing after me with the most playful and determined smile on her face. I dodge in and out of trees, let her get within a foot or two, take off again. I spread out my arms, sound off like a jet engine, and mimic a plane. Willow does the same. At one point, she catches me and the tips of our wings touch, causing us to land facing each other. Willow places her hands on my shoulders and moves eye-to-eye close. Her eyes aren't solid brown like I thought; they're the color of espresso beans with rich reddish-brown flecks. And her scent is different now, sweeter, like something precious long lost.

"Your eyes are beautiful," I say.

She gives me this wide-eyed look and a gentle smile, which I've imagined but have never seen from her before. All else blurs as we slowly inch closer. Then an eye-open kiss, lips barely touching, lacelike, which gives way to a deeper one with hints of apple and caramel. After a time, a boy bumps into us, breaks the trance, and says, "Sorry, mister," before running off to resume his game of tag.

"I didn't think this would ever happen," I say.

"We needed these last months together."

"Finally, a benefit to being fired."

"There are more."

"Like what?"

"You haven't discovered them all yet," she says.

On the way back to the car, her arm looped around mine, we stop for pizza. Up close, the wood-fired oven radiates heat and fills the air with oak-tinged smoke. In line, we talk about whatever, wait to order our pizza and warm apple cider, take in all that's around us. Everyone here is connected by the festival, the beautiful day, and the food, surely by some kind of invisible grace. What would the world be like if connections to something larger, something meaningful, happened all of the time? When our pizza arrives, we feed each other folded slices and sip our cinnamon-infused cider until we've had our fill. It's better than good.

Back in the car, Willow gently pulls my arm across, palm-up, and rests it on her lap. We head down country roads toward Massachusetts, mostly in silence, as she tickles my forearm with long slow back-and-forth strokes. A peacefulness permeates the silence that's different from the one on the way up. We're not off in our respective head lands, and somehow we're both sure that hours earlier, in a sun-filled New Hampshire apple orchard, we forged an inextricable link.

#

My kitchen is large, and since Hannah moved out, unused. It's filled with an eight-burner Wolf stove, a Sub-zero refrigerator, wine cooler, and extra freezer, a Bosch dishwasher and microwave, and a four-spout Gaggia cappuccino maker— all the best appliances in their respective categories, or at least the most expensive. The kitchen has a large island with granite countertops and enough cabinet space to stock an army's worth of kitchen stuff, though the cabinets are depleted now. I'm barefoot, and the radiant heat feels good against my feet. Willow is barefoot, too, with painted red toenails, which I only recently discovered are one of her loves. We've been aspiring chefs these last weeks, as we've spent more time together. When we started, neither of us knew how to cook, but we inched forward one day at a time and made simple dishes together. We've also talked nonstop, laughed at each other's jokes, kissed, and touched often, but we haven't had sex. Yes, we've been building toward it, but I wasn't in any rush given my Hannah history. Take it one day at a time and see where things go. That's been my mantra.

Tonight, we're going difficult and making a classic Italian dish, Rotolo di Spinaci. I bought the ingredients this morning: flour, eggs, San Marzano tomatoes, spinach, ricotta, and Parmesan. The dish calls for large rectangular sheets of homemade pasta that we'll have to roll out by hand. Once rolled out, we'll evenly spread spinach and ricotta filling across the sheets, roll them up, wrap the rolls in a towel, and poach the toweled pasta in a large pan of water. Once poached, we'll cut the pasta rolls into one-inch thick pinwheels, smother the pinwheels in tomato sauce and Parmesan and bake them in a low oven. How hard can that be? Before we start, I click on some music, Damien Rice, whom Willow loves and whom I'd never heard of before Willow. He has a good voice.

I place flour, eggs, egg yolks, and olive oil into the food processor in the exact measures. One of the things I have learned through cooking with Willow is that I'm an exact-measure recipe follower, and she's a feels-about-right one. Early in our cooking trials, we had our first fight about it, which I think I won, though she made some comment about feeding my control-hunger, whatever that means. We process until the mixture doughs, turn it out in a bowl, cover it with plastic wrap, which has to be one of the greatest food-related inventions of all time, and place it in the Sub-zero. Damien sings about cannonballs and volcanoes. Willow whistles along.

"So far, so good," I say.

"Let's do the filling while we wait."

Willow blanches the spinach in a pan of boiling water until it's wilted. She drains it well and squeezes out the excess moisture. I start to finely chop the spinach. Last night, after I took Willow home, I studied this chef on TV masterfully chop onions into perfect little bits, the whole time the gap between the tips of his fingers and the knife was razor thin, and the speed of the blade faster than the eye could follow. I try to mimic him now with the spinach, at first slow with distance, but gradually faster and closer.

"Fuck!"

"Are you okay?"

I put the knife down, bandage the tip of my finger with my tongue. "Just a nick."

She smiles, takes my hand, and kisses my palm. "I'll finish up if you want."

"I can do it."

"I know. But the dough should be ready now, and you're probably better than I am at rolling. Let me get you a real Band Aid."

Bandaged, I remove the bowl from the fridge, divide the dough into two pieces, and flour both. I begin rolling out in random directions. The dough resists my every move but slowly creeps out on the flour-covered granite. Damien is singing about nine crimes, one of which must surely be rolling dough. In some ways, cooking and software are the same: you have to follow a carefully planned process. For Rotolo di Spinaci, a detailed recipe guides our team of two through the complexity and breaks each step into a series of workable tasks. For software, the Agile Method does the same—chunks out the work into manageable stories and sprints that enable the software team to move forward. Willow, finished with her chopping and mixing duties, moves closer to show me the bowl of ricotta-spinach filling. I taste a finger full.

"Delicious," I say.

"I guess rolling is the hard part. Do you want help?"

"I'm okay for now."

I roll more. The thinner and larger the dough gets, the harder it is to manipulate. In some places, I go too thin and create a hole. In others, the dough sticks to the rolling pin and fattens by crease and fold. As I roll, I add more and more flour, which the cooking shows claim will ease my rolling problems. Unfortunately, the flour covers me as much as it covers the dough, and not only my hands; my clothes are ghosted, probably my face and hair as well.

"The dough looks awful," I say.

"We can patch it up. First, I'm going to change the music."

Willow disappears into the living room. The dough problems mount—more holes, more flaps and creases, more displaced flour. It doesn't look anything like a sheet of uncooked pasta and is more Frankensteined than seamless. I gather up my creation and scrunch it back into a ball. It's time to start over, time to master the blob. Willow returns as I'm once again flattening the ball into a pancake and places her hand over mine. Marvin Gaye is singing about healing.

"Want to dance?" she asks.

"I'll get it right this time."

"The heck with the pasta. Let's order Chinese takeout later."

I reach for a towel, but Willow stops me midair and gently pulls me close. As she rests her head on my shoulder, we circle the center island to Marvin, our interlaced hands guiding the way. When the song ends, we stop and hold each other. Willow has this look on her face like she's previously only imagined this place. I gently remove a stray piece of hair from her face, leaving a little flour behind.

"Let's go upstairs," she says.

"Okay."

Arm in arm, we head upstairs, our kisses stopping us after each couple of steps as we press against the wall. At the top of the stairs, I spin Willow around so her back is to me, wrap my hands around her waist, and slowly kiss her nape as I gently guide her into the bedroom.

We stop in front of the floor-to-ceiling mirror. She unbuttons my shirt, top to bottom, kissing my chest and then my stomach, as she undoes each button. When she finishes, she slips off my shirt one arm at a time until it falls to the floor. I bend down, slowly raise her top over her head, and kiss her stomach, her breasts, her lips, and her forehead along the way. We both turn to the mirror and smile. She unfastens my jeans, slides down with them, and kisses my stomach and then each hip and each thigh. I pull her up, turn her around, unbutton her jeans from behind, and inch them down over her hips until they drop to the floor. She steps out of them, turns, and faces me. As we press up against each other and kiss, the warmth from her body and her smell guide me forward. Relationships, like startups, are such courageous acts. We slip under the sheets, and I stretch above the nightstand to turn off the light.

"Don't," she says.

"I'm a little nervous. It's been a long time."

33

"For me, too. That's why I need to see you."

A wave of desire shelters us. The whole time Willow seems completely present—open and giving—and has this balancing look on her face that I imagine only comes after being badly broken and working through it. The whole time I try to open and meet her halfway, but it's too much. I glance over at the light switch and try to will it off.

Later, after we're done, Willow, head on my shoulder, softly strokes my chest with the tip of her finger.

"What are you feeling?" she asks.

"I don't know."

"Are you happy here?"

"More than I've been in a long time."

"Me, too."

Willow moves onto her other side so her back is to me. I pull her close until we're facing the window in a nested fetal position—me on the outside, her on the inside. She reaches above the nightstand and shuts off the light. She's still wearing her Rosewood Mala bracelets, which she's mentioned she never takes off, now I know not even when she makes love. A waxing gibbous moon lights the clear night. We raise our free hands together and enter into a silhouetted dance of sorts, gently weaving our hands in and out, barely touching our palms, fingers, knuckles, and forearms. The beads sound off in an undeniable rhythm that fuels our movements for a long time.

"We're good shadow dancers," I say.

"We are. Do you remember when we first met?"

"Of course."

"First time I ever did anything that bold."

"Must have been the TR6."

"Must have been. Maybe it's time for a second bold move," she says.

"Do I need to get the car?"

"Funny."

"What then?"

"Well, I've been thinking about how well we cook together."

"Next stop, The Food Network."

"Maybe we should do more than cook together. Maybe we should live together?"

Willow turns toward me so I can see she's serious. My gut—no, my whole body—is saying yes, but I weigh anyway. I haven't lived with anyone since Hannah. I'm unemployed. Maybe now isn't the right time? But these last weeks have been fantastic, and we have spent the last six months talking and growing much closer. Besides, I learned long ago at RR that sometimes it's best to take a leap.

"You sure?" I ask.

"Yes. And you?"

"Yes. Okay then, it's settled. When do you want to move?"

"Right away."

"I can rent a U-Haul in the morning."

#

We cross the Concord town line in our rented U-Haul. I could have hired movers, but Willow doesn't have much stuff, and besides, she wanted to move right away. It's a sunlit morning, and the spring air prisms the light the slightest shade of blue. Shoppers are walking Main Street, popping in and out of coffee shops, bakeries, galleries, and toy stores. We didn't need to go through the center of town to get to my house, but the day seems fresh, and I find myself wanting to show Willow the shiny things Concord has to offer. I take a quick left off Main.

"The truck route to the house?" she asks.

"Something like that."

A short time later, we pull in front of Henry David Thoreau's house. I park the truck, and we get out and lean against the hood. The house is yellow with white trim and black shutters. Two brick chimneys, crowned and capped in black, also are painted white and extend well above the roofline on both sides of the house. We could tour the place, but taking it in from this distance is enough. I've never been much of a history buff, or until recently, a poetry buff.

"Do you know that Louisa May Alcott lived in the house after Thoreau?" she asks.

"No. You've been here before?"

"First time. Want to hear my favorite Thoreau poem?"

"Sure."

"*My life has been the poem I would have writ, but I could not both live and utter it.*"

"Nice. I read *Walden* a long time ago, but I don't remember much of it."

"I can recite parts of it to you sometime."

"Sure," I say.

She takes my hand, angles her head my way, and gives me this little smile, the kind that levees so much intelligence that some can't help but break through. I would have never thought that the offer of reading Thoreau out loud could be this erotic.

After a time, we go back to the truck and head toward our house. Two kinds of houses stand in Concord. The old historic ones near the center of town, like the Thoreau-Alcott house, and the newer ones on multi-acre lots out in the country like mine. Hannah and I bought the house only a year before we divorced, which in retrospect was the wrong financial move, but placating at the time. By that point in our marriage, I was clear I didn't want more kids (Hannah did), and the house was my peace offering. My no-kid logic: I barely saw Zack given my work schedule, and I couldn't imagine bringing another child into the world I would rarely see. Way too many Dad no-shows were going on already, so why make it worse? Instead, we bought a 7,000-square-foot McMansion.

Most of the houses on Revolutionary Road, which has the same namesake as the movie, and which I should have taken as an omen at the time but didn't, are large. The road is a big circle, and my house is about halfway in, at the farthest point from the entryway. I stop at the base of my driveway so Willow can snap a few photos and video our arrival. The house, centered on ten acres, is an Adirondack with natural cedar shingles, traditional dark green trim, lots of glass, and large stone columns that support a porch off the master bedroom. I hang out on that porch a lot when the weather is good.

"Do you feel strange moving in here?" I ask.

"No. Why do you ask?"

"Hannah and I lived here."

"Oh, that." Willow takes my hand, raises it to her face, and kisses it softly. "I'm fine, Dan. Honestly, I'm more uncomfortable about the size of the house than about Hannah."

"We could move to a smaller place."

"That's not necessary yet. Let's see how things go," she says.

With the U-Haul parked in front of the house, we unload the photos first. The most striking pieces in Willow's apartment were the three beautifully framed, large photographs of battered women she'd taken over the years, which we had bubble-wrapped and loaded onto the truck last. The first one displays a headshot of a woman with no makeup, wet hair, and incredibly sad eyes, like she'd lost everything and was too tired to continue. The second one shows a woman in a sundress, dancing barefoot in front of a painting of a little girl, her daughter, doing the same. The woman's arms and legs are splotched with black and blue, yet her movement expresses such joy. The third photo presents a woman in a red business suit with a low-cut white blouse highlighting a pearl necklace around her neck. Right above the pearls are strangle marks. When I first saw the paintings, I assumed they were the women who Willow had helped the most, the ones who had made it. But the truth was exactly the opposite—they were the ones who didn't pull through, the ones whose deaths she'd vowed would push her to do better in the future. She—like many people who work too hard, too much— has the push-to-do-better gene.

The Concord house is big, so big that we can have separate offices. We agree the pictures will go in Willow's, though part of me wants to hang them prominently in the foyer or the living room so that visitors can see what's happening to women in this country. The rest of her belongings—a rug, books, clothes, and a reading chair and sofa—unloads safely. In the last weeks, we've talked about how important it was for her to live a simple, honest life, without the boatloads of stuff I've accumulated over the years. I still have a long way to go; I guess somewhere along the way I lost perspective and more became my norm.

In our bedroom, Willow organizes her clothes in one-eighth of her walk-in closet. I sit on the floor in the corner of the closet, legs crisscrossed, which is the closest I'll ever come to a yoga pose, and watch her hang blouses, pants, skirts, and dresses, and then line up shoes on the shoe shelves. I never noticed before, but all of her clothes contain black—some with a splash or two, some almost entirely. Black suits her, places the focus where it belongs, on her face, and compliments her perfumeless scent, which is fresh and intoxicating, already on its way to taking over the entire house, a far cry from Hannah's sandalwood perfume or Olivia's Tom Ford.

"All done. You realize this closet is the same size as my old apartment?" Willow asks.

"It will fill over time."

"I hope not." She walks over to me, reaches out with one hand, and with lips slightly parted, helps me up. Then she whispers in my ear, "Let's."

Later, we're fully charged, sitting on the master bedroom porch in our robes and barefoot, sipping iced teas, and taking in the late spring view. For me, sex has always given an element of release, but not always a recharge. For years with Hannah, that's what we did best; we recharged each other when the world, for one reason or another, used us up. I guess at some point I stopped being an energy source for her, and she found it somewhere else. I can't blame her; almost all of my energy back then went into work, and what little I had left went into Zack. Maybe in the end marriage isn't about whether two people love each other; maybe it's about whether they can recharge each other when most needed.

I stand, reach for Willow's hand, and pull her up. We lean against the balcony railing and survey the yard. After Zack died, I let the landscapers go, and it shows. Everything in the overgrown and unkempt yard has been falling apart for years. The grass is almost a foot tall, and the azaleas, rhododendrons, and Japanese maples have lost their shape and beauty. The driveway potholes have partnered to form an obstacle course with the low-voltage walkway lights I toppled while drunk one night right after Zack died. Off to the side of the house sits a full-size soccer goal with its weathered and torn net barely hanging from the crossbeam.

"It's peaceful today," she says.

"I think I'll cut the grass today and fix a few things."

"I'll help."

"Okay."

"Shall I write a poem first to commemorate move-in day?"

"On the spot?"

"Most of mine are."

"Really? I didn't know that. Well, yes, go ahead," I say.

Willow surveys the woods for a time, sometimes silently mouthing a word or two, sometimes drifting off, sometimes shaking her head yes or no. She's written and published hundreds of poems over the years, and I've read all of them, but this is the first time I've been engrossed by how she works. Moments later, she takes my hand and softly says, "The sun, warmth, fill the woods today with the promise of spring, of a new cycle, of the two of us planting a garden of return."

"That's beautiful," I say.

"Thank you. I have good subject matter."

"Thanks. Are you ready to begin?"

"Planting?"

"Yes, starting with the yard work."

"Ah. In a minute. Do you remember our conversation weeks ago about living a simple life?" she asks.

"Sure."

"Do you think you could live that way, outside the pull of work, just you and me, maybe a few kids? I didn't think I wanted kids, but standing here with you now made me reconsider."

"You could distance from work?" I ask.

"Probably not. You?"

"Maybe."

My foot starts to tap. Sometimes I think my half-baked start-up idea is too much. I've never been the lead executive before. Maybe I was never meant to be more than employee number two. Maybe I should get out of technology while I can still see clearly. Maybe it's time to follow my father's advice and focus on family. He would have liked Willow. But could I bring another child into this world after what happened?

"You went off," she says.

"I did."

"Where?"

"Having another child after Zack would be difficult."

"I wondered about that. One of these days I need to hear the whole Zack story."

"It's hard for me to even think about what happened, never mind say it out loud."

Still holding my hand, she circles her thumb around my palm.

"But I'll tell you soon," I say.

I take Willow's hand and focus again on the soccer goal. Fathers and sons have special places between them, places where unspoken beliefs pass down from one generation to another. That goal, that makeshift field was one of our places. Sometimes I wake at night and swear I can hear Zack playing.

Zen and the AT-AT

On the pilgrimage, I buy sixteen blue balloons filled with helium, one for each of my years at RadioRadio. Right after the purchase, in a large field with Willow at my side, I release them. As they float up, I reach for her hand and interlace my fingers with hers. With time, the balloons drift out of sight, but I can't seem to move off my spot or let go of Willow's hand. We're in the Berkshire Mountains, away for a long weekend right before Memorial Day. Willow is teaching a class at the local Zen center called "The Healing Power of Poetry" and asked me to tag along. The field we're in is filled with maybe two hundred pilgrims, all ballooning, all I'm sure with their own versions of death by Olivia.

Willow releases my hand and loops her arm around mine. With a little tug, she starts us into our walk toward the sparsely furnished building where we're staying. Walking in the field with her has a peacefulness and an effortlessness to it, which is also true when we car ride together, or talk deeply, or cook. Our building, even though spiritual, reminds me of the thousands of concrete buildings all across America that host big corporations. Steel, glass, and concrete rise out of the ground in modern, abstract ways, forming cathedrals where many workers lose their way in pursuit of what exactly? Money? Power? Certainly not happiness.

Right after we unlock our room door and enter the alcove, Willow wraps her arms around me and says, "My class starts tonight and goes until around ten and then picks up again tomorrow for the whole day. You're more than welcome to attend, but instead you may want to wander around and see what comes up."

"You sure?"

"That's really why I asked you to come."

"Oh."

"Nudity and sheets?"

A few hours later after an enterprising N&S afternoon in our Egyptian cotton sheets, Willow kisses me good-bye. She'll be back in a few hours after her stint in poetry land. Part of me is tempted to stay in our room the whole time, to savor the evening, to work, and to read-nap, but I don't. Ever since Willow sent that poem last year, the one I modified on fire day, I've trusted her judgment on deep spiritual stuff. I don't even modify her poetry anymore.

I leave our room under a lingering afternoon spell and head out to watch pilgrims, maybe even talk with a few. On the car ride out to this place, Willow asked me if I'd ever been on a pilgrimage. Apparently, all of these famous ones exist around the world. The Camino de Santiago, or St. James Way, in Spain. Shikoku Pilgrimage in Japan. Bodh Gaya in India. Route of Saints in Kraków, Poland. Salt Satyagraha in India. She's been on most of them, starting back when she was in her twenties. She said they changed her, opened her, and helped turn her into a poet, a healer. I was so fascinated, so impressed that she had pilgrimed, that over a bag of nuts and a bottled water at a Mass Pike rest stop, I had to look up the definition of a pilgrim on my phone and read it out loud to her. "According to Dictionary.com, a pilgrim is a person who journeys, especially a long distance, to some sacred place as an act of religious devotion, a traveler or wanderer especially in a foreign place, an original settler in a region, one of the band of Puritans who in 1620 founded the colony of Plymouth, Massachusetts, a newcomer to a region or place." I especially liked the newcomer definition. From that point on in the car ride, I started referring to our little trip as a pilgrimage and the people we were about to meet as pilgrims. I figured a spiritual center in the Berkshires was as close to the real thing as I would ever get, so why not?

It's already dark outside, so I decide to people-watch in the grand hall. The place truly is grand—a football field long and wide, with one entire wall of glass facing the mountains. A bunch of cushy chairs line the glass wall and, during the day, provide a place to rest and view. At this time, all I can see is my reflection in the glass, which I judge as short-term satisfied, long-term restless, and a vast improvement over last fall. Where to sit? Most of the glass wall-facing chairs are full, except for one, next to an older man. Another area in the center of the great hall, near the main entrance, has a couple of sofas facing each other, one empty, and provides a much better vantage point for watching pilgrims. I make my way toward the sofas, but when I'm almost there, I have a change of heart and head toward the older man. A minute later, I sit next to him. He's staring into the darkness with a closed book on his lap, with "Fearlessness" in the title. I pull out my phone and begin to read an article about the future of social networks.

"What brings you to the center?" the man asks.

"My girlfriend is teaching a class."

"Ah. That's all?"

I place my phone on the arm of the chair, stroke its smooth glass with my finger, and try not to look annoyed. The entire place is filled with an earthy incense smell that I can't identify, which I just noticed. Although I was open to pleasant talk earlier, I lost interest after the article caught my attention. At this point, I may be better off excusing myself, going to the sofa, and getting back to my article, or to people-watching. The benefits of scoping out passersby are numerous. First, it's outward focused instead of inward focused. Second, I don't have to talk. Third, I can make up stories about the people I watch that make my current problems pale in comparison. For example, I'm sure many people here have lost everything multiple times. Multiple deaths. Multiple divorces. Multiple firings. Yes, the sofa is a better choice. As I slip my phone into my pocket and get ready to leave, the man smiles.

"Do you know what kind of incense is burning?" I ask.

"Tibetan. It's based on the ancient Ayurvedic texts and is supposed to have healing power."

"I like it."

"Me, too."

"Back to your earlier question about what brings me to the center, today I released blue balloons."

"That's one of our best rituals."

"It is. Though if you asked my girlfriend, she would say I'm here because I've had a few rough years. I divorced. My son died. I recently lost my dream job. But I'm working on something new and will be fine. And you?"

"I teach here."

"About fearlessness?"

"Among other things. Three separate deaths in such a short time. I'm so sorry."

"Thank you."

"Though if you go through them, what a gift," he says.

There it is again, that word. Why do poets and spiritual people always seem to talk about gifts? Hearing it out loud is much more annoying than reading it in one of Willow's poems. A swell right below my stomach spreads up through my body, toward my mouth, where it surely will morph to invective. Luckily, at RadioRadio, I went to a management development class once to learn how to navigate idiotic comments, and at least on business topics, I'm quite good at it. These swells happened all the time on budget, people, and software product issues, and because of my training, I know how to turn a fuck-you-in-the-making into something calmer. I take a deep breath. Another, until the fresh air caps the anger, reshapes the fuck-you. Then I say, "That's one way to think about it."

The man crosses one leg over the other, angles himself toward me, and folds his hands over his book like they're a Ouija board planchette trying to tell him something. "Sorry, I didn't mean to upset you."

"No problem. I just don't think of loss as a gift."

"I know it's hard to accept. Soon, I'll spend three months in silent retreat where I'll open, touch, and release my own deaths."

"That sounds extreme."

"We all experience many deaths in a lifetime if we're willing to see them."

"I don't have that much emotional capacity," I say.

"Experiencing death of any kind is the hardest thing we do as humans."

"It is."

"If you don't mind, I have one more question."

"Sure. One more. I have to get going."

"Do you think your losses have broken you open?"

Broken open? What a strange question. I broke, yes, that definitely happened, badly. My divorce. Zack. The final takeaway, RadioRadio. But he asked the question as if being humpty-dumptied was a good thing, almost as if I needed more cracks instead of more love, instead of more work, almost as if I was better off because I fell. What kind of spiritual teacher encourages you to fall and break?

"I don't know. Maybe. I thought I was on the mend until I lost my job. Most of my focus now is on trying to figure out what to do next," I say.

"Ah, the universe."

"What?"

"It took away your favorite drug."

Swell or no swell, fuck him. Really, fuck him. This is why I've stayed away from this spiritual crap all these years. Drug? Just as I'm about to launch into a rampage about work not being a drug, another man approaches and tells the man his students are waiting for him. The man stands up, grabs his book, extends his hand, and warmly smiles. "By the way, I'm Dylan. Take care of yourself. May your work going forward be filled with openness."

And like that, Dylan leaves. My blood pressure slowly releases. Did divorce, death, job loss break me open? And what exactly does openness mean? If I did open, and if I stay that way, doesn't that mean it's much easier to get hurt again? Why would anyone stay open for long? I remain in the chair and devour every article I can find on social networks. Subscription models. Number of users. Way too many new and useless sound-bite social networks. Nobody is talking about anything close to my start-up idea, which isn't exactly a social network, but related, which isn't exactly anything fully formed yet. When I'm done, I look up; my reflection is doubled off the black window, translucent like a ghost, and preferable to my normal reflection. I spend a moment trying to locate the source of the doubling, but I can't.

Later that night, back in bed with Willow, I tell her all about my conversation with Dylan. She thinks she knows him, but she isn't sure. When I get to the part about death and gifts, she perks up and wants to discuss both, but I'm tired and tell her we'll discuss in the morning. As I drift into sleep, I'm surprisingly looking forward to spending the next day alone.

#

The sun-drenched room wakes us early, kindles us under the down comforter. An hour later, we grab an organic-everything breakfast and send each other off into the long day ahead. The guy at the front desk gives me three choices for trails to hike—short, medium, and long—and encourages me to take the short one because I'm not an experienced hiker. I'm feeling ardent, so I ignore him and decide to go long and hike the twenty-mile Grace and Bottoms Trail, which was named after the two women who years ago donated the thousand acres that the trail navigates to the Zen center.

Right from the start, the trail has a calmness. As I walk, the sun mottles the way with the help of large oak leaves, a stream gracefully wends down a small hill, and I don't pass a single soul. Now and then, large rock formations set the direction of the path, like someone placed them there for a reason, which I contemplate briefly. Twenty miles is a long way. If I average three miles per hour, with plenty of rest stops, I should finish in eight hours and be back in time to meet Willow for dinner, which is perfect, because we're leaving tonight for the three-hour drive back to Concord. Tomorrow, she'll be back to helping victims, and I'll be back full time, trying to flesh out my start-up idea.

The first part of the hike passes. I make steady progress, stopping to rest when I need to drink some water, eat a protein bar, or snap a photo of something unusual or beautiful. Small rocks someone stacked like a pyramid. A particularly majestic white birch. Another stream in full flow after the storm. At the stream's edge, I kneel and wet a dozen or so different mature green leaves. I place them on the water like water lilies, shape them into a floating arrow, and launch it. At first, caught in a small eddy, the arrow floats slowly, almost as if it believes it has a say in the inevitable, but then the main current grabs it, and it races off in the only possible direction, until a fallen tree branch downstream shatters it back into leaves.

About ten miles in, I come to a poorly marked fork in the trail. I slip my phone out of my pocket and check for a signal. None. That raises a flag, but not enough to turn around. Onward pilgrim. One path seems slightly more traveled than the other, so I take it. I'm sure it's the right way, and if not, it probably parallels the other trail. I have the same direction-gene most men do, which is a good thing this deep in the woods.

Miles later, after the trail narrows to an overgrown footpath, after the sky overcasts, and after I've done everything in my power to validate that my direction-gene hasn't failed me, I admit I'm lost. I check the time—six hours since I left. Even if I turn around now, I won't be able to make it back before dinner or nightfall. I'm still calm though occasional waves of fear threaten to dig in, forcing me to ward off each one soon after it arrives. Is that what Dylan's book meant by fearlessness? When the waves come, you push them back and soldier on?

At the next inflection point the woods open. The trail hugs the edge of the mountain and rims a gully maybe fifty feet deep as it pushes up and out of sight. It's not the way home, but it's breathtaking. How did I get so far off track? A hundred yards later, I turn around and start jogging back toward the Zen center, slowly at first, then with purpose and pace. Right before I re-enter into the woods, I slow. What's that at the bottom of the gully? It's rectangular, maybe two feet by three feet, with colors that have been washed by the weather. It's lodged between two large rocks, almost like it was placed there on purpose, part of a man-made altar in worship of I-don't-know-what. I take a step toward it and stop just short of the trail's edge. What the heck is it?

The drop-off into the gully is steep and rocky. Should I go down? I bet I can make a path. Carefully, I angle my body so that it's perpendicular to the gully and begin my slow descent by repeatedly leading with my left leg. Even so, I slip multiple times along the way and barely avoid falling. Every so often, I stop and refocus on the box, trying to discern it. When I'm close, I make out a red logo in the top left corner of the box, which is barely recognizable. Lego? What would a Lego set be doing out here in the middle of nowhere?

When I reach the box, I kneel down next to it and wipe caked dirt off the front until the image of a Star Wars AT-AT Motorized Walker Lego set is clear. This one promises to walk and bob its head up and down and looks like a metal turtle with long plodding legs. Zack liked the AT-AT, but not as much as the Falcon.

A few years ago, I gave Zack a Star Wars Millennium Falcon Lego set. We'd watched all of the Star Wars movies in a row the previous summer, and from the marathon on, he dropped not-so-subtle hints that a Star Wars Lego set was all he wanted for Christmas. After he unwrapped his present on Christmas morning, he was so excited that we spent the rest of the day building it together. I was pretty excited, too. The finished Falcon still is hanging from the ceiling in his room.

I open the AT-AT box. All of the pieces are still there, mostly in their exact pre-use positions. I notice an unopened envelope, although it's hard to make out the handwritten name, which has smeared over time. Jimmy? Jack? Julie? I open the envelope and pull out a birthday card that reads: *Son, on your birthday, there's one important thing to keep in mind . . .* I open the card. *You're another year closer to conquering the world!* Then in cursive handwriting, the same as on the envelope, this: *James, I love you. Let's build this set together soon. Dad.*

I drop to my knees, shake my head, and repeatedly pound my fist on my thigh as I scream, "Fuck! Fuck! Fuck!" The fucks echo through the gully, the Berkshires, the state, the country, the world, the universe, searching for something. But instead, all that comes is a wave of grief, the kind that promises to get it all out but can't, the kind that in the end can only confirm that some acts aren't forgivable.

After Zack died, I did grieve some, late at night when no one else was around, with loads of scotch, but most of the time I didn't. Instead, I worked. And worked. And worked. I tried with little success to get what I'd done out of my head, but nothing at RR calmed the chronic cycle of guilt and pain. What causes that cycle, causes people to spin, day after day, year after year, on their mistakes? Who keeps pushing the repeat button?

I pick up rock after rock—big ones and small ones—and hurl them as hard as I can at nothing. They barely make a sound when they hit. Should I smash the AT-AT? Rocks are as potent as a sledgehammer when leveraged properly. Maybe that's why the set is here in the first place—a failed attempt at destruction that I can now set straight.

After maybe twenty minutes with the AT-AT, I need to leave. It's a matter of survival. At night in western Massachusetts, the bears, bobcats, and gray wolves own the woods. But what should I do about the set? Should I take it with me or leave it? If I carry it back, it may slow down my jog, which is a problem this late in the day. But I can't leave it.

I return the letter to the envelope, pack the box up so that it's close to how I found it, and put it back in exactly the same location. As I stare at it, it's clear that's not good enough. I flip over, and on all fours, I start to dig. The soil is soft, the rocks I hit are manageable, and the loose dirt smells like incense. In no time, I dig a shallow hole and secure the AT-AT in it. As I'm covering it up, I say, "May you both find peace, wherever you are now."

I get up, pausing for a moment, before I climb out of the gully sure-footed. As soon as I'm on the trail, I start to jog briskly toward the Zen center as fast as my heart allows. I don't think I can run all the way back, but I have to try. I have to get out of the woods. I have to get back to Willow. As I pass rock formations, streams, and increasingly ominous oaks and maples, I can't stop thinking about the dad and James. What happened to them? Did the dad come out here and throw the set into the gully? Did the son? Did I do the right thing?

My phone rings.

"Are you okay? I was worried about you," Willow asks.

"Yeah. Fine. Long story. I'll be at the room soon."

Back in the room, as I'm telling Willow the Lego story, I start to choke up. She holds me close, gently strokes my back, and chokes up herself. Then she says, "It will all be okay, Dan. It will all be okay."

As she's holding me, I feel this strange warmth next to me, almost as if Zack is by my side, or James, or the dad, or all three. Their presence directs me, and for the first time since we arrived at this place, I understand. Then I say, "I need to leave on my own pilgrimage as soon as we get back to Concord."

PART II—*The Pyramids*

The Pilgrimage

Zack and Dad are buried in the same cemetery, not too far from Concord. That's where I am now at the crack of dawn. I leave the Prius running and securely fasten my backpack, which contains everything I'll need for the next three months, which has no practical use in a cemetery. The grass is dewed over, and I almost hate to walk on it, like it's a piece of art that must be saved. I haven't been here in a long time, and I won't stay more than a few minutes now—there's still too much charge. This just seemed the right place and time of day to start my pilgrimage.

I go to Dad's tombstone first. Mom has been recently; wilted flowers are glazed over, and underneath the dew the plot is perfectly landscaped, just the way Dad would like it. The place smells cold and damp, shortening my breath. I rub my finger along the arched top of the tombstone, which is unfinished and rough like it was chiseled this morning. From my pocket, I pull out a few pennies and place them at the apex of the arch. What would Dad say to me now about my start-up idea, about any idea that places work above family? Probably not to do it. Take my money and live a peaceful life away from it all. Marry Willow, have more kids, plant a garden. Live a simple life, like Willow suggested weeks ago. Let go of the hi-tech dream after a good-almost-to-the-end run. Maybe I could do something creative. Paint? Or sculpt? Or write? Though I have no experience in anything but technology. Or maybe I could spend time with Willow and grow our family.

Family was different once, larger, all-American. Sunday dinners were jazz; with the clan gathered around the much-too-small dining room table, with every square inch filled with food, we riffed off each other on topics ranging from politics to poker. In the fall after each feast, the men, following some long-handed-down tradition, watched NFL games. Dad was a Patriots fan. Zack too. Glued to the television, mostly silent, we only spoke when some random statistic came to mind, which the three of us had a knack for retaining, or when a hunger pang called, which was often. I loved those days.

I say good-bye to Dad, walk across the cemetery to Zack, and destroy more art along the way. Can the dead sense what I've done? I reach Zack and stand in my same spot, the one where I witnessed them lower him into the ground. At one point that morning, I had my arm around Hannah, trying to comfort her in the way that divorced people sometimes do in crisis, like we suspended our disbelief for a time, like a real connection between us still existed. But after a moment, she pulled away and instead took the hand of her new husband. Olivia must have witnessed the entire pull-away, because she reached her arm around me and, with grace, gathered me in. Now, all three of them are gone—my love, my son, my work. Sometimes, like in this moment or in the woods with the AT-AT, I glimpse the enormity of what has happened these last years, but I can't stay there long.

I take a step closer to Zack, start to tremble, and hold back. I read the tombstone, checking to see if the facts are still right. *Zackery D. Underlight. Born March 5, 2000. Died October 20, 2010. He loved with all his heart.* Then I hear myself say, "I didn't mean to cause you harm."

Dozens of polished gray and white stones rest at the base of his tombstone. They're spread out randomly and look like egg-shaped marbles. Someone must have put them there, though I can't imagine why. I get down on my knees and gather them up. Right in the center of the tombstone's base, below *all* and *his*, I use them to build a stone pyramid, alternating gray and white stones with the base eight inches square and the height about the same. It's arresting, even though it won't last, even though time will eventually knock it down. When I finish, I kiss the tips of my fingers, touch the tombstone, and say, "I'm so sorry, Zack. I wish I could trade places with you." Slowly, I get up and walk away, turning back a few times to take in the pyramid.

Securely buckled into the Prius, I motor out of the cemetery and make my way toward the Mass Pike. For my pilgrimage, I'm not going to follow any of the famous routes that Willow took. Instead, for inspiration, I've decided to visit the corporate headquarters of many of the Fortune 500 companies across the United States. Only then will I know if my half-baked start-up idea has any legs. The current five hundred are bunched on the East Coast and the West Coast, but plenty exist in between. General Electronics. The automakers. Sears. The oil moguls. Dozens in Silicon Valley from Intel to Google to Peach. Microguild. Starbucks. Walmart. Coca-Cola. The financial guys on Wall Street. The New England companies. I'll drive the Midwest route first, and then make my way down through Texas into the Southwest until I hit Southern California. From there, I'll make frequent stops up the West Coast to Seattle. On the way back east, I'll zigzag across the country until I reach Florida. For the last leg of my trip, I'll drive up the East Coast and make my way home. I've mapped out the entire path. At first, I used mapping software to help me calculate the most efficient route, but I abandoned it—it's not that kind of trip. Overall, about twelve thousand miles, thirty-two states, and 234 companies. With a little luck, I'll finish in four months.

Along the way, I'm going to stop and see my old professor, the one who persuaded me to take a risk with RadioRadio all those years ago, the one who, other than Olivia, shaped my views on technology the most. I haven't seen her since I joined RR.

#

My first stop is General Electronics in Schenectady, New York. Although Schenectady isn't the corporate headquarters anymore—they make turbines and batteries here these days—it is where Thomas Edison started it all at the turn of the century, so I opted. I park, open my trunk, slip on my gray Patriots sweatshirt, and fill the large front pocket with stones. At the city boundary, I passed by a marble and stone quarry fronted by a store. About a mile later, I turned around, backtracked to the store, and zeroed in on these one-inch gray and white pebbles. I purchased as many as I could fit in my trunk—three hundred pounds' worth.

The two main GE buildings, which are probably a hundred years old, are set off the road in a campus. The one on the right has a giant "General Electronics" sign over it with the "GE" logo on top of that. Both sign and logo are wired and bulbed, capable of lighting up at night like a Christmas tree.

I slip through GE's front gate. A park bench about halfway invites me. From there I watch a number of folks hurriedly walk by. Even so, everyone is friendly, and we exchange "Good morning" and "Have a good day." Unlike some of my previous people-watching sessions, where I attributed all kinds of negative stuff to everyone that passed, I like these people. An older man wearing a derby. Guys in jeans and work boots. Women with kind smiles. They're all normal hard-working folks who are looking for a fair shake, who love this community, whose parents bought into the middle-class dream when it was still real. President Obama was out here a couple of years ago and gave a speech, which I'm sure he believed, about American jobs and restoring the middle class. I bet many of these people drank the Kool-Aid.

Here's the thing—the middle-class jobs this country was built on are gone. As long as the corporate mantra is faster, cheaper, and better, as long as globalization is king, all of those jobs will remain overseas, which is approximately forever. Lots of pundits are saying the same thing these days, so maybe it's slowly seeping into the American collective conscious, if such a thing exists. What most don't know, however, is that even once-abundant hi-tech jobs are dwindling at an alarming rate. Twelve kids out of college today can form a start-up for virtually nothing and write an application that's sold for billions in only a couple of years. It took thousands and a lot of time to do that twenty years ago. Where is the country headed? I'm not sure, but the change won't stop with dwindling numbers. The next revolution forward won't be a return to the hi-tech glory days, or about hi-tech at all, or about any one leader. Thomas Edison-less, it will be about something else.

A suspension bridge about halfway up joins the two GE buildings. From this distance, I can see someone making her way from one side to the other, probably on her way to one of the infinite meetings that dominate corporate America schedules. On the ground below the bridge, right at the center—the core—is where I'll do it. GE has an air to it; I can see why it was the birthplace of a revolution. It's ordinary, yet it's not. The air, oil-tinged, is filled with the tail end of greatness. Maybe that's why I like these people— they're holding on to something lost long ago with faint hope of a return.

Under the bridge, I kneel, reach in my pocket, and run my fingers through the smooth, hard stones. A young man walks by, glances my way, and smiles, before continuing into the building. I pull two handfuls of rocks out of my pocket and start to build a pyramid, like the one I built for Zack. Stone by stone it takes shape, rises out of its concrete foundation, pointing up toward the bridge. About three rows up, I leave a space for one rock in the center and slip a quarter into the space instead.

The pyramid only takes a few minutes to complete, and I'm grateful I finished without anyone noticing. Back on my feet right above it, I imagine red laser lights shooting out of the capstone, dancing all over the belly of the bridge, the buildings, the campus, the city, in life-saving surgery.

#

"They've turned the water off."

"Don't they realize the city is bankrupt? I mean, people want to work; there's just nothing here for them, not even water."

"The whole country is a profit-driven corporation now."

I'm in a run-down breakfast joint just outside of Detroit, in the process of visiting the automakers and their suppliers in Michigan: Autoliv, Ford, General Motors, Penske, TRW Auto Holdings, Visteon. The two guys next to me can't get over the fact that the utility company is systematically shutting off the water each week for thousands of families who can't pay their utility bill. The restaurant hasn't been renovated since at least the eighties. The walls are paneled, and the simulated wood paneling is covered with old photos and plaques. AFL-CIO. Masons. A youth baseball team the owner must have sponsored. From the outside, the restaurant looks like an oversized train car with large rectangular windows cut into its side. A row of booths with heavily pockmarked linoleum tabletops lines the windows. I'm in one of those. Another row of equally pockmarked stand-alone tables are next to the booths and a counter most likely full of regulars is next to the tables. The place smells like bacon and coffee, like morning in my childhood home.

As I'm eavesdropping on the men, I have a hard time processing their conversation. Do we live in a country where families are denied water? I return to my scrambled eggs, pancakes, and morning *Detroit News*. As I flip through the sections, sure enough, I come across an editorial titled "Water For All," which confirms what the booth-men are saying. More than 300,000 of the city's customers, including schools, commercial buildings, and residential accounts, haven't paid their bill. There really is a city-led campaign to shut off thousands of accounts weekly. Social services are threatening to remove kids from homes unless bills are paid and water is restored. Temporary jobs for contractors willing to help get the city's water crisis under control exist, but the editorial equates workers taking these jobs to scabs crossing an imaginary picket line.

I finish my breakfast, refill my coffee cup, and approach the men at the next table. "Excuse me, I heard what you guys were saying about water. Do you mind if I join you and ask you a few questions?"

"You a reporter?" one man asks.

"No, just passing through. I'm having a hard time believing that something like that could happen in the United States."

"You ever been to Detroit before?"

"No."

"All right, buddy, pull up a chair. What's your name?"

"Dan."

"I'm Will. This is Jimmy."

I grab a chair and slide up to the end of their table. Both Will and Jimmy are gray, probably in their forties. Both are wearing jeans, Carhartt sweatshirts, and work boots. Will has a beard; Jimmy doesn't. There's no food on the table, and they're each nursing a cup of black coffee. Life has leathered their faces.

"Where you from, Dan?"

"Massachusetts."

"Bet they have plenty of water in Massachusetts."

"I have a well. Water is free."

"That's the way it should be. Detroit is bankrupt. There are no jobs. We both worked at the GM plant for years, but those jobs are long gone. Now we work odd handyman jobs when we can find them, like the painting job we're headed to now."

I sip my coffee, wondering about the costs to provide water to a city: piping-in costs from the reservoir, purification costs, employee salaries for engineering and administration. These are real dollars, and someone has to pay. It's certainly much more complicated than pulling water out of a well in the backyard. Still, it seems un-American to deny people water. Or inhumane. I've been so caught up in my own problems, in turning my crash into something positive, that I had no idea what was going on here, or for that matter, anywhere in the country. "I guess it does cost money to provide water to a city. Someone has to pay. But overall, I agree with you guys."

Jimmy glances at Will, says now-I-understand with his eyebrows, and for the first time since I joined them, I'm other, different, white-collar, someone with money, part of the problem instead of a concerned citizen. Then Jimmy says, "Let me tell you a math story, Dan. When I was working full time, my wife and I were pulling in $60k per year. We had a home. Nothing fancy. Three-bedroom over on K Street. About a thousand-a-month mortgage payment on a modest house. We shared two cars, junkers, but you know, good enough to get me, my wife, and our teenage sons where we had to go. Sure, a little more money would have been nice, but none of us was complaining. We were happy. Then I lost my job."

"When was that?" I ask.

"Right after the crash. Early 2009. Things got real hard for us after that. But I'm getting ahead of myself. Here's the math from when I was still employed. You good at math, Dan?"

I nod.

"Okay, on the 60k, take 15k off for all of the taxes—federal, state, local. Long-term deductions like for Social Security and insurance like workers comp and my, luckily, small piece of healthcare. Now we're at 45k. From there, take 12k off for the mortgage, so now we're at 33k. You with me so far?"

"Yes."

Jimmy finishes his cup and then signals over to the waitress for a refill. I haven't had to worry about money for such a long time. That's one of the lures of hi-tech where the basic deal is, *Give us your life, all of your hours, and you'll never have to think about money again. We'll even write apps to help you manage it.* These guys, like most people I guess, have to plan out every last dollar.

Coffee cup in hand, Jimmy continues, "Okay, so we're at 33k. Now there are things like heating oil. Winters in Detroit are cold. Then there's gas, mostly to get back and forth to work, and Internet, which the boys need for school, and electricity, and of course water. That gets us down to around 20k, which brings me to the last part of the story."

Jimmy sips his coffee. For the first time I look over at Will, who's been quiet the whole time. His eyes are teared up.

"You okay?" I ask.

He looks out the window.

"Don't mind Will," Jimmy says. "After he lost everything, even more than I did, he can't talk about what happened anymore."

"I'm sorry."

Will turns my way, looks me straight in the eyes, and says, "Thanks."

"Okay, financially, we're in the fourth quarter now, so to speak. I have 20k left. Family of four. We still need to buy food, clothes, supplies for school, even a Christmas present or two. Even if we spent all the money on food, which we mostly did, that's roughly thirteen dollars a day for each of us. Not enough, so we still had to dip into the credit cards each year just to cover unanticipated expenses. So, Dan, even when I was working, the math didn't add up. When I lost my job and we used up our limited savings, there was no way I could pay for most of those things anymore, never mind water."

Is this the new norm in America? Good hard-working people, who are making what has to be an average salary, can't make it? And then they lose their job, and all the government can do is stand by and charge them for water as they're losing everything? "Thank you. I get it now. I'm sorry it took me awhile."

"That's okay, Dan. Most of us are trying to hold on, hoping for a way out. That's the American way, right? But we're losing ground every day."

"Isn't there anything you can do to fight it?"

"Fight it? Everyone with power thinks we're the ones at fault. The city put a property tax lien on my house for not paying the water bill and is now trying to foreclose. Do you believe that? I told them to get in the lender line. I mean, what kind of country denies its citizens water or tries to take away your house when the country is in so much trouble? Who do they think is going to buy it?"

"I wish there was something I could do," I say.

"There isn't. We don't have a voice. What do you do, Dan?"

"Right now, I'm unemployed. I'm working on an idea for a software company."

Jimmy glances over at Will again. "Being unemployed knocks you down, doesn't it?"

"It does."

"Will your new company provide jobs?"

"Some."

"If it's one of those websites where you can post pictures or little blurbs about nothing, don't bother. We live in an era of cacophony, Dan. Don't add to it."

For the rest of my cup of coffee, we switch to more familiar ground. All three of us love the NFL. They argue Matthew Stafford is statistically better than Brady, that Calvin Johnson, Megatron, is the best receiver ever, that Barry Sanders is the best running back in the modern era. I counter on Brady, but am not in the mood for a statistics war, so I let the rest go. At the end, we exchange names and numbers, during which I promise to let them know how my little venture turns out and to send them condolences when the Patriots win yet another Super Bowl.

As I return to the hum of the highway, to my pyramids-across-America gig, I can't get *We live in an era of cacophony* out of my head. What's needed is not only about giving people a real voice; it's about giving people a collective voice that cuts through the noise.

#

I enter, my backpack heavy with stones. The campus is like no other. Sprawling, perfectly landscaped with tropical trees that thrive in California—mulberry, lychee, passion fruit. Throughout the three hundred acres, the reflecting ponds, fountains, and man-made lakes perfectly complement the ten earthquake-proof steel, glass, and concrete buildings, each a triumph of modern architecture. At the back of the campus, an amphitheater, the Peach Center, seats ten thousand. It's used not only for all-hands company meetings, but also for regular free-of-charge concerts. Coldplay headlined here last month. On the walkways, on the volleyball courts, and in the numerous outdoor restaurants that feature almost every kind of food, young men and women, who make up the highest concentration of hi-tech geniuses in the world, recharge before they resume building great products.

For the last fifteen years, the campus has been the home of Peach, the most successful, most admired, most innovative company in the world. Peach has disrupted the phone, computer, watch, and television markets and is the envy of the industry. During said time, the company has accumulated more than 200 billion in cash, enough to buy many of the hi-tech giants that I've already visited in this state. What's more impressive is when Peach started its current run, which has no end in sight, most pundits and competitors had written the company off as a has-been whose heyday had passed.

I've been in California for more than two weeks and have pyramided, among others, Intelligence, Cisco, eBay, PhotoPhotobook, Google, McKesson, NetApp, Oracle, and Yahoo. California has fifty-three companies on the Fortune 500, most of them technology firms, so I've been pyramiding nonstop. The raisings went well, and I'm to the point now where I've perfected my construction skills. As I layer stone after stone, I carefully assess their size, shape, and brilliance to determine proper placement. As a result, my pyramids have grown larger and more vibrant. At PhotoPhotobook, I built one two feet wide and two feet tall that glistened in the California sun.

Peach is not only at the pinnacle of American business, but also at the pinnacle of worldwide business. The company has great software and hardware, a great team, and a great culture. Folks, including me, literally love its products. In addition, Peach is vertically integrated and controls every piece of its supply chain, which goes against industry norms, which results in best-in-class profit margins of forty percent. And although Peach tries to stay away from social issues, at a closer glance, the company clearly cares about the work-life balance of its people and about the broader communities in which it operates. Part of me believes that if my start-up accomplishes a fraction of what Peach has achieved, it would be a miracle. But part of me is after something different, not bigger, but more connected, more relational, more socially relevant.

Behind the amphitheater stands a large cypress tree with two hand-carved oak benches facing the tree, two of the many artisan pieces throughout the campus. Right next to the tree, I slip off my backpack, dump out the pebbles, and begin to construct a pyramid stone by stone, larger pieces on the bottom, smaller ones on top. A short time later, the pyramid complete, I sit on the bench, pull out my Peach phone, and snap a picture. This is the first time, and probably the only time, I'll photograph my work. The pyramid seems to belong here, like it has instantly entered into a symbiotic relationship with the cypress.

"Did you make that?" a woman asks. She's standing in front of the other bench about to sit.

"Yes."

"It's beautiful."

"Thanks."

"You work here?"

"No, just passing through looking for a little inspiration."

"Ah, do you mind if I sit?"

"Not at all," I say.

The woman sits on the other bench, pulls an apple from her briefcase, and starts to read a book, A *Simpler Way*, by authors I don't know. The woman is thirty-something with long flowing brown hair and wire-rimmed glasses circa the late sixties. She's wearing a flowered dress and sandals, and though we've only spoken a few words, she exudes intelligence, and a strength in her eyes pulls at me in a familiar way. After she reads a few pages of her book and finishes her apple, she asks, "Why do you do it?"

"Build the pyramids?"

"Yes."

I've been asked this question multiple times during my trip. My favorite answer: I'm an artist celebrating corporate America. Our companies and their achievements are in every way as monumental and everlasting as the pyramids, so I'm shedding light on that fact by building pyramids at most Fortune 500 companies. People seem to buy that answer. Strangely though, with this woman, on this campus, I don't want to sell. Instead, I say, "My son died in an accident when he was ten. It was my fault. I'm doing it in his memory."

"I'm so sorry. I didn't mean to—"

"It's okay."

The woman closes her book. She angles her body toward me, smiles, and lightly strokes her forearm with her index finger. She looks like she wants to know more and, at the same time, is smart enough not to ask.

"Are you in hi-tech?" she asks.

"Yes. I worked for RadioRadio for sixteen years. I left recently."

"That was a great company."

"It was."

"Did you know Olivia?"

"A little."

"There was a time when I aspired to be like her."

"Many people did."

"Though she was more of a marketing genius than the brains behind their products."

"I guess."

"Well, I better get back to it."

The woman reopens her book and immerses herself. I return to my pyramid. Is what she said true? Was I the brains behind RR? Olivia was clearly the public face, but we made all the big decisions together. Our initial products, based on my high-level design. The timing of our IPO, based on my analysis. Our cloud and big data strategies, based on my research. Right up until the last year, I was involved in every major corporate decision, and ninety-nine percent of the time Olivia accepted my initial recommendation.

"Sorry to bother you again. Are you looking for work?" the woman asks.

"I'm not sure. I'm trying to figure out my next step."

"Would you like me to sponsor you at Peach? I'm sure we could find something for you here."

I study the woman to see if she's serious. She is. Part of me wants to say yes. This place has such a familiarity—like what RR could have been. Maybe that's why I took this trip, to find the real RR, the one Olivia and I promised ourselves we would build all those years ago. Maybe I need to go no farther than Palo Alto, join this team, ride the wave they've already launched. I don't need a job as big as I had before. I would be happy to help implement somebody else's vision. But there is my start-up idea, now almost fully formed, now a bona fide big idea. Finally, I say, "That's generous of you, but I think I'll pass. I've got some stuff I need to do on my own."

"If you ever change your mind, give me a call." The woman gathers her stuff, stands, extends her hand, and smiles. "Nice meeting you. Take care." Then she hands me her business card that reads, *Sarah Fordiano, Executive Vice President, Products*, before disappearing into the vastness of Peach.

#

Hitchhikers give me the willies. Something with the whole proposition is unbalanced—an offer of help on one hand, a potential ax murderer on the other. Yet, here I am, pulling over to the side of I-5, for a kid with long blond hair, who reminds me of Kurt Cobain. Since Zack died, anytime I see a hitchhiker I pick him or her up, willies and all. Mostly hims. Mostly short distances within Massachusetts. Mostly okay. One time a shadowy guy subtly threatened me for a twenty, so I handed him a hundred and sent him on his way. But that's about as close as I've ever gotten to the ax.

I just finished my pyramid ritual at IQ, and I'm heading up toward Washington to visit Microguild and Starbucks. The IQ campus reminds me of RadioRadio toward the end of my run there. The beauty is unparalleled, and at the same time an undercurrent of ruthlessness, left over from the days when the company was unstoppable, permeates everything. IQ caught a big wave, didn't even create it, but it knew how to harness and manipulate its power. For decades in tech, it was impossible to introduce a new software product that didn't run on an IQ hardware platform. But now the once mighty IQ has largely lost its strength. Mobility, cloud, and big data made the company an afterthought and another victim of the innovator's dilemma.

I've been on the road a few months and have pyramided more than a hundred and fifty companies so far. Everything is exactly as planned, though the repetition is starting to wear on me. Maybe 234 is too much? Plus, I've hardly spoken with Willow. I miss her; I miss home. Before I left, we agreed to a text-only pilgrimage. Actually, at the start, she proposed no contact at all, made some poignant point about the power of solitude on pilgrimages, but I didn't fully buy it.

When my car comes to a full stop, I roll down the window. Kurt Cobain picks up his backpack, catches up to the car, leans against the door, and smiles.

"Hey, there. Where are you headed?" I ask.

"Portland."

"I'm passing through there. Jump in."

"I'm Jack. Thanks for the ride."

Jack gets settled. I can tell a lot in the first few minutes of any hitch. His backpack appears to be brand new. He's clean and smells like Old Spice, so he's only been on the road a short time. He looks right at me when he speaks with honest eyes and a sincere smile. I judge him safe.

During our conversation, I learn Jack is a recent college grad on his way to Portland to visit his girlfriend who's still in school. He grew up in Seattle but moved to Sacramento a few years ago. People tell him he looks like Kurt all the time. He's surprisingly easy to talk with for a young male, so I open up and tell him about my cross-country pilgrimage to visit big companies, even about the pyramids.

"Why pyramids?" he asks.

"I don't know. I guess the originals were such an epic achievement. And they were all over the world. And they pointed to the heavens."

"They sound cool, man. What do you do for a living?" he asks.

"I'm thinking about starting a software company."

"Oh, that's cool, too. Hopefully, different than the ones around here."

"Why do you say that?"

"They don't hire people like me. Have you seen the statistics on recent college grad hire rates? They're not pretty. I was a liberal arts major in school. About the only option open to me right now is to go back to school. It's sad."

I glance Jack's way and nod before returning to the road. Has the United States reached a point where we've intentionally devalued areas of study that have zero economic value? Have we unintentionally extended the age at which our youth enter the workforce? Part of me could get behind entering the workforce later—that way people would have more time to explore what mattered to them. But part of me scoffs at the idea because I knew exactly what I wanted to do right out of school.

"Sometimes I think the whole model is broken," Jack says. "Unfortunately, there's no way to talk about what we're all feeling.

No one cares about youth protests anymore. Anyone who tries to organize is radicalized and dismissed."

"I was in Detroit a short time ago. They turned off the water because families couldn't pay."

"That's messed up."

"Exactly."

"Good song."

"Yeah." I increase the volume. When I picked up Jack, I was playing an old Police album, *Synchronicity*. The song "King of Pain" started a moment ago. At RadioRadio, I played this game with up-and-comers called King for a Day, where I asked them what they would do with RR if they were in Olivia's shoes. Even though I played it hundreds of times over the years, I was always amazed by the quality of ideas and opinions generated during the game. Olivia hated KFD and said she didn't need employees to do her job for her, but for me, nothing was as powerful organizationally. After I explain the game to Jack, I ask, "So what would you do if you were king for a day?"

Jack goes silent for a time and then starts tapping his finger against the window intermittently like he's entered into a Morse code exchange with an unknown accomplice. When he returns, he says, "You know, it's pretty simple for me. First thing I would do is trust the scientists, which when you think about it, it's insane that we don't. So that would mean things like a global plan for climate change and for going green and sustainable in every way we can with a focus on water, food, and energy. After that, I would focus on education. A lot of our problems today stem from lack of education. How do we raise the collective education levels of the world so we can have more meaningful conversations? I have no idea how to do that, and it would probably take forever, but it's needed. Then I would make healthcare a basic right for everyone. Why that one isn't obvious . . . ?" Jack pauses again, taps the window more with his index finger, and then shakes his head no. "Okay, so I know what I'm about to say is super-idealistic, but, whatever, I am king for a day. I would let people work at what they love and somehow pay them enough to live comfortably for whatever loving thing they contribute to society, even if it's not a money-maker. And lastly, I would encourage people to protest more. There needs to be a constant questioning going on if we're going to make it another century. Change should be king, not for a day, but for every day. That's my list. My parents were second-generation hippies, named me after JFK. Must've rubbed off."

I take my eyes off the road again and glance over at Jack, who is back to tapping the window, this time with a smile on his face. "You came up with that on the spot?"

"Kind of. It's been brewing."

"Do you think society could handle people working at what they love?"

"Sure. Fewer people might be in the garbage-collection business, but otherwise, people would gravitate."

"The country wouldn't function without those kind of businesses."

"We'd figure it out, man. Robots. Whatever. My main point is the era of money rules is almost over."

"A lot of people would disagree with you on that one."

"Mostly people stuck in the past," he says. "By the way, I need to make a pit stop. Can you pull off at the next exit?"

"Sure."

I silently listen to more of The Police, replaying my conversation with Jack a few times until it settles in, until I believe his main points. If a twenty-something kid knows what to do, if many of us know what to do, what keeps us from moving forward? Is it lack of leadership? Do we need another Kennedy? Or Martin Luther King, Jr.? I read once that what made King so effective was that everyone listening already knew what he was saying was true. What he did was voice the collective conscience of millions. But we haven't had anyone like him for almost fifty years. Or maybe it's not about leadership. Maybe it's that we know what to do, but don't know how to manage the complexity required to do it.

I take the exit ramp off the highway. Unfortunately, no gas stations or restaurants come into view when I reach the stop sign. I offer to go to the next exit, but Jack suggests we drive a little down the country road and see what we find. A short time later, in a patch of forest, I pull over to the side of the road. Jack gets out, says he'll be right back, and heads into the redwoods. There should be a place in my new company for folks like Jack, folks who are smart and have learned how to reason in school, folks who are socially responsible but don't have technical credentials. Maybe that's why the United States has gotten into this predicament—too much focus on business and technology and not enough on the humanities?

When Jack returns to the car, I say, "I think I'll go, too. Be right back." I head into the woods and find a suitable tree. I'll have to ask Jack for his contact information when I drop him off. Maybe I'll be able to hire him down the road. He'd be a good fit. A moment later, as I'm zipping up, I hear something behind me and turn around. Jack is pointing a gun at me with one hand and holding a set of license plates with the other. My plates.

"Give me your wallet and keys and phone," he says.

I try to say "What?" but nothing comes. My heart races, and the thought crosses my mind that I may die of a heart attack if he doesn't shoot me first. So Jack's the one. After years of uneventful hitches, I'm going to die in the woods in Northern California at the hand of a millennial hitchhiker who will probably get away scot-free. The headline: *Failed software exec killed by unknown assailant. Finally gets what he deserves.*

"C'mon, man, give me your wallet, keys, and your phone. Don't worry, I'm not going to hurt you. I only want your cash and your car." Jack throws the plates on the ground.

As I hand Jack the things he requested, sweat prickles my forehead. How could I have been so wrong about him? He seemed so solid, so clear.

"This was all a setup?" I ask.

"This is what I do. I steal cars."

"Why not steal out of parking lots?"

"I don't know. I like getting to know people before I rip them off."

"Did you mean any of that stuff you said when you were king for a day?"

"I threw you a bone, man. It seemed like you needed one. None of those things will ever happen, which is why I do what I do. We live in the era of every man for himself. At your age, I'm surprised you don't already know that."

Jack throws my phone on the ground and smashes it with the heel of his boot. Then he throws my cashless wallet on the ground and backs away with exactly the same smile he used on me when he first leaned up against my car.

#

After the robbery, I stood in the woods stunned for a time. Having a gun pointed at me made me realize two things. First, no matter what I had done, I wanted to live; I wanted to serve; I wanted to take what had happened with Zack and flip it into something positive. If not for me, for others. Second, I was done with hitchhikers. What was I thinking? I picked up my plates and cashless wallet and jogged what must have been a good five miles to the nearest strip mall, where I was able to get a new phone and call Willow. During a conversation where I couldn't soak up her voice fast enough, we figured out my recovery plan: contact the insurance company, report the car stolen, get a rental car, buy a plane ticket. We did briefly discuss continuing the pilgrimage, but I'd had enough after Jack and wanted to get home. At Willow's urging, I did decide to meet with my old professor before returning to Concord; at least that much of the trip was salvageable. Last thing Willow said to me on our call: "Everything is emerging exactly as it needs to."

Well.

In a rental car, I slip into a parking space in front of a restaurant, an Indian place close to the Duke campus. I'm exhausted because I didn't sleep on the red-eye, but also excited to see my brilliant former professor, Vidya, to hear what she has to say about my big idea. Last time I met her, I was deciding between going into business with Olivia or accepting an offer from Microguild. She teaches at Duke University these days. Close to twenty years ago, when she was a professor at M.I.T., I enrolled in her advanced software algorithms class, and after that class, I took every software course she taught. I even signed on as her graduate research assistant in my final year. Her brilliance attracted me, for sure, but also her ideals. She was the one who first convinced me that software would eventually eliminate many forms of suffering on the planet—from poverty to lack of education to adequate food and water for all.

Vidya is waiting for me and waves as I get out of my car. With the exception of her gray, striated, shoulder-length hair, she looks exactly the same—fit, not an inch taller than five feet, dark brown skin, wearing one of her signature perfectly tailored business suits. I've never seen her in anything but one of those suits, not even on long weekends when we were in the middle of a code-a-thon. Even from this distance, she still has the same smirk on her face, the same penetrating eyes that she had all those years ago. It's like we're the only two people in the world in on the big secret, the one that will change everything.

After a hug, I kiss her on each cheek. We enter the restaurant, talking nonstop about how it's been too long, how we both look the same, how we've followed each other online. The hostess greets Vidya as though she's a family member and shows us to a secluded table in the back of the restaurant. Vidya asks me a few questions about my food preferences before ordering our dinner in her native language. Even though I haven't heard her speak Hindi in a long time, I'm as surprised by it as the first time I heard it because her teaching voice is perfect Oxford English. When she graduated from university in India, she did study at Oxford and obtained her PhD in engineering. After graduate school, she accepted her first teaching job and settled in the States with the last fifteen years at Duke.

For the first part of our conversation, we continue to catch up. Robbery recap. Willow. Her three kids are grown and established. Her husband will retire from the bank next year. She'll teach a little longer, though she's making a fortune on the side consulting with hi-tech companies. She seems genuinely happy. As we're talking, an ambrosial spread of food arrives: Vegetable Samosas, Chicken Korma, Shrimp Vindaloo, Bhindi Bhuna Masala, and plenty of naan. We dig in. I tell her about my recent time at RadioRadio, about Olivia, about the end game. Vidya listens with an incredulous smile, on occasion saying "No!" or "How could she?" or "Sali Kutti!" or "Chodu!" Why haven't I seen this woman in years?

Eventually, we come to the big idea. Right before I begin, Vidya's face blanks and her eyes penetrate even more than usual, which means that she's entered technical feasibility mode, the mode that all brilliant software engineers enter when they're trying to assess whether an idea is bullshit or not. I'm grateful and begin with the high-level constructs. My software will connect billions. It's based on deep ecological systems theory and will shift the power structure to the masses. From there, I deep-dive into the technical details: how to extract meaning from so much data, how to build an effective user interface, how to construct breakthrough software algorithms. She hardly says a word the whole time I'm speaking except to ask a few clarifying questions. She's the first person I've been confident enough to speak with in any detail about the idea.

When my pitch is complete, she says, "Why don't you get back to your food and let me think a little more?"

For a few minutes, I nibble in silence, dissecting the food on my plate, on occasion glancing at Vidya to see if she's leaning toward a bullshit or no-bullshit verdict. If she doesn't believe in what I'm trying to do, it's probably time to give it up. After all of these years, after working with thousands of smart people, Vidya is still the smartest person I know, and I trust her technical judgment. One of the things I admire the most is how she links technical prowess, honesty, and gentleness when she's assessing an idea. She's capable of detailing why I badly screwed something up and, at the same time, making me feel good about it. My favorite example, which I told many times to my employees over the years, happened when I was a graduate student. "Dan, that code is awful, but here's what you can learn from it. If you make these changes, it will turn these clumsy segments into art, into a tool that will serve you well for your entire career. What an opportunity, a gift!" Well, I don't remember if she said the gift part, but everyone else is saying it these days, probably.

Finally, Vidya says, "You ready?"

"Yes. By the way, good choice on the food."

"This is my favorite place." She looks directly at me and folds her hands on the table. Her eyes contain so much strength that I almost have to look away. "Your idea is intriguing, Dan. There's a tremendous amount of technical innovation required, but it's feasible with the right team and a lot of work. And the goal is noble, which is unique given the times we live in. That said, I don't think you should do it."

"Really? Why?"

"There's no viable business model. You can't make money at this."

"That's a problem I need to work on."

"Why bother? You can make a fortune if you go back to corporate America."

"It's not about the money for me anymore. I want to do something masterful, something that will help people, something that will change the world."

Vidya continues to look right at me as she sips her tea. She's deep in thought, almost like she's trying to access ideas she hasn't thought about for a long time, like she's trying to bootstrap herself out of resignation. She stays this way until she finishes her tea, and then as she's refilling her cup, says, "I used to think people like us could change things, but it's just not possible in the world we live in today. There's too much entrenchment at every level—individuals, corporations, the government. Many people have tried something bold before you. Most of them failed or sold out, or worse, took too much venture money. If I were you, I would take the next ten or twenty years and stockpile as much cash as you possibly can. We're headed for a dark period in human history, and I'm afraid only people with enough money are going to come out of it unscathed. You owe it to yourself and to Willow. At least, that's what I would do."

I nod, but I'm having a hard time processing. Is the woman sitting across from me the same woman I once knew? Her advice to me now is to make more money? How could that be? What happened to her? Did time wear her down like those guys in Detroit or something else? "That's not what I was expecting to hear from you. It sounds like you've changed your views on the power of software in the last twenty years."

"We've lost, Dan. I'm sorry to say the hopes I had all those years ago have faded. These days all I care about is taking care of my family. And unfortunately, that means making as much money as I can before I retire."

"I'm glad you think the idea is technically feasible."

"That's the least of your problems."

"What do you mean?"

"No one will fund you. What you're proposing is a threat to the existing power structure. Many people will try to crush you if you go down this path. On the other hand, if you go back into corporate America, they'll hail you as a superstar, as one of their own, and reward you handsomely. It's not much of a choice from my perspective."

The Big Idea

As soon as we're back in the Concord house, after a long embrace at Logan International, after an even longer kiss, after a much-needed, face-to-face, catch-up conversation about Vidya and the big idea on the way home, I take Willow's hand and lead her up the stairs toward our bedroom. We're past the talk point, full of desire. In the bedroom, clothes fall off, cover the floor, and form an after-the-fact aisle to the altar. Willow slips under the sheets, but I pull them all off and throw them on the floor. After the pilgrimage, Jack's robbery, and Vidya's vote-of-no-business-model, I need to uncover.

We start, building slowly. For a moment I marvel at how, in only a few months, she's learned the details of my body. She knows just how to soft-hard kiss, how to touch the middle of my back in the place where stress builds, how to interlace our fingers and draw circles on the palm of my hand with her thumb. It's like those months of handholding through my crash let her see the invisible, let her labyrinth in now.

Willow rolls over on her stomach. At her side, with my head propped up on one hand, I gently stroke her back—fingertips on the way down, back of my fingers on the way up. Her skin is soft and white, almost translucent, and her shoulders are covered in freckles that match her auburn hair. At the base of her spine are two small tattoos in Sanskrit. The one on the left says "Strength" and the one on the right says "Resilience." She had them done a long time ago but hasn't told me their story yet. "I'll tell you when you tell me about Zack," she said when I asked her months ago.

I make my way down her legs with long, slow strokes and eventually to her favorite part of the massage, her feet. I slide off the bed onto my knees and then start by circling my thumbs around each side of her ankle. From there, I move to the top of her foot, where I work from her ankle to her toes, stopping on each one to give it its due. From there, I move to her arch. As I'm working up and down, kneading with my thumbs, I say, "I think we should go for it. Let's live simple lives away from it all. Let's have a child together."

A grin spreads across the half of Willow's face I can see from my angle, daring me to flip her over and skip the rest of the massage. But then she stills and remains that way for a long time, which isn't the response I expected. More like, *That's what I want too, Dan,* followed by an amazing lovemaking session where we conceive triplets: Tara, John, and Amantha. As I'm about to ask her what she's thinking, she gently slides her foot out of my hands and rolls over. In one fluid movement, she pushes up against the back of the bed, pulls her legs up to her chest, and covers herself with a sheet.

"And what about your big idea?" she asks.

I crawl up on the bed next to her, slip under the sheet, and take her hand.

"My idea didn't work out. At best, I'm a number two executive, not a number one."

"I don't believe that."

"The robbery and Vidya are signs," I say.

"Is this what you really want?"

"I think so."

"But you've worked so hard," she says.

Willow pulls her hand out of mine and uses it to push off the bed. Without looking at me or saying a word, she slips into her jeans and pulls a T-shirt over her head, but instead of putting on the sandals she was wearing, puts on and laces up her Nikes. She doesn't look at me or say a word the entire time. When she's fully dressed, standing in the bedroom door archway with her thumbs looped into her pockets, she asks me to get dressed. I locate my jeans, my T-shirt, and my matching pair of Nikes we bought together right after she moved in. I'm not sure I've ever seen Willow this way before. Is she angry? Isn't this what she wanted? Confused, I shadow her down the stairs and out of the house.

A giant sycamore tree, the natural centerpiece of the entire property, fifty feet tall and almost as wide, a hundred years old, stands in our front yard. The tree's base looks like a bundle of gravity-defying arteries that stretch up and out. Before I can stop Willow, she's climbed the sycamore and is hovering at ten feet. As she dangles from a branch, she asks, "Do you think I can make it to the top?"

"It's dangerous."

"Do you think I can make it to the top?"

"No one can make it that high. I don't want you to get hurt."

Willow smiles and resumes climbing. With sure feet and hands, she moves from limb to limb. Where did she learn to climb so well? At the halfway point, she latches onto a branch that I'm sure can't hold her weight. I move closer to the trunk and, with outstretched arms in catch position, ready myself in case I have to break her fall. But I don't. In no time, she's monkeyed to the next branch, and is, for the moment, out of danger. I discourage her from going any higher, but she ignores me with a little smile and continues until she reaches the top of the tree. As the branch she's holding sways a little, she bolsters the cloudless sky.

"Why don't you join me?" she asks.

"Where did you learn to climb like that?"

"C'mon, Dan, at least meet me halfway up."

I know what she's doing, and I can think of less dangerous ways to make a point, but something is pulling me to go up, to meet her halfway, to play along with her much-too-dangerous game. I calculate the midpoint of the tree and visualize the route. It's not too bad. If I'm careful, I can make it, and from there, we can come down the rest of the way together. When we're back on the ground, she can tell me why she traded a perfectly good massage with a potential follow-on lovemaking session for an impetuous climb just to make a point that won't change my decision.

The first few steps of my ascension aren't too bad. The trunk and the lower branches are thick, and even if I slip and fall, I won't get seriously injured. As I move from branch to branch, I occasionally glance at Willow. She's coming down to the midpoint effortlessly, almost like she's gliding down steps to make a grand entrance at the ballroom dance. About a quarter of the way up, I lose my footing on a branch that's slipperier than the others. Luckily, I have a good grip on another branch and pull up to safety. I've never been this close to a sycamore before. There's beauty in the infinite variations in the bark, the sun-seeking shape of the branches, the lace-like formation of the leaf veins. The leaves, in full maturity, murmur in the breeze and smell surprisingly redolent. When I reach the midway point, Willow is already there. Zack, too. He would have loved this climb.

"How was that?" she asks.

"Not as bad as I thought."

"Now we'll go the rest of the way together. Follow me."

Against my better judgment, I follow. I move much slower and more deliberately than I did during my midpoint ascent. As my breath deepens, every ounce of me wants to turn around, to ground, but Willow keeps climbing, keeps checking in, keeps pushing me up and up, and I've apparently surrendered motor control of my body to her. At the three-quarter mark, she wraps her arms and legs around a branch and lets me know the last part is the trickiest. "Make the same moves I do, and you'll be okay." My heart steps up even more, and the beads of sweat morph into rivulets. I wipe my forehead, dry my hand on my pant leg, and glance down again. Galactic mistake.

Light-headed, I squeeze the branch tighter with both hands. I then slowly reach down with one hand and pat my pocketed cell phone through my jeans. Maybe I should call 911? The fire trucks can be at the house in no time, and the rescuers can lower me to safety. Willow will understand; we have so much else going for us.

"Want to hear the story about my tattoos?" Willow asks.

"Now?"

"Not now. When we make it to the top."

"I can't go any farther."

"Sure you can. We're almost there."

I glance down and then up. I can still call the fire trucks at the top if I don't die along the way. The headline—*Man falls from tree and dies a sudden death. Girlfriend says revolutionary new software idea lost forever.* But there isn't that much more to go. I can make it, and I'll feel better when I do. I branch up slowly, religiously following Willow, who's a few feet ahead of me. With each step, I become a little less stiff, a little faster, a little more confident.

Fuck!

Everything races past me in a blur as I wildly grasp for a branch, for a foothold. After I've fallen a few seconds, I bang into a large limb and catch hold. I steady myself, up, down, left, right, and then assess: a few arm scrapes; no sharp broken-bone pain; burning palms from bark scrapes; my heart pounding in my head. I've fallen back to where we started. The branch above, the one I was standing on seconds ago, the one that held Willow right before me, is dangling by wood threads.

"Dan, are you all right?" Willow asks.

"Yeah, I'm fine, but I need to go to the ground for a bit."

"Are you sure?"

"Yeah."

"I'll go with you."

And with that, I back down the tree, limb by limb, sure grip by sure grip. The way down is much easier. When I get to the ground, I'm going to plop down, stretch out my legs, prop myself up on my elbows, and repeatedly run all ten of my fingers through thick grass until the cool dirt calms me. A little farther down, on a thick, secure branch, I pause. Willow is right above me, waiting for my next move. Part of me wants to continue to the ground, where I'll be safe, where Willow can join me in the soft grass under our spectacular sycamore, and we can continue what we started in the bedroom. But part of me doesn't. I learned enough the first time to give it another go—the solid footholds, the branches to avoid, the importance of planning well. I've never been one to quit at first failure, even when the task at hand scares me to death.

"Let's give it another try," I say.

"Are you sure?"

"Yeah."

And with that, I reverse direction and begin my reclimb, my redo. I follow Willow's every move, but before I do I visualize each foothold, each hand grab, and every possible angle, misstep, and contingency. At first, I inch along, but as I move up the tree, my speed improves. With no ill effect, I even look down a few times. When I do opt for an alternate path, it pans out. With Willow's support, I reach the top faster than expected.

"Couldn't you have picked a safer way to make your point?" I ask.

"Would that have worked?"

"Where did you learn to climb like that?"

"It's what I did as a girl."

"You're amazing."

"You are, too, Dan. I knew you would make it," she says.

She smiles, puts her hand on my shoulder, and gently squeezes it. It's a clear day, and toward the east, Boston, with its ever-increasing number of skyscrapers, readies itself to rival any of the bigger American cities. In the near distance, the church steeple from the Concord Unitarian Church ascends toward uncertain heavens. Even closer, our house is enormous, much too big for a family of any size.

Willow moves her hand off my shoulder and takes my hand. "I climbed to get away from my father," she says. "He was an alcoholic, and when he drank, he liked to take it out on me. I felt safe in the trees. It all started one day when he came home on a real bender. I was in the backyard of our house swinging on the set he bought me in one of his rare lucid moments, and our dog, Captain America, was smelling around the grass nearby. Dad started yelling and waving his arms, and then I realized he had a gun in his hand. I don't know if he was truly trying to kill me, but in his drunken stupor he fired a couple of shots my way, and one hit Captain America and killed him instantly. I was so scared that I jumped off the swing at the high point and ran to the big oak tree in our neighbor's yard. Frantically, I started climbing, but I was seven, and my father pulled me down after I'd only made it a few feet off the ground. After that, I got skills, and when I turned eighteen, the tattoos."

"I'm so sorry, Willow."

"It was a long time ago."

"Where was your mom?"

"He beat her, too. She'd left by then. I never saw her again." Willow goes quiet and remains still. Then she starts roll-tapping her fingers from pinky to index on the branch she's holding, harder and harder, like the bark is a drum head, and she's hitting it with ever-increasing confidence.

"Want to hear my first poem?" she asks.

"Yes."

"*If you could go back to before, to the playground, to the swing, would you still jump off at the highest point, try to touch the sky?*"

"It's beautiful."

"First time."

"For what?" I ask.

"I've always climbed alone."

"Ah . . . I'm glad I'm the one."

"You know, we're not meant to be together to live a simple life," she says. "We need to reach for the spectacular. I know that now. I would love to have a child with you, and we'll have a beautiful one when the time is right. But this year if I'm sure of anything, especially now that you've told me more about your idea, it's that you need to start your own company. And you don't have to do it alone. I've got you."

I'm grateful. For the vote of confidence. For the climb. Is what Willow said after the pilgrimage right? Is everything emerging exactly as it should? I would have never predicted, well, anything from the last year. Yet here I am, fifty feet off the ground on top of a tree next to the woman I love who's just convinced me to go for it, to take the biggest risk of my life.

"I love you," I say.

"I love you, too."

"I'm not sure where to start."

"Who do you trust businesswise?"

"I know a few."

"Then start by asking them for help."

#

Zia, Maggie, Charles, and Willow are sitting in our living room. We're in a star formation. I'm rocking in a chair at the top of the star, opposite the fireplace, and my friends are sitting facing each other, two per sofa, between me and the fire. I'd built a fire before they arrived, so the hearth radiates warmth and smells of burning oak, as it battles an unusually cold fall evening. Something about the fire demands attention, pulls me in. It morphs endlessly, in shape, in color, in heat, waiting for someone with the right decoder ring. Six months of hell began a year ago, worse than the divorce, almost as bad as Zack's death, which I didn't think humanly possible, followed by six months—Willow moving in, the aborted pilgrimage, the tree boost—all leading to this moment, this meeting, this big idea that may bounce. Or brick.

We're about to start the first, maybe the last meeting of the Wednesday-night-save-the-world club. This is not the formal name, just something Willow mentioned in passing this morning in bed and repeated to the others upon their arrival a little while ago. Everyone seems to like it, or at least finds it amusing.

I push out of the fire and scan the star clockwise.

Zia is reading email on her phone, trying to squeeze in a few more minutes of work before the real conversation begins. She's still at RadioRadio, responsible for marketing its flagship enterprise software package. Thirty-five, I think, though I'm not good at remembering birthdays. She's beautiful, elegant, and well-dressed, wearing a similar silk scarf to the one she had on during our first conversation years ago where I asked, "Are you sure you want to talk with me? Are you feeling okay?" She laughed this deep guttural laugh that the entire building heard. With a laugh like that, how could I not befriend her, make her part of my inner circle, ask her to join me now?

On weekends, she jettisons her corporate persona, lets her dark red hair bloom, and races her Aston Martin, which I've done a few times with her, or rock climbs shear mountain walls without a safety rope, which is nuts, or jumps out of planes, which she's been trying to get me to do for years. Not going to happen. She goes out with a lot of different guys, though she calls me after most of her dates and we laugh together about how so-and-so wasn't strong enough for her or didn't meet her adrenaline requirements. She has no idea I've been staring at her for more than a minute.

Maggie catches my eye, pulling me away from Zia. She's on the same sofa, one leg crossed over the other, with her hands in prayer position on her lap. Apparently, she was studying me while I was studying Zia, and for a moment, I'm sure she's captured my Zia-thoughts, which is okay because she already knows all of that stuff. Tonight, she has a fresh flower in her hair and is wearing a flowered peasant dress and leather knee-high boots. With short brown early-Beatles hair and chestnut-brown skin, she looks like she just got off the bus in 1969 Haight Ashbury. Points for that.

"Nice flower," I say.

"Thanks."

"How's work?"

As she walks me through work small talk, she reaches up with one hand and rolls her necklace between her fingers. No matter how she's dressed, she always wears this heart-shaped gold locket, which encases a black-and-white picture of her and her lover, Zooey, taken at their place in Cambridge. Maggie is the baby of the bunch, a true millennial, out of M.I.T. only a few years with a PhD. Like me, she's a software engineer. She did her thesis on enhanced voice recognition and contextual understanding and is the foremost expert at RadioRadio on those topics. Also like me, she captained her college debate team. For a while, I fancied that I would mentor her at RadioRadio, but somewhere along the way it clicked that a one-up-one-down relationship wasn't going to fly with someone as driven as Maggie. So we leveled it, and after that, we became close.

With small talk complete, I switch sofas. Close to the fire is Charles, who's been on the phone ever since he arrived in a heated conversation about budget cuts. His face is red, and even from this distance, sweat marbles on his forehead. Charles is in RR finance. He's one of those people who you can ask to multiply any two numbers, and he'll immediately give you the result. 369.47 times 609.51? I have no idea, but he's never wrong. He's older than all of us, maybe in his late forties or early fifties. He's the only older man I know at RR who dyes his hair. Gray isn't beautiful, he always says. A long time ago, at thirty-seven, his wife died of a massive heart attack. It wrecked him, and if not for his kids, he wouldn't have made it through. Back when Olivia was still Olivia, she set up a college fund for Charles's two kids that paid for the first year. The kids, twins, are sophomores now, so much of Charles's earnings are going toward their education. He recently got remarried to a schoolteacher.

Willow is next to him, picking a piece of cheddar off a tray of cheese and crackers that's resting on the coffee table. She smiles, nods a you've-got-this my way, and for a moment, we're back at the top of the tree holding hands. It was kind of her to sit in on this meeting given her own workload and the fact that she doesn't want a role in my new company. She loves her current job too much. About the best I could do was get her to acknowledge that the door will always be open.

Trust between colleagues is the most critical thing when starting a company, and all of the people I trust are now in this room. Well, except for Nessa. Sometime after the breakup with Hannah, after I caught her in a compromised position with a twenty-something colleague of hers, Zia, Maggie, Charles, and I became close. During a three-month daily review of our big data, software-as-a-service, and cloud-computing strategies, the four of us spent almost all of our waking hours together. Although the strategy document that emerged from those sessions was a competent piece of work, one that had the potential to fuel RR for the next decade, the late-night conversations about love, about loss, about how to make a difference in a world resistant to change, are what cemented our relationship.

I push off the rocker, and at my overstocked bar grab the Spanish wine, which I had decanted before folks arrived. It's outstanding value for the money. As I fill the last glass, Willow's, I say, "I'm glad you're all here."

"You're the reason I'm in this business. Of course I'm here," Zia says.

"So how are you?" Maggie asks.

Back in my chair, I rock a little faster and sip my wine, looking into the fire. "That's a good question." All of them know I crashed, but at my request I haven't spoken with the three RadioRadioers at length since I left RR. An occasional text, something like, Hi, just checking in. How are you doing? Fine. Digging out. Still a few months to go on the pilgrimage. Or Working on the big idea. Talk soon. But that's all. Now, it's time to catch them up.

"I'm okay. So much of my life was linked to Liv's and to RadioRadio that I had a hard time believing RR was over. Actually, for a time I felt like my professional life was over. Then Willow and I got together, and I went on the pilgrimage, and I fleshed out the big idea, which you'll hear about in a few minutes."

"We're glad you're okay now," Zia says.

Maggie drinks what remains in her glass, puts it down, stands up, and walks over to me. With one hand, she forklifts my glass out of my hand. With the other, she pulls me out of the rocker, pushes up on the balls of her feet so she's my height, and pulls me in. Zia follows suit, and a moment later all three of us are hugging. Willow, who's had a monopoly on touch since we've been together, smiles from the sofa. Charlie smiles our way, stays puts, and checks something on his phone.

After we return to our seats, we continue catching up. The headhunters have been calling me nonstop, but the opportunities are more of the same. Zia has been out with dozens of new guys—all losers—since I last saw her. We all agree the woman needs an astronaut. Maggie has been flat out with the new RR software release scheduled to go out next month, and Zooey is giving her a hard time about the long hours. Even though Charlie is in serious budget mode, he still managed to squeeze in a campus visit with his kids last week. In general, no big news, almost like my months in exile never happened.

But it did. And now it's unveil time. I take a deep breath and place my hand over my pocket to make sure the paper is still inside, still in one piece. "So . . . I've been working on an idea for a company, ConversationWorks. There's still a ton to do, but I'm at the point where I'd like to share my thoughts with the three of you and get your feedback. Willow's already heard it."

"I like the name," Maggie says.

"Me too," Charles says.

"It came in a dream early on."

"No kidding?" Zia asks.

"Really. The five of us were all at a coffee house in Cambridge, and everybody in the place started talking about the shooting of those kids in Newtown, Connecticut, and what to do about it. In no time, we all agreed on a plan. It was amazing how quickly a roomful of strangers converged. As I was walking out of the coffeehouse, I said to one of you, 'You know, conversation actually works.' And there it was."

"Cool," Maggie says. "So let's hear the idea, but let me get my journal first."

From her backpack, Maggie pulls out a journal and a pen. The cover is brown distressed leather and seems more like a Bible than something you would write in. At my request, she passes around the journal. I undo the journal's leather ties and open it to an empty page. Touching the page, I imagine my pocketed-speech written there for a few seconds, before closing the journal and passing it to Zia.

After the journal returns to Maggie and is opened to a fresh page, she nods that she's ready, and I begin. "Okay, so here's my pitch. ConversationWorks is a local problem-solving network with global scale. It's software that allows small group conversation to scale all the way from coffeehouses, to towns, to cities, to the world, with the primary goal of collectively working on problems that matter to its users."

"Isn't that a social network on steroids?" Charlie asks.

"Good question. Not really. The main difference is that the conversations are active and focused on solving problems instead of socializing. The idea is that all real change happens from small group conversation, but there hasn't been a way to scale these conversations to everyone interested in them or to do something productive with the outcomes. ConversationWorks facilitates those conversations, builds consensus across all stakeholders, and helps implement an action plan. I guess the social networking companies could go there, but it's not their sweet spot."

"Sounds more than cool. Did you develop use cases?" Maggie asks.

"Yes. Give me a second." As I'm picking the best of many good examples, I can't help but smile. It's good to speak in my business voice again, good to sound competent, good to work in a group. Although I wouldn't trade these last months for anything, I've missed work. For a time after Zack died, I thought work was my only great love, but now thanks to Nessa and Willow, I know that was the pain thinking; I know all of us are capable of many great loves.

"Okay, here goes. Say the entire state of Massachusetts wants to make its position known on climate change. Not only make it known, but also collectively agree on the best way forward. How would six million people do that? Today, you can do polls, and small groups can get together, but there's little real power or consensus in the results. What if the entire state could enter into a problem-solving session on climate change, for as long as needed, one where all voices are heard and contribute to the solution? That's what our software will allow them to do. Now, if we're successful, the software will allow conversations to scale to an entire country, or even the world, or scale back to any problem that requires a group of people separated by time and distance to solve. I don't want to kid you though; this is an incredibly ambitious goal."

"I don't think you can build it with existing technology," Maggie says.

"Probably not. There's a lot of invention required."

"How will you fund it?" Zia asks.

"I'll sell this house, and even with the divorce, I've saved over the years. I'm willing to risk everything to do it, especially because I don't want to take venture money and lose control."

"And you want us to be employees two through four?" Charlie asks.

"Yes. The three of you are the best I know in your respective fields."

"Have you given any thought to how you monetize the platform yet? Advertising?" Zia asks.

"Advertising or subscriptions. It's a big decision that we'll make together if you decide to join. Honestly, I'm conflicted."

"It will be hard to make money in the long run if you don't take advertising dollars."

"I know."

"The three of us have noncompetes, so we need to be careful how far we take this initial conversation," Charlie says. "Plus I'm not sure if I can afford a start-up given my personal situation."

"I agree we'll need to manage the noncompetes. On money, for the first two years, I can pay you what you make now, plus options. After that, we'll know a lot more."

"Can we invest, too?" Zia asks.

"Of course."

"There is one more thing I want to share tonight." I pat my pocket, slip my hand into it, and pull out the folded piece of paper. After I unfold it slowly, I scan the words like they're an article from a spiritual journal, like they're not mine. But they are. This warmth emanates up from my stomach into my chest, like the fire has jumped from the hearth to my stomach, where it acts as fuel. It's the best I've felt in, well, years. I glance over at Willow, who nods me into a start. "Now that you all have a basic feel for what ConversationWorks is, I want to say a little more about what kind of company we're going to build. Here goes. ConversationWorks helps people live their lives each day in service, with more kindness, compassion, and equality. The company is a new kind of technology organization, one that treats employees and customers with respect, one that doesn't believe community is a dirty word, one that's about much more than stock price and profit, one without executive high priests, one that makes a real difference in the world by allowing all people to participate actively in change, regardless of their social or economic position. We believe the true measure of a company is its ability to serve its stakeholders equally, even in times of unforeseeable difficulty. We believe ConversationWorks offers the promise of true democracy on the broadest range of problems, with never-before-seen solution sets only limited by our users' collective imaginations. At ConversationWorks, we believe we are at the forefront of defining the company of the future, where the contribution is based on intrinsic value instead of profit at all costs."

Maggie stops writing and puts her journal down on the coffee table. We all go silent as the journal catches the light from the hearth. I imagine my words rising off the page and intermingling with the smell of burning oak, with the warmth, and with the light in the room, like they've rediscovered their brothers and sisters, like they too are natural elements created long ago. What are my former colleagues thinking? They're deep in thought, their faces expressionless. Is it the same for them as it was for Vidya?

"What do you all think?" I ask.

"RadioRadio started off just as idealistic," Maggie says.

"That's true. But Olivia caved," Zia says.

"Why do you think that happens?" Charles asks.

We hypothesize for a time. Why does a company or leader cave? I don't know, but I've come to believe that there are a few times in a leader's life where she's right up against it, where everything changes based on a single decision. At the fork, she goes left or right. In the boardroom, she pulls you closer or pushes you away. Against insurmountable odds, I create a new software category or I follow established money. It's only in those moments that you truly see the strength, the integrity of a leader. The rest of the time is, well, sixteen-year window dressing.

"How many engineers to start?" Maggie asks.

"Ten, but that will be up to you."

"And I would own all aspects of marketing? Branding. Outbound. Inbound?" Zia asks.

"Absolutely."

"We'll need huge datacenters if it takes off. And I bet there are hundreds if not thousands of patents in this thing. It's engineering nirvana," Maggie says.

"I hope."

"This is exactly the high-risk, high-reward thing I've been waiting for," Zia says.

"Building something like this is a once-in-a-lifetime opportunity," Maggie says.

In advance, I knew Charlie would be the most skeptical of the three. For him, it's all about his kids and new wife, and he has to be sure it won't jeopardize their futures in any way. Still, I need him if we're going to pull this off. When you're an executive long enough, you learn you can't do it all by yourself. You learn one of the most important decisions you'll ever make is how to complement and enhance your skills. Zia knows more about marketing than I ever will. Though I'm a software engineer by training, Maggie can do stuff with code that wows me. And Charles can run a P&L better than anyone I know.

"What about you, Charles?" I ask.

"Let me sleep on it, Dan. I need to weigh a few things," Charlie says. "You realize that if the company is successful, we'll create many enemies."

"We will. Olivia. The software giants. Probably a few governments. If we pull this off, this really is the first meeting of the change-the-world club."

PART III—*Build from the Sky Down*

The Aha Moment

Starting a technology company is like early romantic love. The team spends loads of time together, and the interactions are effortless, filled with hope, possibility, and even joy. The only real difference is that, instead of large quantities of lust-filled sex, colleagues collectively becomes pregnant with a product idea, which it turns out, is every bit as fulfilling.

Nine months ago, shortly after our first meeting of the change-the-world club everyone agreed to join CW, even Charles. My three friends resigned from RR and only managed to ruffle a few Olivia feathers in the process. "You're making a big mistake." Or "You're walking away when RadioRadio is about to enter a huge growth period." Or "Dan doesn't have it in him." Pretty mild, overall. Together, we picked out and rented a suite in a rehabbed warehouse in Cambridge, one with lots of exposed brick and high ceilings, and furnished it openly, with few dividers and with all the normal creativity-fostering hi-tech toys—a Ping-Pong table, a video game console, a Buddha Board—to name a few. My favorite: a red Gaggia Deco-D three-spout cappuccino maker.

With the office space and toys in place, we hired ten of the brightest M.I.T. and Harvard software developers we could find, five women and five men, which wasn't easy to balance, and gave them each a piece of the company. Not nearly as big a piece as the four of us, but enough to ensure they were all in. One of Zia's first tasks was to have the CW logo designed—a pyramid built from blue and white pebbles next to our abbreviated name, CW, also in blue and white. It's perfect.

During the week, all fourteen of us virtually moved into the warehouse. Twelve-hour days, minimum, with every possible form of takeout food brought in for lunch and dinner, we laser-focused on the product definition. Sometimes much to the dismay of Zooey, Maggie worked the whole night with her engineers, trying to figure out never-been-done-before technical details on enhanced voice recognition, on understanding the context of a conversation, or on combining similar results from different conversations. Often during our first months, Willow came to hang out with us at night, and we soundboarded our dailies off her. For someone who isn't tech savvy, she judged well, especially on how small groups might work together. Last month we even got profiled in *Start-up* magazine. The headline: *Dan Underlight was the key behind RadioRadio's early growth. Can he do it again?* That must have been well received by the Ms. O.

Minutes ago, we finished our product definition phase review, which is the first of many big milestones for CW we must successfully navigate before launch fifteen months from now. T minus fifteen months. Zia, Maggie, and Charles have stayed behind with me in the Retool the World Conference room to debrief. One of the lessons I learned at RR was not to write a line of production code until the team members were clear, with sufficient detail, on what they wanted to build. That was much harder to accomplish than it seemed, especially because RR was filled with brilliant engineers who believed they could build anything based on a cursory requirement or two. Unfortunately, I learned that one the hard way. We had this cool idea for a product that we thought would take the market by storm. We were so excited about it that we set the engineers free to build it as quickly as possible, but software is like building a house; you have to get clear on the architecture before you set the builders free. Once, when version one of the RR product was done, the team had built an exquisite turn-of-the-century Dutch Colonial when what the market called for was a midcentury modern masterpiece. We had to scrap the product and start again. At CW, we can't afford to make that kind of mistake, and today's phase review should help us avoid one.

"How do folks think that went?" I ask.

"Well. At a high level, we know what we want to build now," Maggie says.

"Hopefully, all this up-front work will keep the requirements churn at a minimum," Zia says.

"That's key to managing our costs," Charles says.

"I agree on all points," I say. "We should take the team out to celebrate."

As Maggie, Zia, and Charles toss around a few places for a party—a pool hall that also serves food and alcohol, a movie theater, a bowling alley—I go big picture. Every month, the four of us have an informal high-level conversation about the company where we answer two questions with radical honesty: What's going well and can we make it even better? What's not going well and how can we address it? We're about due for our next one. At the start, Olivia and I did this at RR, but over time, we spent less and less time on the what-wasn't-going-well part. It was like our success made us forget how we'd gotten there, and instead of constantly changing in anticipation of the market, we settled into the past. Why does that happen to so many corporations? Is it inevitable?

"The pool hall is a good choice. Let's go next week," I say. "Before we leave, let's do our monthly check-in and talk about how things are going in general. Our normal questions. Who wants to start?"

"I will," Zia says. "What's going well? Technology journalists are interested in what we're doing, even though we can't tell them much yet. That has more to do with our credentials from RR than anything we've done at CW. And the NDA focus groups we've done are positive on the vision. On negatives, the press continues to poke at our relationship with RR. Since Dan and Olivia were close, they're clamoring for an Olivia Strikes Back story—not much we can do about that one except ride it out. In the focus groups, our biggest issue is that most folks want our product to be free and don't want us to take advertising dollars. Even when pressed, they're not willing to help us resolve that issue."

"I'll go next," Charles says. "How we eventually make money is still our biggest issue. We need to decide on a pricing model with uplifts by country for both consumers and corporations, on the advertising issue, and on what channels and routes to market we'll fund. Everything else financially is going well. Our burn rate is good. We still have two years of cash before we need to raise more. We're spending our money in the right places. All of our legal and corporate filings are done."

"We'll refine the business model soon. You all know my position on advertising dollars," I say.

"I think that's a mistake," Zia says.

"Me, too," Charles says.

"I know you both do, but I'm convinced people are willing to pay for value. What could be more important than giving people access to a platform where they can work to change what's important to them? Anyway, we're not going to resolve the advertising issue today, but we'll go after it soon. On the other issues, the four of us are pretty close. I favor uplifts for corporations by country. For consumers, I favor currency equivalent pricing, so ten dollars per month in the US is equal to ten pounds per month in the U.K. And I'm fine with multiple routes to market as long as they're mostly self-funding and as long as our partners don't rebrand our stuff. Maggie, what about engineering?"

"On engineering, you all heard where we are in the review. I think we're okay for now with no major gotchas. I do have one non-engineering issue worth mentioning. I'm not sure. Have any of you heard from your RR contacts or friends?" Maggie asks.

"Not a word," I say.

"It's dried up recently," Zia says.

"For me too," Charles says.

"Zooey and I had our closest friends over this weekend, and both still work at RR. We had a little too much wine, and at one point, one of the women mentioned that she overheard a conversation she wasn't supposed to hear. Apparently, Olivia was talking about CW and using all kinds of expletives as she detailed how she was going to crush us, and in particular, Dan. My friend had never seen Olivia so full of vitriol. Have any of you seen her that way?"

"She can't handle the idea of CW being successful while RR is struggling," Zia says.

"She thinks she still owns you," Charles says.

"She did fire you. What did she expect you to do?" Maggie asks.

"She expected him to take a smaller job somewhere and fade into oblivion," Zia says.

"Have you spoken to her, Dan?" Charles asks.

"No."

"Can she hurt us?" Maggie asks.

"Don't worry about Liv. You're right, Zia. RR still isn't doing well. Olivia has much bigger things to worry about than a start-up that has no revenue. And besides, what could she do?"

#

It's a warm summer day, T minus fourteen months, and after a rare quiet weekend together on the heels of the product phase review, Willow and I opt to take Gordon Bell into the city. With the top down and the wind and morning sun in our faces, we blast an old Fleetwood Mac album, *Rumours*, and sing along. "Dreams." "Don't Stop." "Go Your Own Way." Long before we met, we memorized the lyrics. We've been together a little more than a year now, and to be honest, I'm afraid the initial shine is wearing off. Why does that happen to couples? We're still good, though. It's just that our respective work commitments have taken over, and there's much less time for the two of us. That's all. As we slow to a stop and double-park in front of Willow's center, "The Chain" ends.

"I'm sorry I got so angry last night. I don't know why I did," I say.

"Don't worry about it, Dan. I don't even know why we were fighting. We're good."

"Are you sure?"

"Yes. These last months we've been consumed and stressed with our work. It's a rough patch that will pass."

"I hope so. I love you," I say.

"I love you, too. I have a dinner tonight, so I'll see you at home late."

"I'll be home late, too."

She pecks me on the cheek and a moment later disappears behind the large entranceway door to her Back Bay building. I accelerate until Gordon Bell flows with traffic, and minutes later, bridge across the Charles River toward my other love, ConversationWorks. Willow is right—we have been working around the clock these last months. She's in major fund-raising mode, and I remain in major start-up mode. Sometimes I think it's impossible for people like us to stay in love while working at different companies. There isn't enough time in the day.

When I arrive at work, everyone is already three-cappuccino-busy. There was a time when I would have been the first and last person in the office, but ever since Willow and I started fighting, I'm trying to pull back a little. Even so, I'll be here until ten tonight given that she has another dinner. After saying hello to everyone, I head over to the Deco-D and fill my cup with four shots. Much to the delight of my team, I've become an expert at frothing art these last six months, drawing something every day to finish off cappuccinos, this time for me, but often for anyone who asks. Today I draw stars like Van Gogh.

Each morning, we arrange fourteen chairs in a circle and start with a big-boulder check-in. Big boulders are the biggest problems team members are working, the ones that are best pulverized together in circle. Sometimes the problems are technical; sometimes they're about how we make money. Lately, they've been about the best ways for our users, our conversationalists, to work together, to problem solve, and to take action. There's a lot of trial and error, a lot of invention, a lot of one-step-forward-two-steps-back as we collectively try to knock the boulders down to size. Sometimes we think we have something that works, but then it doesn't scale; sometimes we're too US-centric in our thinking given that we are building a worldwide product; and sometimes we understand why the social network companies stayed away from trying to solve complicated problems.

"My big boulder for today is love," Maggie says.

The room rumbles a bit and makes a few cracks. "Maggie loves Zooey." Or "Late night?" Or "Love is more of a galaxy than a big boulder," which I wish I could claim as my own. Maggie weathers the barrage with a smile like we all do when the rumble turns our way. That's the other thing about CW—we spend an inordinate amount of time laughing, giving each other a hard time. There was some of that early on at RR, but toward the end Olivia was too far gone to let laughter take hold.

After the room settles, Maggie says, "For the record, my night was better than you could imagine, and even though it would exponentially increase all of your knowledge of the Kama Sutra if I detailed it, that's not what I want to talk about. My big boulder has to do with what it collectively means to love."

"Like in a commune?" one of the engineers asks.

"Stop. What I mean is more about community. If our software is going to work, if millions of different problem-solving communities are going to work, people need to feel committed to the communities, they need to feel love for them. If they do, the possibilities are endless."

The room goes silent. This is where our breakthroughs always start—the aha moment. Some days I am the instigator. Some days Zia or Charles is. Some days it's an engineer. Today is Maggie's day, and she's on a point, one the team just got, that all hi-tech people dream of achieving with their products—love.

"Like Peach has for its products," I say. "Yes, Peach's products are great, but there's also a disproportionate goodwill toward those products. After you cross the goodwill threshold, even when you screw up, the customers stay with you and help you get it right the next time."

"That's much harder to do with an app than a phone or tablet," Zia says.

"Maybe. Maybe not. We want users to feel like they're in the trenches together," Maggie says. "We want them to feel like what they're doing will not only make their lives better but a lot of lives better. If we can garner that feeling, we'll generate love."

We get into what generates love for a time, though I remain silent. The user interface is key. The conversation aggregation technology, too. Identity authentication and security are critical;

users need to trust that what they say is secure and private. And, of course, the quality of the software has to be high. These days my role is not so much about coming up with the ideas. It's more about creating space so that ideas bubble and about amplifying the good ones when they do. That's the way I can help the team the most; that's the way I can minimize all that I've risked getting this far. When a person risks everything financially to start something new, when his whole life is wrapped up in that thing, when he can't bear the thought of losing someone or something else, the most important lesson is to listen and not to act. Nothing in the world is more generative.

The room quiets again. At first, I think I missed another aha moment, but then I realize it's only the folks facing the elevator who've gone silent. I twist around in my chair and join them, half expecting to see our regular pastry delivery guy from the local shop.

Olivia steps off the elevator and walks toward the circle, arms at her side, head tilted slightly down, her eyes more focused than usual. She's carrying a large manila envelope. Always dressed well, she looks majestic today—a black skirt and matching black low V-cut blazer. One silver tie clasp, right below her breasts, holds the blazer closed. No blouse or necklace—actually, it appears she doesn't have anything on under the jacket. She's wearing large diamond stud earrings and a matching diamond bracelet. She's in taller-than-usual black pumps, maybe four inches, though they're still that brand with the red soles she favors. Her hair, normally pulled back, is flowing down one side. As she gets close, Tom Ford perfume marks the room.

I stand and extend my hand. "Olivia."

"Dan." She hands me the envelope. "I wanted to deliver this to you personally. I'm suing you for stealing ideas you developed at RadioRadio. ConversationWorks is a sham, and soon the intellectual property you stole will be returned to its rightful owner."

"But I didn't steal—"

"That's for the courts to decide. And oh, by the way, I've asked my legal team to make this their top priority and to spare no expense."

"Olivia, can't we work through this?"

Instead of answering, Olivia turns her back on me and heads toward the elevator. She walks slowly, in control, as if she's patented power. When she reaches the elevator doors, instead of waiting, she continues past them and pushes the door to the stairs open. Seconds later, the door punctuates shut.

As I walk back to my circle seat, I study the floor. Even though Maggie warned something like this was coming, nothing prepares you for that kind of an entrance-exit. It's like she was saying, I made you. You'll never be as powerful as me. You'll always be second-rate. Well.

"I'm sorry you all had to witness that," I say.

"How should we respond?" Maggie asks.

"She doesn't have a case. She knows that," I say.

"Why then?" Zia says.

"She's trying to bankrupt us with legal fees," I say.

"And she has the resources to pull it off," Charles says.

The collective fidgeting and chatter in the room skyrockets, and for the first time since we formed the company, fear thickens. I'm not sure how to calm down the team or how to handle Olivia. She really could bankrupt us before we have a product out the door. That's the truth, and one of the CW values we set at the start of the company, which we've followed to a T so far, is to never shy away from the truth. When the chatter has stopped and everyone is looking my way, I say, "I've got this. You all get back to work."

#

Nessa opens her door and smiles me in. In the years since Zack's death, these weekly sessions have darned my life. At first, they were about Zack, then about losing the job, and then about starting over with Willow, about pilgrimages and pyramids, about CW. Honestly, I can't imagine my life without Nessa. She's the only one who knows the whole story.

I take off my jacket, assume my normal chair, and place my phone on the arm. A new painting on the wall catches my eye. In the top half of the painting, upside-down skyscrapers tower down and touch a snowflake-filled sky in the bottom of the painting. A poem is written in the sky. *Build from the sky down / Not the ground up / Let dreams form from fractal snowflakes / Nimbus clouds / Memories ballooned up / Forgotten.* Sounds like something Willow would write.

"The new painting is cool," I say.

"Thank you. I like it, too. How are you?"

Good question. I catch Nessa up on Olivia's surprise visit to CW. Even though it's not top of mind, it rises quickly, and I find myself going through the whole story in movie-script detail down to the red-sole shoes. After Olivia parachuted in this week, I spoke with my lawyer. He's a friend and said he'd squash the suit and RR's lawyers at a significantly reduced fee. I trust him though Olivia is a more than formidable opponent. The whole time Nessa listens attentively. On occasion, her eyes widen or she nods, adding an occasional "No way!" At the end of my story, which has unexpectedly eaten up a good chunk of our session, she says, "Olivia pulled out all of the stops, didn't she? The first of many who will try to knock you down."

"Isn't it sad that we live in a world where one measure of success is the number of people who try to knock you down?"

"It is."

"It's not that I don't believe in healthy competition; it's more that we've gone way past that in the last thirty years to the point where it's stained us, where we've lost perspective."

Nessa nods.

"You know, companies shouldn't just be about profit and growth. They were always meant to serve the broader community. Anyway, enough about CW. I want to talk about Willow for our remaining time. Something's going on with her, and I'm worried. She's been staying out late a lot in the last month."

"Has she told you where she's going?"

"Dinners with donors."

"And you don't believe her?"

"I have my doubts."

"Ah."

There it is— the famous *Ah*. We've worked together long enough that Nessa sometimes slips out of therapist mode with an *Ah*. First time this happened, she told me that she hoped there was enough emotional capital between us for what she was about to say, said we'd probably be friends if I weren't her client. Then she went into some bit about the dangers of *storylines* and *ego* and *shoulds* and *musts*. She even mentioned this famous dead therapist, whose name I can never remember, Ellis I think, who coined the term "musterbation." That part made me laugh. After I left her office, I spent the rest of the day on-and-off trying not to say should or must, and instead worked on accepting things as they came up. Strangely, in doing so, my mood lightened. Now, when the *ahs* come, I welcome them as the Emotionally Corrective Opportunities, or ECOs, that they are.

"Okay, let's hear it," I say.

"Well, it's just that between Hannah and Olivia, it must be hard to fully trust a woman again."

I hadn't noticed before, but more rabbits have invaded the room: Buddha Rabbit. Abstract Rabbit. Dancing Rabbit. And the original ones are in different places. When did that happen? Yes, it's abundantly true that I'll never trust Hannah or Olivia again. How could I after the betrayals? Here's the thing about betrayal—it corrodes a person's memories, burns, melts, and rusts them until a melted pile of rust is all that's left. I'm sure there were vulnerable times with Hannah and Olivia over all of those years, but since the betrayals they've slowly melted away. But Willow's not like them, and I do trust her. Well, except on this one thing.

"There are women I trust, like Zia and Maggie," I say.

"They're different. They work for you."

"The rabbits are multiplying. When did that happen?"

"A month ago." Nessa locates a few new ones and seems to draw some strange focused energy from them like they're there to help her manage randomly planned dead ends and redirections, like they're there to help her further penetrate labyrinth island. Then she turns back to me and says, "There's one other thing I'm wondering about. Did you ever tell Willow about how Zack died?"

"Bits and pieces."

"Ah."

"You're only allowed one *Ah* per session."

"So you both have private lives."

"Sorry. I don't respond after the second *Ah*. But I will say this. She'll leave me if I tell her everything."

"You didn't intentionally cause harm, Dan."

"Intentional. Unintentional. There's no difference," I say.

I stretch my neck left, then right, glance at the clock next to Nessa's chair that luckily shows only a few minutes left before I can mist my way out of here. Early on in our sessions, Nessa offered to keep track of time, and I accepted her offer. But it's been hard for me to do week after week. The table clock is facing me, round, old school analog, so I'm always aware of where we are in the session. And besides, I want to be respectful of her time, so I'm really tracking for her. "Looks like we're almost out of time. Let's stop now and mist."

Nessa's brow furrows a little before it unfolds. She smiles and walks over to the box of blue bottles. I stand up and slip on my jacket. She once told me that emotional patterns follow the laws of karma—it's best to deal with them right away, because if you don't, they'll strengthen and hit you harder down the road. She may be right about that one, but easier said. She approaches me with the box of mists and holds it out. I run my fingers back and forth over the bottle tops until I blindly select the Fifth Chakra Expression Mist. After I hand it to her, she sprays over my head, at my sides, and around my heart until lavender, rose, and sandalwood cradle.

#

Here's the thing about being well-off— you can afford to hire a good private detective. Not one of those sleazy ones you sometimes see in movies who chain-smokes and works out of a seedy office, mostly on intuition. No, you can hire one who uses state-of-the-art technology—phone taps, telescopic cameras, and online mining software.

As soon as I left Nessa's office, I called Technology Detectives and spoke with Barry Porcelaina and hired him on the spot after only a fifteen-minute conversation about what his cool toys can do. He confirmed what I'd suspected for a long time—if you have money, there's virtually no one you can't spy on in the Internet age. I contract with him to find out what Willow was doing at night, who she was meeting, what they were talking about. Pictures. Voice recordings. Text messages. All of it.

I didn't lightly make this decision. It goes against everything I believe about relationships, especially the part about not being a possessive, controlling asshole, but I have to know if there's something or someone behind a month of fights and late nights. If I tell Nessa, which I won't, she wouldn't approve. If Willow finds out, she'll compare me to those creepy guys that women come to her center to get away from, and it will mean the end of our relationship. But she won't find out.

A mid-workday weekday, I'm heading across Harvard Square now to meet Barry for coffee at the Starbucks right off the Square on Church Street. When he called, he said he had something he wanted to show me, but he wouldn't give me any of the details, just that he'd finished his snooping. It's only been two weeks. The Square is bustling with students, musicians, and magic acts, but what strikes me the most is how the suits and skirts appear filled with hope and possibility, and how little of it is likely to translate after they go back inside their cubicles. For workers, lunch hour is a time to stand in the Cambridge sun, be who they really are, and grant themselves a reprieve from the corporate drudge. Critics call this city The People's Republic of Cambridge, but to me, that's an okay name. What's wrong with a place that concretizes we the people?

The Starbucks has two floors, and Barry is waiting for me on the second at a corner table out of the way, expressionless, wearing a cheap black suit and a button-down shirt unbuttoned much too far. As I move closer, his abundant cologne pollutes the smell of dark roast. He ordered me a venti cappuccino at my text request, though now I wish it were a Highland Park Eighteen-Year-Old single malt. On the table is a large, unmarked manila envelope, which looks identical to the one Olivia handed me a few weeks ago.

"Barry," I say.

"Dan."

"Thanks for the coffee."

"All of your answers are in the envelope."

"Thank you. Your work is done?"

"Yeah," he says.

I pull out a much smaller envelope filled with hundreds from my blazer pocket and slide it across to Barry. It strikes me that this may look underhanded to onlookers, if there are any, but I pay for many things with hundreds and rarely use credit. Dad never believed in debt, and though he never made enough money to dole out hundreds, I guess he did pass the no-debt gene along. I stand up, grab the dirt-filled envelope, thank Barry for his hard work, leave behind the unopened cappuccino, and return to Gordon Bell. Engine running, at first I place the envelope on my lap, staring at it for a long time. Part of me needs to see what's inside, but part of me doesn't.

A handsome young man floats out of the envelope until he reaches eye level. Then an older gray-haired father figure. Then Willow's long-lost mother, still young like in her photos. Then a real donor. When the envelope stops launching holograms, I place it on the front passenger seat, Willow's seat, and head back to CW with the flattop still up. On the way, I mostly think about a connection algorithm that's stumped our engineers for more than a month, occasionally glancing at the envelope.

#

Willow and I are watching an old movie, *Chinatown*, to take-out Spicy Szechuan Chicken with Peanuts, Peking Ravioli, and Spicy Broccoli. We're in our home, in our theater, in a cushy reclining love seat strategically placed in front of a 120-inch screen surrounded by seven surround speakers. On occasion between chopsticks heroics, we pass judgment on one aspect of the movie or another. There's no comparable actor to Jack Nicholson. Water will be the new gold fifty years from now, which doesn't bode well for my friends in Detroit. Detectives like Jake Gittes serve themselves, not the common good.

A week has passed, and I still haven't opened the manila envelope. I'm not sure why I would pay someone thousands of dollars to produce evidence that I won't examine, but so far it's a no-go. I locked the envelope away in my home office and have spent quality time with Willow this week. I left the office early a couple of nights, and she dropped in a few times to visit me. We've been good. Maybe it's enough to know I have the envelope available to me if I ever need it; maybe we're going to be okay. Though dinner with donors continued one evening this week.

When *Chinatown* ends, I'm unsettled. Why did she pick a movie where the lead character is a detective? Does she know? How could she? A wave of remorse, dark and suffocating, flows over me like black tar. I have to tell Willow about Barry, about the manila envelope, before the seep-in is complete. What was I hoping to gain by hiring Barry anyway? If I tell her, will she forgive me? If I don't, I'm perpetuating a big mistake by violating one of our fundamental agreements—on the big ones, always tell the truth.

"I'll be right back," I say.

"Okay, hurry."

I make my way to my office to my safe. I punch in Zack's birthday, 11-12-20-01, pull out the manila envelope, and double-check that it's still sealed. Should I open it? Unopened, there's no damage done, right? That should make it easier for Willow to forgive me. As I leave the room, I pause and wipe dust from the top edge of a framed picture of Zack on my desk. He's in his soccer uniform, number 7, and is pressing a No. 5 soccer ball against his side with one hand. It's my favorite photo, one I'd taken a month before he died. He scored a goal that day. When I snapped the photo, he was beaming, the way a boy does when he's mastered a skill and is truly seen by his father. A month later he was gone.

Zack steps out of the frame, juggling the ball.

Do you think I should tell her? I ask.

Yes.

But she'll leave me.

She may. But you have to tell her.

Chinatown was a sign.

It was, Dad.

Willow taught me that the universe sends signs, and I believe my conversations with Zack are signposts. Ever since I hired Barry, I've been seeing and chatting with Zack more. It's comforting. Once, early on, Nessa said I still had access to Zack and that I could speak with him anytime I wanted, but I never believed or followed up on that one until recently. I was too ashamed. But now, these conversations happen often, like New England rain. Having him near me is good, as ConversationWorks takes off, as Willow and I figure out a path forward.

When I return to Willow, her clothes are strewn all over the floor. She's powered the love seat down to full recline and is propped up on her side, her head on her hand with a blue blanket over her lower body. She smiles, opens one side of the blanket, and beckons me in. I slip out of my clothes, place the envelope next to them on the floor, and join her. Both on our sides, bodies entwined, we kiss. With hands, tongue, and words, she builds toward more, but the envelope is weighing on me and despite my best effort, I can't go with her.

"Are you okay?" she asks.

"Yeah, I'll be fine."

"What's in the envelope?"

"Nothing. We can talk about it later," I say.

As she canvasses my face, the softness in her face stiffens. Gently, she pulls away from me, the whole time watching me closely for a sign. When one doesn't come, she pushes off the reclined love seat. Blue-caped in the blanket, she looks down at the envelope and then up at me, asking me one more time to divulge the contents. Time slows. Then she swoops down, grabs the package, and tears it open. From the envelope, she pulls out a bunch of 8x10 photos, a CD, and a few pieces of paper. As she's cycling through each item, her face distorts and tears build up. Then she drops to the floor like a marionette whose lines have been cut and gathers and crisscrosses her legs. From there, she gently circles her fist on her knee as she holds one of the photos with the other hand.

"I can explain," I say.

"You had me followed?"

"I'm so sorry. I brought the envelope so I could come clean."

"Why didn't you ask me?"

"I don't know. I'm sorry. I should have."

"Do you realize what a violation this is? Do you realize how many women I've counseled to walk away under similar circumstances? Do you realize this is how it starts? You think you can control us? You think because I had dinner with someone, it has to be something negative about us? What the fuck, Dan?"

"I haven't even looked at the contents."

"Here," she says.

Willow throws the pictures, the CD, and the papers at me. Two of the photos stick to my body like 8x10 rectangular leeches that hint of Barry's cologne. I'm hesitant to look, but slowly I gather all the photos and cycle through them. In each one, Willow is sitting across a restaurant table from an older man. I recognize one of the restaurants, Bondir, which is high end and one that Willow and I visited early in our relationship. The man is older, maybe fifty, with a full head of white hair and black-rimmed glasses. He's clean-shaven, and in each photo, he's impeccably dressed in a dark suit, a silk tie, and a matching folded handkerchief in his pocket. In one of the photos, the only one where his hand is in view, he's wearing a wedding band.

Willow's body seems to have crumpled in on itself. Her head is lowered, and her neck has disappeared underneath the blue blanket. The color has drained from her face, and though she opens her mouth a few times to speak, no words come. I've never seen her this hurt. Though we've talked about it before, for the first time I truly internalize that trust is much more important to her than even love. Without absolute trust, she can't be in a relationship. It's like I unintentionally zeroed in on the one true nonnegotiable in the relationship and, in a single and irreversible swoop, fucked everything up.

"Not that you deserve to know, but his name is Brian Young. I've known him since I first entered the business years ago. He's one of my biggest donors and wants to make another large contribution to the center. We've been talking these last weeks about how to best use the money."

"I messed up. I know that. Isn't there anything I can do to fix this?"

Willow lets the blanket roll off her shoulders and stands. As she dresses, the sadness in her has an inevitability to it, like she knew this moment would come, but didn't expect it this soon. On the way out of the room, she says, "I'm going to spend the next few days with friends."

I dress and move my side of the love seat so that it's fully upright again. There's still wine in the bottle and food in the take-out containers, so I refill my glass and plate, and empty both in no time. Then I open a new bottle of Highland Park and pour four fingers. As I slowly sip, a few tears find their way into my glass and salt the scotch. I wipe my face dry, down my drink, and refill. With the remote, I dim the lights until the room is completely dark, turn the sound way down, and start *Chinatown* from the beginning. As the opening sequence plays, Zack appears in front of the screen.

She'll come around, Dad.

No, she won't.

Why did you hire Barry?

For some reason, I didn't trust her enough.

Just you and me again?

Just you and me.

Distorted images of Jake Gittes's color Zack's face.

Spectacles and Halos and Code

The following week Willow officially moved out of the house. I guess I knew it was coming because I prepped like I had to deliver a fifty-slide long-shot presentation. I rehearsed my pitch over and over and developed solid counters for every possible leave-argument Willow might make. It will never happen again. We're good together. Let's see CW through until the end. I love you. But when we met, the slides abandoned me, and I hardly said a word. Willow only said a few.

"I have to leave, Dan."

"Are you sure?"

"Yes. There's no way forward when trust breaks."

"I do love you."

"I love you, too. I hope someday you'll truly let someone in again."

We both teared up, gently hugged.

"Do you need help moving?"

"I have it covered."

I've replayed that sequence a million times since then, each time reciting it exactly as it happened, down to the inflection points, each time searching for something I missed, something that might change the outcome, each time ending up in the same place. I have no one to blame but myself. This time, for sure, I caused harm to someone I love. Well, last time, too.

A short time after The Conversation I moved away from Revolutionary Road. I closed on the house, which sold at full asking price, and rented a loft in Cambridge close to CW. Before I moved, I sold most of my stuff: Gordon Bell, my 500W Class A component stereo system with my B&W 802 Diamond Speakers, the movie theater components including my Runco projector, almost all of the furniture. Even the sledgehammer went for five bucks during a yard sale. I guess there was something about driving Willow away that made me lose my appetite for material things, made selling things the easy part. The hard part was cleaning out Zack's room. At first, I packed everything Hannah didn't claim. But in the end, the only things I kept were the Millennium Falcon, his soccer trophies, and a few rocks and arrowheads we found once on a hike.

Driving Willow away also had an air of familiarity. Some people are most comfortable around family, or with a lover, or traveling, or working, but these days I'm most comfortable around loss. Everything slows down, and there's a sweet and sad quality that lodges in my chest. When that happens, I know there's little in the world I can't accomplish. I know that what I'm about to do, which started with stacked pebbles, is going to skyscraper.

Today, the sweet-and-sad is thick, and I've dialed it up a notch with caffeine. I'm heading into the office with a singular focus, without distractions, ready to put this feeling in my chest to good use. As I exit the elevator, I'm the first one in the office, and that too provides comfort. I power up the Deco-D and inject more, read my email, and check the tech news for anything related to what we're doing at CW. Still nothing like us out there. Then, sitting on my chair, I roll out into the open space so that I'm in the exact middle of our as-yet-to-form morning circle of chairs. There, I spin even after the elevator door rings open.

"Having fun?" Maggie asks.

"Much."

"How are you?"

"Okay."

"Can I join in?"

Maggie rolls up and, in silence, we spin together. As she spins, she lifts her feet off the ground and her hands over her head. This is one of many things she does where she's present and free. Writing code, anything with Zooey, and eating Almond Joy ice cream are a few of the others. How did she figure that out at such a young age? How does anyone figure that out at any age? Eventually, we both stop and face each other.

"That was fun," she says.

"Much needed."

"I can't imagine losing Zooey."

I take in my engineering VP. She's wearing jeans, Keds, and a T-shirt with I *do* stenciled across the front. She looks like she's still in school down the street at her alma mater. For her, CW is only possible because of Zooey. Yes, work is important and an integral part of her life, but at her core, love for Zooey fuels everything she does. I guess I recently proved we're reversed that way.

"I'm okay. She was right to leave," I say.

"And you still don't want to talk about it?"

"No. Other than it was my fault."

Maggie looks at me like she's not sure what to say. Instead, she starts to spin again. Clockwise. Counterclockwise. I start too, and we hold a short competition to determine who can complete the most full spins off one push. She wins with four by cleverly balling up in the chair to improve her momentum. We both have such strong compete-and-smarts genes—they will carry us through the coming time if they don't get corrupted. I spin one final rotation and catch the wall clock at my nine. Everyone will be here soon, and we'll get into the technicals, but for these last connected moments together, it's comforting to know Maggie is willing to spin with me.

The elevator door opens again, and Zia walks in with a big yawn. She's dressed in one of her many business suits, this one red, and her hair is pulled back off her face, which is perfectly made-up and almost hides her exhaustion. "What is it with you engineering types and morning? It's much too early." She heads directly for the Deco-D and fills a large mug with espresso. Then she wheels up a chair and joins us.

"How are you doing, Dan?" she asks.

"Okay."

"No word from Willow?"

"No."

"I guess it's good for CW. Back to your old work habits and all."

"I guess."

"I would spin with you guys, but I'm overdressed."

Maggie and I break out laughing.

The three of us talk the business side of shop for a time, teeing up some of the bigger topics for road-map discussions with the larger group. Should all of the conversations be English-based at the start? Can we eventually incorporate language translation into the software? If so, when? Until then, how do we, if at all, aggregate results of two conversations if each one is in a different language? We've been circling on these topics for a long time, which isn't unusual given their magnitude, though I'm inclined to reduce complexity at launch and stick with English. Addressing multiple languages is a requirement for version three or four. When we're done with the language topic, surprisingly, Zia starts to spin. Maggie and I join, and for a time the three of us synchronize.

The elevator door opens again and Charles enters. "Did I miss an early meeting?"

"No, just spinning, " Maggie says.

"Glad I'm a little late."

Charles heads toward the cappuccino maker, which gives us all an opportunity to refill. Gathered around the machine, there's an undeniable bond between us. This is how it all started—just the four of us. Well, Willow too. Will we launch something new thirteen months from now, something revolutionary, something that will redefine how the world conducts business? The affirmation—Hell yes! The truth—we don't know. We'll either make or break CW. We'll either be on the covers of all the tech magazines or we won't. We'll either change the world or fail big. Regardless, it's good to know three other people share the boat with me. And if we do fail big, at least I know they'll be okay. They're exceptionally talented; they'll find something else. Coffee in hand, we return to our chairs and circle.

"I have an idea," I say.

I propose giving the rest of the team the day off, so that the four of us can hang out and focus on our big issues. All agree. We spend the next hour, as folks trickle in, giving them the good news, sending them on their way, and mapping out an agenda for the day. Every employee says no first, there's too much work, but in the end takes us up on our offer. After the last employee leaves, we circle in the center of the office again.

"What should we talk about first?" I ask.

"Lately, I've been waking up in the middle of the night worried about something pretty fundamental," Maggie says. "I don't think it's possible for our users to have a meaningful conversation given our current product definition."

"Why is that?" Zia asks.

"Look at the four of us right now. We're sitting in a circle. We can talk with words with hand gestures and facial expressions, and we use them interchangeably when needed in the conversation. So much of what happens in conversations isn't spoken at first, yet there's a richness that those other things add that builds trust and moves the conversation forward. We can't emulate in-room gestures and expressions with our software, and although we use video and texting to let people feel like they're together talking in a room, they're really not. As we all know, when people aren't in the room together, civility breaks down."

"You realize that if you're right, we don't have a company," Zia says.

"Let's sit with Maggie's point for a bit," I say.

Is Maggie right? There's no doubt that what she's saying, if we could build it, would make the conversations seem real. There's no doubt that the current design relies on readily available devices—desktops, laptops, tablets, mobile devices—to enter the conversation. It would be better if there were a way to use a more seamless device to immerse the user in the experience. But how?

"Zia, what do you think?" I ask.

"Maggie's right. We're screwed if we don't fix it."

"Charles?"

"I agree. The whole company is based on the user feeling like he's in a real conversation. We have to fix it."

"I agree, too. Okay, any ideas?"

We spend the next couple of hours tossing around ideas on how to best represent the user in our software: realistic avatars in a fully animated conference room; split-screen movement triggered video; various combinations of text, video, and animation. All of the options have pros and cons, but none have the wow factor; all of them are variants on what we're already doing and aren't truly immersive. That's the thing about what we're building. If we're going to get the whole world in conversation, we need technology that allows people to connect in a visceral way. They need to feel like our product is indispensable, like they can participate in changing the world by using it.

"How about conversation glasses?" I ask.

"Say more," Zia says.

"Well, what if a user could put on a pair of glasses that would transport him or her to a virtual conversation circle where he or she could see all of the people in the conversation, regardless of their location? And what if those glasses, through laser-sensing technology, could project facial and body expressions of the person wearing them to all the other participants?"

"It's like highly advanced holographic video conferencing," Maggie says. "We're at least a decade away from that kind of technology."

"Feasibility may be a showstopper. Still, talk about a leap forward."

"So we'd expand to be a hardware and software company if we could pull it off," Zia says. "Do any of you know anything about hardware?"

"I do," I say. "Don't forget that we had a hardware business at RR focused on cloud infrastructure. I was heavily involved in the manufacturing and supply chain issues when we started that business."

"I know hardware, too, from my M.I.T. days," Maggie says. "Robots and voice recognition and contextual understanding tend to go together."

"How much would something like that cost?" Charles asks.

"We'd need a lot of cash to build a prototype, assuming it's even in the realm of possibility," Maggie says. "And building a manufacturing site will be expensive, too, even if we go to China."

"I don't want to go to China," I say. "It will cost around 50 million to get the manufacturing site up and running in the US. How much for the prototype?"

"Another fifty million. I know this guy doing postgraduate work at M.I.T. in virtual reality. If anyone can build the glasses, he can," Maggie says.

As Maggie is telling more about the M.I.T. guy's research, my phone rings.

"Hey, Dan, got a minute?" my lawyer asks from the other end of the call.

"Sure."

"It looks like Olivia is serious about the lawsuit and won't settle. In the end, I still think we'll win, but it's going to cost a lot more money than I originally anticipated. I'm sorry."

He walks me through the exact interactions that he's had with Olivia's lawyers—one three-hour meeting with him on one side and five RR lawyers on the other. They're requesting a mountain of data, and their strategy is to spend money at an alarming rate to obtain it. He thinks Olivia is trying to weigh us down in legal fees and detail before we ever get to court. As expected, she knows she can't win in court, but she has no problem trying to get us to cave by bankrupting us along the way.

When I hang up, I shake my head. The rest of my time with the three of my colleagues has little to do with the technology conversation we just had. The lawyer's call rattled me, and that's clear to them. Instead, we spend the time working through cash burn-rate scenarios. How much will development cost given the current product definition? Do we really need a hundred-million to build and manufacture the conversation glasses? What's the upper-lower for how much it will cost to win the lawsuit? No matter how we cut it, we keep reaching the same conclusions: we need more cash, and we need an outside investor.

#

Willow emailed me a poem the other day: *Loss has its own light / In the throng / I can always pick out the ones who've been hurt the most. / They're faint beacons toward a distant, more kindhearted world.* Right after we started living together, she caught a poetry wave and wrote almost every morning. When she finished a poem, she'd read it out loud to me, and each time, I felt honored that I was the first: the first to hear her shiny new words, the first to hear what was in her head, and the first to see her love for a newborn. I miss those mornings. For this poem, she said she woke up with the first line in her head, thought of me, and wrote the whole thing in about a minute. I guess it was a reach out of sorts, but it's not like she wants to get back together given my gargantuan screw-up. That's the way it is when you love someone and don't trust him—you can have moments of kindness and of true connection, but stringing those moments together into something more is no longer possible.

Today, I'm heading into Boston for a first-time face-to-face with a potential investor. With start-ups, cash and control are king. An entrepreneur can have a game-changing idea, but if he runs out of cash, the idea will never come to fruition. Or he can have a vision for where the company is headed, but if he gives up too much control to the money guys, he won't realize it before he's pushed out. When we started CW, I was adamant that we not take money from outside investors. But now, with the lawsuit, with the glasses that we've tentatively named CSpectacles, I have no choice.

I'm on the T, the red line into the city, which I picked up near my apartment in Kendall Square. Ever since I moved to Cambridge, I've used public transportation. There's a lot to be said for it, which I never thought about before. It's cheap. It's energy efficient. It mostly runs on time. Sometimes I miss Gordon Bell, the house, my larger-than-a-dollar-a-year salary, but not that often. As I'm crossing over the Charles River, a downpour pings my train car, which along with the noise from the T and the hum of people talking, backgrounds thoughts of CW for the first time in days. Zack sits down in the empty chair next to me.

Dad, we haven't talked in a while.

Work's been all consuming.

Like the old days.

I'm sorry. I'm here now. What should we talk about?

Women. I think you need one.

When did you start thinking about girls?

I'm at that age. You know, hormones. What about Zia? She's pretty.

It's not like that between Zia and me. We're just good friends.

Too bad. She's pretty. Where are you going?

To sell my soul.

Zack would have been fourteen this month. On the day of, I agreed to go over to meet Hannah at the cemetery first thing, which has been our ritual since Zack's death, but I punted at the last minute. I haven't been since my pyramid-building visit, and it's unlikely that I'll go again. I'd rather have a conversation with him than stare at his name on a stone.

I get off the T at Charles Street near Beacon Hill, which is where I'm meeting Jason Knight. Jason is the head of an up-and-coming venture capital firm, Knight Technology Ventures. Ever since he heard about CW, he's been trying to invest. He's a believer, which is good, though he also runs a billion-dollar venture fund with an average annual return of twenty-five percent. That part worries me.

As I enter the restaurant, Jason is waiting for me in the lobby. He's tall, well dressed in a black blazer, white polo shirt, khaki slacks, and alligator shoes that match his belt. All the venture guys dress like this. It means: I'm rich, but casual; I have power, but will wield it only when you fuck up. He must be six-foot-five and two-sixty, more a former starting defensive end for the Crimson than a technology venture guy.

He extends his hand, says my name, and squeezes like a vice grip for a second. He's strong, and his skin leaves a faint oddment of oil. We exchange introductory pleasantries and make our way to a secluded table Jason reserved in advance. The restaurant, high-end nouveau, is full, which is strange for midafternoon, and for a second, I consider the possibility that the place is filled with hi-tech spies who've gotten wind of our meeting. I do a quick scan for Barry Porcelaina.

After we order our food and an apparently expensive bottle of wine, an Altamura Cabernet, we begin in non-earnest. I catch Jason up on the Olivia lawsuit, which he'd already heard about from his sources, and walk him through our plans for CSpectacles. After the four of us met that day at CW, Maggie met with the engineering guy at M.I.T. We did a series of all-day deep dives to determine the feasibility of building CSpectacles. The conclusion: there's tremendous risk in pulling it off, but if we do, we'll have a product with the wow factor we all believe we need to be successful. We hired the guy from M.I.T. to help Maggie with the design and a supply chain guy to help us ramp up manufacturing in South Dakota. With these two on board and Maggie's software expertise, we have all the pieces we need to move the company forward. Except for the money.

When I'm done with the update, Jason remains silent for a time as he looks me in the eyes, trying to determine if I'm bullshitting him. That's understandable. I can't count how many times I've shaken my head after hearing about a venture investment made in some hare-brained technology start-up. Less than ten percent of them amount to anything real, but when one hits, it more than makes up for all the losers.

"Are you sure about the hundred million?" he asks.

"As sure as one can be at this point."

"I'll need to meet Maggie, the glasses guy, and the manufacturing guy."

"No problem."

"If you pull this off, you'll change everything. The applications are endless. You'll disrupt the airline, communication, gaming, and a host of other industries."

"Down the road, yes, but not right away. First, we want to get the world talking. How much do you want?"

"You're in for?"

"Twenty million."

Jason taps his knife on the table as he tries to figure out the appropriate ask. He knows I need the money, but he also knows I don't want to take it. If he goes too high, I'll walk and look elsewhere, but if he goes too low, he'll potentially leave money on the table. So he'll start high, but not ridiculously high, and come down from there.

"Sixty percent," he says.

The anger-swell starts to rise. I cut into my steak and eat a few pieces. Then I sip the wine, which lives up to its price. Part of me wants to get up, tell him to fuck off, and leave. But part of me knows we're not that far off. Jason wants sixty percent of the company, which will give him control on all the important issues. I can't give him that much, but for the amount of money I need, giving him a substantial piece is necessary. "I can go fifty-fifty. Can you squash the Olivia thing?"

"Fifty-fifty is agreeable. I'll handle Olivia. I'll have a term sheet for your review in a few days. We'll need to set up a formal board that oversees your progress. I'll be chairman."

"That's workable as long as all hiring and firing decisions are exclusively mine."

Jason drifts off for a time as he eats a portion of his extra-rare veal chop. Then he says, "Except for you. I'm sure you're going to make us both a fortune, and it will never be necessary, but we have to have the ability to fire you if you don't meet the requirements detailed in your employment contract. Anyway, we're getting a little ahead of ourselves. First thing is to meet Maggie."

#

My CW office is the same size as everyone else's. A ten-by-ten cube along an outside wall, modestly furnished with a company desk and two standard chairs in front of it for impromptu meetings. A few pictures, including a Munch print I like, shelter the lone brick wall. The one liberty I did take on office selection day was the window. It's big, provides full afternoon sun, and has a view of Kendall Square. Dill from last night's Sam La Grassa's deli sandwich spices the air and reminds me of how much Zack loved Sam's pastrami.

Zack sits down across from me, leans back in his chair, and puts his feet up against my desk.

Dad, you need to develop a code.

Since when are you interested in developing software code?

Zack laughs loud. *Daaad! Not that kind of code, I mean a code for how to work. You're going to be the most powerful businessman in history. Many have come before you and lost their way. You need a code to keep you on track. Like the one we had on our soccer team.*

I liked that code.

Me, too. I miss being part of a team.

Me, too.

When Zack was part of FC Concord, the team had a code. Respect your teammates, work hard, play fairly, that sort of thing. Being part of a team and living by a simple code taught him more than I ever did. When I think about lessons from Dad, I guess there were a few, but there could have been many more if I hadn't spent so much time Radio-Radioing.

Now that we've taken venture dollars, now that I'm building a company with big aspirations and big profit pressure, a code might help during those inevitable times when Ventureland or eventually Wall Street forgets that money is a means to an end. Or during those times when competitors come after us with shadowed corporate violence. Olivia and I chatted once about developing the RR Way, which had all the makings of a code, but the talk never advanced. We were busy, doing well, and had no time to take ethics and integrity beyond the mandatory training class RR required.

How to develop the CW code? I could pull everyone together. We could have a conversation about what belongs. In many ways, that's exactly the right process. Get everyone brainstorming. Get buy-in. Get our own compass, our own version of true north. But there are business tasks that the CEO does do alone, tasks that are more about leading than teaming, more about defining moments than living in them, and this is one of them. Besides, Zack wants me to do this on my own.

For a long time now, my best thinking comes to light while I'm driving alone on the open road. I discovered this as an undergraduate, right before my Morals and Ethics final. When everyone else was in one of Harvard's infinite number of libraries studying, I borrowed my roommate's car keys and drove north a couple of hours to contemplate what I'd learned during the semester from Plato, Aristotle, John Stuart Mill, and Nietzsche. It worked better than any study group or set of comprehensive notes, and I aced the test. Ever since, driving and deep thinking have been inextricably linked.

The only thing is, for this trip, I'll have to borrow a car, preferably a fast one. On my way to Zia's office, I let folks know I'm going on a think retreat and I'll be back tomorrow. It's not the first time I've done one, so folks kid me about the dangers of overanalyzing while driving, which I seem to do even more since I've become CEO. When I reach her office, she's sitting at her desk transfixed by something on her computer. She's wearing the most beautiful silk scarf that contains brightly colored and variegated concentric circles that seem to pirouette off of the silk.

"Nice scarf."

"Thanks. I had it made. African. Adinkrahene."

"It's lovely. Hey, I need a favor. Can I borrow your car for the day?"

"Sure. Time for another strategy drive?"

"Yeah. I'll be back before dusk."

Zia flips me the keys, tells me where she parked her Audi RS5, and wishes me luck. I thank her and a moment later I'm on my way. At the elevator, the door opens, but I don't go in. Instead, I retrace my path, past the water cooler, past the fresh hires already hard at work, to Zia's office. She's staring at her computer, like she was a few minutes ago, and doesn't sense my return. I tap on the wall divider and ask her if she wants to take a ride. Without hesitation, she says, "Absolutely."

In the car, Zia pulls a gold clasp out of her hair. Red whorls drape the scarf and meld with the concentric circles, confirming the power of unadulterated beauty. Moments later, we head out of the parking lot in her dark green RS5, which, with an almost 400 horsepower engine, is more than ready to race. We pick up 93N and cruise out of Cambridge toward New Hampshire. As we drive, Zia updates me on some of her recent one-and-outs: a technology executive vice president, a lawyer, a musician who writes beautiful emotional songs. "He should have been a girl." When she finishes telling me everything, she says, "You know, I'm not girlfriend material. Can't sink to that level." I can't help but laugh. I'm not boyfriend material. Or husband material. Or father material.

"What's today's think retreat about?" Zia asks.

"The code."

"The code?"

"For how we run the company."

"I don't like rules."

"Me, neither. Not so much rules, more like living, breathing guidelines for sorting through things," I say.

That said, Zia is onto something. Is a living code an oxymoron? How can we create one and not have it come across as dogma and as a rigid inflexible set of rules, or worse as a set of clichés that employees joke about more than they use? Yet there is a need for some level of direction, for helping people productively manage through their days. So much of what we did at RR, especially as we grew, was inefficient. Too many meetings. Too many presentations. Hours spent on topics when only a few minutes where necessary. Too much focus on the short term versus the long term. Too much unwarranted conflict or politics. Why does that happen as a company ages?

"Maybe the first point in the code should be about each employee making the code their own?" I ask. "We want people to believe in what we're doing and not just follow. If they don't push back on the code, make it better and make it their own, then they won't buy in. And if they don't buy in, the company will fail."

"Don't you think we should involve them in the code's creation then?"

"I need to do the first pass myself, with you as my sounding board."

"Why?"

"I just do. Trust me on this one."

Zia taps her finger on her knee, apparently processing possible reasons I might want to do this myself. In general, I've been highly collaborative at CW—after all, that's what the company is all about. Even when I've done think retreats in the past, I've always come back with a suggested process instead of an answer. But this time, it's different.

With Zia's favorite band, Rage Against the Machine, blasting through her Bose sound system, I take the exit for I-89 North. It's a less-traveled road and allows me to open up the S5 to a little more than a hundred. New England has few roads like this, few opportunities to enter the speed-cocoon. Racecar mode and "Wake up" shut down the conversation as we focus on the highway, on speed, and on the spoils of superior engineering. After a good fifty miles, Zia's radar detector goes off, so I hit the brakes and shut off the stereo. Sure enough, around the next bend we drive the speed limit by a state trooper who, laser gun still pointing, has pulled over another German-made vehicle, apparently not blessed with an Escort RedLine Radar Detector.

"There's an honesty to speed," I say.

"Like hi-tech, if you mess up, you're toast."

"Maybe that's a piece of the code. Be direct and honest about everything."

"All companies say they do that today, but few do it," Zia says.

Zia turns and looks out the window. We pass a large lake that kisses the highway, probably a reservoir. The maples and oaks swoosh by and say their good-byes as evergreens slowly replace them. Occasionally, a home or a farm dots the landscape, but mostly little competes with the forest. If nature were building a new company, how would it organize, what kind of code would it put in place, wouldn't it by definition be honest?

"By the way, where are we going?" Zia asks.

"Do you have your passport?"

"Always."

"Let's go to Montreal then. I know this place, Beauty's Bagels."

"We're driving six hours for bagels?"

"Don't judge until you taste one," I say.

Even after years on the East Coast, where I've experienced every kind of bagel, nothing could have prepared me for my first

Beauty. One day, during the first months of RR, Olivia said, "Let's go for a ride." I asked her where, and she smiled. "Trust me." Six hours later, after three delicious bagels that I downed in record speed, I understood. I even took home a dozen with me, which I savored each morning for the next week. Thinner than New York bagels, with a one-to-one crust-to-interior ratio and a generous amount of sesame seeds, the bagels had so much flavor that I ate mine without cream cheese or butter. In fact, I liked them enough to try on multiple occasions to have local Boston bagel makers reproduce them, but to no avail.

We get to work on the code and eventually come up with the next piece: Celebrate Failure. This one is tricky. Valuing mistakes is a critical component of building a great product, but if the company makes too many mistakes, the market or venture guys will squash it, and it will never get the chance to make it right. So what kind of failure do we want to celebrate? Not the kind when people don't work hard or don't think through a problem. More the kind where team members go all in, where everyone believes the proposed product or solution is the right one, and, in the end, the market crushes them. Understanding those kind of failures in detail and learning from them are just as important, maybe more important, than the successes. Though with a company this young, we'll need to string together a few successes first.

Why, as companies grow and age, does success breed skirmishes instead of continued success? Companies turn inward, and employees often find it easier to focus on the *them* in *us versus them*. The Product Management Department laments: if only Marketing did their job. Engineering complains: if only Product Management did a better job with requirements. And Marketing whines: if only engineering was more innovative. For some reason, it's easy to forget that everyone is connected, that we work best when we focus on the things we can control. This leads to the next part of the code. Deemphasize us versus them and focus on what you can control.

After Zia records what we've done so far, she tells me a story from her childhood about the time her father took her to a Celtics game. The Celtics were playing the Lakers for the championship, and although she didn't know the game or the players, one thing her dad said stuck with her. "Zia, the great ones slow things down under pressure. It's not that they're more athletic; they're just calmer than everyone else. That's why they're great." She and her dad share season tickets to the Celtics now, and she goes to as many games as she can. I've known her all of these years, and I had no idea.

#

Beauty's is a corner breakfast and lunch shop on Mount Royal Street at the base of Mount Royal Park, the famous one with the giant cross on top. The shop has been there since 1942. Even though we arrive during nonpeak hours, most of the booths, with their signature royal blue leatherette seats and white linoleum tables, are filled. Luckily, the hostess leads us to an empty one in the back. In no time, an abundance of food fills our table, enough to satiate us through the creation of the remainder of the code. Before finishing, we need to eat. Zia takes a bite of her sesame bagel covered with cream cheese and her mish-mash omelet and confirms that they're both delicious and every bit worth the drive. I devour my bagel and my eggs and bacon, confirming how much I missed this place. In between bites, bagel superlatives roll: Perfect texture. Impossible to create a better crust. Each bite is like a long-awaited payoff.

"Waiting for the payoff," I say.

"What?"

"Creating long-lasting value is something that many American companies have lost their appetite for over the years. The pressure for achieving quarterly results, for placing profit above long-term value, and for having immediate and constant success has clouded value creation. When we eventually go public, the pressure will mount for short-term release, and we'll need to fight it."

"Easier said."

"How about this one? Do the unquarterly thing."

"Do you think you can sell that to Jason now or eventually to the Street?"

"If I don't, we'll end up no different than RR or anyone else."

Zia takes out her phone and adds this last one to a note she started when we were in the Audi. "So here's what we have so far. One, be direct and honest with your colleagues, especially when the conversation is difficult. Two, take time for yourself in retreat to map out ways to constantly improve things in your sphere of influence, which I added given it's what we're doing today. Three, mistakes are our greatest teachers. Value them and accept their lessons. Four, rage against us versus them. Concentrate on the things you can control by setting goals that are crisp and achievable, and don't dwell on what others aren't doing. Five, do the unquarterly thing."

"Cool. You took our fragmented thoughts and enhanced them a lot. I like number two."

"I'm your VP of marketing. That's what I do. So, I know this is your show, but I have one suggestion. How about something like, 'Strive every day to build products that connect people in ways previously impossible.'"

"Let's make that one number six. And back to the Celtics, how about, 'When stress comes, practice calming yourself.'"

"Pretty good. How about stepping it up to 'When conflict comes, deescalate while staying true to what you believe.'"

"That's better."

We each finish our third bagel and get ready to leave Beauty's. We'll spend the night in Montreal and leave early in the morning.

That way, we can come back to Beauty's first thing, have breakfast, and take a few dozen back for the folks at CW. It turns out that, even though she's never been to Beauty's before, Montreal is one of Zia's favorite cities. She makes the Grand Prix and the Jazz Festival most years. As a result, she offers to show me the city for the rest of the day and to take me shopping to buy a change of clothing and toiletries. While she gets on the phone to make a dinner reservation, I grab the bill and head to the counter.

As I'm paying at the old-fashioned cash register, a mother, father, and their maybe five-year-old daughter come into Beauty's chatting in French. The little one is blonde and is hugging her daddy's leg. The dad has his arm around the mom, and both of them look deeply in love. Once inside, the three unattach. The woman hugs the hostess and then kisses her on each cheek. The man shakes hands with a few men behind the counter. The daughter runs between tables and says hello to grandparents, fathers, mothers, sons, daughters. All three of them—the man, the woman, the child—are exuding love; all three of them are part of the Beauty's community, of more. I look over at Zia, who's now standing next me. She sees it, too.

"That's what we need at CW," I say.

"That's what the whole world needs."

"Do you think we could do that at CW?"

"Maybe. If we don't screw up too bad."

"Let me try this one. How about, 'With your chosen work, your chosen family, your chosen community, love widely'?"

Zia reaches out, takes my hand, and squeezes tightly.

#

Maggie, Zia, Charles, Jason, and I are sitting in a circle at CW. At first I said no to Jason participating—it was too soon—but he insisted so

I caved. We're about to slip into our respective CSpectacles, which are wirelessly connected to our servers. It's early morning, and the rest of the team is anxiously standing outside the circle waiting for us to begin. We've hooked up a few large flat screen TVs so they'll be able to observe our virtual selves in the conversation room. The room warms as each moment passes.

During our session we plan to test the prototype, which thanks to Maggie's around-the-clock efforts was developed in nine months, much faster than any of us thought possible. We've been in business now for eighteen months, and it's T minus six months until launch. It's hard to believe time has gone by so fast, but that's the nature of hi-tech companies. Now and then a big milestone marks progress and problems, and everything in between is a blur of work.

In a few moments, we'll each slide on prototype versions of the glasses, which look like multi-antennaed clear helmets with Ray-Bans glued on. Hopefully, when we power up, we'll be transported to a virtual room, where we can hold a conversation about our chosen topic: lack of drinking water in Detroit. Today's the first time we're trying the glasses with more than two people. Maggie and her team have done the test runs to date, which have been short and mostly bug-free, but the complexity and processing power increase exponentially as you add more users. It's also the first time we'll try out Maggie's summary and aggregation software, which, if it works, will summarize our conversation, broadcast it through to the CW world, and automatically identify other conversations with similar outcomes. Because none of those conservations exist yet, we made some up as test cases.

When I talk to folks about CW, most gravitate to CSpectacles, where the value proposition is simple to understand. Put on a pair of glasses and get transported to another world; there you can do stuff with people located anywhere. Even though we're limiting the world to a conversation room for now, folks can easily imagine extensions and licensing deals. Why travel for business when you can use CSpectacles to conduct your meeting virtually? Why play a game on a TV screen or computer when you can actually be in the game? Why use a phone or Skype to talk with your child who's studying abroad when you can sit in a room with him and have a conversation? Many more use cases exist; our total addressable market is gigantic. We just need to put a lot of thought into prioritizing them.

Although CSpectacles are innovative, the real power of our company is most evident when the glasses are combined with the rest of the hardware and software. There are two main pieces of hardware, the glasses and a cylinder, and three main pieces of software, a summary engine, an aggregation engine, and a change engine.

The glasses, CSpectacles, allow a user to immerse herself in the conversation room and see her colleagues. But when we thought about what a user would see, we identified two problems. First, if a colleague is sitting in a chair in say Africa, what's the best way to send that live feed to the conversation room and make it look like the person is actually in the virtual room? Our solution was to add motion, image, and sound detection cylinders above and below each chair, which allow us to capture real-time images of the person, transmit them as a hologram over a fat Internet pipe, and not only re-create it in the conversation room, but enhance it—give it flesh and blood so to speak—by using a complicated fractal algorithm the team developed. This leads to our second problem—the African colleague would still be wearing her glasses after materializing in the conversation room. With glasses on, we'd lose an important part of body language, the eyes. To solve this problem, we digitally enhance the image by removing the glasses and fill in the gap with a live feed of the person's eyes. To capture the user's eyes, we installed miniature cameras in each pair of glasses facing the user's eyes. If the glasses and cylinders work as planned, a group of people will be able to sit across from each other in a virtual conference room like they're actually there.

The summary engine does pretty much what the name implies: summarizes the conversation the team had into a set of crisp recommendations. Those recommendations are fed to the aggregation engine, which looks for similar conversations in the CW database, and gives users the opportunity to combine their results with those conversations. After a group of conversations, ranging from two to many, has agreed on a set of recommendations, the change engine helps them translate the recommendations into an actionable plan.

Even if all of the technology works, we know that we have a lot of privacy issues to solve. Over time, we'll know the views of everyone who has any sort of conversation on our platform. We'll know these folks' detailed preferences and positions and, with that much data, we'll have a great deal of power and responsibility. We can either make the world a better place by disrupting many different markets or we can cause great harm if governments, corporations, advertisers, even us, misuse the data. Could what people say in a conversation be held against them? Could we unintentionally usher in a new Orwellian era? Will people truly be free to say what they believe in a meeting without repercussions?

I put my CSpectacles on. At first, all I see is a black screen with the CW pyramid logo in the middle. Soon after that, I'm transported to a room with four empty chairs. One after the other, Maggie, Charles, Zia, and Jason materialize, yes, like in *Star Trek*. As each one appears, a wide grin spreads across their face, which means the glasses and cylinders are working, and we're all seeing each other. Zia moves her hands, like she's been paralyzed for a long time and is shocked she's regained movement. I do the same, and sure enough, my virtual hand movements track my real hand movements perfectly. The image of each of us is so realistic, so detailed, that for a moment I'm convinced I'm really in the room. We don't look like holograms or animations; we look like real people sitting in a room about to have a conversation.

"This is so cool," Jason says.

"Shall I begin?" Maggie asks.

We all nod. One of the limitations of this version of the software is that you must designate a supervisor for the conversation at the start of the session. When the supervisor says the appropriate phrase, the software transitions from capturing and analyzing the conversation to accepting voice commands from the supervisor. Prior to the conversation, we all agreed that Maggie would be the conversation commander for our maiden voyage.

"Supervisor mode," Maggie says. "Today's topic is the water crisis in Detroit."

"That's a cool topic!" the computer, which we've named Darra, says in a perfect female Boston accent. "Please begin."

"I'll begin," I say. "I think water, like air, is a basic human right, and people shouldn't have to pay for it, even in large cities."

"I agree," Maggie says.

"Me too," Zia says.

"I don't know," Charles says. "It does cost money to purify and ship in the water to Detroit. Someone should pay for that."

"That is how we built this country," Jason says. "You pay for what you use."

"Given the water problems around the world, water will be the new gold in fifty years," Charles says. "People need to get used to paying now."

As the conversation continues, what strikes me is not the different points of view, which I could have predicted for this particular set of folks. Instead, I'm drawn to just how much of the conversation is nonverbal: a frown, a tapping of the finger, a nod, a smile, arms folded across a chest, furrowed eyebrows, hands animated next to Maggie's face. We're each cueing off words and body language, and this combination propels the conversation forward and makes it feel like we are friends having a debate on campus instead of executives at a start-up.

"I don't know," Maggie says. "You have to ask yourself why a country exists in the first place. I mean, it's to serve the people, isn't it? Food. Water. Healthcare. Education. Jobs for anyone who wants one. They should be basic rights."

"You sound like a socialist," Charles says.

"Maybe we need a little more socialism," Maggie says.

This starts an intense debate on capitalism versus socialism, which is off topic, which has no chance of reaching consensus, and which is divided along expected lines. Jason, Charles, fifty percent of Zia on one side. Maggie, fifty percent of Zia on the other side. I stay neutral, CEO-like, though Jason almost hooks me a few times with a conservative rant. After we've gone on for a bit, the computer interrupts us, saves me from an imminent outburst at Jason, and asks if we're off topic. This feature of the summary engine is one of my favorites, one that uses a complicated heuristic algorithm to determine if a conversation is off track. Without this feature, our fear was that many conversations wouldn't reach their potential. Maggie lets the computer know we agree we're off topic.

"I think there's probably some place in the middle where we can all agree," Zia says. "To run the country, we collect taxes at multiple levels. And those taxes go for all kinds of things from educating our kids to paving roads to defending the country. All we need to do is agree what's in the bucket for everyone, regardless of location, and what's not."

"If we agree everyone is entitled to water regardless of location, then that would eliminate any municipal water crisis," I say.

"How much would that cost?" Jason says.

"The place to start for me is to ask what are our basic needs as a society, what should be handled as a national issue versus local issue, and then go from there," Zia says.

"Are we agreeing that water is a basic need for our society and that all should have access to it regardless of location?" Maggie asks.

"Not yet. What about places where there isn't enough water?" Charles asks. "If we give everyone free access, then it will cost us a fortune and people will waste it because they no longer value it."

"That's a good point. To guarantee water for everyone, we would have to build a culture of conservation, so that everyone understood that their tax dollars only went so far," Maggie says.

For a time, we loop on the points we've made so far, refining them along the way, clearly identifying where we agree and disagree. Not all conversations will have this much structure. In fact, many will be much messier, but for our maiden voyage we wanted to give the computer every opportunity to succeed. After all, what we're attempting is incredibly complicated.

"Let's see where we are. Supervisor mode," Maggie says. "Summarize agreements."

Summarization is the hardest part for the software. To get it to work, we built in state-of-the-art, artificial-intelligence algorithms. The program has to comb over the entire conversation, extract relevant parts, look for meaning, check factual accuracy, and summarize what was agreed to, often in a way that's crisper than what was actually said during the conversation, almost as if a manager was in the room listening the whole time with the sole purpose of documenting our agreements. For our current CPU-intensive version of the software, summarization is maxing out our servers and is slow. We'll have to speed it up significantly before launch, but for now, the important thing is to see if it works.

After twenty minutes, Maggie pops out of the conversation and asks one of her engineers to check the servers and see if they're hung. A short time later he returns, says they were in fact down, and that he had to reboot. Maggie rejoins the conversation and repeats what we overheard, but catches herself when we all smile. "Hopefully, the computer captured our entire conversation and even drew a few conclusions, but we may have to start all over."

The rebooted computer processes for a long time and seems hung again. Just when we're about to give up, it returns and says, "The group CW Trial Run has reached the following agreements. Water is a basic human right for all in the United States. To make this happen, the cost of providing water to all will be absorbed in a national tax. To keep this tax as low as possible, an extensive water conservation plan must be developed and implemented. Is that correct?"

"Yes," Maggie says.

"Agreements saved. Searching the CW world for similar outcomes," the computer says.

Maggie beams. We all virtually applaud and hear everyone else who's watching the trial at CW applaud with us. To take what was maybe an hour conversation and boil it down to a few summary agreements is an impressive piece of engineering, even with the hang. But we're not done yet.

The next piece is the aggregation engine. The software is searching the database, looking for similar outcomes. After all the matches are found, there are a couple of choice points. If the outcomes are identical between our conversation and another group's conversation, we can combine the results. That way, instead of the two five-person teams agreeing on what to do about the water crisis, one ten-person team is in sync. If the conversations are fifty percent similar, the groups have the opportunity to hold a joint conversation to see if they can agree on their differences. Our hunch is that the greatest learning will occur in situations like this. If the conversations are significantly different, less than fifty percent, they're not aggregated. Our hunch is this is where the greatest polarization will firmly root. Of course, the aggregation process scales. All similar conversations, from two to millions, will have an opportunity to aggregate. In this way, large groups of people who are connected only by our software have an opportunity to agree on a course of action for almost any topic. Across CSpectacles, the cylinders, our summary engine, and our aggregation engine, we've already filed for fifty-seven patents.

Even though many business uses exist, what excites me the most about CW is the possibility of significant social change. The CSpectacles and cylinders have a wow factor for sure. And we just confirmed the wow of the agreement summary part of the software as well. But for social change, building one small conversation into an overall movement that can bring about change is key. That's why the aggregation engine is so important; without it, the conversations don't scale. It's also why the fourth piece, the change engine, is critical. We don't know how the change piece will work yet, and it's our biggest hole. For a time, I considered calling the change engine the So What? engine. After all, if you're going to hold all of these conversations around the world focused on change, you had better have a good way to mobilize the change after you've agreed on what to do. Otherwise, why bother?

After several minutes, the computer says, "There are no other conversations with similar results at this time. Your conversation has been stored. You'll be notified if similar conversations to yours happen in the future."

The body language in the room deflates.

"What happened?" I ask.

"Don't know. We stored ten conversations with similar results. Darra should have found them, done the comparison, and given us the opportunity to combine the conversations," Maggie says.

"We all knew the aggregation piece would be difficult," I say. "There were bound to be glitches. We'll get it right next time."

I look over at Jason, who is smiling. "At least the hardware worked well."

#

During the days and almost always late into the evenings, I'm with CW people: Maggie, Zia, Charles, and the broader team, which in the months since Jason's infusion of cash has swelled to fifty. But when I'm not working, I'm alone. Sometimes I walk the city early in the morning, before the workday has started, take in the homeless as they roll up their sleeping bags from store alcoves, venture down into a mostly empty T-station to watch the trains whoosh by, or admire the street cleaners brush away the dirt. All of it seems to fuel me for the workday, like some uninvented form of hi-octane gas that gives an average car one hundred miles per gallon. Sometimes I walk the streets with Zack at my side, and we talk about different things. How did the homeless fall? Zack's answer: *Slowly, like a lobster boiling in a pot.* What connects the people in a city beyond the trains, the jobs, the sports teams? My answer: Not much. Who will start at forward for the New England Revolution this season? Zack's answer: *Diego Fagundez.* Why, after building so much, does the suffering seem to be at an all-time high, and does every generation think that or is it truly worse now? My answer: It's worse now. Is Christina's ice cream better than Kimball's? Zack's answer: *Nothing is better than Kimball's.*

Tonight, I can't sleep. It's 3 a.m., and I'm walking Cambridge Street toward Harvard Square, which is still a couple of miles away. It's not much different now than early morning. Darker. A little quieter. A little less populated. Shut down, instead of bootstrapping. Sporadically, different vehicles pass by—a police cruiser, a few taxis, a black BMW with dark windows. The smells—restaurant garbage, wet asphalt from a heavy late-night downpour, vehicle exhaust—citify the air.

As I walk, I spin keys. In the last weeks, I've taken to it. I attached my apartment keys to a long blue and white beaded key chain Zack made for me when he was five. Spelled out on the beads are "I love my dad," only the word "love" has been replaced with a heart shape. He made it extra long, about a foot, so I can spin it, let it wrap around my index finger, and momentarily stop the circulation. There's a peacefulness to walking, to spinning in the middle of the night; the concrete and the darkness ground me.

So far, taking the venture money from Jason has worked out. Everyone is working around the clock, and the buzz around CW is everything you want in a product start-up. We've made incredible hires, not just in the leadership, but also in every level of the organization. If all goes well, we'll launch CW in six months. T minus six months. We still have a ton to do between now and then: finishing the software, ramping our US manufacturing site, debugging our supply chain, running beta trials, conducting some buzz marketing. Maybe after my walk I'll go straight to the office.

About halfway toward the square, I notice a couple arguing on the corner of Cambridge and Norfolk. She's pretty and blonde, dressed in a short black dress and black pumps, adorned with lots of jewelry. He's tall, muscular, with shoulder-length dark hair, well dressed in a blazer, slacks, and Oxford shirt. They look like they're in their twenties or early thirties, probably heading home after a night of clubbing. Their fight has a weariness to it, like they keep repeating it and hoping for a different outcome, like they've loved each other for a time.

As I slow my approach, I whirl my keychain faster, till it propels, sounds off in the air. Clockwise. Counterclockwise. Their argument escalates, passes the point of no return, until they appear to have blocked out their surroundings like lovers sometimes do in the middle of a knock-down-drag-out. That used to happen to me with Hannah, even with Olivia during our best work fights, but never with Willow until the end. I hear bits of the man and woman's argument. The man says, "You flirted." Or "Aren't I enough?" Or "I'm done." The woman says, "You're too jealous." Or "You never let me do what I want." Or "Please stop." For a moment, I swear the night air has traces of Willow's scent.

The man grabs the woman's arms at her biceps and shakes her. She strains to get away, tells him to "Fucking let go." But he doesn't. Instead, while continuing to hold her with one hand, he raises the other and slaps her hard across the face. She struggles more and tries to wriggle free, but he tightens his hold, raises his hand again, hesitates, and yells, "Don't make me do this. Don't make me do this."

Upon hearing those words, she stops trying to get away, stands up straight, and looks right at him like she knows what's coming, like she's resolved to meet the violence with defiance. Then, laser-fast, he fists her in the jaw so hard that I'm sure he's broken it. She reaches up with her free hand and covers the punch spot, mumbles something I can't hear. This enrages the man even more, and without hesitation, he punches her in the stomach. She staggers back like a rag doll and drops to her knees a few feet away from him. He steps toward her, crosses his arms, and statues himself. Looking down at her, he spits on her face. Slowly, she wipes the spit from her face and says, "No more."

Right. I let go of my unwound spinning keychain and watch it fly into the street, making a quick note of its location. Then I sprint toward the man. I know that it's best to strike silently and forcefully, while he's still blinded by his own violence and before he senses mine. When I'm a short distance away, he turns toward me, but before he can defend himself, I barrel into him and knock him down onto the concrete. There, I repeatedly pummel him. Hard. In the face. In the stomach. Wherever I can land one. Blood starts to ooze from his nose and his lip and, in no time, covers his face to the point where I can no longer see him.

The woman gets up off the concrete, latches both hands around my shoulders, and pulls. "Mister, I'm okay! He's my boyfriend! We just had a fight! You're hurting him!"

I can't stop my barrage. It's almost like someone else has taken over my body and my inhabited self's life depends on beating the shit out of this guy. The woman stops pulling on my shoulders and starts pounding my back with her fists. She's repeatedly screaming, "Stop it." The mantra gives me, real me, motor control. I jump to my feet and meet the woman's gaze. She steps back. Her lip quivers. There isn't a trace of thanks on her face. Is she afraid I may hurt her, too? The man remains on the ground, almost unconscious, still shocked and awed. The woman kneels down and wipes the blood from his face with her hand. Crying, she says, "John, I'm so sorry. I love you. I didn't mean to hurt you." She turns back to me. "Mister, leave us the fuck alone!"

At first, I'm hesitant to leave them. He could hurt her again. No, he will hurt her again. But then I notice someone across the street who appears to be filming the entire thing on his phone. This freezes me until I muster enough strength to turn away and start to jog. I stop for a second to search for my keychain on the road, locate it near a storm drain where I tossed it, and swoop it up with my blood-soaked hand, a hand that confirms I beat a man, that I would have continued beating him if the woman didn't stop me. The headline: CEO *of up-and-coming start-up, ConversationWorks, kills innocent young man. YouTube video goes viral. CEO sentenced to death by lethal injection. Company folds in disgrace.* Yes, the man had to be stopped. Yes, he was extremely violent and that can't be tolerated. But I might have killed him. Does anyone deserve that kind of sudden and absolute punishment? At the intersection of the next block, Cambridge and Elm, I speed up, and with keys in hand, I change direction toward CW, toward safety, toward Zack.

Fall, the Day of

Can you pick Zack up after soccer practice today? I ask in text.

I'm outside a conference room at RR, and Olivia just called an emergency meeting after learning our quarterly numbers were less than stellar. Zack went right from school to soccer practice and needs a ride home at six, which I committed to do, but now I can't. I'm sure Hannah can cover for me. Even after the divorce, she always does.

In the conference room, the Gordon Bell, a dozen people—Olivia, a few division leads, many finance types—are sitting in black leather executive chairs evenly dispersed around a U-shaped maple table. Olivia is uncharacteristically disheveled, like she's been up all night. Even though the building is smoke free, residual cigarette smoke taints the air and strengthens as I go deeper into the space, confirming Olivia is smoking again. She gave that up years ago. One wall of the conference room is floor-to-ceiling glass and provides a now-undeserved view of New England on a late fall afternoon. I join the table at my normal spot—the head right next to Olivia. As is our custom for big meetings, we all shut off our phones and place them in a basket in front of her. Before we begin, the room goes pin-drop silent, solemn. In all of my years at RR, I've never seen such sadness.

"I hoped this day would never come, but now that it has, our top priority is quickly to develop a bulletproof recovery plan. We'll only get one chance to fix this," Olivia says. "Ideas?"

For the next two hours, until it's pitch-black outside, we brainstorm. The finance guys argue unpersuasively for budget cuts and layoffs and drag us into the quagmire of the RR P&L. Top line was unexpectedly flat. We missed consensus earnings per share estimates by more than a dollar per share, which is huge. Our cash position is strong, with more than ten billion in the bank. As they speak, I cycle between tuning out and wonder. Tuning out because if a company builds great products, the numbers normally take care of themselves. Wonder, because even in crisis, we have so much power. We control billions of dollars, and more than the government, the state, and the towns, we have the means to shape our future, the wherewithal to weather storms like this one.

The division leads argue the way out is top-line growth. After the appropriate waiting period— to support the illusion that I was initially neutral—I side with them. I mention a number of new product introductions that will allow us to move some of our applications to the cloud and implement a subscription-based, software-as-a-service model. Once implemented, SaaS will provide a more regular source of income and safeguard us against bad quarters like this one.

At the end of the meeting, the growth-faction, my faction, wins, and we agree on a plan to weather the storm by focusing on the future. In the meantime, we'll cut back on discretionary travel, encourage people to use their accrued vacation, and freeze salaries until profitability returns. Olivia and the division leads are laughing, albeit tentatively, and even a finance guy or two smiles. On the way out of the room, which is no different from all the conference rooms at RR, I'm struck by the amount of steel and glass all around me. As

I'm running my finger along a steel girder, Olivia pulls me aside and says, "Nice job."

At the door, I reach into the phone basket, which Olivia's assistant moved here moments ago, and pull out my phone. After I turn it on, the phone text beeps and voicemail buzzes. The first text message is from Hannah. *I can't pick Zack up. Stuck at work. You'll have to get him. I'll drive Zack to school in the morning. Will pick him up at 7:30 sharp.* Fuck. What else? I have two voicemail messages, one from Zack, which says, "Dad, where are you?" and one from Hannah moments ago that says, "Call me when you get this."

I start jogging toward my office to gather my things. As I do, I dial Zack's number. No answer. I text him, *Running late. On my way.* No response. Why did I send my secretary home before the meeting? After securing my briefcase, I run toward the parking lot. In Gordon Bell, I race out of the parking lot and call Hannah to confess.

"I got stuck in a meeting. I don't have Zack," I say.

"You what?"

"I'm sorry. Heading to the soccer field now."

"Did you call him?"

"Yes, no answer."

"I had a missed call from him, but he didn't answer when I called him back. I'll meet you at the field," Hannah says.

"I'm only an hour late. I'm sure he's waiting for us. His phone probably died."

Twenty minutes later, we comb the soccer field for Zack. It's dark with no signs of life. Hannah calls a few moms whose kids are friends with Zack. I call the soccer coach. Zack's friends didn't notice him leave. Practice ended on time. Pick-ups seemed to happen in a timely manner until everyone was gone. One of the rules the coach has is to stick around the field until everyone is safely away. That's saved me in the past when I was running late, which was often, but this was the first time I totally messed up. So someone gave him a ride. Or he walked.

"How could you forget to pick him up?" Hannah asks. "It was your turn."

"I got stuck in a meeting. I figured you had him."

"I had him? I told you that I couldn't do it. If you read your fucking text messages instead of getting all caught up in your latest crisis, you would have known that fact. This is why we divorced; this is why I did what I did. You loved your job more than me. The only thing you love more than work is Zack, and you're fucking that up, too."

"Let's focus on finding Zack."

Hannah turns away to make another phone call. It's true that I drove her away. There was a time when she loved me more than I thought humanly possible. Often, it didn't matter what I said or did—she was just happy to be with me. She laughed at my jokes; she didn't know where we were headed, but she knew we would figure it out together. She had this most amazing look of contentment, which I didn't have to do anything but be myself to earn. How does someone love another, other than a child, that much?

I did love Hannah, though not in the same way. At some point, RR and Olivia took over. I'm not sure how it happened. At first, I was an hour late. I missed a special dinner or date night got canceled. No big deal. Then it was two hours, three, four. Then I agreed that weekdays wouldn't work, that marriages for hi-tech executives were not unlike those of US Senators—gone during the week, home on weekends. I wasn't working for the money or power. I think mostly I was doing it for Olivia. She had this hold over me that made me believe the enterprise-software-good of the many was more important than my wife.

Zack's birth was a reprieve from work. I would sneak out at lunch and sit in the corner of his room and just watch him sleep.

Or, laugh as he tried to reach up from his crib and touch the mobile dangling above him. Whatever, it didn't matter—it was enough to be around him. When he was older, on weeknights, I would come home before he went to bed so I could see him, play a video game with him, give him a hug goodnight. Then I'd go back to work or log on and read email.

I remember one time when I arrived home and found Zack and his friends playing video games in the family room. He was so happy to see me, beaming really, so eager to show me off to his friends, which he promptly did. Dad has a very important job that's changing the world. Dad brings home cool stuff from different countries. Dad drives a fast car. But it wasn't those things that got to me; it was the look on his face, the my-father-is-a-great-man look. I'll never forget his expression, his wide eyes, the cracked smile, the glow and softening of his face. After being put on a pedestal like that by your young child, I guess there's no place to go but down.

Hannah ends another call, turns toward me, and says, "Nothing."

"I'll call the police."

Tears start to roll down her face.

I reach out and take her hands, pull her close, and hug her. "We'll find him. Everything will be okay." I kiss her on the forehead.

Leaning against the car, I dial the police with one hand and hold Hannah's hand with the other. Her skin is soft and clammy. "Hello, my name is Dan Underlight. My son is missing. He's ten years old."

"Just a minute, sir," the receptionist says.

Within a few seconds, a man picks up the call and says, "Dan, my name is Detective Blackledge. We've been trying to reach you. There's been a terrible car accident."

"Is he okay?"

"I'm sorry . . . He's at Emerson Hospital. I'll meet you there."

I glance over at Hannah, clutch her hand. Everything slow-motions. I push my back into the car as hard as I can and slowly lower myself to the ground. There, I pull my legs in close to my chest and start to tremble and shake. Ghosts pass through me like dry ice, drain whatever life energy exists.

Hannah drops to the ground in front of me, pummels my shoulders, and starts to scream cry, "No" and "This is your fault" and "Why didn't you pick him up?"

"We have to go to Emerson. Zack's body is there."

On the silent ride to the hospital, I keep replaying my last conversation with Zack. Homework all done? *Always, Dad.* Have a good day at school. *Big math test today, Dad. My favorite.* Will see you after practice tonight. Score a goal. *Probably three, Dad.* What should we have for dinner? *Pizza, Dad.* Love you. *Love you.*

Inside the hospital, a man is sitting next to the detective. He's tall and thin with long brown curly hair. He's wearing a cheap suit and a loose tie. When he sees us, he turns completely white, stands up, and looks down. Hannah's face contorts until it's red, veined, and violent. I wrap my arm around her, both to comfort and hold back. All I can think is that I need to see Zack.

The man steps forward. "My name is Frank. I'm so sorry. I didn't see him."

"You fucker. You're going to rot in a jail cell for the rest of your life for what you did," Hannah screams. She goes after Frank and starts to pound her fists on his chest. I pull her away, redirect her fists toward me, and let her hit me until she breaks down.

"Where's Zack?" I ask.

A doctor and Detective Blackledge take Hannah and me to Zack. Blackledge tells us the man was driving home from work in his Ford F150. He was texting about some work thing and didn't see Zack, who was walking along the side of the road in the dark. Few sidewalks exist outside the Concord town center, and some of the roads are narrow and pitch-black at night. When I didn't pick up Zack, he must have figured I got stuck, and he could walk the three miles to our home. He was like that; he never wanted to be a burden. In a thirty-mile-per-hour zone, Frank hit Zack at fifty miles per hour. The doctor says Zack was most likely killed instantly.

Zack looks like he's sleeping. He's still wearing the number seven Cristiano Ronaldo soccer jersey that I bought him on a recent trip. Blood from multiple scrapes covers his arms and legs. He has a large contusion on his forehead. I take his hand, bend down, and kiss him on the forehead. He smells like dried sweat, like Zack after a soccer match.

From the other side of the bed, Hannah takes his other hand and kneels down in silent prayer. I do the same, though instead of praying, I whisper, "I killed my son. I killed my ten-year-old son."

#

The First Parish Unitarian Church in Concord is full. Between RR people and townies, it's standing room only. Soon I'll get up and at the sermon podium deliver a eulogy about Zack I've been working on. Some discouraged me from doing it, said it was too much for any parent, but I needed to speak.

When Frank hit Zack, he was driving home to his family. He has two boys about the same age as Zack. The detective said we could put him away for a long time. Manslaughter by motor vehicle carries a maximum sentence of twenty years in Massachusetts. That's what Hannah wants to do. Same for all of the relatives. Olivia, too. Mostly, everyone I know. But I'm thinking that this has already destroyed one family, why two? Yes, Frank killed my only son. Yes, he was texting while driving. Yes, part of me wants to destroy him, to cause him as much pain as he's causing me. But what good will that do? I once read that forgiveness is the only real way out of tragedy, but I'm not ready for that either. Maybe work? Maybe if he goes out and does some good in the world and dedicates his life to helping people who've lost everything, then maybe that would be better? He's not a bad man. He just made a terrible mistake.

As I walk up to the podium, the room goes pin-drop silent and the Frankincense takes over. My mouth is dry, my heart is thrumming in my ears, my knees are wobbling, and my legs are tingling. At the podium, even though I've memorized my speech, I slowly unfold the paper that contains it just in case. I sip a bottled water and look out into the sea of black suits and dresses. Hannah is already crying, and her husband has his arm around her. Relatives from both sides fill the rest of the first pew. Olivia is in the second row, and as she always does, radiates strength. My close work colleagues, Zia, Maggie, and Charles, are on the other side of Olivia. The soccer team and coaches, in full uniform, are sitting farther back.

I take a deep breath. "Thank you all for coming.

"Zack lived a full life in his ten years on the planet. Too short, yes, but full. Today, in this place filled with history, amongst all of you, I find myself focusing on how blessed I was to have ten years with him. I could share with you so many memories, so many stories today: stories of family, hope, and strength; stories of video games, ice cream, and soccer. But for me, one in particular stands out.

"When Zack was about eight, we went for breakfast together one Sunday morning on Main Street. That was our routine then. It wasn't long after the divorce, and we both looked forward to our Sunday breakfasts together. That particular Sunday was a beautiful day. I parked pretty far away from the restaurant so that we could bump our way down Main Street and window shop. We bumped into each other all the time when we walked. It was our way of hugging without hugging. About midway down the street, we stopped at

Zack's favorite store, The Toy Shop of Concord, and talked in detail about his favorite toys on window display.

"As we were discussing the relative merits of K'nex and Legos—Zack liked Legos while I'm a K'nex man—we heard voices from across the street. A man and a woman were the only two sitting at an outside table of a coffee shop, Arturo's, and they were vehemently debating something. As we watched, the debate escalated into a full-blown fight with animated hands and occasional shouts of "No way" or "You're just wrong." At first, I smiled. How many of us have had a conversation like that with our partners or business associates over the years? After my I've-been-there moment, my inclination was to mind my own business and move on the restaurant, which is exactly what we started to do. We crossed Walden Street briskly and passed by the man and woman, at our closest point still twenty yards away. They probably didn't notice us at all.

"Just after the man and woman were out of view, Zack said, 'Dad, I'm going to go talk to them.' At first, I discouraged him. 'What will you say?' And 'It's not our business.' And 'Breakfast is waiting.' But Zack had made up his mind, and if I'd learned one thing about my son over the years, it was to support him in moments like that. So I let him go and followed him back to the corner of Main and Walden. There, I watched him as he closed the remaining gap to the man and woman. When he reached them, the man and the woman stopped arguing and turned toward Zack. Here's what Zack said.

"'Hi, my name is Zack. You two seem to be having a fight about something and I thought I could help.'

"The woman smiled. 'Nice to meet you, Zack. How do you think you can help?'

"'Well, I'm captain of my soccer team, and you know, sometimes a couple of players on the team get into it. One of my jobs is to help them work things out so they can get back to playing together.'

"The man smiled. 'How do you do that, Zack?'

"'I tell them the best teams don't fight about their differences; they're curious about them.'

"The man reached across the table and put his hand over the woman's hand. 'That's good advice, Zack. You're right, we are on the same team. Thank you.'

"'You're welcome. Have a nice day.'

"Zack ran back to me and gave me a big hug. I told him I was proud of him and that he was a big help to the man and woman. We went to have a delicious breakfast where we ordered extra pancakes, bacon, and waffles, and devoured them like we'd never seen food. During the entire breakfast, we talked and talked, mostly about sports. Only one time did he come back to the man and woman. He said, 'You know Dad, the world would be a much better place if people talked more.'

"If we're lucky, we all have great loves in our lives. A husband or wife. A friend or family. Work. Zack was a great love of mine. What do you do when you lose a great love, when that deep-core place that defines you breaks? Can you ever recover, fully heal from that kind of loss? These last days, I must admit, I was sure the answer was no. But then, as I replayed over and over stories from my ten years with Zack, the no unexpectedly changed a bit. Yes, I did break at the core, as I'm sure many of you would. Yes, in many ways, I'll never be the same. But Zack lives on with me in that broken place. And while I'm not sure how, I am sure that broken place is a teacher, if I let it be. And, really, if we are to live full lives, what choice do we have but to learn from the broken places?"

I fold my speech up, put it back in my pocket, sip the bottled water, and glance out into the room. Some are crying. Some are nodding. Some, I'm sure, are thankful it's not their child. As I walk back to my chair, I'm not comforted from finishing the speech or from the warmth emanating from the relatives, friends, and souls in the room. Instead, guilt speaks in loops. This is all on you. It's your fault. You killed your son and ruined lives. All of that stuff about broken places being teachers is bullshit. Repeat.

I freeze midway back, look to the rear of the church, see a woman quickly exiting, and want to run out with her. I didn't want to say anything about my culpability—this was meant to be about Zack. But now, I'm frozen and can't move another step forward.

I turn around and pause for a moment, looking out into the sea of people. Their what's-he-going-to-do-next expressions are as unsure as I am. Slowly, I put one foot in front of the other and return to the lectern, look down at its oak top like there's a speech waiting for me. I take a deep breath and then another. Then I say, "I killed my son, and I'll have to live with that for the rest of my life. Some things aren't forgivable, and this is one of them. All that stuff I said at the end of my eulogy is flat-out wrong."

Weight presses down on my shoulders and crushes me, leaving me in exactly the state I deserve. Strangely, from that crushed place, I'm able to briskly walk to the rear of the church, exit, and look for the woman who left before me.

Launch

Naked, sheetless, I'm in bed, staring at the ceiling fan, which is spinning slowly. It's three in the morning lift-off day, T minus nine hours, and I'm stuck in the middle. I can't sleep even though I downed sleeping pills and a scotch hours ago, both staples of my diet these last six months, and I can't get out of bed to begin my day. At noon, at the office with invited press and guests, we'll officially launch ConversationWorks featuring CSpectacles and CHalo. CHalo is what we're now calling the 3D imaging and motion-detection device that seemingly hovers above each user. It really does look like a four-foot round halo. Maggie printed T-shirts the other day that said, *At CW, we enable angels.* I like them.

These last six months have been a whirlwind. The Olympic part of our work plan turned out to be bulletproofing the software and hardware, both full of push-the-envelope invention and intractable bugs. On our software, we enhanced Darra's speech recognition and context-understanding code, debugged the summary and recommendation engine, sped up the aggregation engine so that it produced results in only a few minutes, and developed a good-enough change engine for a version one product. On the hardware, we shrunk CSpectacles in size to the point where they're now elegant in a sixties thick-black-glasses way, and we ramped our manufacturing capacity in South Dakota so that we'll be able to meet even the most optimistic demand. Sometimes when I consider all we've done these last two years, I can barely fathom it, although none of our challenges seemed insurmountable as we were building the products. That's the thing about breakthrough technology—the overall odds are so low that you have to have an unwavering belief that your odds, given your team, are close to a sure thing.

In addition to the technology challenges, we put The Code to good use multiple times on direct and honest conversations, on mistakes, on doing the unquarterly thing, on love. Once, I stopped a meeting right in the middle of too much indirect conversation about money, jumped up on the conference table, and started dancing, which immediately corralled everyone. From atop the table I said, "Why can't we say directly and honestly what we're thinking?" Turned out that half the team wanted to make boatloads of money and shift focus to high-return markets, while the other half wanted to remain focused on enabling community through meaningful conversations. The money-making half was afraid to say it out loud because they knew I was part of the other half. One of the most important things I've learned as a CEO is to encourage people to push back and fight for what they believe in, especially when they disagree with you—kind of the Socratic method for big business. I'm not against making money—we have to grow exponentially—I just want to do it in a way that's consistent with our values. When I said what I've learned out loud for all in the room to hear, I could almost hear the release valve go off.

Another time a software engineer made a monumental coding mistake that cost us a few weeks in our schedule. At first, Maggie and the engineer's peers ripped him apart, but soon after Maggie caught what she was doing and changed course by referencing The Code. She flipped the conversation into a teaching moment where the whole team learned from the engineer's mistake. The engineer, more than grateful, worked night and day for a month to recover the lost time.

On another occasion, we used The Code to do the unquarterly thing. For our business model, we finally agreed on a two-tiered model. For business users, we'll charge a monthly fee of twenty dollars, a thousand dollars for each pair of CSpectacles, and four thousand dollars for each CHalo. For consumers, we'll charge a ten-dollar-a-month subscription, significantly discount the CSpectacle and CHalo prices, and spread their total cost over their expected useful life of five years, much like the phone companies do with a new Peach phone. Yes, improving our cash flow by recouping our hardware costs sooner would be nicer, but we're trying to build a community. During that same meeting, we finally decided against taking advertising dollars. How could we take them from a pharmaceutical company while there are ongoing conversations about reforming said company? How could we accept political advertising dollars when the whole system is broken? How could we run food industry ads when the integrity of our food is in question? The list of problems with ads was endless. Not taking advertising dollars was the only way to safeguard the consumer conversations, the only way to give big change a chance to root.

My favorite use of The Code happened months ago. It was around midnight, and Maggie and I were the only two left in the office. We were both working separately in our cubicles when I heard her start to cry. Soon, I found myself standing next to her. She'd smeared her tears and was staring out her office window into the night.

"What's wrong?" I asked.

"This is the hardest thing I've ever done. I'm not sure I can pull it off."

I placed my hand on her shoulder. "You can, Maggie. If it wasn't so hard, it wouldn't be worth it." Then I moved my hand from her shoulder and interlaced it with her hand. "Come with me for a second. I want to show you something."

Sometimes, when I'm in the office alone late at night, I stargaze from the roof. I'm not an expert, but I've learned a few constellations: Ursa Major, Cepheus, Draco. We know so little about the universe. Big Bang. Sure. Stars and planets and galaxies. Check. Some greater design? We don't know. Part of me thinks that's the true promise of CW—some greater design, but not of the universe, of humanity. One that we all create together. Is that too big a request for any we, any company? Maybe, but why bother if we're not willing to go big? What does a brand-new spick-and-span design of humanity look like? I have no idea, but I do know that it can't be won, dictated, or done in isolation or hierarchy.

On the roof, Maggie and I sat right next to each other. We put our feet up on the ledge, leaned back, and gazed up into the night. A gentle breeze cradled.

"The sky is so clear tonight," I said.

"There are so many stars."

"They're so far away, yet connected."

"In ways we'll probably never understand," Maggie said.

"Somebody does, though."

"You think that kind of brilliance exists?"

"I know it does."

Maggie went deeper into the stars for a time.

I've worked with a few people over the years, brilliant like Maggie, who at their pinnacle of doubt needed nothing more than to be gently reminded of what was already inside of them— an inexplicable pool of creativity capable, when coupled with determination, of fueling true invention. Sometimes I wonder what CW, or the world for that matter, would be like if people could tap into that pool on their own?

When Maggie returned from the stars, she placed her hand over mine, and said, "Thank you, Dan. You're a good man."

If being a good man was only about management.

I push out of bed, make my way to my spare bedroom, and strap myself into my rowing machine, one of those top-notch wooden ones where the wheel is filled with water. In rowing position, forearms resting on my thighs while I hold the rowing bar, my eyes trace the abstract shapes on the rug directly below the machine. Squares, circles, rectangles, triangles, lines, all brightly colored, struggle to form something recognizable, something true. That's always been the problem with design. How do you do something relentlessly new, push the envelope, and at the same time create technology that resonates in the deep recesses of a collective mind? There's a balancing to it that has to be just right. Go too far into the future, and no one goes with you. Don't go far enough, and your work will ho-hum into me-too oblivion.

Other than rowing, it's been difficult to exercise this year. I tried personal trainers and old school gyms but gave up after a short time. By the time I walked to the gym, worked out, and showered, it was almost two hours of my day. I couldn't afford it. Instead, I bought this rowing machine. My record for a thirty-minute workout is seventy-five hundred meters, which I may break this morning. The trick to a high score is not more strokes; it's long, powerful strokes where the upper and lower body perfectly coordinate push-pulls. These days, rowing is the only place where the work chatter goes away, where algorithms and business models are replaced with sweat and breath and ebb and flow. I bet Willow would love this sport.

After eight thousand meters, a shower, and a morning protein smoothie, I arrive at my office right on schedule at 5:15 and light up the place. The cubicles—filled with computers, pictures of loved ones, binders, and ballpoints—glow alive as though they've forgotten they're inanimate objects, as though they know that after today nothing will ever be the same. A career comes down to a few moments, a few events or choice points that change one's course, that, on the days I believe Willow's view of the universe, are exactly as intended. Today, I'll set off to change the world, or I'll fall and shatter.

At my desk with a triple espresso in one hand, I place my other hand on the two-inch-thick launch binder. It's smooth like a Manchester United soccer ball. When Zack was eight, I took him to see Manchester United in the UK one weekend. I even got him into the locker room with the team after the game, where they all signed a ball for him. It cost me ten thousand, and I remember thinking that it was only money, that I was a good father, that someday he would do the same for his kids.

While my team has diligently prepared for this day for more than a month, I still need to go through all of the details myself one last time. We'll only get one shot at the launch, so overpreparation is impossible. I open the briefing package to the first page and read out loud, "ConversationWorks. Connecting the world one conversation at a time." For the next two hours, I review every detail of our launch. Our launch won't be big like the stadium-filled ones Peach sometimes holds. Instead it will be spread out through the day. The press release, which is concise and catchy, will go out first. Next, the social media campaign will simultaneously begin on PhotoPhotobook, Twitter, Pinterest, LinkedIn, and YouTube. During the morning, I'll hold briefings with influential technology blogs, magazines, and mainstream newspapers that are unable to attend the live event. When key press and technology analysts arrive later, we'll ask them to participate in a live conversation on the water crisis in Detroit, minus the speed and bug problems we had the first time. We believe press and analyst participation is the best way to maximize the probability of positive coverage.

I close the binder. Everything is in place. I gaze over at Zack's picture on my desk, an 8x10 of him eating pancakes at our weekly place in Concord. He's still in his FC Concord uniform after a three-to-one win that morning where he scored a goal. He's stuffing a forkful of four buttermilks into his mouth and has developed a syrup mustache from the previous bite. His eyes are full of wonder.

Today's the day, Dad. Don't be nervous.

You know, I did this all for you.

I know. Thanks, Dad. You're going to change the world, but the cost.

What cost?

The light is coming your way.

I'm at my desk first thing on a Monday morning skimming a new Gartner report on emerging software trends, one where we're profiled as a company to watch. It's yet another endorsement to add to our list. A month ago, the launch went off without a hitch, with most of the financial and technical headlines weighing in positive. *The Wall Street Journal*: ConversationWorks has unlimited potential. *The New York Times*: ConversationWorks may just connect the world. *Forrester*: ConversationWorks is the next big thing. The blogs and technical press suggested all of our use cases couldn't be anticipated, then across multiple articles pieced together industries begging for disruption, from politics to pornography. A few articles suggested that in a couple of years we would become a multibillion-dollar-acquisition target. Or go public. Or both. The only truly vitriolic review came from this woman who's covered RR for a long time, someone who until said review I considered a friend. She compared CW to the sixties idealism and predicted the company would fail in the same way that the decade did. She didn't substantiate her claim, but she was certain CW would unfold as portended. That one got me.

My computer beeps with a new email from Charles titled Monthly Sales Trends. I click it open. In the attached spreadsheet, a strange pattern graphs its way across the screen—multinational corporations are buying our stuff in droves, much more than consumers. For multinationals, the total cost of ownership, even when higher prices are factored in, is low—so low in fact that they're buying subscriptions for everyone in their companies. Their main use case: travel reduction. They're setting up conversation rooms at their worldwide locations by repurposing their conference rooms and using the rooms to replace travel and to connect more of their companies to themselves and their partners. Maggie sent me an article the other day from an airline industry trade magazine where the CEO of JetOrange called us an existential threat. That's cool.

Besides multinationals, conversation coffeehouses are trending modestly. CW-enabled coffeehouses are sprouting up around the world, some as retrofits of existing coffeehouses and some as brand new. To use them, a customer only needs a subscription. The coffeehouses absorb the hardware cost, which they're more than happy to do given the increase in customer traffic and average duration of stay. In fact, this use case has been successful enough that last week we caught the attention of a major coffeehouse chain and have initiated talks with it about a pilot program. That would be huge. Similar opportunities exist for bookstores, health food chains, and drop-in work chains, pretty much any company that's interested in building a community.

As I'm finishing my review of sales trends, an unmistakable knock at the entrance to my office interrupts me. Three taps, soft to hard, and a familiar fragrance. I look up, and she's motionless there, smiling, hair flowing down well below her shoulders, dressed in jeans and a Nirvana T-shirt. When was the last time I saw her smile that way? She looks young and unfettered, much like I remember her at the start. For a moment, I forget.

"Dan."

"Olivia."

"I've been reading the press and analyst coverage. Pretty impressive."

I lock my computer and ask her to come in and take a seat. First, she helps me clear the stacked-to-the-tipping-point binders and books on both of my guest chairs. How did they pile up so quickly? Olivia once told me that CEOs have no time to read books, but I've found the opposite to be true during my tenure. I'm constantly looking at futures, at trends, and at potential companies that may creep in and fuck us over.

"I'm surprised to see you," I say.

"I wanted to congratulate you in person. ConversationWorks is going to make you a fortune. I brought you a little something."

She hands me a gold-wrapped bottle, which at first I put down on the desk, but soon after with her encouragement, carefully unwrap. Inside is a fifth of Dalmore Fifty-Year-Old scotch, which is legendary, which may be the best scotch in the world, and which probably cost her ten thousand.

"Thank you. That's more than generous."

Olivia glances over at my bookcase that has four scotch glasses lined up in a row. They were a gift from Jason and have come in handy multiple times since he gave them to me. I push off from my chair, grab two of the glasses, and pour us each two fingers. Olivia raises her glass and taps it against mine. I sip the scotch, which is the best I've had, which if I were to buy and consume at my current rate would bankrupt me. Why the scotch? Why the visit? Why the return to Nirvana?

"I want you to know I still visit Zack in the cemetery once per year. A couple of visits ago, I saw the pebble pyramid. Using it as the

ConversationWorks logo was a nice touch. You should tell the press that story," she says.

"You still visit?"

"I loved him, too."

That catches me.

"Not my style to tell the press something like that," I say.

"You'll sell more."

"Could be. Still."

We both sip our scotch.

"Switching topics, can I ask you a question?" I ask.

"Shoot."

"Why did you drop the lawsuit?"

Olivia crosses one leg over the other and wraps her hands around her scotch glass, as though she's trying to understand what's behind my question, as though she half-expected me to already know the answer. She looks into her glass as she takes another sip. I do the same. Soon after Jason invested in CW, he called one day to tell me that he'd made good on his promise: Olivia had dropped the lawsuit and our RR trouble had passed. When I asked him why, he said he had appealed to her higher values, which I thought strange, but because it was welcome news, I didn't push.

Olivia returns from her scotch and says, "That's old news, Dan. I was angry you didn't come up with the idea for CW while you were still at RR. We certainly could have used an innovative product at the time. But you and I have too much history, so I let it go. By the way, I wanted you to be the first to know that RR is fully adopting ConversationWorks internally."

"Really? Thank you."

We finish our scotches in small talk. RR has rebounded with a record quarter and a host of new products. Olivia met a man, a doctor, who is the first one she's been serious about in a time. She suggests the three of us should take in a Patriots game soon at the

RR box. On the way out, standing at the entranceway to my office, she gives me a hug, kisses me on each cheek, and says, "I'm so glad we reconnected, Dan."

As she walks away, I find myself wanting to believe in the sincerity of everything she said during our visit. We do have too much history. She did let go. She is happy for my success. But I know Olivia Whitmore all too well.

#

We built a stealth monitoring application into CW. It captures a conversation's location, complete content, and aggregation results. In a way, it's not stealthy because we documented our intentions in the CW Terms and Conditions document, a pop-up screen that asks a user to read three pages of legalese, and then requires her to hit the *Accept* button to continue. But consumers don't read those things. And while corporations do, we gave them the option to opt out of monitoring. Many of them took that option, but some agreed to allow monitoring so that we could improve our software.

To protect all of the information, we had to find an ultrasafe home for our data in the short run. In the long run, as we grow, we'll build new datacenters to house the conversations, but for the next couple of years we opted to partner with a company who has already made the investment in big cloud datacenters. We shopped around for the best deal, and in the end, after a heated debate among senior staff, after a narrow in-favor straw poll, I went with RR.

This wasn't a light decision. Since our congratulatory meeting in my office, Olivia has been nothing but supportive. We started talking again on a regular basis with weekly check-in calls, and I even asked for her advice a couple of times. We did take in that Patriots game together, which was a throwback. Still, part of me doesn't trust her. Can I ever truly trust someone who suddenly and ruthlessly screwed me? And if I do, aren't I a schmuck, certainly not a competent CEO? But another part of me longs to trust her again. After all, hi-tech was forged on second chances, and even if forgiveness after big betrayal is one in a million, well, we did have all of those years together. Besides, I have an ironclad contract with RR. As long as we are both making money, there's minimal risk.

We're occupying the two sofas and the rocking chair we sat on more than two years ago when I first pitched CW to the three of them. I couldn't bring myself to get rid of the sofas when I moved, and now, surrounded here by my dearest friends, it's clear I made the right call. Each week, Zia, Maggie, Charles, and I meet to review sales trends in our target segments and data from our monitoring application. That's what we're doing today, though instead of meeting in the office, we agreed to meet at my apartment. It's more private, not to mention a welcome change of pace. Zia had two dozen Beauty's flown in from Montreal, and I signed up to provide the rest of the food and an ample supply of espresso. I'm rocking slowly, in rhythm, sampling a small piece of a bagel, no butter. Zia, Maggie, and Charles are in the middle of their own bagel moments. When we've had our fill, I suggest we begin by getting into the monitoring data first and then moving on to market segmentation.

Maggie checks a text message on her watch, mutes her phone, opens her laptop, and projects the monitoring data on the wall. In hi-tech these days, almost everyone is multideviced, though I remember a time not long ago when all I had was a desktop system. Sometimes I worry that my time has passed, that I'm already too old to change the world, that all of the great hi-tech leaders of the past fifty years started their companies at a much younger age.

"The monitoring from businesses is routine with lots of corporate meetings on standard topics," Maggie says. "As we expected, corporate users are deploying CW to eliminate travel. They're channeling portions of their travel budgets our way, and many of them are commenting that we'll save them fifty percent per year."

"That's what Olivia is predicting at RR," I say.

"We should leverage her statement in our marketing collateral," Charles says.

Zia gives me an uncomfortable look, as if she's trying to hold back. It quiets the room. When Olivia offered us the datacenter deal, Zia vocally opposed it during one of my staff meetings. Her rationale: Olivia can't be trusted; she has ulterior motives; she's not a good person. But Zia didn't stop there. After the staff meeting, Zia pulled me aside and pushed further. My judgment clouded when it came to Olivia. My trust in that woman was borderline delusional. I did carefully listen to Zia—she's always been a good judge of character—but in the end I had to go with my gut.

Finally, Zia says, "We can leverage Olivia if you want."

"Good," I say.

"Shall I continue?" Maggie asks.

"Yes, please."

"Outside of corporations, the conversations have been all over the map," Maggie says. "For example, politicians in this country are starting to use CW as a recruiting tool. Sit down virtually with your favorite politician for a chat and then donate megabucks. That sort of thing. In addition to conversations on almost every topic, from domestic violence to climate change, there are also radical groups talking. The anarchists. The Communists. The revolutionaries. Homeland Security contacted us the other day about access."

"What did you say?" I ask.

"That our data is fully protected and that we would cooperate if there was a clear terrorist threat on the country, but we haven't seen one to date."

"Good," I say.

The mention of Homeland Security quiets the room again. One of my biggest fears about our company is data security. Not technical security, which is rock solid, but political security given the times we live in. Will the United States commandeer our data under the guise of averting terrorism? Will China let us in at all, and if they do, will citizens truly be able to speak openly in our conversation rooms? Will Russians believe our security is strong enough to keep out Putin's thugs? All I know is that the people who create the conversations must own them, believe they're secure, and have complete control over how to share them. Anything short of that will break trust and won't lift off. Anything short of that will fold our company.

"There haven't been any break-ins, have there?" Charles asks.

"No. Many cyberattacks, but none were successful," I say. "Because we build such an extensive profile of our customers, many cyberthieves covet our data."

"We'll only be successful if we remain secure and neutral," Zia says.

"Conversation neutrality is the other key piece. We need to stick with our current neutrality strategy. We safely enable conversations, that's all. If change comes about because of those conversations, it's about the conversationalists, not us," I say.

"That's key," Charles says.

"It may be, but it also may mean that we can't go after the big problems," Maggie says.

"Why is that?" Zia asks.

"Because without our own champions in certain big areas, like climate change for example, the conversation will polarize along familiar lines and nothing will happen," Maggie says. "We need to take a stand."

We debate Maggie's point. Is neutrality, a strategy we've had in place for over a year, the best way to change things? Or should we not take a stand on issues and only facilitate? Maggie has evolved her thinking over these last months. She would have us pick and choose causes to support, would hire champions, and would have us ban certain conversations that were inconsistent with our ideals. Part of me agrees with her. So many things are broken in the world; we don't have time for a rigged system that fabricates two equal sides to every issue. However, part of me believes that the best way to move forward is not to judge or exclude, to get the world talking on divided topics, to trust that most people want to move forward, if for nothing else, their kids' sake.

"We need to stick with neutrality," I say.

"I thought you wanted to change the world," Maggie says.

"I do. What you're saying is tempting, but we're not smart enough to know what course folks should take. We need to let them figure it out themselves," I say.

"I agree with Dan," Zia says.

"Me, too," Charles says.

We go silent again. Maggie, who appears deep in thought, excuses herself. When it's not unanimous between the four of us, I've learned to let silence help a decision sink in. I have so much respect for Maggie. It's only right that we wait for her until she's ready to move on. When she returns, she sits down on the sofa, crosses one leg over the other, and rests her hands in prayer position on her lap.

"Okay, I'll defer to the three of you," Maggie says.

"You sure?" I ask.

"Yes. I strongly disagree, but I'll get over it," Maggie says.

"Okay then. Anything else worth mentioning from the monitoring application?" I say.

Maggie gets into the numbers. Since we launched, there have been ten million conversations, but so far only five percent have opted to take advantage of aggregation. Apparently, even outside of corporations, people are using CW more to replace traditional face-to-face meetings. They're not yet reaching out and problem solving with others in wide numbers. We're not sure why this is true, but Zia agrees to do a focused program on marketing the aggregation features to our users.

We're at a good break point, so we gather around my small kitchen. I click to stream the Motown channel. "The Tears of a Clown" by Smokey Robinson and the Miracles gets us all tapping utensils, the granite countertop, or coffee cups. I crack a dozen eggs into a mixing bowl and whisk them yellow. Earlier, I placed a ton of bacon in a slow two-hundred-degree oven. It's crisp and brown now. Combined with scrambled eggs and Beauty's bagels, it will make the most delicious sandwiches. After I scramble the eggs, we construct our sandwiches and refill our coffees. The perfect sandwich is an art: eggs first, bacon, a slice of avocado, some cheddar, a little salsa, and black beans to kick it up.

When we're a few bites in, "I Want You Back" by the Jackson 5 starts. Maggie puts down her sandwich, taps her finger on the counter, and smiles. Seconds later, she's dancing. She's good and fluid; her hips, arms, and head move in elusive natural ways. Soon after, she reaches out with both hands and pulls Zia, Charles, and me into the dance. Not that I often compare, but Charles is worse at this sort of thing than I am. The four of us dance around the kitchen and the living room, trying to sing lyrics none of us know.

I slow a little. In the corner of the living room Zack is moonwalking. He's good. I've never seen him dance like that before, and part of me wishes I still owned a video camera. Surrounded by good work, good friends, good food, good music, and Zack, I have everything I need. Well, not Willow. Has it really been more than a year since I've seen her?

After the song ends, we grab our sandwiches and coffee and return to our seats.

"We should dance more," Maggie says.

"We should," I say.

"I need lessons," Charles says.

"Me, too," I say.

"You're both fine. There's no right way to dance," Maggie says.

"Right. Okay, enough on dancing. Let's get back to work."

"Well, on market segmentation you already know about the coffeehouses, travel, and politics," Zia says. "In addition, the phone companies are licensing CW as a high-end way for family-to-family communication. That's been slow so far, but it's only a matter of time. There's also a movement to use CW for online dating. Seeing a potential mate virtually is a powerful selection tool, especially because it's easy to take off your glasses if you don't like someone. Probably the most troublesome use case so far is pornography."

"The porn sites are pushing CW to their users big time," Maggie says.

"Anyone have an issue with that?" I ask.

All uncomfortably move in their seats. Willow once told me that in Sweden they've virtually eliminated prostitution by criminalizing it for the johns and decriminalizing it for the women. They treat prostitution as abusive to women, which it is, and have implemented an extensive program to help women move away from it. Because prostitution is illegal here, we don't allow CW conversations that are veiled forms of solicitation. But should we do the same for pornography? If users agree to use a conversation room as if they're reading a holographic porn magazine or watching a holographic porn video, should we censor them? Is it our role to exclude certain industries, even when they're legal, just because they're degrading?

"I guess if we're going to be neutral, people can use it for whatever they want," Zia says.

"Everyone agree?" I ask.

Charles nods.

Maggie gets off the sofa, stands behind it, places her hands on top of the cushion, and nods slightly. "I did get one interesting request. One of the porn companies wanted to know if it was possible to merge halos, so that a user in one halo would be able to reach out and virtually touch a user in another."

"Is that possible?" I ask.

"With work, I think so," Maggie says. "The big issue is how to simulate touch."

"So a grandmother in California would be able to virtually hug her grandchild in Boston?" Zia asks.

"Yes," Maggie says.

"That's not what the porn industry has in mind," Charles says.

"It ups the connection level," Zia says.

"Let's do some advanced development and see what's possible," I say.

Is it the right business decision to add features that make the experience more realistic, even if those features may enable a degrading industry? I'm not sure, but we should clearly do some advanced development on touch to see if it's even possible. I'm also not sure about our earlier conversation. I keep coming back to Maggie, to what we're trying to do, to Willow. What would she say to me now? That women have been degraded for much too long, that neutrality is often a cover for cowardice, that our only hope is a world where power and control are replaced by guided equality and compassion.

"Maggie, I made a mistake," I say. "We need to reverse course and ban pornography on CW. I'm not sure how we'll police it, but I'm sure you'll figure that out."

Maggie smiles. "Thank you, Dan. I'll get right on it."

#

The door opens. "Come in, come in. I'll be right back," Nessa says. As she walks down the hallway, one of her infinite supply of pashmina shawls covers most of her back and cements my view that she's really the superhero, Pashmina Woman, Clark-Kenting as a therapist. Her shawls are capes, designed to, well, I never understood the purpose of those capes. No matter, her real superpower is helping me bring my stuff into plain view, where, after an epic battle, I may or may not let it go. I've missed her.

I go into her office, sit in my normal chair, and place my phone and keys on its arm. Everything is as I remember it: my chair, her Harvard diploma prominently displayed, the floor-to-ceiling bookcases filled with too many ultradense impenetrable psychology books, my old friends, the rabbits. The place smells like health food, with hints of wheat grass and faro. Overall, it's as designed, comforting in a therapeutic way. Though the first thing Nessa does in our sessions each week is leave. It's always bothered me, though I could never put my finger on why. Women who leave? Everyone leaves? I haven't seen Nessa in the three months since the launch. Due to critical CW meetings, I canceled a total of twelve sessions at the last minute.

When Nessa returns, she smiles warmly, slips off her shoes, and sits cross-legged on her chair as she often does during our sessions. "It's good to see you, Dan. How have you been?"

"It's been crazy."

"You've had quite the run. All the positive press."

"We've been fortunate. People seem to like our stuff, but there's still tons to do," I say. I catch her up. Press. Analysts. Initial sales trends. Olivia's surprise visit. Maggie, Charles, and Zia are thriving. I even mention that a number of therapists are interested in establishing conversation rooms for their practices. Wouldn't it be something if CW revolutionized online therapy? I go on for a long time, much longer than expected, and eat up a good chunk of the session.

"That's all wonderful news, Dan. Who knows, maybe Olivia does want a relationship again. Have you heard from Willow?"

"Just a text to congratulate me."

"That was kind of her."

"It was."

"And how's Zack?"

"He's well. We still talk every day," I say.

Before my hiatus, I confessed to Nessa about my visits with Zack, telling her everything, down to the last detail: the pebbles, the *Chinatown* conversation, the I-need-a-woman pep talk. I asked her if it was wrong to interact with my dead child all the time, asked her if I should stop. The whole time, she listened carefully, didn't judge, didn't lean one way or the other. When I finished, she encouraged me to learn what I was meant to learn from him and reassured me that everything was happening exactly as intended. Honestly, I was relieved. The other day I had a long heart-to-heart chat with Zack. The net-net: *Dad, go back to therapy. You love her. She's good for you, and CW isn't everything. Tell her how you feel.*

"Zack was happy with the launch," I say. "Though he did say the cost for me would be high. Something about the light coming."

"Ah. What do you think he meant?"

"I have no idea. Whatever the cost, doing CW was worth it."

"Building the company is such a wonderful way to honor his memory."

Nessa has a new neutral-colored rug. A Berber I think, which I didn't notice when I first arrived. From the rug, a swell, faint at first, launches and races up through my feet, legs, the base of my spine, through my stomach, chest, throat, on its way to more. At the last second, right before strong words come out, I cap the swell by pushing my thumbnail into my index finger as hard as I can. My neck stiffens and weight pushes down on my shoulders.

"Where did you just go?" Nessa asks.

"You know, I actually see him. I know he isn't real, but he's more than a memory."

"What does he look like now?"

"Like a hologram. Like a fourteen-year-old boy."

For some reason, saying his age out loud sets me off. Tears form and stream down my face. And as if streams aren't enough, sonorous, guttural, alien sounds exit my mouth at irregular intervals and escalate uncontrollably. E sounds. I sounds. O sounds. Nessa hands me a box of tissues, which is standard therapy practice in moments like this. Somehow the gesture, kind and appropriate, is facile. I want her to dry the streams and contain the uncontrollable. I want her to prescribe good drugs or share a bottle of scotch with me until neither of us can walk. Doesn't she understand that some things truly are unforgivable? No therapist, not even Pashmina Woman, can redeem me. There is no lasting release. After a few moments, I wipe my face, blow my nose, ball up the tissue, and, with perfect form, sink a shot in the wastebasket a few feet away. I then cross one leg over the other, fold my arms across my chest, and take a deep breath.

"I don't know where that came from," I say.

"From truth. You know, your body never lies."

"So you've said."

"After your release, your entire body lightened."

"It was temporary."

Over our time together, when I was inconsolable, when I had a strong physical reaction to the past—a tightening in my shoulders, a headache, a limpness that made it hard to get out of bed in the morning—Nessa suggested that my body was always right, that it never lied. At first, I had no idea what she was talking about, even after she patiently explained it multiple times, but eventually it came to mean this: whatever I'm thinking during the time I'm having a strong physical reaction probably isn't true. In therapese, my primordial monkey mind is working overtime to protect my ego-based storyline at all costs. Apparently, the treadmill-spinning monkey would have me believe my bullshit and loop with him in pain forever instead of facing the truth. Which is what, exactly?

"When you see Zack, does he seem wise and loving?" Nessa asks.

"Yes."

"Do you feel any pain in your body when he's with you?"

"No."

"That's important to pay attention to."

"I guess."

I glance over at the clock. Only a few minutes remain. I place my hands on the arms of my chair, one hand covering my keys and my phone. The keys jiggle as the phone vibrates the arrival of yet another text message. I hold back a strong urge to read it.

"There's one other thing," I say.

"What's that?"

"I love you," I say.

"I love you, too, Dan."

"I've missed you, too. You've been so helpful these last years. I don't think I would have made it this far without you. I got all caught up these last months. I'm sorry."

"No need for sorry. You know, it's been an honor to witness you do your work so far."

"I guess. Okay, see you next week."

Nessa smiles. "Mist?"

"I think this is a mist and chocolate day."

We both lift off our chairs at exactly the same time. Nessa picks up a bowl of chocolates and moves in my direction. A wave of warmth cradles me. Is love the primary outcome of therapy? If you love and connect with your therapist, yourself, then can you love and connect with your friends, with your colleagues, with your company, with the whole world? Could be, but does love also absolve? Nessa offers the box of chocolates. I pull out a piece wrapped in blue, which I hand to her. She opens it and hands me the chocolate. It's sweeter than usual today. She reads the wrapper to herself, smiles, and then says, "Know your own mind with honesty and fearlessness."

At her desk, she secures the wooden box full of mists with two hands. They've become an important part of my life over the years, and I've come to believe they're guides in a way, always a few steps ahead. She offers me the box, and without hesitation, I lift a bottle out and hand it to her.

"Tourmaline Mist. That's for protection and grounding." She mists.

One of these days, I'm going to give Nessa a hug and thank her. One of these days, I'm going to ask her more about her. One of these days, we're going to dance like it's, well, whatever year it is.

ConversationWorks

During one of our executive check-ins early in the development of CW, Maggie proposed creating software aliases. Her idea was simple: the four of us would have virtual plastic surgery so that we could participate in CW conversation rooms with altered voices and faces. That way none of the conversationalists would recognize us as CW employees. I agreed with her proposal and figured it would be invaluable diagnostically. My one edict: participation was limited to research purposes only. Otherwise, our presence might alter the outcomes. After I made the decision to move forward, the four of us had a hoot coming up with our personas. Zia became an aspiring physicist concerned about global warming, Jamie Wyatt, younger but not nearly as pretty, brunette instead of a redhead, with thick black glasses for intellectual emphasis. Charles became a lobbyist working for big oil, Bill Tatesworth, an ex-Marine with a thick southern drawl, a shaved head, and way too much muscle. Maggie became, well, Zooey, a Harvard grad student finishing her PhD in economics, a Steinem-esque feminist, petite with cropped blonde hair and magazine-cover blue eyes. I became Dan Derico, a recent college grad, unemployed, trying to find my way in the world, with long flowing blond hair, better looking than I am.

Unfortunately, after months of working on the alias project, all Maggie had developed was the ability to bypass the authentication software and change our names. For example, this allowed me to log in as either Dan Underlight or Dan Derico, but in both cases I looked and sounded as I do now. Virtually changing a person's face and voice turned out to be more challenging technically than originally anticipated. We had to backburner the project.

Inside one of my haloes, the one at my apartment, I slip on my CSpectacles, log in as Dan Derico, and search for a conversation. Thanks to Zia's aggressive *Citizens Unite!* marketing program, thousands across the world are scheduled to start on the hour, and many are looking for additional participants. I short-list *Creating Jobs for Millennials* and a local Nashua, New Hampshire, conversation on *How to Stop Violence toward Women*. It's a difficult choice, but I've been thinking of Willow lately, so I opt for nonviolence. She still sends me a poem now and then, the last one after I texted her that I beat up that abusive guy: *Let the need to purge those without a clue go / Replace it with curiosity, kindness, love / Otherwise there will be no one left.*

Sometimes, she's the bigger idealist.

I log out—it's not right to go into a conversation around violence toward women with a fictitious name—then log back in. When I materialize, six women are seated in the conversation room, their full names and locations virtually displayed in front of them. There's a Donna, a Judy, two Janets, and two Marys. We built a retinal scan security protocol into CSpectacles to authenticate folks, so no one (other than the four of us) can use fake identities. When people sign up for the service, instead of selecting a password, we scan their retina and save the results. During any future login, we compare a new retinal scan to the one we initially stored for that user, and then we display their verified names and location in front of them for all the conversationalists to see. It's bulletproof.

The seven of us introduce ourselves, and during that time an eighth, Cindy, joins. After some light conversation, it's clear that the rest of the participants are skeptical about Dan Underlight. Do they know who I am? Instead of reading recognition on their faces, I read, *What are you doing here?* and *Are you one of the violent ones?* Well.

At first, I let it go, thinking it will right itself during the conversation. Then I look at Cindy, who glances down at her tapping hand. She seems genuinely afraid of me, the way people do when they rule out a class of people, and her look causes my confession. In gory detail, I share the story of the man and woman that I messed with in Cambridge.

"You saved her," Cindy says.

"But I can't condone the violence," Judy says.

"Maybe this conversation isn't right for you, Dan," a Mary says.

"Sometimes violence is the only way to stop these guys," a Janet says. "I want Dan to stay if it's okay with the rest of you."

Some of the others nod. Some remain silent.

"I can leave if folks aren't comfortable," I say.

"That won't be necessary," Cindy says.

With Cindy as moderator and with trust at least temporarily in delicate balance, we launch into a conversation about violence toward women in America. To start, each of us rattles off statistics. Every ninety seconds, somewhere in America, someone is sexually assaulted. Less than half of domestic violence incidents are reported to police. Factoring in unreported rapes, about six percent of rapists will ever spend a day in jail; fifteen out of sixteen will walk free. Approximately 1,270,000 women are raped each year in the United States, thirty percent younger than seventeen. Almost two-thirds of all rapes are committed by someone who is known to the victim, and about one-third of female murder victims are killed by an intimate partner. The costs of intimate-partner violence against women exceed an estimated six billion. Victims of sexual assault are three times more likely to suffer from depression, six times more likely to suffer from post-traumatic stress disorder, fourteen times more likely to abuse alcohol, twenty-six times more likely to abuse drugs, and four times more likely to contemplate suicide. For the women in this conversation, the facts and statistics are almost second nature, and their darting eyes, tapping fingers, and occasional sighs give away that each of them is also a statistic.

Many of the facts I kick in are taken from my lengthy conversations with Willow. I remember being shocked when I heard the numbers for the first time. How could this happen in the United States? Willow's answer: *It's about power and control. There's something called the Deluth Model that details what abusers do: intimidation, emotional abuse, isolation, denial, and blaming. Abusers use the children to make a woman feel guilty, use male privilege, use economic abuse, and use coercion and threat. All of these escalate the violence. To start to fix this, the law must give women equal power.* What's the government doing about it? *Not nearly enough. It's hard for men to accept responsibility for what they've done either implicitly or explicitly.* What can we do? *First thing, get the facts out. Second, educate from an early age. Third, get a few concrete big wins fast.* Fourth, beat up assholes who hit their girlfriends.

"Darra, please verify our facts," Cindy says.

"I'm on it. I'll be back soon."

Verification is a recent CW feature, implemented by a brilliant engineer we hired who's an expert in analyzing big data. Sometimes I shake my head at the caliber of talent we've attracted to the company. We developed verification because users in earlier conversations fabricated things and called them facts, and then based conclusions on those supposed facts. We had to address that issue to maintain platform credibility. In our latest version, only verifiable data in a conversation is considered factual. Things like *There are 600,000 people in Cambridge* is a verifiable fact. Things like *The Freedom*

Caucus is destroying the country is not. After the facts are verified, they form the basis for the rest of the conversation. Anytime someone makes a claim inconsistent with the baseline facts, Darra interrupts and corrects. Some love this feature, believe it's the only way forward, believe that certain things are incontrovertible and that manipulators need to be called on bad behavior. Others hate it.

"Your facts are accurate except the percentage of abused women under seventeen. That number is actually higher at 35 percent," Darra says. "With this correction, do you agree that this is your baseline set of facts?"

We all nod, so Cindy says, "Yes."

Facts verified, we move into the discussion and recommendation part of the conversation, which is where the true promise of CW begins. I tell the women what Sweden did about prostitution. All gravitate to that idea, are impressed with the after-implementation statistics, agree that men and laws are the problems and not the prostitutes. It easily becomes our first recommendation. Don't arrest prostitutes for solicitation. Instead, only arrest the johns. Implement a comprehensive program to help women move away from prostitution toward healthier, nondegrading professions. From there we meander through additional ideas— education, tougher laws, more government funding—until the conversation settles on the ERA. I come back to the Deluth Model and make Willow's point: *to start to fix abusive behavior, women by law must be given equal power.*

"I agree it all starts with the Equal Rights Amendment," Donna says.

"Until the government passes the ERA, change will be difficult," Mary says.

"Darra, can you give us the exact wording of the ERA and add it to our dataset?" Cindy asks.

"Working ... *Equality of rights under the law shall not be denied or abridged by any state on account of sex.*"

"That's it?" I ask.

"There are two other sections on enforcement, but this section reflects the main content. Would you like Darra to read the other sections?" Donna asks.

"No. I'm okay for now. I guess I don't understand why this is controversial," I say.

"Because many men don't believe in equality but are smart enough not to say it out loud," Janet says.

"We only need three more states to ratify the 1972 proposed amendment. Thirty-five already have including Massachusetts and New Hampshire," Cindy says.

"Of the remaining states, Illinois, Virginia, and Arizona are strong candidates. We should see what folks are organizing there and help them," Mary says.

All agree that's a good idea, so we spend time looking at ways to help these states. Darra details the abundant number of the linkage points, and we agree to participate in CW conversations sponsored by those states to help in-state organizers go door to door to solicit support, to raise more awareness money, and to get the word out through online press and other social networks. One of most profound lessons from CW so far is that there's not a lack of folks trying to help, there's a lack of connection. Our conversation today is not so much about differing opinions, it's about participating in a movement, rising up, and playing the long game to stop further violence. It's about connecting like-minded people instead of resolving conflict between opponents, but this kind of conversation, on many CW topics, is not the norm.

When the conversation ends, we wait for Darra to summarize our recommendations and look for opportunities to aggregate. Here's another thing we've learned: sometimes the opportunities for aggregating extend beyond the stated topic. As we're waiting, I learn the other participants heard about ConversationWorks through the Director of the Nashua Center for Domestic Violence, and they trust me enough now to confirm they're all victims themselves. They tell me CW is spreading across the domestic violence centers in the US, and victims are using it as a tool to unite. Does Willow know?

When Darra comes back, she does an excellent job of summarizing our conclusions and recommendations, and then she says, "There are 532 conversations that have reached similar conclusions on Violence against Women. Would you like to share your recommendations with them, aggregate them where appropriate, and schedule follow-on conversations with these groups?"

All nod, so Cindy says, "Yes."

"Also, there are 149 conversations where the participants support the ERA. Would you like to add your names to the list of Americans who support the ERA?"

"Yes."

"Finally, there is one other conversation on adopting what Sweden did on prostitution. Would you like to connect with that group?"

"Yes."

"Should we make this a working group and stay connected?" Donna asks.

None of us want to stop after one conversation. Coming together in meaningful work has tapped into a much deeper human need to connect and lift the world, a need that can't be fulfilled after one meeting. We agree to form a working group that will meet regularly. Sometimes we'll work on a particular prearranged topic. Other times we'll independently go into other sessions where we can better understand what another group is doing. All are committed to help move our recommendations forward or to help further similar recommendations in the CW network. One of the things I theorized at the start was that optimal size for most conversations was eight, which, after this conversation, seems true.

With our action plan in place, we say our good-byes. None of these folks know who I really am, but I guess I'll have to tell them at some point that I run CW. My vision, back at the start, was to connect folks in meaningful conversations, to let the people figure out their own solutions, and to enable people to change the world one conversation at a time. Even if CW never solves anything except for the women's equality and domestic violence issue, I would consider it a major success. But we can do much more.

I log out, remove my CSpectacles, and remain sitting inside the halo. On the end table next to me is a stone arrowhead that Zack found a long time ago while we were hiking in the Harton Woods. We were collecting all kinds of things that day—arrowheads, riverbed stones, colorful fall leaves—but only the arrowheads and a couple of stones survived. The arrowhead is about three inches long, two inches wide, serrated, gray-blue.

I pour myself a large glass of scotch and take a few sips before shooting down the rest. My chest and stomach warm. I pull off my shirt. Pressing the arrowhead to a patch of unmarked skin right below my ribcage, I push it in like a surgeon's No. 10 blade. I catch my breath, and then pull it slowly for about an inch in a straight line. The sting, the burning, is like the one that comes from a tattoo gun in the hands of a true artist, like the one who tattooed Zack's image on my upper arm years ago. Directly from the bottle, I drizzle scotch over the cut, bruise marks, past punctures, past cuts. Blood and scotch pool over the fresh cut. I close my eyes.

#

The four of us CSpectacle in and materialize at the same time. Zia as climatologist Jamie Wyatt. Maggie as Zooey Caulfield. Charles as Bill Tatesworth. Me as Don Derico. Going in together is against the CW rule we put in place around the number of employees who can participate in any one conversation, not to mention that we're going in with fake identities, but we're trying to understand a knotty problem that's cropped up. What does Darra do when a conversationalist commandeers and refuses to accept points the rest of the folks are making and ignores facts even after Darra sets him straight? What happens when multiple obstructionists participate in a session, and they're locked and loaded before the conversation begins? What happens when, no matter how the rest of the participants try to move forward through compromise, there simply is no movement? We're not sure why people would enter into a problem-solving session if they're already locked in, but that seems to be happening in spades. Maybe the threat of a meaningful conversation where folks let go of fixed ideas and change is too much for the obstructionists. Maybe for them it's better to stay in the past, or it's as simple as we live in an era of cacophony.

Two men and two women who are all from the same town in Texas join us. John and Bob. Rose and Joann. They're dressed well, professional, and likable after small talk. John agrees to be the moderator. The particular conversation we've chosen is on one of the more difficult conversations on CW, climate change. Zia prepared extensively for this session, consistent with her persona. In the United States, after megasessions on the topic, the two camps on climate change are evenly divided between those who believe the scientists and those who don't. In the rest of world, almost everyone believes the scientists.

"Shall we get into it?" John asks. "You know, the climate has changed before. We've had ice ages and warm periods for millions of years, and some of the warm periods were warmer than now."

"That's true," I say.

"It is," Jamie-Zia says. "It's also true that greenhouse gasses—mainly CO2 and methane—directed most of the climate changes in the earth's past. When emissions were lower, the global climate became colder. When they were higher, the global climate became warmer."

"Yes, and to John's point, the planet survived the warm periods," Rose says.

"Yes and no. The real issue is the speed of change. When greenhouse gas levels jumped rapidly, the warming that resulted was highly disruptive and caused mass extinctions. We're emitting today at a rate faster than the most destructive jumps in the earth's past, and as a result, we're not giving the planet a chance to adapt to the warmth as it did during successful transitions in the past," Jamie-Zia says.

"That sounds like a convenient explanation," John says. "Darra, do you agree with Jamie?"

"Give me a minute," Darra says.

When verifying a fact, Darra checks all available data on the topic, correlates it, and looks for credible opposing views. We've built a massive CW repository from as many reliable sources as possible—research papers, scientific findings, blogs, government data, whatever. When possible, Darra comes back from the repository with a total verification, but on difficult topics sometimes she'll express her answer as a percentage. If eighty percent of the data supports a point made during a session, Darra considers it a CW fact; if less than eighty percent, she doesn't. In both cases, she articulates the opposing view.

"Ninety-seven percent of the scientific community agrees with Jamie. No national or major scientific institutions anywhere in the world dispute the theory of anthropogenic climate change. A few independent denialists and adaptionists disagree," Darra says.

"Really? It's hard to believe there are so few. Anyway, there are other communities besides the scientific one to consider," Joann says, who's sitting directly next to John.

Bob and Rose nod.

"Okay, let's agree to disagree on that one and move on. How about this one? It's a fact that there are more sunspots in the last thirty-five years. That's my take on why the planet is warming," John says.

"I read that too," Joann says.

"I didn't know that one," Bill-Charles says. "Why is that happening?"

"No one knows, but it's probably a natural cycle," John says. "This is all a natural cycle."

"Actually, over the last thirty-five years, the sun, even with more sunspots, has shown a slight cooling trend," Jamie-Zia says.

"Don't more sunspots mean a warmer sun?" John asks.

"No," Jamie-Zia says.

"Darra, can you verify?" John asks.

"Give me a minute," Darra says. "Jamie is correct. The sun has cooled during the time frame considered, and no correlation exists between the number of sunspots and global warming."

"I find that hard to believe," Bob says.

"And even so, how do we know the climate warming is bad? I mean, there have been multiple times in the past where a warming trend was good for people. It's actually cooling and ice ages that are bad," Joann says.

John, Bob, Rose, and Joann go into an animated conversation that feels more like a combined denial speech about climate change. Point one: more CO_2 will help plant growth. There will be greener rainforests and enhanced plant growth in the Amazon and increased vegetation in northern latitudes. Farming will shift north to new areas that are now too cold. There will be increased plankton biomass in the oceans. Point two: for humans, a warming planet is better for the elderly because they'll live longer. The Texans call it the Florida Effect, say the entire country will have the same climate as Florida. Point three: even if the sea rises, people will migrate to higher ground. That's what happened in the past with other species. Point four: there will be financial benefits because the arctic waterways will open up to business. Point five, which they're even more adamant about: new technologies will save us as they have in the past.

Who are the four Texans? Their positions are so well orchestrated. They've clearly met before and are in the conversation not to learn, but to push their joint agenda, which we all are to some extent, but still. I glance over at Zia, Maggie, and Charles, and I can tell they're in the same place. Zia is disjointedly moving her hands on the arms of the chair, tapping faster than the visual recognition software can handle.

"Okay, let's look at all the pieces of what happens when the planet warms and see if what you are saying is true," Zia finally says. "Let's start with agriculture. Although CO_2 is essential for plant growth, agriculture depends on steady water supplies, and climate change will disrupt those supplies through floods and droughts. You suggest that higher latitudes may become productive due to global warming, but the soil in Arctic and bordering territories is poor, and the amount of sunlight reaching the ground in summer won't change because it's governed by the earth's tilt. Plus, agriculture will be disrupted by wildfires, and changes to grasslands and water supplies will impact domestic livestock grazing. So for agriculture, warming is not a win.

"Now, let's look at human health. Warmer winters would mean fewer deaths, particularly, as you say, among vulnerable groups like the aged. However, the same groups are also vulnerable to additional heat, and deaths attributable to heat waves will be five times as great as winter deaths prevented. Add that warmer climates will encourage migration of disease-bearing insects like mosquitoes and the bottom-line health prognosis isn't good for anyone, including the elderly.

"Now, let's look at polar melting. Even though the opening of a year-round, ice-free Arctic passage between the Atlantic and Pacific oceans would have business benefits, the negatives outweigh them. The loss of ice causes the ocean to absorb more heat, which warms the waters and increases the glacier and Greenland ice cap melt, as well as raising the temperature of Arctic tundra, which then releases methane, which is much worse than the CO_2. Now pile on that the glaciers will also melt, and things get even worse. One-sixth of the world's population depend on fresh water supplied each year by natural spring melt and regrowth cycles of glaciers and those water supplies will fail.

"Now, let's look at sea-level rise. Many parts of the world are low lying and will be severely affected by modest sea rises. You talk about the Florida Effect, but most of the state where the population currently lives will be underwater. Seawater will contaminate rivers as it mixes with freshwater further upstream, and aquifers will become polluted. Migrating hundreds of millions of people inward without severe loss of life and the resources necessary to sustain life is impossible. With the whole planet changing so quickly, there's simply no place to hide."

"Wow, Jamie. What a speech. I guess we know where you stand. Remember this is a conversation," John says. He laughs a little, looking at the others who join him. "Are you even open to another view on the topic? Don't you believe in American ingenuity? Even if you're right, we'll figure something out. We always do."

"I'm open, if it's based on facts," Jamie says.

"Some things are unknowable," John says. "Sometimes you have to take a leap of faith."

"Yes, but many things are knowable if you believe in science," Jamie says.

"Why don't we have Darra check Jamie's statements?" Maggie says.

Darra lets us know that it will take a few minutes to check Jamie's statements. She asks us to go off topic until she returns. Darra, for the most part, can't analyze and listen to a conversation at the same time; it's a limitation of the software that we'll have to fix in future releases. As we wait, I survey the room. The four Texans launch into a fact-and-statistic-based conversation about the Dallas Cowboys' chances of winning the Super Bowl. Jamie-Zia is flexing her fingers in a circular motion, and her eyes are strained. She's done her homework, and like many new converts, she doesn't believe climate change has two valid sides. Maggie and Charles have pushed back in their chairs and have folded their arms across their stomachs. They don't have the same data as Zia, but they've clearly labeled the Texans as obstructionists. We all come from a technology world where the ability to think critically is, well, critical. Without disciplined thinking, the product fails. Simple as that. Is it really true that the ability we take for granted in hi-tech doesn't translate to the general public? The four seem well educated and sincere, yet they're unwilling to critically analyze the data. It's like they've decided what's true and are looking for data that supports their conclusion. Why would professionals do that? Because there's no easy solution? Because they judge as serious only those problems for which actions can be taken? Because climate change threatens the survival of the human species and they're in denial? Or because we live in an era of cacophony and polarization?

When Darra returns, she verifies Jamie-Zia's data. The four Texans remain silent for a long time, apparently trying to plot their next round. While they clearly prepared for this session, they didn't expect Jamie. Finally, John says, "I read recently that the planet has been cooling since 1998."

"That plus the fact that we've gotten some giant snowfalls and record-breaking droughts these last few years leads me to believe the planet isn't warming," Rose says.

"Even after the data Darra verified says otherwise?" Zooey-Maggie asks.

"The data Jamie presented does seem to overwhelmingly make the case for climate change," Bill-Charles says.

"You know, for me it's not so much about science. I mean, scientists thought the world was flat for a long time. It's more about faith that God wouldn't let us destroy our beautiful planet," Rose says.

There it is. Before we entered the conversation, we heard that some were using a religious argument in the climate-change sessions. People clearly have a right to do so, but the whole premise of CW is that fact-based conversations can help move issues forward. For many conversations it's doing just that, but there are few places a person can take a conversation after a faith-only argument is made. You can either agree or you can stalemate.

"Are you saying that regardless of what the data says you won't accept it because of your religious beliefs?" I ask.

"Not exactly. My religious beliefs lead me to trust certain facts more than others, even if they're not mainstream," Rose says.

Jamie-Zia shifts in her chair and crosses one leg over the other. She looks like she's about to erupt. "For the record, the planet hasn't been cooling since 1998. Even if we ignore long-term trends and only consider record years, that wasn't the hottest year. The year 2005 was hotter than 1998 and, globally, the hottest twelve-month period on record spanned 2009 and 2010. And climate change is entirely compatible with droughts and large snowfalls; after all, they're just weather.

"Besides, for climate change, the long-term trends are key. Those trends are measured over decades, and they show that the globe is clearly warming. By the way, there's a tendency to concentrate on air temperatures, but ocean warming given its size is a better indicator. The oceans absorb about ninety percent of global warming, and the ocean-warming trend shows that the planet will warm between two and four degrees Celsius, which will take the planet back to an ice-free world not seen for thirty-five million years. Given that the average lifetime of a species is three million years, there's no reason to believe that there won't be mass extinctions."

The four Texans go silent. They've shut down to Jamie-Zia's facts and aren't going to budge. Our conversation has stalemated. Critics of our CW vision believe the problem-solving aspect of CW is intractable, and those critics have no particular demographic; they represent different political parties, different genders, different races, and different ages. About the only thing that unites them is the fact that they don't want the people to unite. For them, the stalemate confirms that a class of problems has no solutions and that the existing power structure in the world, even with all of its problems, is the best we can expect. To be clear, most do support one aspect of what we're trying to do—they believe CW should focus on simpler, less change-oriented stuff, which is shorthand for holographic videoconferencing. But beyond that, they consider changing the world—Dan's folly.

"It's such a complicated problem. I'm not convinced the models are reliable," John says. "Models are full of fudge factors that are fitted to the existing climate."

"You're right. This is clearly a complex task, so models are built to estimate trends rather than events," Jamie-Zia says. "A climate model can tell you that it will be a hot summer, but it can't tell you what the temperature will be on any given day. Climate trends are weather averaged out over thirty years. All models are first tested in a process called hindcasting—"

"Jamie, let me stop you there," I say. "I don't think we need more data at this point."

"I agree," John says.

"I think it's fair to say that the four of you would take no particular action to combat climate change at this time. Am I right?"

The four Texans nod.

"And the four of us support Jamie's data and would do all that is humanly possible to stop climate change. Yes?"

Zia, Maggie, and Charles nod.

"So I guess we're officially stalemated."

#

Charles and I are heading to our first board meeting since the launch in his brand-new car, a BMW electric car. I've been so busy with the product details the last six months that I haven't spent much one-on-one time with him. No matter, he's kept all of the financial stuff moving forward, which isn't where I naturally gravitate, and even prepared and briefed me on the presentation I'm about to give.

We park underground and take up the escalator. The board meeting is at Jason's company, right in the heart of Boston, at the top of one of the many new office buildings. Unlike the CW offices, the space is plush with mahogany built-ins and hi-tech gadgets everywhere: flat screen TVs, a wireless stereo system, tablets on the coffee tables instead of magazines. We're early and are escorted down a long main hallway lined with magazine covers and start-up logos from Jason's other investments. At the end of the hallway, the CW logo is on display. We arrive at a large empty conference room, which rivals the size and decor of the RR boardroom. Computer-generated spa music pollutes the background.

One by one the board members join us. A technology guy who was an early member of PhotoPhotobook, who knows what it means to scale software, who apparently has too much time and too much money on his hands. A retired US general with strong connections into the military hierarchy who believes the morale boost CW could provide for our soldiers is huge. A former CEO of a Fortune 500 communications giant who believes CW has the potential to revolutionize the phone business. We mingle, drinking espresso. Since the board formed, as I've gotten to know each of them, we've cemented our relationships.

Jason beelines in last with Olivia by his side. The two are chatting in the way Olivia and I used to when we were in the know about something. They're dressed, well, like senior executives; their business suits, handmade and black, appear tailored by the same designer; their hair is perfectly styled; their jewelry has no practical value. They swarm our way.

"Dan, Charles," Jason says.

"Jason, Olivia," I say.

"Olivia has been gracious enough to accept my offer to join our board. In addition to being my largest investor, she knows software, knows how to build a company, and knows you."

"I'm looking forward to working with the two of you and the broader team," Olivia says.

Right.

We make nice for a while, doing our best at smiling over the razor-bottomed undercurrent. Even though I've perfected the skill over the years, it takes every last ounce of strength to navigate this time. So that's how Jason did it. The lawsuit went away because he let her buy in and offered her an eventual seat on the board, and the universe knows what else. That explains the scotch, the football tickets, the weekly calls—she's going to attack from inside.

With the board seated around the far end of the table, I PowerPoint. In the months since the launch, revenues have grown exponentially. Sales to corporate clients are strong, and the early adopters on the consumer side have demonstrated unusually high enthusiasm. Our three-year product road map calls for a major release each year chock-full of new features. The culture we're building with the help of The Code is vibrant and connected. Costs are in line. I reach the last slide, having received few questions and many nods along the way. I unbutton my blazer jacket, rest my arms at my side as I was taught in business finishing school, which essentially is a Miss Manners for technology executives, and smile.

"That concludes my prepared remarks. Thank you for your time. Questions or comments are welcome," I say.

"Congratulations. I can't imagine a single corporate client, even small and medium businesses, who won't buy our product," Olivia says.

"If we play our cards right with the phone companies, our hardware could eventually replace in-home phones," the former communications CEO says.

"Maybe we can eventually build a whole house or room halo so users can move around," the former PhotoPhotobook guy says.

"Maybe," Olivia says, "but part of me wonders if the best thing is to focus on the corporate clients first?"

"Why?" Jason asks.

"They have money, and that market is huge, and it isn't fraught with the same technical and political issues the change-the-world portion of CW is facing. Honestly, I don't know if that part will ever work," Olivia says.

Well, at least she's transparent now. Before Olivia, the board once mildly debated this topic, and Jason as chair let the debate ramble on. But now, with her on board, the balance has shifted. She knows the consumer side of CW is my brainchild, and she's going to try to take it away with facts, figures, and years of self-promoted business intuition. How did I once love this woman? How did I let her back in after launch? Her comments kick off a long debate among board members around the merits of building a worldwide, citizen-driven, problem-solving network versus focusing on multiple corporate market segments. During this whole time, I remain silent, which I've learned is the best approach in these situations—let them wear themselves out.

Finally, when the debate slows, Olivia asks, "What do you think, Dan?"

As if she didn't know. I collect my response; both words and tone are important here. This is as much about power as it is about content, and any emotional break in my voice will confirm in front of the whole board that Olivia is the pack leader.

"It's tempting to focus on the holographic communications market. It's large, and combined; CSpectacles and CHalo are leaders in that space. In fact, our hardware produces such realistic images that calling them holograms is a misnomer. With that said, I believe brand loyalty will come predominately from successfully implementing the problem-solving network. If we can do that well, we'll give so much power to people that they'll fully vest in our success, to a point where we become ubiquitous."

Some in the room nod, some don't. Jason, who fully understands that the lines have been drawn, that war has been declared, that in the end only one CEO will be left standing, makes a motion to adjourn the meeting with some innocuous comment about revisiting this topic when we know more. Olivia smiles as if the blood is already on her teeth.

#

The doorbell rings, and I buzz Katie up. I've been seeing her since the launch. On the way to the door, I mirror to check that I'm presentable, not that it matters. I haven't shaved in a few days; my new wire-rimmed glasses match the black puffy bags underneath them; my graying has stabilized at striated.

Katie pushes the door from one-inch to wide open. She doesn't dress or look like any of my previous women. She's model beautiful instead of quirky beautiful, with long flowing blonde hair, cobalt- blue eyes, overly white teeth, and no more than one hundred and thirty pounds on a five-foot, ten-inch frame. At twenty-five, she's the youngest person I've been with since I was her age. Today she's wearing jeans, flip-flops, and a black sleeveless pullover, which reminds me of summer in Harvard Yard. Once inside, she pushes and pins me up against the wall, kisses me for a long time, the deep, intense, aggressive kind that signals what's to come. Her perfume, new and ample, hints of citrus.

We don't speak all the way to bed where I lift off her shirt and unbutton her pants, before letting her take over. She strips me fast and pushes me down to the bed. Before she joins me, she reaches under the bed and pulls out two black leather belts, which she expertly loops and tightens around my wrists and the bedposts until I'm crucified from the waist up. In bed, with her on top and in control, our silence continues. Today, like much of our time together, will be to the point.

These last months, what I've liked best about Katie are two things. First, she covets being in charge. With curiosity, she leads, builds, and lights the fuse each time I see her, and all I have to do is submit. When I do, she's taken me to places, well, I've never gone before: tie-me-up places, alleged Kama Sutra places, places I'd only previously seen on porn sites. Second, she doesn't judge how much I work, the amount of scotch I consume, or the bruises, cuts, and scars on my stomach. Each time we're together, she traces her finger on my stomach, searching for new wounds, and then balms them with gentle kisses. Afterward, instead of smoking cigarettes in cliché, we down a fifth straight up.

After I'm done and unbuckled, I push up against the headboard. Katie joins me and drapes her leg over mine, as she often does at this point. That's her signal to pour us two glasses of Macallan Single Malt from a bottle I have next to the bed. Like all Katie-in-bed requests, I comply. Drinking after sex with Katie generates a buzz that's sweet and edgeless, and for a time, I forget.

"You were very efficient today," I say.

"That's what you needed."

"How did you know?"

"I just did."

"We're good together that way."

"We are," she says.

I sip my scotch until it's gone, pour another glass, and top Katie's off. When I'm honest with myself, when the alcohol lowers my guard, it's clear. With Hannah, with Willow, even with the women before Hannah, I was relationally inept. One thing or the other— boredom, emotional incompetence, distance, fear—messed me up. With each of my lovers I didn't have the same joy I got from work, or later the joy of being a dad I had with Zack. The truth: my best romantic relationship, if one judges such things by length, was unromantic. I saw Olivia almost every day for sixteen years, and I loved her. Together we were better than we were alone. We had a vision and a purpose; we built something that lasted. The only difference was we didn't have sex. Meaningful work can keep you in a relationship for a long time if you let it, at least until you get fucked and the hate takes over.

"Maybe you should come over more," I say.

"That would be great."

We finish the bottle of scotch and for an encore settle on a nap. We scooch down and wrap our bodies together. In no time, I'm in Argentina, in Patagonia, working for this tall guy with a pockmarked face who is presenting at a conference on advances in grieving technology over the last five years. In a nutshell, this little black box that costs a mere thousand sends electrical currents into a patient's skull while she sleeps. With beta and theta waves manipulated, the grieving time is cut in half. Apparently, little, black-box therapy works well for everyone except those patients who've become addicted to sadness, whatever that means.

Pockmarked man can't find a cable to project his grieving pitch, so he has me running all over the hotel, the countryside, and the country for anyone who might have a ThunderVolt wire. Even though the vast majority of people I come in contact with are using at least one Peach product, no one has the wire.

Well into my search, I run across a young woman whose face I can't see. Apparently she's worked for me for a long time, and we love each other the same way Olivia and I loved each other. She says, "Did you hear my news?" The man she loved came through for her after lots of ups and downs, so she's cutting the business portion of her Patagonia trip short, which I fully support. How many people does pockmarked man need running around on his behalf, anyway? Instead, faceless woman is going to marry her love in a quaint church, a picture of which she happens to have on her phone. St. Augustine's has white stone walls and a green thatched roof; it holds maybe twenty people. It's beautiful, peaceful, and mystical, and a far cry from the Unitarian church in Concord. She asks me to stand up for her, and right before I leave, she hands me her ThunderVolt wire.

Next thing I know I'm on a conveyer belt and about-to-be-married woman is ten yards in front of me, talking and laughing on the phone with her lover as she moves at a steady pace toward oblivion. A short time later the woman passes Willow, who's on a parallel conveyer belt talking and laughing on her phone, presumably with her new lover, presumably headed to the same destination, albeit at a slower rate. The women wave to each other and say a few words I can't make out. When I reach Willow, the belts stop, and she covers her phone with her hand.

"Just a donor," she says.

"Did you hear the news?"

"Yes. I'm so happy for her. He's a good man."

"Yeah, they're good together. How about you?"

"I'm also happy, Dan. What's done is done. You can't change the past."

I turn over on my side and yawn awake. It's morning. Katie is already dressed in fresh clothes from the abundant supply she keeps at my place and is sitting down on the bed next to me, incandescent in the morning sunlight, like Ophelia in that famous painting. She kisses me on the forehead. The citrus has been showered off and replaced with Dove.

"I've gotta go. I'll see you in a couple of days," she says.

"Why don't you stay a little longer?"

"Can't today, but next time."

She pushes off the bed with one hand while gently holding my hand with the other. Slowly, I let go of her hand and open my nightstand drawer. I pull out a white letter-sized envelope filled with a large number of one-hundred-dollar bills and hand it to Katie. She folds and tucks the envelope into her jean pocket.

Story to Dither

Maggie phoned early and woke me from a sound sleep. "Dan, a video you're in went viral. I just sent you the link." The video, titled "CEO of ConversationWorks beats the shit out of innocent man," showed only part of what happened that night. Apparently, the videographer didn't push record until I charged the guy, so the man repeatedly hitting the woman wasn't captured. What's on screen: Dan tackling and pummeling the man, the woman pulling Dan off the man and yelling at him to leave them alone, Dan running away from the scene. Not good. At the time, I hoped it was dark enough that my face wouldn't be captured on video. More recently, I figured I was in the clear because nothing had surfaced since the incident. With mega Internet video views over the weekend and trending, I was wrong on both counts.

CW has rocketed in the year since we launched. While the growth on the corporate side has been steady, consumer sales have passed corporate sales for the first time. As a result, I've been plastered all over magazines, blogs, and cable television, all of which are heralding the change potential of CW and my arrival as the next hi-tech golden boy. Now, the same media will swarm for a takedown, fueled by a high story-to-dither ratio. When you're a CEO with ascending power, when your aspirations are sky-is-the-limit and driven by idealism, when you beat the shit out of an apparently innocent man, your ratio skyrockets.

It's midmorning, and I'm walking to work. Though I've taken the same route each day since I moved to Cambridge—Central to Cochran to 1st Avenue—today's the first time I've noticed the stores. I stop at an Indian restaurant and read the extensive menu posted in the window. At a drugstore, I buy razor blades in case I decide to clean up at the office. At the local bagel shop, the black coffee smells better than it tastes. From the shop, I call Maggie, tell her I'm on the way, and say that I want to meet with her, Zia, and Charles upon my arrival.

I can't remember the last time I went in this late. After Maggie called, I got out of bed and watched the video alone in the bathroom a few times. How had I gone so far over the top? Why hadn't I stopped after the first punch? Then I slipped back into bed, pulled Katie close, and did, well, what we do best. When we were done, I confessed and shared the video with her. As she watched the beating, she said she'd seen worse, wished she had a Dan Underlight around for the times when a creep went nuclear on her, and said the bastard had it coming. She's good that way—there's support, no judgment, and, other than cash, no expectations.

When I get off the elevator at work, everyone is waiting to greet me. Maggie's doing, no doubt. We now have employees on multiple floors of this building, and soon we'll occupy the whole thing, but today all have gathered on my floor. On the way to my cubicle, I shake mostly familiar hands and repeatedly hear, "It will be okay." Or "We know what really happened." Or "It will blow over when the woman comes forward." Well.

Maggie, Zia, and Charles follow me into my office and semicircle around my desk. We chat about everything but: the new software release, the Celtics, Zooey. I'm glad they're near. My entire adult life I've untangled certain Gordian knots by myself, often for other people. Bring me Problem X, and in no time I'll knock out Solution Y for you. It's probably why I did well with Olivia and not so well in my personal life. Olivia wanted me to anticipate problems, fix them before they mounted, and when they did, make them disappear. Hannah wanted me to listen to her, hold her, and support her until she figured out things on her own. But listening like that was never a strength of mine. I couldn't sit still; I had to come up with a fix.

Zia excuses herself and leaves the office to make me an espresso. First time that's happened. By the time she returns, she not only has my espresso, but she's made one for Maggie, Charles, and herself. She's also managed to commandeer a box of Italian pastries, which is filled with Cannoli, Zeppole, and Sfogliatella. In general, I'm trying to limit my sugar intake, but today's an exception. As we're eating, drinking, and chatting more in hi-tech, the phone rings.

"Dan, I assume you've seen the video," Jason says.

"Yes."

"What do you plan to do about it?"

"Nothing. It will pass."

"I think you need to put out a press release saying it isn't you."

"But it is," I say.

"Who knows that?"

"Too many people."

"I'm going to call a special board meeting to discuss."

"Is that necessary?"

"Yes."

I update Zia, Maggie, and Charles on the fifty percent they didn't hear, though they've already pieced it together. As I speak, one by one, their expressions go from we've-got-this to we're-worried, confirming what all four of us already know: this is a big one. Olivia once said, "When bad things happen, and they will, a leader either lines up behind consensus, folds, or goes all-in. The first two are certain death, and the third may be."

My computer buzzes. I excuse myself to email and lose myself behind a much-too-large monitor. My three closest friends move to the conference room next to my office to wait for me. I scan a page of new messages and open an unimportant message about last month's costs, which contains information that Charles has already briefed me on. As I'm staring at a spreadsheet of numbers, the screen morphs to Zack. He's wearing his only suit, the one we buried him in, and his hair is long and slicked back like he belongs to Young Entrepreneurs of America. He's alternating between rubbing his forearm and tapping his index finger on a leather shoelace-bracelet he made years ago at school. His eyes are widened, his smile is filled with compassion, and for an instant his love transcends all boundaries, even the ones I've imposed.

In my first fifteen years at RR, when a crisis kicked off, the turns saved me. Until Zack died, they forgave almost all the time. Major product slip: turn it around with a fourteen-hour-a-day push. Not enough budget: turn off discretionary expenditures and voila, freed-up money. Missed an important family event: turn it into a positive by handing out expensive gifts. Then during the lead-up to his death that day, I remember thinking with each piece of news, okay, that's not good, but things will right themselves at the next turn.

Dad, you did nothing wrong. Just tell the press the truth.

They won't believe me.

Yes, they will. Why wouldn't they?

It's a bigger story if they don't.

But you've done so much good.

All the more reason.

When I join Zia, Maggie, and Charles in the conference room, they've shaken off the Jason call and regrouped. They're huddled over a laptop and are in the process of crafting a statement that will truthfully detail what happened that night. As soon as I sit, I'm hit with a barrage of questions. Why were you out walking late at night? What did the man do exactly after the woman fell to the ground? Why didn't you stop hitting him? Why did you run away?

Hours pass as we hone the statement. We go through every word and every sentence multiple times, and we don't move on until all of us are comfortable. We drink an inordinate amount of coffee, even by our standards. We order in lunch from the local Indian place I passed earlier. As the afternoon progresses, the room takes on the smell of curry and sweat. Two things are going on with my friends. First, they're truly trying to help me craft a statement about what happened. Second, they're trying to get their heads around the fact that their CEO, their friend, a person they thought they knew well, beat another man senseless.

When we're done, the final statement reads, *A YouTube video emerged recently that shows Dan Underlight assaulting another man in Cambridge, Massachusetts. What the video didn't show were the events leading up to his involvement. In an act of senseless rage, the man had violently attacked the woman and had brutally struck her multiple times. In the heat of the moment, Dan intervened and kept the man from further violence. While Dan does not, in general, advocate the use of violence, what unfolded that night was egregious enough that he had to act swiftly and decisively to save the woman. Dan would welcome the woman coming forward to corroborate the events of that evening.*

#

"Hi, Dan."

"Hey."

"I saw the video."

"Oh."

"Would you like to meet for a glass of wine and a chat?"

Willow and I agree to meet after work at an Italian restaurant near her office. I haven't seen her since she moved out a little more than two years ago. From her end, she's sent a few text messages and a few poems, but that's all. From mine, I've driven past her office building multiple times, visited the *About Willow* page of her company's website, and, on countless occasions, picked up the phone only to partially dial her number. Sometimes I have to remind myself that I'm not trying to reconcile with Willow; we're past the point of romantic return. Instead, these acts are more about staying connected from afar, more about the fact that, even if I were never to see her again, I'd still love her. These last years, I've come to believe the energy required to build a company like CW was the same energy required to truly be in a relationship with Willow. I couldn't do both; I had to pick. But now and then I remember, get lost in might-have-been, snatch a few Willow moments, and recharge. ConversationWorks is helping so many people now; wasn't that worth giving up the one? Because that's what I did, I gave her up, sabotaged the whole thing in a single act. Why else would I push away the adult I connected with the most, the one I truly and deeply loved?

I enter Lucca's, which is unusually warm. Garlic and freshly baked bread permeate the air and remind me of this restaurant in the North End that Willow and I frequented, Prezza, when we were still thick with hope. On the way to Lucca's, I rehearsed what I was going to say, but it was disjointed at best, and I couldn't settle down enough to piece it together. Do I want forgiveness? Do I want her to understand my actions? Do I want her to discourage the arrowheads, the scotch, Katie?

Willow is already seated and reading something on her tablet. She glances up, smiles, and waves me over. She's wearing a sleeveless black dress and a white pearl necklace. Her face is radiant, and her hair is pulled back and tame in a way I've never seen before. She looks as though her personal life is on the upswing. When I reach the table, she rises to greet me, and we exchange hellos and gentle embraces. She smells different than I remember her, like the backyard honeysuckle vine from my childhood home.

"You look well," I say.

"Thank you."

"How are you?"

"Good. I'm writing a lot of poetry, and the center is doing well. You?"

"Pretty good. Until this latest snafu, we were firing on all cylinders."

"The press before that was outstanding," she says.

A waiter comes to our table, fills our glasses with water, and hands us two menus. We order the house wine and send him on his way. Then we catch up. I talk about CW and about what happened the night with the man and woman. Willow is more than sympathetic, says I did the right thing. She talks about loving her small one-bedroom in Somerville, about how the neighborhood suits her, and mostly about her poetry. She's excited that Cove Press will soon publish her book, *Inexplicable Fog.* I'm excited, too. I'll have to buy a copy for everyone in the company.

I open my menu, but all I can think about is how good it is to sit across from Willow. I've missed her. Everything about her: her smile, her eyes, her smell, her touch, how our conversations are effortless. After a royal fuckup, after a galactic push away, after years have passed, how is it possible to still feel so connected to her?

"Did you hear CW is helping a few domestic violence centers across the country?" Willow asks.

"I did. I even sat in on a session. You going to eat anything or just the wine?"

"Wine. I have dinner plans."

"Ah," I say.

So there it is. Willow was never one for indirectness. She always said, "Just say it." If her answer is no, after the initial happiness wave, I guess it won't change anything, but still. If her answer is yes, I'll be truly happy for her. In the end, that's what love is—supporting the person wherever he or she needs to go, even if it's far away. The waiter returns with the wine. I give him our news about dinner, hand him a hundred to cover the bill, and send him on his way. Willow and I toast to old friends. After I take my first sip, I stare into the glass for a time. Then I place the glass on the table, wrap both hands around it, and look directly at Willow.

"So, you seeing anyone?" I ask.

"Yes. And you?"

"Yes."

"It's going well?"

"It is. And you?"

"The same."

"I'm happy for you."

"Me, too," she says.

I consider asking Willow about her new love, but don't. Instead, I create an elaborate cover story for Katie. Some of it is true, but most of it is inflated or flat-out made up. Katie's in hi-tech, too (false). We met one evening at a Massachusetts hi-tech event (false). She too is a Patriots fan (inflated). She makes me laugh (inflated). She's accepting and doesn't judge (true). We both enjoy a good scotch (true). Willow nods and smiles, seems genuinely happy for me, as if she too knows there will always be love here. After I finish, I wonder if my cover story had cracks. Did Willow opt to be gracious? Or have I become so proficient at lying about my personal life that I no longer have a tell? There was a time when the thought of lying to Willow was incomprehensible, when outside of work, she was my one safe adult place.

"So, I was surprised to hear from you," I say.

"After I saw the video, I had to reach out. They're going to try to take you down."

"Who?"

"The press. CW's competitors. People who don't like your change agenda. But you can't let them, Dan. You're a good man. I wish I could help."

"I guess I have to dig myself out of this one," I say.

Willow takes a sip of her wine, and for a time she studies the tablecloth that consists of an elegant pattern of interlocked circles, mostly in red, with an occasional yellow, blue, or green one mixed in. She's right, of course. They're all going to come after me, and I'm not sure if I'll make it through this time. Wouldn't that be something? To fail, not because of our product or business model, but because of my out-of-control personal behavior. Maybe I shouldn't have climbed that sycamore years ago. Maybe staying on the ground was my one shot at a simple life.

"I have an idea," she says. "If you're open to it, I'm willing to give up my position at the center and join CW. A woman is ready to take over for me, and I'm ready for a change. If I join, I can become your spokesperson for women's equality and domestic violence. If the public sees me accept this position, it will speak volumes about the faith I have in your leadership."

I smile. I want to reach across the sea of circles and take her hand, but instead I ask, "Are you sure that's what you want to do?"

"Yes."

"You would be our first champion."

"It would allow me to take my work wider and help you at the same time."

"Win-win."

"Yes, win-win."

"I can pay you well."

"That's not why I'd do it."

"I know, but still," I say.

We spend the next hour talking through the details of working together. The vision: significantly reduce domestic violence and significantly increase women's equality around the world. The goals: educate from an early age, legislate when needed, and enforce the current laws better. The money: twice her current salary though I would have given her more. The start date: as soon as possible, which translates to about a month from now. On the way out, Willow and I hug, agree it was good to see each other, and agree to take a couple of days to let our conversation sink in, to make sure we're doing the right thing.

As I'm walking back to the apartment, my step has a bounce that I haven't felt since she left me years ago. The bounce leads to a jog, one where I can fully breathe in and breathe out, where I glide along instead of pound. At a corner, I jog in place and wait for the light to turn green. I need Willow back in my life. I need to stop arrowheading. I need to stop the scotch. Who am I kidding with Katie?

When I turn onto my street, the strongest urge hits, and I sprint all the way to my apartment. Safely inside and winded, I push the up button at the elevator. Before I enter, I call Katie and ask her to come right over. Halfway up, I hit the stop button, press against the wall, and push myself down to the floor. For a few minutes I remain there until I think about my neighbors and about how I don't want them to wait too long for their rides home.

#

The boardroom is more barren than my previous visits. No food. No coffee. No water. I'm by myself sitting at one end of the executive table, waiting for the scolding. It only took a few days for Jason to pull together the meeting, which has to be a record. After his call Monday, the deluge began. All the newspapers, blogs, magazines, and cable stations that have been covering CW from the start hounded us for an official statement on the video. The first day we ignored them, but by day two we had to respond. Zia ran point and did a masterful job of pushing them off with a promise and a hint. "The official statement will be released in a few days. When the facts are revealed, they will more than exonerate Dan."

One by one, the board members slip in with "Good morning, Daniels." G.I. Joe. Phone Lady. Mr. Social. I made up their nicknames on the way over. A little unspoken humor can't hurt when teetering on the precipice. If things go well with the board today, I'll fall on my sword, commit never to do anything unCEO-like again, put out our expertly crafted public statement, and get back to work. If not, well. Planted in our seats, there's none of the usual banter about stock markets, start-ups, or expensive toys. Instead, we cocoon in our smartphones. I skim the *Most Emailed* pieces in the Times, one of which is about the excesses of power in corporate America.

When Jason strolls in, Olivia is at his side. They make their way to the opposite end of the table, as an invisible toxic cloud of male and female perfume threatens. They're dressed exactly as they were for the last board meeting, in expensive black and jewelry. Sitting close together and aligned, I imagine Jason as that famous dummy from the fifties Dad liked, Charlie McCarthy, and Olivia with her hand up his back, throwing her voice his way. I get up to crack a window.

"Let's get started," Jason-Olivia says. "Dan, please walk us through in detail what happened that night and what you recommend as a response to the video."

Not bad. Her lips barely moved.

Still standing, feet firmly planted hip-width apart and hands initially steepled, I take the board through the blow-by-blow, the exact words the woman shouted at me, and my rationale for jogging away. As I speak, I'm more and more comfortable. My words are clear and passionate, and my hand movements are textbook in emphasizing my points: the woman was in clear danger, the man could have killed her, violence against women has to stop. If I do go down, it won't be because of lack of sincerity. As expected, none of the board members speak or move during the entire walk-through. We all learn in business finishing school to show nothing in situations like this. That way we can keep our options open and, when the time comes, exert maximum control and power, which, of course, is the main purpose of this meeting. For the last fifty years, almost all of American business has been about maximizing control and power instead of serving and connecting people. The pundits swear this isn't true, point to the exceptions instead of the rules, and regularly reel off an impressive list of facts to support their argument, but at their core, they're lying.

"Thank you, Daniel. Does anyone have any questions?" Jason asks.

"Has the Internet chatter died down yet?" Mr. Social asks.

"Not yet."

"Do you think your statement is sufficient?" G.I. Joe asks.

"I have one other idea."

Jason nods as his posture stiffens. He doesn't want to hear more, but he needs to be careful. Even if it's as I suspect, even if he's using this crisis as a power play, an excuse to further Olivia's agenda, he has to make sure none of his actions appear biased. That's the thing about hi-tech. If his motivation is purely to fuck me over on Olivia's behalf, it's best to couch it in a plausible reason. That way employees, customers, and members of the press, some who are demanding blood or at least a righteous fall, will support the decision. That way, no one outside of this room will know Jason is a puppet.

I begin. I tell them about Willow joining the company, about the general need for champions and about how what happened that night was violent, yes, but more a result of my outrage about violence toward women. I tell them we can flip what happened into an opportunity to champion women's rights and the fight against domestic violence, and with Willow's help, we'll have instant credibility. I tell them she's willing to join right away and to stand with me.

I survey the room. Jason and Olivia remain perfectly still; they've already made up their mind though it's not clear how far they'll take my punishment. Phone Lady exchanges quick glances with Mr. Social, who is running his fingers through his hair. Their body language remains unreadable, as it's been since the formation of the board. Luckily, the body language for G.I. Joe has shifted positive. As he taps his pen on the table, he seems to be signaling that sometimes violence is a way forward, that responsible citizenship requires difficult choices and sacrifice. He's the only one I have in my camp for sure.

"Thank you, Dan. I like the idea of champions and I'm sure Willow would help. Okay, now that we've all heard from Dan, I think we should vote," Jason says. "We have to decide as a board if you can continue as CEO."

"I didn't realize that was an option," I say.

"We need to protect our investors, Dan. We're sitting on a company that already has a multibillion-dollar valuation. That's more important than any of us individually," Jason-Olivia says.

Well, there it is. A death-vote. I would argue with his points if they were his real motivation, but this is much more about Olivia taking me down. This is her first sortie from the inside, and she's probably secured enough votes ahead of time. If I'm lucky enough to survive this round, there will be more. I knew this moment might come when I first took money from Jason, but I never thought it would be this soon. In this instance, I expected them to give me a chance to make things right, and only to use a vote as a last resort, but I underestimated Olivia. I scan the room again. Phone Lady is looking down at her notepad. Same for Mr. Social. Olivia is trying to hold back a smile, but cracks. Jason, in his best executive impersonation to date, stills until I'm not sure if he's breathing or blinking, until there's no doubt that he really is made of wood. Then there's G.I. Joe, who continues to tap his pen lightly, who may be my only hope.

"All right, let's get on with it then. I'll make a motion to remove Dan Underlight as CEO from CW effective immediately. Per his contract, his options will vest assuming our current valuation, and we'll buy him out," Jason says.

"I second," Olivia says.

"Let's go around the room. I'll start," Jason says. "Dan, you've done a great deal for the company, but it's time for a change. Too much money is at risk, and even though your performance as a CEO has been acceptable, your actions outside the company are not possible to overcome. I vote Yea. Olivia?"

"Yea," Olivia says. "I want to thank you for your service in getting the company this far. Unfortunately, I don't believe ConversationWorks can achieve the goals you yourself put in place if you continue as CEO."

Right. When it's Phone Lady's turn to vote, she looks across the table at Mr. Social, smiles, and says, "Nay. I believe Dan is the face of ConversationWorks, and we need to stand behind him and see if he can make it right."

Olivia and Jason take it in stride. They knew before the meeting started they didn't have her vote. Or Mr. Social's. After Mr. Social votes "Nay," the room shifts to G.I. Joe, who is deep in thought. He stands up, moves to the window, and stares out at the harbor for a long time. I thought I had him, but he's on the fence. What did they offer him? When he returns to his chair, he picks up his pen and uses it to bridge one hand to the other. Then he looks directly at me and says, "I think we need to give Dan an opportunity to work things out. We may come back to this place if things don't improve, but first we need to let him implement his plan. Nay."

Jason shifts in his chair a little. Olivia does as well. They thought they had secured his vote ahead of time. They'll need to regroup, and I'll need to plan for the next round of a war I never wanted. Round One: Dan Underlight by a split decision.

Time to celebrate.

#

The longing surfaces after a forgotten dream—thick and crestfallen—and lodges in my chest. It's the middle of the night, and my sheets are in a tangle. Outside the bedroom window, semitransparent clouds ghost the moon. From my chest, the craving slithers out until I'm dry sobbing on the in breath, until all I think about is that I failed: With Zack. With Hannah. With Olivia and RR. With Willow. With myself. No one can take that away from me. If relief exists, it's not at CW; it's far away.

Part of me wants to get out of bed and leave the apartment, Massachusetts, the country, and see if I can outrun myself. Maybe I could go to a cabin in the woods in Alberta—remote, shielded by forest, mountain, and snow—with limited ways in or out? Or a studio apartment in a large foreign city where few speak English, where anonymity is easy. I don't have to disappear for long; CW will manage until I emerge.

But part of me, the software engineering part, is curious about why the longing is coming more frequently and staying longer, why it's hijacking sleep and dream time. "There's a solution to every software bug," Vidya used to say. "You simply have to look at things from a fresh perspective." Or as Nessa would say, "Go into the longing and embrace it until you fully learn what it has to teach you. There's a reason the dry sobbing comes after a nightmare you can't remember. Stay with the felt-sense until you know." Right. If only I could follow their advice, I might recharge instead of dwindle.

When Zack died, I couldn't sleep, so I worked all hours. More is better, right? I guess that was the start of the end with Olivia. I used work to numb the loss, and even though I thought I was doing great stuff, well. Back then, Olivia wasn't a monster. To her credit, at first she tried to give me space. "Take whatever amount of time you need, Dan. I'll cover your work." At one point, she even suggested that I take a leave of absence, and she did that at a time when RR had started its own descent. But I refused, took on more work than I should have, thought that work and only work could make the pain go away.

I turn over on my side, prop my head up on my arm, and watch Katie soundly sleep, as she's prone to do after one of our sex and scotch binges, binges that have been nonstop since the board meeting. She's peaceful, like she's overcome her past or at least has squashed it while she's around me. After I had met with Willow at Lucca's, I thought I would stop seeing Katie. Instead, like the longing, we've escalated. Twice-a-week sleepovers went to three, then four, and lately, I've been thinking about asking her to move in. If a prostitute moves in with you, is she still a prostitute?

Katie seems to sense she's being watched and slowly stirs awake. She reaches over and strokes my arm from shoulder to elbow. "Up again?"

"Seems to be the norm these last weeks."

"Want to—"

"Not now."

"You sure? It might relax you."

"Yeah," I say.

I stay that way for a long time, watching her as she falls back to sleep. Her breath is slow and easy, satisfied somehow, and her body has relaxed into nothingness. Her face is wrinkle free, and her eyes, almost closed, look peaceful like she's decoded how to soak up the sun, like she has no desire to be anywhere else but here. How is that possible?

At night, there's a background hum in my apartment building, most likely manmade. I've tried to figure out the source a few times with the building manager, but we never got far. A generator? A furnace? It isn't grating. It's quite the opposite; part of me likes the consistency. Tonight, it's more pervasive and threatens to extend out beyond my apartment building, the city, Massachusetts, on its way to distracting the entire country.

The Army of Ego

The Suits are black, genderless, and fill the elevator. As they slowly unload, walk toward my office, they scan everything—the flash-frozen employees watching their entrance, the desks filled with proprietary info, the cappuccino maker that would never make its way into one of their government offices. Maggie, who is standing next to me, who I insisted attend this meeting despite her strong objections, turns ashen, and a fidget subjugates her hand.

Upon closer inspection, I count five Suits—three men and two women—with few distinguishing features beyond pack and formation. It's clear from their V-shape that their leader is Ed, the guy I spoke with on the phone yesterday. During that call he wouldn't give me any details, just that it was urgent that we have a face-to-face meeting as soon as possible. Ed is rangy, with gray Marine-Corps hair. He looks like he doesn't smile often and would say So? if anyone asked him why.

After formal intros and after the Suits respectfully decline any liquid stimulant, we make our way into the conference room and take our places on opposite sides of the table. Ed, using a technique from Management 101, starts off with common ground, tells us that it's unfortunate some communist and fundamentalist countries have banned our product, states that not everyone values freedom the way we do in the United States. We spend time aligning on the dangers of banning software and on the likelihood that the offending countries are the ones who need CW the most. During the conversation, Ed is clearly pleased with his management skills and is clearly unaware that Maggie and I learned Management 101, well, a long time ago. When the break-the-ice portion of the conversation wanes, Maggie opens her notebook to an empty page. Ed requests that she close it.

"Thanks again for agreeing to meet," Ed says.

"How can we help?" I ask.

"You're working on a technology that interests us—aliases," Ed says.

That catches me. I glance over at Maggie, who is stroking her neck with her index finger. No one outside of CW or the board knows that we're developing aliases, though developing is too strong a word. After we had discovered how difficult it was to build, after we indefinitely placed the project on the backburner given the open-ended investment and the thorny ethical issues, we didn't spend another dollar on it. So how did the Suits find out? No one from inside CW would leak information.

"How do you know about aliases?" Maggie asks.

"One of your board members."

"Ah," I say.

"We think aliases may help us with homeland security."

"You think terrorists are using CW?" Maggie asks.

"Yes."

"And you want to sit in on their conversations with a fabricated identity?" Maggie asks.

"Yes."

I sip my glass of water. Part of me admires Ed's one-word answer efficiency, his actualization of a yes man, but I'm mostly surprised by his claim. We made a firm decision to ban groups or individuals from CW that explicitly broke our code of conduct. No hate groups. No violent groups. No pornography, veiled or unveiled. But we never explicitly considered that terrorists might use an open platform like CW to further their agendas covertly.

"Do you think terrorists trust CW? Darra captures and stores all conversations," I say.

"Most terrorists know their close associates well. You have a videoconferencing-only mode where you can disable Darra, and you've implemented one of the best retinal security algorithms in the world. We're the NSA, and we don't believe anyone can break in with a false identity. We believe terrorists use your retinal scan feature to verify a participant's identity. When they couple scan results with visual identification, they trust the platform. That's why we need aliases."

"You've tried to break in?" Maggie asks.

"I'm not saying that," Ed says.

Maggie engineer-smiles, which is an expression us technical folks recognize. It means: I built state-of-the-art technology and the foremost experts in the world agree. How cool is that? She's right to be proud. She's led the development of multiple breakthrough technologies, and she's done it under incredible pressure. I try not to smile, but sometimes, even after years of practice, the recognition of great technology overshadows a controversial use case. Yes, helping the government stop terrorism is the right thing to do, but if this technology is misused, it would allow the Suits to spy on anyone, anywhere, at anytime.

"What's the current status?" Ed asks.

"We started development some time ago, but we stopped," Maggie says.

"It's expensive and difficult with a limited return on capital," I say.

"We would be willing to fund the development."

"With conditions, I'm sure," Maggie says.

"Yes."

"Like what?" Maggie asks.

"We need it as soon as possible. No one outside of a small group of people can know you are developing it. No one else can use the software. We'll require proper oversight. Because this is a matter of national security, we require you to build the software at cost plus a nominal profit."

"Anything else—" Maggie says.

"Actually, that's enough to get us started. Can you give us a few minutes?" I ask.

We wait for Ed and the Suits to step outside the conference room. Maggie is rapidly tapping her pen on the table, watching me for clues on how to expunge Ed and team with prejudice. It's times like this that confirm The Code as one of my better CW decisions. In this case, *Mistakes are our greatest teachers* may help us erase these guys. When I was at RR, we once took money from the government for a noncontroversial defense project. We hired a bunch of people, went through the hoops to deliver it, agreed to rigorous oversight, and, in the end, delivered the project on time, on budget, and with high quality. The big three in software. But after we were done, we also agreed never to take on defense work again. Doing the work in the first place was a mistake; the margins were razor thin, the work was too specialized, and we had to lay off a good portion of the team when we finished the project. The same would be true now. And for what? A controversial project with the potential to dramatically reduce our civil liberties. No thank you.

"We shouldn't do this," Maggie says.

"I agree. But how we say no is important."

"Why?"

"How much would it conservatively cost to develop?"

"Give me a minute."

Maggie opens her notebook and begins reviewing and jotting down numbers on a page entitled Project Alias. Part of me agrees with her and wants to flat-out say no to the Suits. But another part of me has become a conservationist when dealing with people in power. For sure, at times I exert my power openly and fully, and I just say no, but it's often better to get others to do the work for me. That way there's no backlash. Besides, if we unexpectedly move forward, part of me is interested in aliases. Over a scotch last month, Maggie and I even discussed starting the project up again.

When Maggie returns, she says, "I went over our old numbers. Even with what we've done already, there's still a massive amount of invention. Maybe twenty-five million for a proto, and another twenty-five to produce."

"Okay, how about this? Let's ask them for one hundred million with no oversight and no schedule. We're done when we're done, and our profit is what's ever left over from the hundred million. Let's tell them that we need to use aliases for diagnostics, so they can't have exclusive access. That should be enough to send them on their way."

"Why not just say no?" Maggie asks.

"They'll go to the board, and given recent events, I'll be overruled. It's better to look like we're cooperating and have them choose to walk away."

"I get your point. You know, if they do say yes, there is that one idea you had last month that would be worth doing."

"Ah, didn't think of that one. No matter, they won't say yes. Ready?"

We call Ed and the Suits back into the conference room and make our proposal. They ask a few questions, push on oversight and schedule, say no on our need to use aliases for diagnostics, and try to cut the dollar request in half. When it's clear our proposal is nonnegotiable, it's their turn for some alone time. Maggie and I leave the room and fill up with espresso at the Deco-D. Although we can't make out what they're saying in the room, occasionally the volume increases and a few words break through: one hundred, oversight, terrorist. Apparently the rest of the Suits do have a point of view after all.

After we've finished our espresso, Ed pops his head out of the conference room and waves us back in. He agrees to wire one hundred million into the CW account within twenty-four hours. No contract. Nothing in writing. Only a handshake to cement the deal.

#

Willow's office is on the same floor as mine in the opposite corner. That's where I am now, waiting for her to arrive on her first day at CW. Everything is in place: a new computer, a reclaimed wood desk that CW recently standardized, a round wood table with matching chairs, every possible office supply. Part of me won't believe she's joined CW until she makes this place her own. Maybe she can bring in the three photos she had at our house? Right outside her office, I lean up against the wall and wait.

When she gets off the elevator, she waves and smiles. She's dressed in jeans and a black pullover, and her hair is back to being wild. I meet her halfway and give her an appropriately short office hug. Her skin seems softer, and she smells like, well, Willow.

"Everything is ready for you," I say.

"You didn't have to, but thank you, boss."

After some debate with Zia, Maggie, and Charles, I decided Willow would work directly for me. Yes, we used to be lovers. Yes, she lived with me for a time. But all of that is behind us, and it won't influence our professional relationship; I won't let it. In the long run having all the champions as direct reports is untenable, but she's the first, and it's crucial we get this right.

I help her acclimate: show her how to log in to her CW account for the first time, point out where the online CW manuals are located, help her navigate through the infinite benefit choices we now offer, including HMOs, 401ks, and a stock purchase plan. I'm proud of how many generous employee programs we've put in place in a short time. Yes, there's a well-defined onboarding process for new employees, and even a small HR team runs the process, but I'm happy to onboard Willow myself. An hour later, she's firmly planted at her desk reading details about our company on the CW employee website.

"You good for now?" I ask.

"All set."

"Let's meet at ten a.m. with Zia, Maggie, and Charles in the Retool the World conference room."

I leave Willow and go back to my office where I catch up on the three hundred emails that have accumulated overnight. Most of them are FYIs, which I receive in spades these days. Even though I tell folks that I don't need to see everything, even though I preach empowerment and risk taking, employees want to make sure I'm in the loop on the smallest details. As I read, I find myself returning over and over to Willow as if she's my breath and I'm a beginning meditation student. I want to hang out with her for the day, start working on, well, it doesn't matter—breathing is breathing. But there will be no hanging out today. Instead, I text Katie, tell her to meet me at the apartment tonight, ask her to stop on the way and pick up a bottle of Bowmore, and inform her I have something new planned that will redefine already loose boundaries.

I still have thirty minutes before the Retool the World meeting, so I leave my email and my office, and do some management by walking around. Whenever I get a few moments, I like to check in with as many employees as I can. How are you doing? Anything I can do to help? Are you spending enough time away from this place to recharge? People seem to appreciate my walk-arounds, and I find them calming, as well. In my last stop before my ten a.m., I pop into an engineer's office.

"Hey, Tariq. How's it going?"

"Well, I'm working on the next version of Darra."

"Need anything?"

"No, I'm good. Who's the new employee?"

"Willow. She's our first champion."

"Ah. She has creative hair."

"She does," I say.

In the Retool the World, the reunion blossoms. Willow kisses on each cheek, and then hugs Maggie, Zia, and Charles. After that, there's nonstop catch-up. How's Zooey? What will happen to Willow's center? What kind of adrenaline risks has Zia taken recently? There's also an unspoken welcoming of a long-lost founder. Because that's what Willow is, a founder; CW wouldn't be here if she didn't climb that sycamore years ago. After catching up, we take our seats. I'm at the head of the table; Zia and Maggie are on my left; Willow and Charles are on my right.

"I prepared the press release," Zia says.

"What are the majors?" I ask.

"Pleased to announce Willow is joining CW. She brings a wealth of experience on equality for women and domestic violence and will be working tirelessly to champion our efforts in this area. Here's a copy for everyone."

After we all have copies, at my request, Zia reads the one pager out loud. "*Domestic Violence Expert, Willow Kaye, Joins ConversationWorks.* We are pleased to announce that Willow Kaye is joining ConversationWorks in a newly created role focused on achieving equality for women and dramatically reducing domestic violence. Willow brings a wealth of experience with her that she's built for more than fifteen years at the Domestic Violence Center in

Boston. Given Willow's broad expanse of practical knowledge and ConversationWorks's commitment to investing heavily in this area, we believe we have all of the pieces in place to make significant inroads into achieving equality for women and reducing domestic violence on a national and worldwide basis."

"What do you think, Willow?" Zia asks.

"Good. Maybe add a point about areas I'll focus on: education, legislation, a few early wins."

"Got it," Zia says.

"Someone needs to teach me how to use the CW software," Willow says.

"I can this afternoon," Maggie says.

"And I'll need some budget."

"No problem," Charles says.

The four of them get into the details. Zia runs revised announcement words by Willow. Maggie gives a short speech on how easy it is to use our software in preparation for their afternoon tutorial. Charles asks a few detailed questions about budget and resources. As I watch the four of them, what strikes me most is the chemistry. So much has been written about the science of teams, about what makes them tick, about why they often fail. Yet something special between the five of us isn't textbook. It's hard to put my finger on it, but I know it's generative.

"Let's spend a few moments on our goals," I say.

"I've thought about this more since we last spoke, Dan. If you would like, I can share my initial thoughts."

I nod. Willow opens her notebook to a page covered in her handwriting and gathers her thoughts. Having Willow talk with me as an employee is strange, but that's part of where we need to go. Nessa would say that Willow and I are establishing the boundaries of our new relationship, and even though some of them may seem alien for a time, it's better to have a relationship with boundaries than no relationship at all.

"Okay, I'm pretty flexible, so please push and add to these as you see fit. First goal: pass the ERA in the next three years. Second goal: pass our equivalent of the Swedish law on prostitution in the same time frame. Third goal: cut top domestic violence statistics in half in the next decade through a series of comprehensive programs that we'll need to define. What do you folks think?"

"Those are superaggressive," Zia says.

"But solid," Maggie says.

"Talk about changing the world," Charles says.

"Let's get into them," I say.

What kind of programs, goals, and milestones can we put in place? The team's answer: *For the ERA, let's target critical states. For prostitution, let's pilot in a city and go from there.* Is the timing too aggressive? The team's answer: *No, let's go for it.* What could we do to go even faster? The team's answer: *Speed isn't a question of more money; it's a question of more and more conversations started.* As we converge on a plan, I realize that Charles has been more silent than usual.

"Charles, are you okay with all of this?" I ask.

"I'm fine with the ideas, but I do wonder how active of a role we should take. I'm good with champions facilitating conversations, but shouldn't the goals come from the people having the conversations? Otherwise, we're pushing our agenda, and we lose the perception of neutrality."

"That's a good point," Willow says.

The room goes silent. From the expression on Willow's face, she has never considered neutrality as an issue. I guess when you're dealing with women who are victims, who are survivors, there's nothing neutral in the work. Still, Charles is raising a fork-in-the-road question that will, in part, define our path forward. We have to spend the time to get the answer to this one right.

"We need to all agree on one way or the other, because what we do here will set the stage for future champions," Zia says.

"As you all know, I'm tired of living in a world where neutrality is revered above all else," Maggie says. "Some things clearly need to be changed, and I, for one, think achieving equality for women and wiping out domestic violence are two of them."

"I don't disagree with you, and I'm certainly not neutral on these issues. I do think the change goals should come from the conversation participants, not from us," Charles says.

We debate neutrality, nonneutrality, and something in between. It feels good, like the conversation we're having now is the kind of conversation that's needed across the world on a million different topics. The whole thing has an openness, and no one, not even Willow, is defensive. We're simply trying to figure out the best way forward. When we're done, a simple principle emerges. In cases where widespread violence or suffering exists, ConversationWorks will hire a champion, put in place an aggressive change agenda, and work over time to alleviate the violence and suffering. Pretty much as envisioned. However, while we're fully committed to our change agendas, they're not rigid. If conversationalists have new and better ways to do things, we'll welcome their ideas, incorporate them into our plans, and even let conversationalists volunteer to lead threads of our plan. With this principle in place, I check in one last time with folks. Charles is good. Maggie is good. Zia is good. Willow is good. We've reached a natural stopping point.

"Anyone want to have lunch?" Maggie asks.

"Sure," Willow says.

"How about vegetarian?" Zia asks.

"Okay," Charles says.

"You all go ahead. I have something I need to do," I say.

I watch the four of them exit the conference room and head to the elevator. When the elevator door closes, I leave the Retool the World and head up to the stairs toward the roof. In sunlight, the skyline reminds me of how much I've loved Boston over all these years. The Hancock Tower. The Prudential. One International Place. Sailboats are out in numbers on the Charles, and droves of students are walking, biking, and sunning themselves on the promenade. Up here the breeze filters the city's smell, and a freshness contradicts the night air. Zack is waiting for me, sitting in one of the portable blue soccer chairs I placed on the roof weeks ago. His hair is longer than the last time I saw him; his whorls are now draping his shoulders. He's wearing jeans and a New England Revolution number ten jersey that I bought for him years ago at a game. He has a gleam in his eyes. I sink into the portable next to him.

Willow was the missing piece, Dad.

She was.

You're about to become much more than a technology company.

I hope.

All the people you love are close now.

Yeah.

Your demons and enemies, too.

#

I'm in my normal therapy chair, in what has become, regardless of time of year, my normal therapy uniform: a gray pullover T-shirt, a gray hooded Patriots sweatshirt, a pair of jeans, a pair of Nikes I bought with Willow back in the day. No matter what's going on, I always change into these clothes before my session.

"What a smile," Nessa says.

"Willow started at CW this week. We're all back together again—Zia, Charles, Maggie, Willow, me."

"I'm happy for you, Dan."

"We're going to do great stuff with her at the company."

"More great stuff."

I update Nessa on Willow's first day: on her onboarding hour, on the equality for women and domestic violence agenda we goaled and milestoned, on the chemistry between the five of us in the Retool the World. As I'm speaking, I'm aware not only of the particulars of the day but also of the energy with which I'm telling the story. My voice has a lightness and a bounce to it, and I'm talking a little faster than normal, as though deliverance may be more than a hope.

"It's good to see you like this, Dan. You know, our natural human state is joy."

"So you've said."

"You seem to be there today."

"On work, yes."

"Ah. What else is on your mind?"

Nessa's office has hardly changed in all the time I've come here. The furniture is the same. The desk is the same. The rabbits, Buddha Board, Play-Doh, pipe cleaners, paintings, chocolates, and chakra mists are the same. I have this urge to rise out of my chair and rearrange all the pieces, to take off this gray uniform and show her there's still color underneath, to break out the Buddha Board and pipe cleaners and create something bright and beautiful. But I don't. Instead, I unscrew a bottled water I brought in with me, take a sip, and screw the top back on. Then, as I'm staring at the floor, I say, "I haven't been completely honest with you."

"How so?"

"Well, as you know, I've been seeing Katie for a while now, and she's been good for me in many ways. I care about her. But it's also true that she's a prostitute."

Nessa's breath remains slow and steady. Her hands remain loosely clasped on her lap. Her eyes are soft and filled with light from some deep, unreachable place. I imagine the place only forms after breaking badly in life, after pushing through pain against stacked odds, after enduring a long time before finding forgiveness. How does anyone endure that much?

"You're not mad?" I ask.

"No."

"But I lied to you."

"I don't have an expectation that you're honest with me, Dan. This is your time. It's up to you to decide what to share here."

"Don't you think I'm a hypocrite?"

"Why would I think that?"

"Because I hired Willow to, among other things, fight against the very thing I'm doing."

"You know, most choices we make, especially the gray ones, are acts of courage. It sounds like Katie is exactly who you need in your life at this time."

I nod. Is being with Katie courageous? I'm not so sure. It's more that, since Willow, since I've resigned myself to being alone, Katie lets me remain alone when I'm with her. What's courageous about living my private life in solitude? Besides, Nessa doesn't know the whole story yet. It's too early for her to label me courageous. She'll change her view after I tell her the rest. "One of the things Katie and I do is drink scotch together—a lot of scotch. I told you I stopped a long time ago, but the truth is I'm back to drinking as much now as I did right after Zack died. Probably more."

"I see. Why do you think you started again?"

"I don't know."

Nessa remains silent.

"I guess, something about how each bottle promises both connection and obliteration."

"That's insightful."

"I guess. In the interest of full disclosure, there's one last piece. Do we have time?"

"We have as much time as you need."

I tell Nessa the gory details of arrowheading: how Zack originally found the arrowhead in the woods; the multiple cut lines per week, each doused with scotch; Katie's nonjudgment. The whole time I'm talking there's such gentleness on Nessa's face, as though she's my closest friend and has just been made privy to my chronic, incurable, life-threatening disease.

"Why do you think you mutilate yourself?" she asks.

"I'm not sure, other than to say, and this is hard to admit, part of me likes the pain."

"Do you think the pain helps you in some way?"

"I guess."

"Any infection?"

"The scotch seems to work as a disinfectant. Would it be okay if I show you?"

"It's up to you."

Slowly, I stand right in front of my chair. I'm about six feet away from Nessa, who is still sitting. The weight on my shoulders is crushing and threatens to push me back down. I've never been above her like this. I want to return to my seat and sit across from her like we always do, with neither of us one up or one down. Instead, I hold in a breath to tighten my midsection. Then I inch up my sweatshirt and T-shirt. At first, I try to count the bruises, cuts, and scars, but a total is impossible. Over time, the wounds have blurred together and look more like one giant trauma than many small ones. That's what happens after so much. I let go of my shirt and sweatshirt and let gravity redress me. Then I lift my head up and look at Nessa to see if this last reveal pushed her over the edge. Her eyes are filmed over.

"Are you okay?" I ask.

"Yes."

"You seem upset."

"None of us want to see people we care about in pain."

"No, we don't."

"You know, we feverishly guard our deepest wounds with a highly trained army of ego."

"It's hard to defeat an army."

"It is."

"Though one thing I do know is I need to stop the cutting. And the scotch. And Katie."

Nessa gently pushes off her chair and stands directly in front of it. Are we out of time? I glance over at the clock. Ten minutes. There's a warmth emanating from her that reminds me of the last time Hannah, Zack, and I went to Lullwyle farm. Zack was running through the apple trees, and Hannah and I were holding hands and watching him. That was a happy day, rare by then, but for those moments I convinced myself that RadioRadio wouldn't get the best of us, that everything would work out in the end.

"Is it okay to give you a hug?" Nessa asks.

"You don't have to."

"Do you want me to sit back down?"

"No."

Nessa takes a step in my direction, another, until she closes the gap to a few inches. Then she wraps her arms around me and pulls me into a gentle embrace. As I rest my head on her shoulder, the weight on my shoulders lifts. Against my cheek, her shawl smells like freshly woven wool on a cold fall day and feels like a refuge after too many unkind nights. Silent, we stay connected like that until the minutes run out. Where is the Army of Ego?

PART IV—*The Year of the ERA*

Newsoid

Today, the ERA was ratified and became law. The country is celebrating, and the twenty-four-hour conservative and liberal news channels are replaying the story in endless polarized, stretched-out forms. Sometimes I think the reason real conversations have stopped in this country is because of the 24/7 news cycle; it's like all day news is more an oxymoron than a cycle. While the ERA story is much bigger than CW, almost all of the coverage has positively mentioned our company. A few have even mentioned Willow.

She's been onboard for a year and has worked tirelessly to organize ERA support. We targeted six states—Arizona, Illinois, Virginia, Nevada, Florida, and North Carolina—though we only needed three. Better to be safe. And Virginia, Illinois, and Florida ratified the amendment in 344 days, though our goal was three years. Better to overachieve.

Of her three equality for women and domestic violence goals, only the ERA is a major success. We haven't been as lucky with prostitution, and the annual statistics detailing violence toward women continue to be dismal. Moving the violence downward is like playing whack-a-mole; every time we make progress in one part of the world, we take a step backward somewhere else. On our prostitution goal, what happened in Sweden may be unattainable in this country. Too many American men like their women by the hour or night, and the thought of cracking down on johns as true criminals while treating prostitutes as victims is too radical for most. Even a handful of women's groups have come out against our proposal, citing freedom of choice and high wages as their issues. Like most business leaders, they want to keep demand high while controlling supply.

What was it about Willow's work that made the difference this time? The numbers. In each of the three states where ratification occurred, more than seventy percent of the women in the state participated in CW ERA conversations. And it wasn't only the women; more than twenty-five percent of men also joined in. Ninety percent of the conversationalists agreed that passing the ERA was the right thing to do, and as a result, aggregated their recommendations. Aggregation turns out to be a powerful motivator. Why? Because when a large majority of voters in a voting district specifically recommend a course of action, it's virtually impossible for that district's representative not to honor the recommendation. In each state, as soon as the numbers were clear-cut, the action plan was simple. Each member of the state legislature was approached by constituents of his or her district, shown specific data about local ERA support, and asked to push ratification through the state legislature. To be sure, after they internalized the data, most were eager to support us. But some had to be threatened with losing their jobs before they acted, and some will.

On prostitution, at least I'm not one of the johns anymore. About ten months ago, I ended things with Katie. Strangely, it ended well with her actually thanking me after I told her. "Dan, this is the best gig I've ever had. Thank you for treating me with respect. What you're doing with CW, especially for women, is noble." It probably didn't hurt that I paid her for this entire year, four times a week times fifty-two, which added up to a number I hadn't previously considered. When I handed her the envelope filled with hundreds, she said, "Now both of us have received golden parachutes." It was the least I could do.

To celebrate ratification, Maggie, Zia, Charles, Willow, and I just arrived at Kimball's for ice cream, miniature golf (they have the best course in the state), and water bumper cars. In the old days, I used to do these three things with Zack and Hannah, but that seems like another lifetime now. I haven't had a glass of scotch, or for that matter, any alcohol, during this ten-month stretch, and I safely secured the arrowhead back where it belongs with the rest of Zack's stuff. Even though I still have some level of stomach scarring, at least now I can see patches of clear skin.

At the ice cream stand, we order one Kimball's Special with five spoons. A Kimball's Special is the single largest sundae imaginable, so large, in fact, that if you can eat two of them they're on the house. It's comprised of six gigantic scoops of ice cream, three toppings, marshmallow sauce, whipped cream, and nuts. For our Special, we choose Pistachio, Almond Joy, and Swiss Vanilla Almond scoops with fudge sauce on the Almond Joy, strawberry sauce on the Swiss Vanilla Almond, and pineapple sauce on the Pistachio. The girl who built our Special hands it to me, and it's piled high enough to topple without provocation and must weigh five pounds. Moments later, loaded with napkins, at one of the many picnic tables next to the ice cream stand, we dig in.

"This is delicious," Willow says.

"It is," Maggie says. "I've never had one."

"I have to take my kids next time they're home," Charles says.

"An ice cream toast to Willow," Zia says. She dips her spoon into the Special and loads it with fudge sauce, Almond Joy, and whipped cream. Then she holds the spoon up in the air as she waits for us to do the same. "To Willow. You helped change the world this year, and you did it in a way that embodies everything we're trying to do at CW. You're a wonderful colleague and friend, and we love you."

We down our spoonfuls of ice cream, which starts the long journey toward finishing the Special. Along the way, superlatives about how good it tastes continually enter the conversation, and we wonder, more than once, how any one person could eat a whole one, never mind two. The entire time feels like play, like the time Zack was here with teammates after a big win, like home before the trouble started.

Miniature golf is one of my favorite games. I never had the patience for the real game, but the miniature version pumps me. When I was a boy, Dad and I would go to this place in Hampton Beach during the summer where we'd make a day of it, eating lobster at The Shack right on the water and playing a round or two of miniature. Something about that course I loved—the preciseness of it, the technical wizardry, the salt-scented air, the windmill that scooped up your ball and dumped it within inches or megayards of the hole. Dad and I took Zack to that place once, but he was too young to appreciate the details.

The Kimball's golf course is elaborate. Eighteen holes filled with waterfalls, waterwheels, rope bridges, forbidden mines, and clever trick holes designed to delight novices and pros. Charles is the favorite with a real golf handicap of one. In the summer, he and his wife play every weekend, and other than family and finance, golf is his thing. Zia isn't far behind. She played at Stanford, fell in love with a guy from the men's team who she was determined to beat, one who dumped her after she finally did. She only plays on occasion these days, but it's clear from the first hole she's retained skills. Maggie and Willow, who have played only a few times, are enthusiastically all in.

"You realize, I'm going to crush all of you," Charles says.

"Ha. You know what they say about golfers that talk trash, don't you?" Zia asks.

"That we win?"

"That the game never lies," Zia says.

"They're right about that one."

"I'm much better at board games. Scrabble, Risk, chess," Maggie says. "Zooey and I play all the time."

"This place is cool," Willow says.

"It is," I say.

After nine holes, we take a short break. As expected, Charles is in the lead, Zia is second, and Maggie, Willow, and I are bunched together at the bottom. To amp things up a little, Zia bets Charles weekly car washes, by hand, for a month. Like Zia, Charles is into cars, though he's clearly more of an electric car man than a racecar lover. The two of them shake, and we all resume on the tenth.

For the next five holes, Zia and Charles stay within a couple of strokes of each other, with Charles mostly ahead. But Zia makes a run on fifteen, sixteen, and seventeen, and the two of them head into the eighteenth tied. Much earlier, the rest of us stopped competing and became fans.

"Ready to wash cars?" Zia says.

"Let's double the bet to two months," Charles says.

"This is like taking candy from a baby," Zia says.

They putt their way equally until they're only a few feet away from the hole. Zia is a little farther with a five-foot putt remaining. She squares up, smiles at Charles, and hits the ball. It makes its way on course with pace, reaches the hole, rims around the far end, and comes to a stop a few inches away. She bites her lip and taps the ball in.

Charles's ball is about four feet away from the hole. Not an easy putt by any means, so he loses the bravado, squares up, and concentrates like he's finalizing our quarterly statement. He strikes the ball. For the first few feet, it seems off, too far right, but then it starts to curve back, slowing as it inches up to the cup edge. Then it drops.

Charles releases his putter and enters into a dance in which he's washing an imaginary car, first with one hand, then with the other. Zia isn't amused. She too drops her putter or more accurately pushes it to the ground. Even though we're all smiling, she's stoned-faced, almost pouting, and won't join in.

"To lessen the blow, I'll buy the Shammy, wax, and soap," Charles says.

He takes her hands and pulls her into the wash-the-car. The man has no rhythm, but at least for now, he also has no inhibitions. Shammy to the right. Shammy to the left. Pick up the bucket and circle around. A moment later, Zia cracks up, hugs Charles, and says, "Buy the Chemical Guys J97 paste wax. It's the best." I glance at Willow and Maggie and give them the signal. The three of us drop our clubs and join Zia and Charles. Shammy to the right. Shammy to the left. Pick up the bucket and circle around. As we're dancing, I notice the family queued up behind us on the eighteenth. They're smiling. The boy seems like he wants to join the dance, but uses his phone to film us instead. I hope this one does make the Internet. A few moments later, when our CW No. 10 blue and white racecar is sparkling, we stop. I walk up to the family, give the father my card, and ask the boy to send me the video. Then we move on to bumper boats.

Twelve water bumper boats are in a rectangular pool of water. Each boat looks like a giant inflated truck tire with an attached outboard motor and a seat and steering wheel instead of a hubcap. The five of us buckle into our seats and motor out into the center of the water. At first our bumps are gentle; we're gauging our controllable power. But minutes into our session, Willow begins ramming each of us at full speed. After each hit, she lets out a guttural laugh, like she's tapped into some kind of primordial joy. It doesn't take us long until we're all ramming each other head on, laughing, trash talking one liners, letting the spray from an occasional wave soak us. I can't recall us laughing this much together.

Willow stops her boat in the center of the pool. She's gently stroking the top of her steering wheel, and her eyes are soft and filled with something regenerative. Still holding the wheel, she stands up and steadies herself as the bumper boat rocks back and forth, until she's balanced enough to let go of the wheel. Soon after all five of us are in a bumper-boat circle, standing and balancing amid the gentle waves. Then Willow loops her thumbs into her jean pockets and smiles. One by one, Zia, Charles, and Maggie follow her lead. The other bumper-boat drivers in the pool come to a stop and watch us, like they understand and don't understand what we're doing. Then I stand and join my dearest friends. For a moment, I feel weightless, like I'm in zero gravity.

#

The *Newsoid* team members arrive on schedule with the five of us waiting. After a round of greetings, Zia asks them to set up in the center of the room where we normally hold our morning meetings in the round. In no time, two large spotlights on C-stands hover eight feet in the air, illuminating a row of comfortable chairs. With powdered faces, the five of us take our positions and sit across from our interviewer, Debra Dunham, an attractive woman with an Australian accent and flowing blonde hair made glamorous by a red dress. I'm seated in the center, with Willow on one side and Zia on the other; Charles and Maggie secure the end chairs. The room smells like a smoking cast-iron skillet forgotten on a lit stove.

The session came together quickly. The day after ratification, the *Newsoid* people tracked down Zia and asked to interview me about CW's role in pushing through the ERA. Newsoid is the most popular show in America with more than thirty million regular viewers each week, and it has gained notoriety for two reasons. First, the Noid team consists of top-notch news reporters who thoroughly research their topics and report them accurately using the best journalistic standards. If a story is featured on Noid, the country trusts the content. That was the upside of doing the interview. Second, as the name implies, Noid combine news with tabloid journalism. If there's something behind the story that's juicy, they'll find it. That was the downside. No one is clear why this formula works, but in this age where money and polarization rule, it's the new news paradigm. If I agreed to the piece, Noid would handle all the logistics, come to CW to film, and air the segment on an upcoming show. After my initial wave of tabloid nervousness had passed, I accepted with one condition—Zia, Maggie, Charles, and Willow had to flank me during the interview.

There's a tendency in America to ignore teams and single out the best athlete, the strongest leader, the man on top. Yes, Tom Brady is the best quarterback of all time, but he couldn't have done it without each member of the Patriots. Yes, Lionel Messi is one of the best number tens of all time, seemingly able to score at will, but he couldn't find the back of the net without a team of midfielders, forwards, and defenders supporting him. Yes, Steve Maxwell is a visionary CEO, but Peach wouldn't have been able to disrupt industries without thousands of employees doing their jobs. At its core, our work at CW is about teaming between employees and between all of the folks who enter into a conversation using our product. It's not about me. Although I can't have everyone with me at the interview, I can have the four leaders who were, from the start, critical in building the company.

Zia and Debra agree on simple rules for the interview. At any point, one of us can ask that the Noid team stops filming, and we can do this for any reason: bathroom or coffee break, an urgent call, a nasty question. Anything filmed may end up in the final thirty-minute interview; anything off camera stays off camera.

Debra begins by asking us to check mic levels. Starting at the end of the row, each of us looks into the camera and speaks for a short time. As we go down the row riffing off Dr. Seuss about cats in hats who don't get fat or become rats, what strikes me is how comfortable Zia and Willow are in front of the camera. They're not only at ease; they light up when the camera is on.

"Okay, let's get started then. I'll be on a stool, with a picture of the five of you in back of me and the title, *The ERA and the Quest to Change the World.* I'll talk about ConversationWorks success during the last several years, which will be a positive spin, and we'll work with you, Zia, to incorporate key facts into the intro. It will culminate by suggesting that, with the ratification of the ERA this week, we're just now seeing the true potential of the company. Then I'll start the interview with you, Dan. Sound okay?"

I nod.

Debra signals to the camera operator to start filming. "Okay, we're filming. . . . Dan, over the last several years, ConversationWorks has had a meteoric rise. Millions are using your product, and your company is now reportedly worth billions. Yet, it's probably fair to say that many didn't understand the potential of ConversationWorks until the historic events this week with the ratification of the ERA. Was it always your goal to bring about this kind of change?"

"Yes. We believed from the start that wide-scale conversation would shake things up."

"But that's not a new idea. Many of the big changes in history have started in small conversation. Why do you think it was different this time?"

"The scale and technology. Now people are empowered to participate in both intimate and global conversations about what matters to them. That's never happened before. "

"True, though you've done more than empower. You've invested in champions to help shape the conversations. "

"Yes. That's why we recruited Willow. Without her work this year as a champion, I believe the ERA wouldn't have been ratified."

"Willow, what are your thoughts on your role and why passing the ERA was so important?"

"During my years working as an advocate against violence and discrimination against women, I learned that the two pillars of change were education and legislation. For us, the ERA is the critical piece of legislation because it guarantees that sexual discrimination will receive the highest level of judicial scrutiny like race discrimination now does. Until ratification, the Constitution didn't explicitly prohibit sexual discrimination."

"Even though seventy-five percent of Americans believed it did," Debra says.

"That's right," Willow says. "Unlike other countries who've had the equivalent of equal rights amendments for decades, to fight a sexual discrimination case today in this country was extremely difficult in terms of cost, process, and the emotional toll it takes."

"You must be very proud," Debra says.

"I'm proud that I was part of it. Many capable women organized in meaningful ways to push the ERA forward. They did the heavy lifting. I simply helped them connect."

"Some of your critics would say CW is doing too much of the heavy lifting, that the company should do nothing but enable conversations, and that there's no need for champions. How would you answer them?"

"I'll take that one," Maggie says. "You know, some issues call for action. We as a society have been too neutral over the years, and frankly, every issue doesn't have two valid sides. Violence and discrimination against women need to stop, and we believe that's not a debatable point. With that said, we did extensively debate the role CW should play, including the points our critics raised. Where we ended up was that champions made sense as long as we allowed for flexibility and inclusion when working the causes we take on. We believe taking a stand while being inclusive and open to new ideas is the best approach for a class of problems like this one."

"Speaking of a class of problems, what other ones does ConversationWorks plan to take on?"

"We've hired champions to focus on a range of things from education to climate change to feeding the planet," Zia says. "We're excited to have them onboard, and they're already making a difference. It's also worth pointing out that many conversations are happening each day without a champion, and they too are bringing about real change. The power of CW is enabling millions of conversations throughout the world, champion or no champion."

"In the prep for this meeting, I participated in a few of those conversations, and you're right, they're fruitful. What about giving back financially? Though you're still a private company, I assume your charitable contributions are more than generous."

"Well, we don't discuss financial details publicly," Charles says. "But to answer your question, we don't give a lot to charities."

"Why? Isn't that inconsistent with your values?"

"Not really. A system that relies on the haves to give to the have-nots isn't an equitable one. We would rather heavily fund our champions and try to level the playing field that way."

"You sound like a socialist."

"No, we're not socialists," I say. "But we are egalitarians."

"This is a good stopping point. Why don't we take a break?"

We agree on fifteen minutes. The five of us gather around the espresso maker. The interview is going well, though Debra is following the proven *Noid* formula—news before dirt—and hasn't yet entered tabloid mode. The hard part is ahead of us. What are the gotchas Debra might have uncovered? Well. After we finish two rounds of espresso and chat about gotchas that are minor in relation to the real ones, we encourage each other to stay focused, on point, and to call time-out if necessary. Then we return to our seats and wait.

"Okay, we're rolling. I'd like to shift gears now to a more personal topic. Dan, your son died several years ago in a tragic accident when he was only ten years old. A rumor out there has hinted that the ConversationWorks logo is somehow a tribute to him. Is that true?"

I look down and take a deep breath, counting the oak planks that make up our floor. When I hit ten, Zia asks Debra to stop filming, but I reach out and gently press my hand against hers.

"It's okay. Let's keep going," I say.

"Are you sure?" Zia asks.

"Yes."

"We're still filming."

"Yes, my son died several years ago in an accident. Yes, the logo is for him. I first built a pyramid in front of his gravestone, and the idea to use it as the CW logo came from there."

"Why a pyramid?"

"If he had lived, Zack would have had a life full of meaning, one where he built something that lasted for thousands of years, something like a pyramid. He was that kind of kid."

"I have children and can't imagine anything worse than the loss of a child. How did you manage?"

Well, Ms. Dunham, I coped using various different techniques rooted in the ancient practice of sex, drugs, and a rock shaped into an arrowhead, and although that's exactly the answer your audience craves, I've been well coached on staying focused and on point, so let me commit a sin of omission and say, "I worked."

"As many of us would. Sometimes great change comes from great pain."

"Yes. I still miss Zack every day," I say.

"Shifting again, is it also true that you and Willow were together once romantically?"

"Yes, we were," Willow says.

"Isn't it hard to work for a man you were once involved with? Isn't it an example in a way of something you are fighting against, men with too much power over women?"

Willow throws Debra a few bones about our relationship. We were friends first. The romantic part came later and didn't last long. For most of our careers, the two of us have placed work ahead of our personal relationships. As she's speaking, I look beyond the *Noid* crew to the edge of the room. Zack is leaning up against the wall, arms folded across his chest, smiling. Not now, Zack. I need to concentrate. *I know, Dad, but I didn't want to miss this one. You're doing great.* I try not to smile, but a small crack surfaces. When I return to the interview, Willow is in the middle of an answer sounding defensive.

"I'd agree with you if our romantic relationship started while we were working together, but it didn't," she says. "We made a conscious choice, and the results speak for themselves. I'm one hundred percent sure that I wouldn't have been successful at CW if it wasn't for Dan's unconditional support. "

"And there's no issue for the rest of you?"

"None," Maggie and Charles say.

"I wondered about it at the start," Zia says, "but I'm good now. We're all partners, and I can't imagine Dan exerting inappropriate influence over anyone in the company."

"Okay then. Shifting gears once again, Willow, I know you also tried to make progress with prostitution laws this year, but didn't have much luck. Can you say a little more about that? Will you continue to work on that issue in the coming years?"

"Yes." She goes on to explain the prostitution laws in Sweden, why they worked, and elaborates on the challenges of implementing a similar program in America where she says, in multiple ways, men in power would work to undermine it.

"Speaking of prostitution, Dan, I understand you saw a prostitute named Katie for a long time. Is that true?"

"Let's stop filming," Charles says.

"Dan?" Debra asks.

"Let's stop for a few," I say.

I stand and look out the window, which is awash with rain. The New England downpours are heavier these days. This part of the country has always had abundant precipitation, but now when weather comes it's often extreme: eight feet of snow last year, storms filled with golf-ball-sized hail, three inches of rain in an hour. I haven't told my friends the truth about Katie. Or about consuming large amounts of scotch. Or about arrowheading. While I was hooked, well, addiction doesn't kiss and tell, and after I'd stopped, it didn't seem relevant anymore. How did Debra find out about Katie?

In silence, we fill up at the Deco-D and make our way to the Retool the World. The four of them sit across the table from me, like I'm about to be deposed. I sip my espresso. The far wall is filled with photos, head shots, groups working, and company events, much like the wall in my old family room was filled with photos of Zack, Hannah, the three of us, Dad, Mom, Hannah's family, Olivia.

"Is it true, Dan?" Charles asks.

"Yes."

"What the fuck?" Maggie asks.

"Willow, did you know?" Zia asks.

"No. What the fuck, Dan? How could you not tell me Katie was a prostitute? Do you realize how hypocritical your actions are?"

"I do. I'm sorry. It wasn't just Katie. I was drinking a lot of scotch, too. Not to the point where it messed up my work, but right up to the edge, maybe past it on occasion. And I was harming myself."

"You were what?" Willow asks.

I confess the details of arrowheading: the cutting, Katie's involvement, the discipline required to consistently hurt yourself. As I'm explaining away matter-of-factly with a surprising level of specificity, Willow's face softens. Maggie and Zia tear up. Only Charles looks pained, like he understands, like he is afraid because he does.

"I'm so sorry," Willow says.

"There were a few signs, but I ignored them," Zia says.

"If I'd lost a child, I don't know what I'd do," Charles says.

"Me, too," Maggie says.

"We've got you now," Willow says.

"You're not angry anymore?" I ask.

"If you were still in it, I'd be worried. But some part of you needed to go there exactly the way you did, so you could figure a way out yourself," Willow says.

What exactly is that part? The part where loss craves so much pain that the only way to get through it is by creating pain in your body? Or the part where loss craves regularly forgetting in a bottle instead of fully grieving? Though, in either case, there is something to Willow's point—if one digs deep enough of a hole, only he knows the way out.

"Does anyone else know about the scotch or arrowheading?" Zia asks.

"Nessa."

"Good," Maggie says.

"What do you want to do about the interview?" Charles says. "We should stop."

We discuss the pros and cons of continuing the interview. We all agree Debra is going to come after me though we're not sure how. She may have talked to Katie, and even though I don't think Katie would betray me, my colleagues aren't as sure. Maybe Olivia got to Katie and offered her a lot of money? Besides, Katie is act one. After Debra finishes eviscerating me on prostitution, she's going to come back to the video of the man and woman and the beating. Who knows what she found there?

In the end, my dearest friends believe I should stop. Nothing positive can come from continuing. Keep the interview focused on the ERA. Even the Zack bit was okay. But I can't carry the lie anymore; I've had enough. It's best to tell Debra the truth, at least on the part that she already knows. We built a company based on that principle, and I need to live or die by it.

Back in our seats, we ask Debra to continue from where she last left off. She has this look on her face like she's entered scotch row at a liquor store, and I'm about to lead her right to the good stuff. She repeats her original Katie question.

"Yes, Katie is a prostitute. I saw her multiple times a week at my apartment for a time. It stopped about a year ago," I say.

"If the change you're championing was implemented—treating prostitution the way it's treated in Sweden—wouldn't that shift the focus to you as the criminal instead of Katie?"

"It would."

"Do you see the hypocrisy in what you did?"

"I do."

"Then why did you do it?"

"That's a good question. I was going through a difficult time because of my son's death. Katie helped me cope for a time, and I'm thankful to her. Not that this makes it right, but I always treated her with kindness and respect," I say.

"You're right, it doesn't make it right. And you are a hypocrite. With that said, I do understand grief. We did happen to locate Katie for comment earlier today."

"Dan, I don't think this—" Charles says.

"No, it's okay. I want to hear what Katie has to say."

"During the broadcast, we'll play this video of Katie at this point. Here it is."

Debra signals with her hand to stop filming. Her face blanks as she pushes play on a tablet and hands it to me. The five of us huddle around the tablet. Katie is sitting in an overstuffed leather chair. Is that her apartment? She's dressed in a way I haven't seen her before, in an elegant full-length black dress that highlights a single strand of white pearls. Her hair is pulled back in a side-swept chignon. She looks beautiful, like she's from a different era. Debra asks her a few basic questions about our relationship, and her answers echo my statements. Then Debra asks her what she thinks of me.

Katie crosses one leg over the other, which exposes a black pump with a red sole like Olivia's. She places her hands on her lap, interlaces her fingers, and takes a deep breath. Then she says, "You know, I'm glad I was able to help Dan in some small way. I know it was just a business relationship, but what we had doesn't happen often."

"He never hit you, forced you to do anything you didn't want to do, or in any way abused you?" Debra asks.

"Dan? Listen, Debra, I've been around my fair share of creeps over the years. Dan is not one of them. He's one of the good guys."

"And he in no way paid you off to say these things?"

The camera zooms in on Katie. She looks away for a moment. Does she consider the money I gave her at the end a payoff? When she returns, she calmly looks right into the camera and says, "Look Debra, I'm well paid for what I do, and Dan was generous with me, but that's where it stopped. He didn't pay me off. He's not that kind of guy."

Debra thanks Katie for her time, and the interview screen turns black. There have been times in life when I've been disappointed. I thought I knew someone, and then suddenly I didn't. Hannah. Olivia. Others I cared about less. I'm not sure I'll ever understand why that happens, but it has something to do with freedom. The best relationships, the authentic ones, are where people can come and go freely, where there's no need to explore in secret. Katie and I had that for a time. She saw me drink. She saw me cut. She saw me grieve. And she saw it all without judgment. That's why she didn't disappoint today. Though why did Debra pursue this line of questioning if nothing was there? I scan the row. Willow has this look of warmth on her face. Charles has a little smile. Zia is questioning Debra's intentions, too. Maggie smiles as she rolls her locket between her thumb and forefinger.

"Well, Dan, even though there are many men who think about sex and violence as one and the same, it sounds like you aren't one of them, at least with Katie. Speaking of violence, I'd like to go back to that controversial video of you beating the man if we might. Willow, you've said you believe Dan's story about what happened that night."

"I do," Willow says.

"When the video surfaced all those months ago, one of our local affiliates located the woman in the video. She didn't want to go public at the time, so we respected her wishes. In light of the events this week with the ERA, we went back to her one more time. This time she agreed to go on record. Her name is Eva. Stop filming please. This is where we'll play the video of what happened that night and her new exclusive statement."

Debra queues up Eva's statement on the tablet and hands it to us. We huddle around the tablet again. Eva looks exactly as I remember. Pretty. Blonde. Wearing a similar outfit to the one she wore that night. Debra starts off by asking her, "Can you tell us what happened that night in Cambridge?" I guess Charles was right earlier—she's pulling out all of the stops. If Eva contradicts my version of what happened, even though it's my word against hers, the board will end me.

"That night with my longtime boyfriend was one of many that ended in violence. At first, when Dan intervened, I did what many victims do. I thought it was none of his business. I wanted him to go away. My boyfriend and I would work it out like we did in the past, which meant him making all kinds of idle promises about it never happening again and me blaming myself and promising to do better. Before we went to bed, we worked through it and even had make-up sex. I went to sleep in his arms thinking everything was going to be okay. And things were okay for a few more months. Then one morning, after it had happened again, I woke and felt different. Something had snapped inside me. It's then that I knew I needed to end things. I packed up my stuff and moved out that day. In retrospect, I have Dan to thank. That night he acted, and I now firmly believe his courage helped me move away from a violent relationship."

"Any comments, Dan?"

"No, other than to say I'm happy for her."

"All we have time for is one more question. Dan, if you could say one thing to our television audience, what would it be?"

I take a sip of water to collect my thoughts. I want to say so many things out loud now. To Katie, thank you for having my back. To Eva, thank you for corroborating my story. To Zack, thank you for all the conversations. But above all, I want to thank the CW team, and in particular, the four people sitting next to me. Without them, CW wouldn't have happened. I put my glass down, fold my hands on my lap, recall my one canned answer for this interview, look right into the camera, and say, "We all struggle during our short time on this planet. I'm certainly proof of that. If we're fortunate, our struggles help us make sense of the big things and move us forward with our lives. If we're not, we never truly reach our potential. We started CW years ago because we realized that more and more people were struggling not only with their own issues, but also with issues beyond their control. More importantly, we realized that when we struggle together with a problem, the potential exists for something incredible to happen. We seem to rise above our individual problems and limitations, and collectively we find creative ways to serve the greater good. I'm honored that CW, in some small way, was able to help many of you solve such an important problem as passing the ERA, and I couldn't be prouder of the folks sitting here with me, without whom there would be no CW. With that said, we're just beginning. There are literally millions of problems to be solved, and we're looking forward to working with all of you to create a better world for our children."

Debra thanks us for our time, says it's been a pleasure, and wishes us good luck with ConversationWorks. Later, as the *Noid* team is packing up, she asks if she can speak with Willow and me privately. We make our way to my office.

"Thank you for the interview," I say.

"You're welcome. I bet you wonder why I put Eva and Katie on TV."

"The thought crossed my mind."

"To tell you the truth, when I first started I was going for the kill. I thought Dan Underlight was a violent hypocrite masquerading as a benevolent CEO, and I was going to expose him. But by the time I finished speaking with Katie and Eva, instead of wanting to bring you down, I wanted to prop you up and make you into a hero. Many others out there had questions about what happened the night of the beating, and the Katie part of your story would have eventually been leaked by one of your enemies in a way where you couldn't control the narrative. I decided to get out in front of it and make it clear to millions of viewers that you're exactly and uniquely the right person to run a company like CW. To do that, they had to see all of you. You're not like other executives, Dan. You have compassion and vision, and that's the rarest combination of leadership traits that exists. You can thank me now. I just made you one of the most admired CEOs in the country."

"Thank you," I say.

"I would have never guessed you would turn out to be a supporter," Willow says.

"I am. And a survivor," Debra says.

The Blue Road

The colors wake me from a still sleep. The dawn is mottled with ephemeral pastels, opening gradually into full light. I pull the sheet off, and through the shadowed room, the blues and pinks wash over me. The empty spot at my side, still contoured, no longer holds a charge. All that has come before—the lovers, the weight, the loss, and the different versions of numb, of me—have guided me to this place. I'm no longer lonely; I simply live alone.

I get out of bed, make coffee, row, shower, and dress. In the last months, I've shed many of my possessions. I no longer have a television, or books, or art. I've only a few pictures, a few pieces of furniture, a closet full of identical shirts and pants, and a CHalo. The sparseness of the place has centered me. Until these last months, I didn't understand why monks, priests, or nuns live the way they do. For them, it's about communion with the spirit, the divine, God, and not about the physical and material. I understand that now. For me, it's about communion with CW employees and customers, about a community in communion.

Today is my quarterly board meeting. In the months since the *Newsoid* interview, CW has continued to grow. Debra was right—the interview put a human face on our company, five in fact, and as a result, our subscriber base increased by another ten million. Here's an interesting tidbit—seventy percent of our users are women. That's not a statistic I would have expected when we started. It seems women, almost four to one, are intent on taking the human race off its current course. Men got us into this mess, so maybe women will lead us out? Didn't Einstein say something like that?

According to the social networks, the response to the interview was mostly sympathetic. People had compassion for the fact that I'd lost my son, that I'd been broken when I started the company, that I'd built something out of loss, that I'd done debatable stuff outside of work to cope. Though I no longer think about the stuff as debatable; they were choices, that's all.

Another plus surfaced after the interview: companies from Microguild to Peach stepped up their interest in a potential acquisition. Even General Electronics is in the mix. And all of them have deep pockets. Before that, mild interest existed from a few companies, but nothing like now. To be clear, I'm not in favor of anyone acquiring us—eventually taking CW public is the way to go. Still, knowing that we've built a company with integrity that's also valued in the market is gratifying.

Even though it's a few miles to Jason's office, I opt to walk. I've rarely taken advantage of mornings this spectacular in the past, and today seems like a good day to start. As I make my way to the office, a gentle breeze touches most things—the buildings, the people, the cars, even the concrete—like we've all earned a blessing. At the midway point on the Longfellow Bridge, I stop to admire the sailboats with Zack.

Let's buy a boat, Dad.

You've always wanted one.

A fast one. Red, with two big engines, so that I can ski.

We can keep it on Lake Winnipesaukee.

Yeah! It's time for a vacation!

At one time Hannah and I thought about buying a house on a lake somewhere north. When your marriage is falling apart, at first, you consider having another child. When that doesn't happen, and you're rich, you buy a McMansion. When that doesn't help, you talk about buying another one on a lake. When the talk goes nowhere, your wife has an affair or two. In all honesty, I'm not sure what happened first, the talk of a lake house or the affairs, but at some point the sequence of things no longer mattered—all paths led away. And the lake house wasn't exclusively about our marriage; Zack gravitated to the idea, too. Sometimes I wonder why I didn't buy it for him. Or Willow. When we were together, she talked a couple of times about living on Winnipesaukee, but neither of us could stomach the idea of being away from work for extended periods of time.

When I arrive at Technology Ventures, the board members are already seated and look like they've been in session for hours. After a cursory meet-and-greet, Jason calls the meeting to order. The primary topic on the agenda is our acquisition strategy; it's a closed topic with only the board and me in attendance. Later, Charles, Maggie, Zia, and Willow will join for our standard quarterly update.

"As you know, a number of companies who are interested in acquiring CW have contacted us," Jason says. "What we need to do in this session is agree on an approach for handling those inquiries. Dan, I know you've been thinking about this. Would you like to begin?"

"It's true. I have given this a great deal of thought lately, and here's where I ended up. We can certainly speak with these folks, and who knows, we might receive an offer we can't pass up, but I'd like to continue with our current strategy of building the company organically and going public in a few years. We have enough cash to move forward without another infusion, and the company will be worth ten times its current valuation in five years."

"I hope you're right," Jason says. "Though not everyone shares your optimism. What do others think?"

Social Guy talks about PhotoPhotobook not selling too soon, suggests we should follow their lead. Phone Lady is intrigued by the possibility of cashing out, warns that market valuations are fickle, that there's no guarantee of continued growth. G.I. Joe is on the fence. All three of them sound nonplussed.

"There's another option," Olivia says. "Some of us favor merging CW with RadioRadio."

"You've talked about this before?" I ask.

"Hear her out," Jason says.

"When RadioRadio invested in Jason's fund, part of the agreement gave us the option to pursue a merger with CW if CW's valuation reached five billion in the first five years. We thought that was extremely unlikely at the time, so it wasn't a controversial point in the agreement, but we've now reached that milestone and would like to exercise our option."

I scan the room. G.I. Joe is tapping his pen, and both Social Guy and Phone Lady are looking down at the blank pages in their notebooks. Olivia meets me head-on, as does Jason. The five of them clearly did meet earlier without me. So, Olivia has been attacking on two fronts all along. On one, she tried to push me out for performance reasons inside or outside of work. On another, she negotiated a secret merger clause. That was well reasoned. The warmth on my face threatens to sweat over, so I pour and sip a glass of ice water.

"So, in this scenario CW would be subsumed by RR?" I ask.

"I've given that a lot of thought," Olivia says. "Although it's difficult for me to imagine a world without RR, CW has better brand recognition these days, so we would keep the CW name and over time RR would go away."

Olivia is looking right at me. Her hands are in steeple position, and she's tapping her index fingers. It's her favorite power pose, one I've seen her use hundreds of times, though never from this vantage point. She must agree the company is a bargain and that the CW brand will be worth much more down the road; otherwise, she would never marry herself to our name.

"What are we talking about?" I ask.

"Five billion like Jason mentioned earlier," Olivia says.

"In cash and stock," Jason says. "Your piece would make you a billionaire on more than paper, Dan."

"And my team?"

"We'd ask them to continue in their current roles. They would become rich, too," Olivia says.

I do the math. Maggie, Zia, and Charles would be worth one hundred million each. Willow, because she joined later, would be worth twenty-five million. More than one hundred employees would become millionaires. And of course, they could be worth much more in five years if they don't cash out their stock right away. I come out of my math blur and focus back on Olivia, who's been calmly waiting for me, hands now folded on the table, without a trace of emotion on her face. How long has she rehearsed the answer to my next question? I fold my hands on the table, and after a long pause I ask, "And who runs the company?"

"I would," Olivia says.

Well, there it is—Olivia's I-played-the-long-con-and-fucked-you-over smirk. Only one problem, you bitch, a merger isn't going to happen. I built this company, not you. You could never have pulled CW off. And Jason, this is how you treat the CEO of your most successful investment? What the fuck? And the rest of you, well, those who can't lead sit on boards. They're all fucking assholes. I should have never taken their money. I sip my glass of water. As much as I'd like to go off on them and say all of this out loud, I know that's not the way to play this one. "I propose taking a short break so I can digest Olivia's offer." We agree on twenty minutes.

On the way to the elevator, I stop in the restroom to wash my face and run my wrists under cold water. In the elevator, on the way down to the lobby, I gently tap the steel wall with my fist. Outside, the morning is still spectacular, the sun higher and brighter than before, and the sunlight, filtered peach, colors the concrete, the asphalt, the cars and buses, and the people. Do I have a legal challenge? Did Jason have to inform me about the deal he cut with Olivia? No, that was between RR and Technology Ventures. Still, he could have informed me, but he simply didn't, which is no surprise. Can I play the other interested parties off RR and see if I can start a bidding war? Yes, I can float that idea; it will appeal to the money-hound investors. Either way, at least my team will be taken care of; they've worked hard and deserve a big payday. Maybe they'll even shepherd the product forward if Olivia doesn't get in the way. Is there anything I'm missing?

Across the street, a mom and dad are pushing their little girl on a swing in the park. The little girl is screaming, "Higher! Higher!" and laughing so deeply that I can't help but smile. Then another family enters the park with a double stroller and a leashed gigantic black dog, a Newfoundland I think. The girl jumps off the swing and runs over to the dog who promptly licks her face. A moment later, she triumphantly returns to her parents riding the Newfie, with the owner still holding the leash in tow. I smile. Before I head back to the building, the mom notices me and smiles back.

Back in the conference room, Jason calls the meeting to order and asks me to share my thoughts. Before I begin, I get a pulse on the room. All five of the board members are calm and collected, like true executives right before a major fork in the road. What happens in the next hour will set my direction, the company's direction, and our users' direction for years.

"I had a chance to think about Olivia's offer more. Shouldn't we consider it in the broader context of all the interest out there? It may be possible to get more from one of the other companies," I say.

"It may be, but that's not the way the contract was written," Jason says. "RR has a right-of-first-refusal option. We as a board can say no to her offer with a majority vote, but we must consider her offer before any others," Jason says.

At least, there's an outside shot of keeping CW independent. It's going to come down to how many board members want to cash out now versus how many want to wait a few more years. They all have plenty of money, so this is more about risk tolerance, about who should lead going forward. I gather myself. As I make the rest of my pitch, their body language suggests my battle is up a sheer granite wall that not even Zia would attempt. Still, I press on, make my points using a carefully controlled tone and regular slow, steady breaths designed to both pace the conversation and combat the sick feeling in my stomach. With multiple bidders, we can drive the price up now. In a few years, we'll be worth ten times our current valuation. We have momentum; a change this big might stall our progress.

When I'm done, we put Olivia's offer to a vote, the outcome of which is no longer in question. Jason tallies the results: five votes for moving forward with her offer to my lone nay vote. RR and CW will merge in thirty days with Olivia at the helm. She's once again won, and I've once again fallen. The only task that remains now is to develop an effective transition plan so we don't lose momentum. What's the exact timing? What's the communication plan? Who's in charge of the integration team? Are any financial synergies expected? Do we need a retention plan for key contributors? What's the stock option exchange rate? When do options vest? While questions race through my mind like the reels of a slot machine, I hit the jackpot on this one—will I even be involved in the integration efforts?

"We'll need a full transition team immediately," I say.

"We agree," Jason says. "Dan, we're going to cancel the rest of the board meeting so you can talk with your leadership team. We'll put in place a transition team tomorrow after Olivia has a chance to speak with your leaders."

"We've taken the liberty of pulling together the details of your package." Olivia gets out of her chair, walks slowly to my end of the table, and hands me the package. Is she wearing the same black business suit that she wore the day she fired me from RR? "Have your lawyer review it and get back to me as soon as possible."

"And help with the transition plan?" I ask.

"We'd like you to remain on as CEO for the next month until we're ready to announce," Olivia says. "We'd like you to focus on the deal and externally facing customer issues. We'll jointly sponsor the integration teams though I expect you to consult mostly with your directs instead of actively participate. Are you agreeable to that role?" Olivia asks.

"I will be."

The meeting comes to a close. The good-byes are business formal. "Thank you for all that you've done for the company." "You've made your mark." "Keep us abreast of your next endeavor." After the transition, I'll never see any of them again, but for now I pretend a little longer, thanking them all for their wisdom and guidance. How many times have these phrases been used across corporate America? What would be more accurate? How about, "Dan, Olivia's outgunned you." "Dan, I'm only in it for the money." "Dan, I admire your idealism, but it doesn't have a place in big business." How about a response of, "You fuckers, wisdom and guidance are antithetical to the materialism you all embrace."

On the way out of the boardroom, I phone Zia and catch her in the office. I tell her to gather the others and wait for me in the Retool the World, that I'll be there in twenty and that I have news.

On the elevator ride down to the lobby, I punch the back wall, the side wall, the other side wall as hard as I can, until I'm convinced I've broken both of my hands.

#

"They what?" Willow says.

"I'm out of here," Zia says.

"Me, too," Maggie says.

Charles remains silent.

"What happened to your knuckles?" Willow says.

"I punched the elevator a little too hard."

Willow gets out of her chair first, though the others aren't far behind. When they reach me, one by one, they shake their heads in disbelief, give me a hug, and tell me that we can fight it, that we'll make it through like we have a hundred times in the past. Well. Zia and Maggie are teary eyed. Charles is solemn. Willow is seething. As they're talking, I can't help but admire the Retool the World. The reclaimed oak table made from wood taken out of a Lowell mill. The Herman Miller swivel chairs seemingly designed for our all-day, deep-dive marathons. The photos on the wall of key innovators through the decades: Edison, Tesla, Marie Curie, The Beatles. I'm going to miss this place.

After we're seated again, I begin. "You all need to stay. You have too much money, life-changing money, riding on this, and you've worked too hard to build this company. I'm hopeful that you'll be able to convince Olivia that our current path is the best path forward," I say.

"I don't see how she did this," Maggie says.

"What if we all walk away?" Willow asks. "Wouldn't that make the board reconsider?"

"Your money is tied to staying for at least six months," I say. "If you walk away, you may lose everything. It's too big of a risk."

"I don't care," Willow says.

"You should. Think of all of the people you can help."

"You know, I just don't understand," Maggie says.

"Olivia played Jason well. She knew he was about the money and would never pass up a multibillion-dollar payday for his investors, even when there's potential for a larger one down the road. Plus, I'm sure he'll stay involved in the new company and make even more," Charles says.

My friends go silent for a time. My point about life-changing money will sink in with everyone, even Willow. Part of me would like all of us to walk out together. Every CEO would. But their place is here, and soon, they'll all know that in their guts.

"It's really over? There's nothing we can do?" Maggie asks.

"I'm afraid it's a done deal."

"What will you do?" Zia asks.

"I'm not sure. I'm thinking about buying a house on Winnipesaukee."

"I didn't know you like lakes," Maggie says.

Willow glances at me and smiles; she remembers our let's-move-to-Winnipesaukee conversation. Then, with a distant expression on her face, she excuses herself and says she'll be right back. Maggie, Zia, and Charles shift back to how they can make staying at CW work. Charles will immediately prepare a detailed financial review. Maggie will do the same for engineering. Zia will go through our five-year growth plan for consumers and corporate clients. Even though Olivia has seen the high-level versions of these plans, when she understands the detailed conservative underlying assumptions, she'll be blown away. No competent CEO in the country would change our strategy given said assumptions. If those reviews go well, all conclude they can make it at least six months until their options vest. When Willow returns, they update her on their conversation and encourage her to build a similar pitch.

"I guess I'll go along. I can make it work for a time, and Dan is right. It's a lot of money," Willow says.

"It's settled then. Olivia will be happy to hear you're all onboard. She's waiting to speak with you right after we end this meeting. Are you all ready?"

"There's one more thing," Willow says. "When I was outside the room, I thought about a tradition I implemented for domestic violence survivors who decided it was time to move on. At their send-off, typically a lunch, I would read an original poem. I thought maybe we could do the same thing for you, Dan."

"That's a good idea," Zia says.

"The lunch is still a month away," Maggie says.

"I know, but I went one step further when I was outside the room. I actually wrote the poem."

My friends go silent again. Zia looks my way. Then Maggie. Then Charles. None of them can believe what's happening. Strangely, I'm calm. Something about this good-bye is different, something about it that I'm better able to handle.

"I'm not sure I'm ready yet," Zia says.

"Me, too," Charles says.

"What would you like to do, Dan?" Maggie asks.

"I can go either way. With that said, I've witnessed what Willow can evoke with her poetry, so I'm leaning toward hearing it now. But I can go either way."

After Zia, Maggie, and Charles nod, Willow reaches in her pocket and pulls out a folded paper towel. She opens it, reads what she wrote, folds it back up again, and places it on the table. Then she takes a deep breath, and while looking right at me, says, "The blue road awaits you now / With its slow reveal and its unknown stops / may love take you all the way to the clearing / where you'll build anew from stones age-old / The blue road awaits you now / As a different one does me / soon I'll meet you in that clearing / where love will have no bounds."

Zia, who is sitting next to Willow, reaches over and slides the folded paper towel in front of her. Then she opens it and reads the poem out loud again. Then Charles does the same. Then Maggie. When it's my turn, I look right at Willow and slowly read "The Blue Road."

#

Today is my last day. The news of the merger hit the wire earlier this morning, and I'm about to start an all-hands meeting. I'm sitting next to Olivia, who will speak after I do. Next to her is the rest of my executive team, strategically placed to help with the illusion of a unified front. We now have thousands of CW employees, so the live link from the auditorium will be broadcast to all our locations. Last night I prepared my speech, and this morning, I had Willow, Zia, Maggie, and Charles read it. They all thought it was on point. Of course, Olivia had to approve it, which she did with only a few major changes.

The last month flew. I focused on honoring my commitment on public appearances and working integration issues with my four friends. We built a good cover story, so most employees didn't suspect the truth, and for those required on the integration team, we had them sign nondisclosure agreements before they were brought into the fold. The cover: I'm traveling the world to have face-to-face conversations with conversationalists about what they like and don't like about our software. I actually did some of this, though not to the extent advertised. It was my farewell tour of sorts, except only a few of us knew I was on it.

Despite dire predictions from my friends, the transition didn't hiccup. For the month, outside of the integration team, Olivia acted like she was the CEO of RR and I acted like I was the CEO of CW: no combined meetings, no proposed reorganizations, nothing that might result in a leak and disrupt the revenue flow of the two companies. Inside of the integration team, Zia, Maggie, and Charles stepped up. They'd been around Olivia before, and my advice on how to handle her helped. Be precise and factual; find occasional ways to play subtly to her ego. Willow had a much harder time, participated but not actively, and had no idea how I worked for such a control freak for so long.

I stand and slowly move to the podium. Before I can say a word, I'm greeted with applause and a standing ovation, which reminds me that all planned endings are sweet and sad. When the applause subsides, I begin. "Thank you and good morning. By now you've heard the news that CW and RadioRadio are going to merge. As you know, in addition to these years I've spent with you at CW, I spent the early part of my career at RadioRadio. Because I know both companies so well, I wanted to spend some time this morning detailing why this merger is exactly right for our company at this time. Later, Olivia will get up and share her thoughts."

I run through a bunch of assertions around the benefits of the CW/RR merger, most of which I don't believe, some based on Olivia edits, all a result of the Rule of the Unified Front that was implemented early on at RR. Basically, the ROTUF states that after a decision is made, all executives in the company must appear to agree with the decision and be able to articulate the reasons why, after thoroughly weighing the pros and cons of multiple options, the chosen path is the optimum path. My false assertions: as a result of the merger, we'll have broader reach, especially into corporations; the large amount of working capital will allow us to accelerate development; and all employees will have excellent opportunities, due to crosspollination of the teams.

"While the benefits of the merger are numerous, I also believe what we've accomplished together is much more than anything I could have hoped for when I started CW. I couldn't be prouder of all of you. You're an incredibly talented set of folks, and you've only scratched the surface of what's possible. I'm confident that going forward you'll build on what we started and make the world even more workable.

"I'm going to miss this place, and I'm going to miss all of you. At the risk of being sappy, I want to talk for a moment about love. I love this company, and I love each one of you. We built a community, and we did it in a way that connected us to something bigger. We aspired to make the world a better place, and we repeatedly widened our aspirations and made them more inclusive. And we did it all by honoring a code focused on kindness and compassion, instead of exponential growth, which, by the way, we achieved anyway.

"With that I'll stop for now. Thank you for everything you've done during our time together. It's been an honor to work with all of you. In the coming years, I know I'll be following your progress, and I'm sure reading much more about all that you've accomplished."

I wave good-bye. The room stands and applauds again. On the way back to my seat, Olivia shakes my hand before taking her spot at the podium. Willow, Zia, Maggie, and Charles each give me a long hug before I return to my chair.

As Olivia speaks, I slowly scan the audience row by row. Not everyone out there sees me. Some are listening attentively to Olivia. Others are preoccupied with their phones. But those who do notice, smile and nod ever so slightly.

#

"Last session," I say.

Nessa smiles.

"I wanted to start by thanking you. You were such a big help these last years. I don't think I would have made it without you."

"It's been an honor, Dan."

I'm going to miss this office. Something about doing difficult work through routine and ritual ingrains the change in you. All the familiar objects in the room. The numerous health food smells. The worn texture on the arm of my leather chair. The hum of cars passing on the street below. And Nessa. Her capes, her wide expressions and gestures, the way her smile sources joy. It's hard to explain our relationship to non-therapees. We're not friends, yet we might be if she wasn't my therapist. She's not my mentor, yet I've learned more from her than almost anyone else. I don't want to be with her romantically, yet she inspires me in a way I previously associated with romance. I guess the best way to explain it is that she's my therapist. Simple as that. And what are friend, mentor, lover, and therapist but labels, anyway? Maybe we're two human beings who've come together to do a piece of work.

"You know what will stick with me the most?" I ask.

"What's that?"

"That everything emerged exactly as intended."

"Yes, it did. How are you doing with the change?"

"I'm okay. I'm going to miss that place and my friends."

"You'll see them."

"Yes, but it won't be the same," I say.

I tell Nessa about my last day. After the group meeting, after my speech, the five of us went back to a conference room. Olivia had offered me a good-bye lunch with the top executives and technologists, but I vetoed it, and instead opted to be around Zia, Maggie, Willow, and Charles. We drank one last round of espresso together and ate Italian pastries from Mike's that Zia brought in. For most of the time, we didn't say much. It was more than enough to sit together. At the end, we all broke down.

"They love you," Nessa says.

"Yeah, I guess."

"Is that hard to hear?"

"A little."

"Even though you love them?"

"Especially because I love them."

"Why is that?"

"I feel like I let them down," I say.

An ant making its way across the floor catches my attention. Ants infiltrate homes and offices this time of year in New England like children exploring every inch of their available worlds. I pull out a credit card from my wallet, kneel on one knee, and place the card in front of the ant. With the ant on board, I go over to the window, open it, and lower the ant in a window box filled with purple tulips. The truth is the scotch has been calling almost every day since the board meeting. But I've resisted. And last night I seriously thought about giving Katie a call for the first time in ages; I even partially dialed her number before I hit cancel. And when I packed the arrowhead along with the rest of Zack's stuff, when I held it in my hands, a charge passed through me that reminded me of the pleasures of creating pain. I mean, I did CW all for him, and I lost it. Since his death, is there a bigger thing I could have screwed up? But I'm not going to tell Nessa about my near return to the scotch, Katie, or the arrowhead. This is the last session, and I don't want to go into that stuff right before a good-bye. I close the window and return to my seat.

"You know what else I learned?" I ask.

"What?"

"Everything I needed I already had. It was just clouded over. What a scary thought."

"We're all scared by that one at first."

"After you understand there's no one else to blame, not Olivia, not Jason, not anyone, then there are no more excuses. It's my life and mine alone to live."

"It is."

"So I have a proposal for the rest of the session. How about we dress in pipe cleaners and dance? I brought the music."

"I would love to dance, Dan."

A short time later, we're standing in front of the Bose stereo, dressed in bright, multicolored necklaces, crowns, and bracelets much like we did the first time all those years ago. I snap a selfie of the two of us, and it occurs to me that it's the only picture I have of Nessa. Once at CW, I did a team-building session with pipe cleaners to foster thinking outside the box. The designs were elaborate and accomplished, everything from flowers to jewelry to guitars, and the exercise did help the team generate new ideas. Yet, here today, fully adorned in simple, unaccomplished pieces, it seems I'm headed someplace much farther away than outside the box, someplace, as Willow said, at the end of the blue road.

I plug my phone into the Bose. Last night, I spent hours picking four songs. My main criterion: did I tap my foot within the first ten seconds? My secondary criterion: did I hum along with the main hook? This is a pretty good test for someone who doesn't listen to dance music, who cut his teeth on Guns N' Roses, Pearl Jam, and Nirvana. In the end, I settled on "Ways to Go" by Grouplove, "Coffee" by Sylvan Esso, "Trouble Will Find Me" by The National, and "Got It" by Marian Hill.

I hit play. At first, my movements have an awkwardness. I'm a proven poor dancer, and my discomfort seems more pronounced around Nessa, who's a natural. About a minute into "Ways to Go," her shawl capes and catches the air. It's magical as it flows from side to side, endlessly changing direction and completely unaware of its power. Soon after, I stop thinking, stop being self-conscious, and begin to move freely. It's like I've surrendered to Grouplove, and for now at least, the past and future cease to exist. Twenty minutes later, when "Got It" ends, which has the best groove I've heard in years, we rest.

"You're good," I say.

"You, too. Water?"

"Sure."

"You know, I'm only a phone call away if you ever need me, Dan."

"Maybe I shouldn't stop. I wouldn't if I wasn't moving away."

"We could do calls," she says.

Nessa pours me a glass of lemon water from a pitcher she keeps on her desk and then pours her own glass. It goes down fast, and I ask for another. A part of me doesn't want to go a hundred miles north, a part would welcome regular calls, but there's also a part that needs to start over on Lake Winnipesaukee, to figure out what's next, to sink or swim on my own. I know that I wouldn't have made it this far if it hadn't been for Nessa, but I was in crisis before, and the loss was too much to handle on my own. It's different now.

"I guess I'll stick with the current plan," I say.

"I'm here if you ever need me. Shall we mist today?"

Nessa goes over to her box filled with blue mists, picks it up, and returns to me. From the box, I select a bottle, raise it up without looking at it, and then put it back down. "I think today, we should use them all." Nessa pulls out a bottle, Divinity mist, and sprays above us. After that, she randomly sprays the remaining chakra mists: awaken, creativity, expression, intuition, energy, stability, and compassion. The room smells like long grass in an open field.

We move on to chocolates. I reach into the box, pull out a milk chocolate piece, and hand it to her. She opens the wrapper slowly and then reads, "Conquer your greatest obstacle and you will spread love in unexpected ways."

"Oh, that reminds me. There's one more thing I learned here I forgot to mention earlier."

"What's that?"

"I can't harm love in its purest form."

"That's true, Dan. None of us can."

"That may have been the hardest one to learn."

"I'm glad you did."

"Thank you again for everything."

"Be well, Dan."

We hug and say our good-byes. Then she helps me put my jacket on, opens the door, and shepherds me through for the last time. A few feet into the hallway I turn around, smile, and wave my hand a little from the side of my hip.

The Depths of Winnipesaukee

The lake is calm at dawn. There's hardly any wind and the big boats aren't out to play yet. I'm sitting in the middle of the wide-open portion of Winnipesaukee, engines cut on my red 35-foot Rinker Express Cruiser, watching the sun inch up from the east. The sky is still mostly black though the night knows its work is waning. Below, the water reaches down two hundred feet and pressures lost treasures pining to surface.

After I'd left CW, I bought a house, a cedar-shingled, virtually maintenance-free cape with a decent dock and a small sandy beach. Nothing fancy. It's in a little cove and has a few bedrooms, one bathroom, a small kitchen, and a comfortable living room that overlooks the water. The real estate agent, who apparently knew my CW tenure had come to an end, pitched me this twenty-thousand-square-foot monstrosity on Governors Island, but I squashed her dreams of a big commission quickly. A simple life, Ms. Agent, a simple life.

In my cape, I've taken to reading in my living room at night, sometimes fiction, sometimes poetry. Currently, I'm halfway through *Mrs. Bridge* and have almost finished the new Mary Oliver collection. They're both deep. During the day, I rarely go out, and when I do, it's for staples: toiletries, gas, food. I'm cooking most of my meals, nothing elaborate, protein and greens. Occasionally, I head over to the Tilt'N diner. They do a hearty breakfast, and I've become friends with one of the waitresses.

I also adopted a dog. One day right after I moved in, I went to the local animal shelter in Wolfeboro. As I was walking by the cages, this big black, brown, and white mutt with long wiry hair started barking at me and wagging his tail. Apparently, his previous owner beat him often, so at first he recoiled when I kneeled down and reached out. But soon after, I found these spots behind his ears and scratched them with both hands until we became good friends. He's eight, and I named him Messi. He comes on all of these boat rides with me. Sometimes I throw an old tennis ball off the back of the boat, and he flies into the water to retrieve it, even at his age. It's not only boat rides; he comes everywhere with me. Living up north it's best to have weather-proof transportation, so I purchased an SUV. Messi likes to ride in the front seat with the window down.

Here's the thing about losing the company you love twice— it fucking sucks. This time, I was more prepared thanks to mega therapy, but still. As Nessa said in our last session six months ago, "It's simply another change, one of many that will happen in your life, and in a way, they're all gifts if you let them soak in." True, but doesn't one's skin shrivel if he soaks too often?

Today Willow is coming. She visits every week or two, much like she did for The Firing, Round One. She's still at CW, as are the rest of my friends. According to their reports, the merger has progressed on plan. Customers, employees, and the press have accepted the change and moved on. CW has grown nicely, and some of the old RR products are rebounding. To Olivia's credit, she's left my leadership team in place and has backed almost all of their strategies. She hired new champions, invested more in existing ones including Willow, and funded an aggressive set of new software features. I guess, like me, she was better equipped to handle round two.

To be honest, part of me hoped CW would fall apart after I left. That part believed only I could run the company, that it was mine, that it was possible to possess, well, anything. But part of me knew CW would thrive. From the start, we built the company to last regardless of who's running it. That's the thing about a great company—if you put it together well, it has a life of its own. Birth. Growth. Maturity. Decline. Death. Executives spend all of their time obsessing about growth, exponential growth actually, yet few learn to optimize the whole cycle. It's like our denial of death as humans has spilled over into our corporations. With that said, luckily, CW is still in the growth phase.

The sun has now found the water and covered it with a silvery film that's glistening from the gentle waves. It takes my breath away, makes me believe that nouveau adage there's infinity in each moment, if only one takes the time to notice. A few other boats have glided out onto the main portion of the lake, signaling that the day has begun in earnest. It's time to go home and prepare for Willow's arrival.

Hours later, after I systematically complete a thorough list of domestic chores—doing laundry, vacuuming, cleaning the bathroom, washing the floors, changing the linen, and restocking the refrigerator—Willow pulls into my driveway, gets out of her car, and waves. She looks beautiful, as she always does, as if she's coming home after a long day. From thin white strings, she swings a familiar white box.

"I brought the cannoli," Willow says.

"I made coffee."

Every time she's come to visit, she's brought me pastries from the North End. I've tried a few places up here, even tried to make some myself, but nothing compares. We sit on the two Adirondack rockers on my deck and water-watch as we drink coffee, eat cannoli, and catch up. I go first and, tell her about my week, about the beautiful sunrise, about Messi. Then I go off on the Mary Oliver poems. What a poet. I didn't realize a poem could so profoundly render nature or the other way around. And "The Journey!" I've read it a hundred times. The whole time I'm talking, Willow listens closely, watching my body language, fully present. What is it about her listening this way that recharges me like nothing else?

When I'm done with my update, she says, "Well, I have some big news."

"What's that?"

"I'm leaving CW."

"By choice?"

"Yes. I want to go back to more local work."

"When?"

"Soon. My options vested last week, and the center in Boston wants me back."

"That's great, Willow. I'm happy for you."

"CW wasn't the same after you left."

"I bet."

"The other thing is I want to give away most of my money."

"Really? That's huge," I say.

We discuss the pros and cons of giving away wealth. For Willow, CW was never about the money and always about how she could help women in need through her work. With her current fortune and a top-notch money manager, she'll be able to help women for the rest of her life. And I can help her set things up. We make so much money in hi-tech, more than we'll ever need. At least some of us are giving back, though the whole model, one where vast wealth is accumulated by a few, needs to be disrupted.

"I'll match whatever amount you give away," I say.

"Really? Are you sure?"

"Yeah."

"That's incredibly generous. Thank you."

Willow goes off into her think-place for a time. I can tell she's running scenarios in her head, thinking about what she can do now that her money has been doubled. I give her space by offering to get more coffee and telling her I'll be right back. When I return, I pour her another cup, refill mine, and offer her half a cannoli.

"I have an idea," she says. "Why don't we call it the Zachery D. Underlight Trust to Promote Equality for Women?"

"That's where you went?"

"Yes."

"Why Zack? I don't understand."

"Because you always said he was destined to build something of value."

I reach over and place my hand on top of hers. How did I ever blow my relationship with this woman? As we rock back and forth silently, I remember a time when I imagined that we'd end up in a house like this, that our love would transcend all obstacles, and that we'd grow old together watching sunsets on some remote lake. As we aged, any inevitable loss in our physical powers would be counterbalanced by deeper and deeper emotional intimacy. But then I harmed love in a way that seemed almost foreordained. Why does that happen to many of us? I still love her, and she still loves me, so I guess I didn't fuck it all up. Like Nessa said, it's not possible to harm love in its absolute form. I harmed the romantic part, and that's the only part that's closed off now.

Willow gently slides her hand out from mine, stands up, and leans against the deck railing. As she's looking out at the water with her back to me, she says, "You know, when we were together, this is exactly the kind of place where I thought we'd end up. It's modest, yet big enough for a small family. I'm glad you bought it instead of another McMansion. It suits you."

"It does I guess."

"But?"

"I'm not sure."

"Yes, you are."

"Not really."

"Just say it."

"Well, it's just that sometimes I wonder if we could start over, if you could forgive me for what happened, give me a second chance."

"I forgave you a long time ago, Dan, and CW was our second chance."

"I mean."

"I know. Come stand with me," she says.

I push off my chair and join Willow at the railing. I place my hand on it next to hers so that our hands are barely touching. She raises her pinky and puts it over mine. We stay like that for a time, taking in the lake—the sound of the waves, the fresh smell of the water, the way the cove opens to wider water.

"I think it's better this way, Dan. I'm not sure I can explain it to you, but I'm no longer looking for romantic love. I do love you. You're my closest friend. If I were going to be with anyone again, it would be you. But our main work in life isn't around romantic love; it's around community. You and I are meant to help communities. We're one-to-many people, not one-to-one people."

"I did say that."

"What we did at CW changed many communities for the better."

"It did."

"You okay?"

"A little disappointed, but I'll be fine."

"You still taking a nap on most afternoons?"

"Yeah, I've become my father."

"Let's take one together now."

"Really?" I ask.

Willow smiles and takes my hand. We go over to the large sofa in the living room, rearrange the pillows so there's room for both of us, and lie down. Willow rests her head on my chest and places her hand on my stomach. Willow is right in general—I am a one-on-many person. It's just that I'm not when it comes to her. Plus, my days of being a one-on-many person are over. I had a good run. The question is what does one do after a good run?

"You okay?" she asks.

"I'm good, you?"

"Yes." She taps her finger on my stomach. "Let me see."

I pull up my T-shirt until my stomach is exposed.

"You're almost completely clear."

"Yeah," I say.

I shut my eyes and enter into that still place where sleep isn't far away. It's good to feel her body against mine again; there's such warmth. I'm more than thankful and mostly content. Hours later, when I wake, it's already dark outside. I haven't slept that soundly in, well. I slip out from underneath Willow and head into the kitchen. I'm starving and have this incredible urge to cook. Later, when Willow joins me, she gently places her hand on my back. Then she helps me chop some curly kale for the salad. We haven't cooked together like this in a long time.

"I forgot one other bit of news," she says. "I'm receiving an award in Boston in a couple weeks for my work. Want to come as my plus one?"

#

Willow and I are driving to the "Women Who Make a Difference" awards ceremony, a national event that happens to be in Boston this year. Normally, she doesn't go to these things—she doesn't believe in individual awards—but in this case, CW negotiated her attendance as her last official CW act. Tonight, Willow will be honored as Woman of the Year. After tonight, she'll be free of corporate America.

I drove down from Winnipesaukee this afternoon with a black tuxedo in tow, one I hadn't worn in a long time. At Willow's, I showered, dressed, and cleaned up pretty well, all things considered. But not like Willow. When she first came out of her bedroom made-up, dressed in a yellow sleeveless dress and black pumps and a pearl necklace and bracelet with her hair still as wild as ever, this wave of warmth hit me hard. I wanted to say something poetic to match the moment, but all I could come up with was, "You look beautiful."

As we drive toward the event, it strikes me that the city is more populated at night than I remember, with more people, more cars, and more buildings lit. The gathering is in one of the big downtown hotels right off Copley Square. We could have stayed there for the night, but Willow offered me her sofa instead. She never was a hotel person, and even though I once frequented hotels, that phase of my life has passed. I'll head back to the lake in the morning.

After we valet, Willow takes my arm, and we draft behind a few other couples as the photographers snap away on our way into the hotel. At our table, three women are already seated, all domestic violence survivors and all in attendance at Willow's request. Two of the women are in their twenties. In the car, Willow told me one, Joey, was raped by her father. Another, Samantha, moved in with a guy at eighteen and was regularly beaten. The third, Dawn, is in her thirties. She has two young kids and recently left a physically and emotionally abusive marriage, one where she hardly ate during the end game. Her face is drawn, and though tall, she must weigh a hundred pounds. I sit next to her. A few other guests at the table are deep in conversation and barely acknowledge our arrival.

Throughout dinner the women tell stories—of love turned violent, of resiliency, and of hope. Willow and I mostly listen. The women broke, badly, and survived. They've taken the first steps toward finding their own content places, their own versions of the lake house, their own chosen families. Sometimes I think that's what we're all here to do, to go up against our worst nightmares, to sink into a hole deeper than we thought imaginable, and to fight our way out with tools we didn't know existed, to, if we're lucky, find a home with family, however defined.

"How do you know Willow?" Dawn asks.

"We worked together for a time."

"Oh, I knew you looked familiar. You're the guy who ran ConversationWorks, right?"

"I am."

"If I hadn't met Willow in one of the conversation rooms, I would have never left my husband. Thank you for building such a great company."

"You're welcome," I say.

Dawn opens up about what happened to her. Her former husband is a man's man, tall, muscular, a high-paid executive who resembles the werewolf on *True Blood*. Had I seen the show? No, I don't watch TV anymore. He grew up around guns, knives, and bows and arrows. She knew his father had been violent with his mother, and his mother had eventually left for that reason, but her husband was kind to her at the start. He would never hurt her; he would never repeat. Then after the financial crash he lost his job. He started drinking and took out his misfortune on her. At first, he slapped her. At the time, she remembered saying to herself, "Get out of here, Dawn, this is just the start." But she didn't. From there, things escalated. He became jealous of Dawn's coworkers, one in particular who was nothing more than a friend. That jealousy led to the first punch. Then he started taking out the knives and guns in front of her and the kids. He never pointed, never threatened, only admired. Her marriage, like so many other victims, had times of gentleness, of remorse, of this-will-never-happen-again. For years she kept forgiving him. At the end of her story, she shows me pictures of her kids, and her face lightens.

Dawn has nothing but accolades for Willow: strong and focused in the conversation rooms, compassionate, loving. As I'm agreeing with her latest point, the emcee interrupts us. She's speaking kindly of my closest friend, of the ERA, of CW. At the end of her introduction, she asks Willow to join her on stage. Willow, along with Dawn, Joey, and Samantha, makes her way to the front of the room. There, she's handed a plaque commemorating her as this year's recipient of the Peach Woman of the Year award. She poses for a picture with the plaque and emcee before settling at the podium backed by the three survivors. She adjusts the mic, looks out into the audience, nods, and smiles in my direction.

"Thank you. While I'm honored to be chosen for such a prestigious award, I'm accepting it tonight not as an individual, but on behalf of all women who've fought to make equality for women a legal reality in this country and on behalf of all domestic violence survivors. They are the true recipients of this award. Tonight, I asked a few of them to join me on stage." Willow introduces each of the women, not with the same detail she told me, but with enough to quiet the audience. Cameras flash throughout the room, which seems to have warmed a degree or two.

"As some of you know, I like to write poetry, so rather than ramble on much longer, I thought I'd read you all a poem I wrote for this event. But before I do, I need to single out one person. More than anyone else, his constant and tireless support of my work was critical to all we achieved in the year leading up to the passage of the ERA. He had a vision about how technology could unleash the power of conversation and community, and I dare say in future generations, scholars and common folk will look back on this time and say Dan Underlight was a champion for women's rights around the world. I love you, Dan."

The audience turns my way and applauds. I stand and do the obligatory wave-and-nod that I learned in business finishing school all those years ago. Like riding a bike. As I work the room, Willow looks right at me with so much love that, in my mind, the applause quiets, the individual suits and gowns fade to throng, and her scent, lemony tonight, reaches me from the stage.

After I return to my seat, Willow gathers herself with a deep breath and looks left and then right, letting the audience know she's ready to begin.

"Go down now, deep inside
to that place where the unimaginable took hold
to that place where you broke a thousand times over.
There, kiss the pain; embrace it as a child
until you can release into a gentle breeze,
one that carries you far out onto the ocean.

When you can see no land behind you,
when there's nothing in front of you but water and sky
lift off and soar high above the past
closer to the sun and moon than you've ever been.
Stay there as long as you need
until you take them both inside,
until you forgive not only those that harmed you,
but yourself,
until you know you already have all you need.
It was only clouded over for a time.

When you return to shore,
may you know that the love you send out

to all those who hate,
to all those who suffer,
to all those stuck in judgment,
to all the daughters and sons
will one day heal the world."

The room remains silent, as though the attendees need time to let the words settle, as though applause is somehow inadequate. But the applause does come, as does an overwhelming wave of emotion. I'm proud of Willow. I'm honored to have worked with her. I love her. She's watching me, barely holding back. She takes a step in my direction before catching herself. Then she squares back up to the podium and thanks everyone once again for the award, shakes the emcee's hand, and hugs Dawn, Joey, and Samantha. When Willow and her friends return to the table, I give Dawn, Joey, and Samantha a gentle hug before they sit down.

"You okay?" Willow asks.

"More than. You?"

"The same."

During coffee and dessert, none of us have time for either. Instead, a constant flow of people stops over to speak not only with Willow, but also with all five of us. Many simple congratulations are directed Willow's way, and many thanks for starting CW are directed mine. A few women share their stories with Dawn, Joey, and Samantha and hand out their business cards with open-ended offers to help.

When the event comes to an end, the five of us walk out together. All the women are happy they attended, including Willow. They agree to stay in touch, starting with a dinner in a few months. Joey and Samantha live in Southie, so they say their good-byes and share a cab. Dawn lives only a mile away, so she'll walk. We each give her a hug, and then send her on her way.

"Dawn, wait a minute," Willow says. "We'll give you a ride."

"No need, I'm fine."

"It's no trouble. It's on the way."

Dawn smiles, turns around, and joins us. A few moments later we're in my SUV heading toward Dawn's apartment. Dawn and Willow are talking about the night, about the ERA, and about the inherent difficulties associated with men becoming less violent. The truth is men spin out, hooked by their own history. They're unable to exorcise their own pain, so they create more to mask their own. While the ERA will help, violent men will only stop when they learn to heal their pain instead of using it to fuel more violence.

We pull up to Dawn's apartment, which is one floor of a brownstone on a quiet side street in Back Bay. Her kids are with their grandmother for the night, so she's looking forward to some alone time. Outside the car, Willow and Dawn hug. I roll down my window, and Dawn reaches in and gives me a goodnight peck on the cheek.

As I start to pull away, Willow says, "Wait." I slow to a stop. She points to a man who just turned the corner. "It's him." Her face strengthens, as though she's gearing up for a battle.

"The former husband?"

"Yes."

We both turn and watch Dawn, who, with keys out, is about to open her front door. The former husband calls her name. She freezes, turns, tucks her keys away, and comes back down the steps of her brownstone. She meets the former husband on the sidewalk, on the opposite side of the street, twenty yards in front of our car.

"Should we get out?" I ask.

"No. But roll down your window." Willow leans across me and shouts out the open window, "Dawn, I forgot. I'll call you in the morning to finish our discussion."

Dawn turns toward my SUV and says okay. Her face is blank; I can't tell if she's resolute or terrified. She starts a conversation with her ex. They both appear calm as they speak, though the ex's hand gestures widen as time goes on. I can't hear all of the conversation, but from what I can garner, he's not happy about the event. He had a friend attend. How could she go out into the world in public and announce to the world she was a survivor? Something about his work reputation, the kids and child support, his new girlfriend. Willow has her hand on the door handle and is ready to intervene if things escalate further.

Then the ex reaches into his coat pocket and pulls out a large hunting knife.

"Call 911," Willow says to me.

"Is this what you want?" the ex shouts. He turns the knife and places the tip on his heart. "Finish the job and push it in, you bitch."

I call 911. Willow gets out of the car and slowly walks across the street until she's within ten feet of Dawn and the ex. Dawn is crying now and has taken a few steps back.

"Hugh, there's no need for the knife. Why don't you give it to me and we can talk this out?" Willow asks.

"Get out of here, bitch," Hugh says. "None of this would be happening if it wasn't for you and your fucking conversations. You've ruined our family."

I get out of the car. Willow takes a step closer to Hugh, hands up. He turns the knife away from himself and holds it in his hand. "Hugh, there's no need for a knife," Willow says. "Why don't you put it down?" If I rush him now, he'll turn toward me. I've done this before. I can do it again. I can take him down.

"Hugh, I'm Dan Underlight," I say. "I started ConversationWorks. If you need to be angry at anyone, be angry at me."

"As one executive to another then, you're a fucking asshole. You ruined my marriage with your we-can-talk-through-anything crap."

"Hugh, I understand. Many men are going through the same thing as you. We can get you help."

"I don't need help. Get the fuck out of here," Hugh says.

Hugh takes a few steps in my direction. He looks like he's on the verge of tears or about to explode. Willow nods my way and slowly backs toward Dawn. When she reaches Dawn, she puts her arm around her and whispers something. They back away toward Dawn's apartment. The police should be here in minutes.

"I saw pictures of your children tonight," I say. "Your son is about the same age as mine. He looks like you. I bet he loves you very much."

Hugh's face softens a little.

"And your daughter, she's beautiful. I bet she loves you."

"I know what you're doing. It won't help."

A police car turns the corner, only a hundred yards away. Hugh screams, "You fuckers," drops his knife, runs in the opposite direction, and disappears around the corner. The police car doesn't give chase. Instead, it stops to make sure that we're okay. After the officer secures the knife, after he assures us that Hugh will be arrested as soon as he's located, we file a full report. Then we spend time with Dawn in her apartment, settling her down and helping her pack a few things. She'll stay the night at her mom's home.

Later, in Willow's apartment, we settle on the sofa with our feet up on the coffee table and a bottle of wine wedged between us, our glasses filled.

"You did good tonight," she says.

"You, too."

"I don't want to be alone."

"I'm not going anywhere."

"No, I mean."

"But I thought?"

"Just tonight."

#

The scotch goes down rough, like it contains a billion nano arrowheads designed to microlacerate my esophagus, my stomach, and my intestines, on the way toward a bloody exit. It's dark out, and I'm sitting on my boat in the middle of Winnipesaukee next to Messi in a bright orange bathing suit like a lifeguard. In front of me are three bottles of Bowmore, one of them almost empty. A waning crescent moon is on the verge of going out, threatening to leave a sky that rivals the depths of Winnipesaukee.

Between drinks, I arrowhead. Not one cut like in the past. Many, like I'm donning full body war paint in preparation for the last stand. At first, I cut and douse. Each wound soaks in the scotch, and for a moment I wonder if this alternate path into my bloodstream is better. Later, I skip the dousing part. Why waste perfectly good booze? Messi is attentive, mostly waiting for the next biscuit I'll pull out of the box. One per drink. He's had half a dozen already and neither of us is showing any signs of slowing down. Occasionally, he tries to lick a wound, but I push him away. When I finish bottle one, it'll be swim time.

Loves are like lost limbs. Sometimes you swear they're still here, that you're going about your day connected, that you're in sync to the point where you take them for granted. And then you remember the sever—the affair, the divorce, the firing, the deaths—and the fact that you're sitting on a boat alone without another human in sight. How does one stay afloat limbless?

Dad, you're drinking too much.

I'm tired, Zack. I've had enough.

Why don't you go back to the house and rest?

After my swim.

I don't think that's a good idea.

Just a quick dip.

I down the remainder of my Bowmore, stand, and go to the stern of *Willow Tree*. As the boat rocks, my legs and arms are heavy with scotch. I decide that I'll take a quick dip first. Messi likes to swim; he'll jump in right after I do. How far could it be to the bottom? Afterward, I'll go back to the house, get some food in me, settle into that father-and-son road story that the barista at the coffeehouse recommended, and wait.

I dive in and fin down. When I reach maybe twenty feet, I swim in place. Below, the water is pitch-black. Above, a small spotlight makes its way across the surface. Part of me wants to go deeper, touch bottom, burrow into the muck. Part of me could stay here forever if my air held, in this suspended place where I'm closer to loss but still separate. Part of me is attracted to the movement above, to the small light. I can probably hold my breath for another thirty seconds.

Almost out of breath, I opt for movement. When I surface, I gasp for air in the middle of a blinding spotlight where the air smells like sweet lake water and gasoline. A dozen yards away, Messi sees me and paddles in my direction. Behind him is a New Hampshire Marine Patrol boat commanded by an officer, Jim, I've spoken with a few times in the past.

"Everything okay here, Dan?" Jim asks.

"Yes. Just went for a swim. I'm heading back to shore now."

"You sure? You look a little dazed."

"I'm fine. Just out of breath."

"Okay. Have a good night."

The officer watches as Messi and I swim the short distance to *Willow Tree*. I help Messi on board, climb the ladder, and quickly wrap myself in a towel. I wave to the officer and send him on his way. When the patrol boat is out of range, I pour myself another glass of scotch and give Messi a biscuit. Then I fire up the engines. On the long route home, the boat cuts through the water at a slow, steady pace close to the shore. Even at night, the lake has a great deal of activity: parties, picnics, young and old lovers. At one point, I stop the boat, taken by a much older man and woman walking the citronella-lit shoreline and holding hands.

When I dock at my house, the living room lights are on, and a car that I don't recognize is in the driveway. Is she here already? I wasn't expecting her for a few hours. I enter the house carrying the two bottles of Bowmore. Messi trails behind.

"You're early," I say.

"I made good time."

"Want a drink?"

"Yes, please. Your shirt is bloody."

"Yeah."

"Are you okay?"

"No."

"Let me help clean you up. You'll feel better around the others on Wednesday."

"I don't think I can do Wednesday," I say.

I put the bottles down on the coffee table, pull Katie to her feet, and kiss her deeply. Then I guide her hand down over my fresh cuts into my lifeguard orange trunks. In no time, she steers me back to the moment. We build like that for a time until she slows us down and says she needs to dress my wounds. Soon after, we're back at it, completely naked in my bed with the scotch at our side. It's clear that we haven't lost what we had more than a year ago—sex and scotch, scotch and sex. They're equally weighted, like justice, and require few words. Of all the methods of cauterized forgetting, they're my favorite.

Later, after the craving has subsided, Katie rests her head on my chest and closes her eyes. I wrap my arm around her. With my free hand, I reach over and pour myself a drink. Wednesday is Willow's funeral. I won't be attending. How could I go? I wasn't there for her when she needed me the most. Instead, I was here in my house by myself, doing nothing. I could have stayed with her a few more days. I could have waited until they caught Hugh. I could have made sure Willow was safe, but I didn't. She wanted to go back to her routine, said she'd handled her fair share of Hughs in the past, said she was more worried about Dawn than about herself. Hugh killed Dawn first. He broke into her apartment while the kids were at school and then stabbed her multiple times with a hunting knife, similar to the one he had the night we talked him down. When he was done with Dawn, he waited for Willow in front of her office building in his hooded Patriots sweatshirt. Then he stabbed her in plain sight before running off unchallenged. An onlooker filmed the whole thing on his phone and posted it online as soon as it happened. They said Willow died on the way to the hospital.

I run my fingers along Katie's back. It's smooth and familiar and has this uncanny ability to temporarily hold loss, as though it knows a respite is the most I'll ever be able to accept. Katie stirs a little and opens her eyes.

"I like it when you rub my back," she says.

"Me, too. Thank you for coming. I needed to see you."

"You're welcome."

"At first, I wasn't sure you'd make the drive. It's a ways and it's been awhile."

"I get why you chose this place. It's nice up here. You know what I've been thinking?"

"What?"

"In the past, I accepted you as is and never asked you to do anything for me."

"You did."

"But now I do want you to do something for me."

"Anything."

"I want you to go to the funeral, and I want you to tell everyone how you feel."

"Except that," I say.

Katie straddles me, gently grabs both of my hands, and pulls them against her chest. She has this calm, firm look on her face that for an instant reminds me of Willow. I try to pull her close, but she doesn't budge. She's right, I guess. When I was young, Dad taught me that there wasn't anything to be afraid of at a funeral, that it was part of life, that it was important to say good-bye. But I can't do another one after Zack; I can't accept that the two people I love the most in the world are no longer physically part of it.

"Why do you want me to do this?" I ask.

"You already know why."

"I can't face her. It was my fault she died. Just like Zack."

"No, Dan, it was Hugh's fault. He's a violent, disturbed man like many others out there. You can't let him win. She would have wanted you to continue fighting for all that you both believe in. And she loved you and you love her. You need to say good-bye so that everyone understands how much love exists between the two of you."

"I don't know if I'm that strong."

"What would have Zack wanted you to do?"

#

When we arrive at Saint Teresa's, the press is waiting. Willow's and Dawn's deaths have triggered an outcry from women around the country with nonstop coverage, vigils, and peaceful protests. In a thinly veiled dismissal, some are comparing these protests to the recent Occupy Wall Street ones, but these are different, well-organized, chock-full of a collective restlessness that's been stirring much too long.

Katie and I get out of the limo. We're both dressed head to toe in black—black hats, black glasses, black suits, black shoes. I'm sure someone will notice who she is, and our pictures will make the tabloids. The headline: *Former ConversationWorks CEO brings prostitute to ex-lover's funeral after tragic murder.* On the way into the church, all I can make out are cameras, protesters, and police officers. The cameras are for the Catholic Mass, which will be broadcast on local network TV. The police officers are for the protesters, mostly women, who pose no real threat, and for Hugh, who is still at large. One protester's sign says, *Willow Kaye died so we can finally be free.*

The cathedral is full and smells of sage. The press is standing in the back, next to two TV cameras from competing networks. As Katie and I walk down the aisle, I recognize a few of Willow's colleagues from the Center and many familiar faces from CW. And there's that older man from the Zen center, Dylan, who smiles my way as I pass. Nessa is in a middle row. Though she can't legally acknowledge me in public, I'm thankful for our numerous conversations over the last couple of days. In the front row, Zia, Maggie, Charles, Olivia, and Jason are waiting for us. We all hug. Zia, Maggie, and Charles offered to come to the lake right after the news hit, but I told them I wasn't ready. I needed to drink and cut first.

I haven't been in a Catholic church in many years. Dad tried to convince me to go back a few times, saying it would be good for our family and for Zack. Eventually, he gave up when I made a crack about work being the new religion in America. I knew Willow was raised Catholic, too, but we never talked much about it. Once we had a conversation about how much she admired one of the modern-day Christian mystics, Lilian Staveley, but that's as far as we ever got. Willow's half sister, who I only met once and who along with the rest of Willow's family has populated the opposite aisle, made all of the funeral arrangements. I spoke with her briefly a few days ago when I was far into a bottle. She spoke with Willow years ago about her wishes. Willow wanted a Catholic service. She didn't want a wake. Too morbid. Had Willow ever spoken with me about death? At that point, all I could do was go along.

After the family settles, all the mourners collectively turn toward the entranceway. Willow has arrived. Her casket is covered with a cream-colored cloth adorned with an ornate gold cross and rests on a church truck. I recognize some of the six pallbearers, three per side. Willow's sister asked me if I wanted to be one, but I declined. Slowly, the pallbearers wheel the casket down the aisle toward the altar until it stops a few feet in front of me.

The Mass begins. Some parts of the ritual are like riding a bike—The Gospel, Prayers of the Faithful, Our Father. Even though I'm not listening to what the priest is saying, I mouth, "Amen," at the appropriate times. When the priest finishes his homily, he waves me up. Katie whispers in my ear, "Just be yourself." I stand and make my way to the podium. When I've spoken in the past, an adrenaline rush normally occurred right about now. The first time I was in front of hundreds of people, I thought the rush was about fear and froze, but over time I learned it was more to get me ready for the performance. Today there is no rush.

At the podium, I survey the room. It's filled with friends, colleagues, Willow-admirers, relatives, and the press; many are radiating grief, outrage, and love. I take all that in. When I spoke at Zack's funeral, I said a lot of things I thought should be true about loss, but I didn't believe them. I was searching for wisdom instead of vulnerability; I was trying to make sense of the inexplicable. But it didn't work. Today, in front of all of these people, in front of God, spirit, the mystics, the universe, and Willow, I'm going to say what I truly and deeply feel. I take a deep breath, notice my finger is tapping as fast as it will go on the podium, glance at the front row, and begin.

"I loved Willow Kaye with all of my heart. There are few people you meet in a lifetime that you know you can love deeply. There's something between you, something you can't quite put your finger on—a spark, a look, whatever—that penetrates you. You're meant to learn something from them, if only you can keep fear or convention at bay. Willow turned out to be one of the two great loves in my life and one of my greatest teachers, and for the brief time we spent together, my dearest friend. Contrary to popular views, our love deepened the most when we were no longer together romantically. Here's what I learned from her.

"First, a Triumph is a magnet for women with wild hair. When said woman walks up to you while you're driving your TR6, tells you that she loves your car, and wants a ride, accept that the ride you're about to go on has nothing to do with fast cars.

"Second, apple blossoms are the stuff of mystics. When Willow and I spent a day in their presence, they helped us bloom in ways previously unimaginable and in ways that guided us forward toward our true selves.

"Third, when everyone doubts you, when you doubt yourself the most, climb a sycamore tree with your love and hold hands. Up there, the clutter subsides, the air is clearer, and you can see what you must do to live and breathe when you return to the ground. When we climbed our tree together, we glimpsed the birth of a company, the elimination of violence toward women, and a love that I now know will transcend death.

"Fourth, when you love someone, when you are most afraid she will hurt or betray you, surrender instead of surveil. Trying to secretly verify your worst fears only strengthens them and dishonors your love. And chances are, opening up to your partner will not only help you calm down, but also will deepen your love. Willow understood this long before I did.

"Fifth, when you can, jump off a swing at the highest point and fly for a time. For many of my work years, I thought work was about the team, about building great products, about customers who loved your stuff, about the conversations. I guess all of that is true. Look around you and think for a moment about what CW accomplished through our conversations, products, and teams. Now, though, I realize work, at its best, is about more than those things. It's about loving partnerships, ones filled with seeds of possibility, ones that can help you fly even when you face huge obstacles. I had a loving partnership like that with Willow, and she's the one who taught me obstacles are like swings. You can either jump off them at the highest point and go higher, or you can stay on them, and let them hold you back until you no longer have enough momentum to soar. With Willow, I learned how to regularly go higher. With Willow, I learned how to jump off at the highest point and fly.

"Finally, know you can do almost anything when you have a friend who is your equal, who inspires you, who sees you, and who writes beautiful poems that sometimes infuriate you and that you sometimes want to shred into a million pieces. Except I never did. Instead, I invariably asked myself, 'How did she know that?' or simply said, 'Thank you.' Pass an amendment, unite a movement, help make the world more workable, love fully, heal. All of these things and more were possible with Willow.

"Willow's favorite Thoreau poem was just one line: *My life has been the poem I would have writ, but I could not both live and utter it.* She lived her life that way better than anyone I've known. If she was to give us one bit of advice, it would be to live our lives fully, and as she recently said, to do it in a way that sends love out to all of the daughters and sons, so that one day they heal the world."

When I return to my seat, Katie puts her hand on my thigh and pats it a few times.

"Did that go okay?" I ask.

"Better than okay."

The Good-bye Return

Jason steps into the boat, wearing his white yachting cap with his pipe lit, and tells me that he's smoking tobacco—a 1776 Boston Whaler blend—he bought especially for this trip. He's wearing a blue blazer, a pink oxford shirt, plaid pants, and midship boat shoes. He opens with the standards: it's good to be here, lake life suits me, what happened in the boardroom Was Only Business. WOB. What other harm has the man caused under the guise of WOB? After I ward off a violent urge, we undock and head out into the main portion of the lake. There, I full throttle *Willow Tree*. The wind presses up against my face and, in harmony with the autumn sun, grants immunity from money and power.

After the funeral, Katie and I stayed the night and spent time with Zia, Charles, and Maggie at Zia's new brownstone downtown. It's modern, fit for a goddess, one of the many spoils of CW's success, and for a short time made me remember Revolutionary Road. In her living room, we didn't talk much about Willow. Instead, we played Scrabble well into the early morning, drank a lot of cabernet, made sure we held hands often, and thanked the Scrabble gods whenever someone had a triple word score. At one point, I started making up poem fragments from words on the board—simple life still, garden of begin, death comes softly—but I gave up quickly. Willow is the

323

only poet in this family. Eventually, we all fell asleep on the sofas; I guess none of us could handle another good-bye, even an I'm-headed-off-to-bed one.

Back at the lake, I settled into a routine. Each day, I digested a book of poetry, toured with Messi around the lake, and slowly built stonewalls around the perimeter of the property with abundant rocks in need of purpose. I gave up scotch. I gave up arrowheading. I gave up anything that might numb the grief and slow going through. In retrospect, that could have been part of The Code: no matter what, do not numb. Occasionally, one of my three friends came to visit, but it wasn't as often as in the past. Olivia kept them more than busy. Katie did stop in one more time after my return for what turned out to be our second good-bye. Somehow Willow's death changed us, and our rekindled arrangement no longer made sense. To be clear, Willow's death didn't distance Katie—I would do almost anything to help her if she was in need. We just won't have sex again.

In the middle of the lake, I kill the engines. *Willow Tree* slowly coasts to a stop as I pull out a beer and a bottled water from the fridge. A moment later, Jason and I are at the back of the boat, sitting across from each other. Messi is at my feet, trying to decide if he should nap or guard. As the boat rocks back and forth, I hand Messi an energy biscuit in case he needs to guard. Jason is taking it all in, sipping his Sam Adams Octoberfest out of a tall glass.

"The lake is beautiful. I should buy a place on Governors Island," Jason says.

"It is beautiful."

"You seem calm here."

"I'm okay."

"You know, I think about Willow often. Her death was hard for all of us."

Right. I thank Jason for his kind words, and we both agree that she was one in a million. How cliché. Then he switches topics and asks me more about Winnipesaukee. What surprises most visitors when they first come to the lake is its size, 44,500 acres with 178 miles of shoreline, and the number of islands, 258, all of which have a certain charm to those of us living alone. Rattlesnake Island has a four-hundred-foot cliff I recently climbed with Zia. Nine Acre Island is actually thirteen acres. A few times these last months, I've thought about buying one of the islands, but in the end I couldn't bring myself to leave my current place, to abandon all that's stored there. Later, after we finish Wikipediaing about Winnipesaukee, one of the giants passes, a 1949 fifty-three-foot Chris Craft Conqueror with rare triple engines. Its wake causes us to balance our drinks until the water settles.

"I didn't know you could have boats that large on the lake," Jason says.

"There are a few."

"I'll have to buy one right after I buy the house."

Jason uncrosses one leg and crosses the other. He takes his time filling his pipe, packing in the tobacco in a way, he tells me, that maximizes the smoking experience. In the lake breeze, the pipe struggles to catch the fire but after a few tries sucks it in. Jason takes a deep hit on the pipe and then blows out a fleeting smoke cloud.

"Ever think about getting back in the game?" he asks.

"Not really. CW was it for me."

"I figured. Just thought I'd ask."

Jason pushes up off the arms of his chair, asks me if I want another drink, and puffs toward the fridge. Even if I wanted to get back in, which I don't, I don't need Jason anymore, and I can't imagine a scenario where I would. Money? I have enough. Advice? Always, but not from him. Connections? I have my own. What is it about folks like Jason that makes them forget history? The headline: *Jason Knight's management opus, The Book of Money and Forgetting, debuts at number one on the New York Times Fiction Bestseller List.*

When Jason returns, he hands me an unrequested Sam Adams and asks, "What if you could come back to CW?"

"You're kidding, right?"

"No."

"What about Olivia?"

"Olivia's done well with the company, and the board is happy with her progress. With that said, the outcry after Willow's and Dawn's deaths and the way you handled them has led the board to conclude that you're the right person to take the company forward. Have you followed the press and the protests and how your eulogy has gone viral? After you pledged the billion last month to educate the masses on domestic violence and sexual discrimination, the press, the protesters, and many of our consumer customers, seventy percent of whom are women, canonized you. Even that woman from Newsoid who went after you on national television, Debra Something, called for your reinstatement."

"Debra Dunham."

"Right. Then the other day the new CEO of Peach called one of the board members and mentioned in passing that CW will always be your company whether you're at the helm or not. That got us thinking."

"Who's their new CEO?"

"Sarah Fordiano."

I haven't followed current events since I left CW. Friends forwarded on pieces, but I only skimmed them sporadically and without real interest. I did hear that Debra Dunham called for my reinstatement, hadn't heard the protests had escalated, and didn't know Sarah was the new CEO of Peach. Funny how a conversation on a park bench with Sarah years ago helped create a potential tipping point now. Seventy percent of CW consumer customers are still women—that's why Jason's here. The board is afraid—very afraid. I wouldn't be surprised if a bunch of female customers organized and threatened CW with pulling their business unless their demands were met. That's what CW taught them to do—converse, organize, act.

"I assume Olivia has a hefty contract," I say.

"We'd have to buy her out."

"The old RR board members support this?"

"Enough."

"The nonsupporters would have to go."

"We agree."

"I'd require complete control with no possibility of removal."

"We're agreeable to that as well. The company is yours to run for the next decade."

"Olivia will fight it."

"She will, but she's already lost. We have the votes," he says.

After another beer, another pipe, and more talk about lakefront property, we head back to shore past Governors Island where a few of the homes have *For Sale* signs. Jason asks me how much they're worth, and I ballpark them. Three million. Five million. Ten million. He writes down the phone number for the ostentatious oversized ten-million-dollar one. What would Willow say about Jason's job offer? *Take CW back, Dan. It's poetic justice. The board is right. CW will be your company for as long as you want to run it. There's so much more good you can do.* Or maybe, *Live a simple life, Dan. Find yourself a woman and have a boatload of kids. Find local work that inspires you.* Or maybe, *It's your decision, Dan. Only you can make it. I'll fully support whatever you decide.*

After we dock, I walk Jason to his car where I tell him that I'll sleep on his offer and make a final decision in a couple of days. If I do go back, at least I know what must be done. The board must be reconstructed. The integration of the two companies must be accelerated. The product road maps must include more big bets. If I do go back, the key will be my contract. Every critical point has to be in writing with no wiggle room. I require complete control and a board that's primary purpose is to rubber-stamp my big bet strategy, a strategy that includes a much wider distribution of wealth to employees. Would any board be willing to give away that much power and wealth?

Later, I put on an old Marvin Gaye album *What's Going On* and open a bottle of Willow's favorite wine, a nine-dollar Columbia Crest cabernet. "Who needs a hundred-dollar bottle of wine when this stuff exists," she'd say every time we opened one. It would be hard to leave this house. When someone leaves you, by choice or in death, the suffering is more bearable in certain places, places that somehow connect you to both loss and kindness. In those places, at least you can ask your questions. How do you go on when your son dies, your company and wife abandon you, and your true love leaves you once by choice and once by violence? How do you let go? How do you forgive? In fact, who am I supposed to forgive? In those places, I find peace in routine, even love in the small things I encounter each day—the wind against my face on open water, the loyalty of a dog, the majesty in the rocks. Maybe this is where I belong?

One thing I do know for sure now is that I was wrong that day I spoke at Willow's funeral. There have been three great loves in my life—Zack, Willow, and CW.

#

Messi and I get off the elevator at the CW corporate headquarters building in Concord. After the merger, Olivia declared the old RR headquarters the new CW headquarters. Some of the CW people from the city protested the change, but not much; the campus here is pastoral and possibility provoking. It even has a barista-operated

Nuova Simonelli Aurelia Digit Three Group Espresso Maker on every floor.

Familiar faces from premerger RR and CW line up and applaud our arrival. I haven't seen most of the RR people since I left this building years ago. Messi doesn't discriminate as he works the crowd with kisses, paw shakes, and tail wags. I draft behind him, alternating between hugs and handshakes on my way to my new corner office, the same office that Olivia inhabited during her RR and CW tenures.

As part of the transition, Zia had the office remodeled. Everything in it has that new product smell: the desk, the leather chairs, the fresh coat of white paint, the new Brazilian cherry hardwood floor. But what draws my attention is the view. It's as beautiful as I remember. The fall leaves are dotted with rich reds, bright yellows, and burnt oranges, though today I'm drawn to the greens. They're living fully in the morning sun, aware and unaware of the endless rebirth cycle that lies ahead.

At my desk, sitting in what has to be the world's most comfortable executive chair, I wait. Olivia will be here soon to do a contractually obligated transition meeting. She didn't take her firing well. Who would? She tried every trick in the book to hold on. Apparently, she got word that a coup was in progress from one of the board loyalists, and as a result clandestinely attempted to swing support her way ahead of the formal board meeting. In the end, though, Jason was right; we had enough votes: five yeas to four nays. Once ousted, Olivia threw a tantrum in the boardroom. She hurled pens and pads at board members, threatened to expose certain members' transgressions, and finally stormed out of the room, beet red, after knocking over a few empty chairs. In all of her years in hi-tech, she'd never been fired.

After boxes with my personal belongings have been delivered and after I've hung photos of Zack, Willow, my family, and my CW family, my secretary, Annette, pops into my office and asks me if I'm ready for Olivia. Well. A moment later, Olivia enters dressed in a royal blue business suit, black pumps, and white pearls, carrying herself more like a presidential candidate than a dethroned CEO. In front of my desk, she sits down in the chair directly across from mine, crosses one leg over the other, and rests her hands, fingers interlaced, on her lap. She's wearing a new perfume I don't recognize, one unsuccessful in concealing her dolor.

"Dan."

"Olivia."

"I've made a list of all the issues I was working at the time of the change. Shall I go through them for you?"

Olivia opens a portfolio filled on both inside pages with handwritten work items. As she walks me through each item— cultural integration of the two companies, quarter-to-date financials, cash position, pending R&D decisions, merger and acquisition activity, new executive hires—she's calm and collected, at her best. Seeing her like this, professional and articulate, exuding intelligence, reminds me of a time years ago, on the day RR went public, when I was sure she'd take over the technology world. Who would have predicted? This time her professionalism is about cash. She's about to become wealthier, much wealthier, and this meeting is one of the last gates to a huge payday. A couple of hours later, after we've covered the forty-seventh item on her list, she closes the portfolio and squarely places it on my desk.

"Thank you. That was helpful," I say.

"You're welcome. CW is a revolutionary company, the culmination of everything we talked about all those years ago. But you already know that."

"I do."

Olivia stands up, walks over to the window, and presses her five fingertips against the glass as if she's trying to touch the untouchable, as if there's a face of a little boy on the other side of the glass instead of a forest. As she drifts in thought, her face blotches slightly red in a way I haven't seen before. I stand and join her. She lowers her hand to her side, turns her head to the right, and focuses on a particular patch of woods.

"The view was always my favorite part of this office," she says. "Do you see that big oak over there?"

"Yes. It's majestic."

"It reminds me of my childhood home before Dad died. We had an oak like that in the yard that he loved. He'd go out and sit under it in the summer with my mom, and the two of them would talk for hours about things like their garden, crossword puzzles, and the Red Sox. My father loved the daily crossword puzzle and finished them in no time. My mother loved the Red Sox and listened to the games under the tree on this broken-down radio she refused to replace. And they both loved their garden. In their later years, it was their refuge. After RR had moved into this building, every time I struggled with a decision, I turned to that oak tree for an answer, and it rarely let me down."

"What a beautiful memory," I say.

"I've never told anyone that story before."

"I'm glad you told me."

"You know, we've known each other for more than twenty years now."

"I was thinking the same."

"We were so close," she says.

I nod and put my hand on Olivia's shoulder. Without looking away from the tree, she slides her arm around my lower back. I slide my hand off her shoulder until my arm matches hers and is around her lower back. We stay like that, silent, in a sort of connected reverie, as though we're waiting for the oak tree to guide us. Olivia holds a distinct place in my heart—we're old friends and old enemies, and twenty years is a long time. Most of it was good, but the odium in recent years stained the rest. Why does that often happen between close friends, colleagues, lovers?

"As I was walking over here, it occurred to me that your firing was one of the best things that ever happened to you," she says.

"Someone once told me loss is the biggest teacher if you let it be."

"I'm still struggling with that one."

"We all do."

Arms back at our sides, we focus on the tree. It borders the woods, and at some point, a landscaper cleared many of the trees around it, giving it room to spread out over time. It's now almost as wide as it is high. A few of its leaves have yellowed, but most are green. The only things that have fallen from it so far are acorns, and when winter arrives, it will be the last to shed completely. After everything that's happened, after the beginning, the good years, the betrayal, the combat, the love, the hate, it's good to stand next to Olivia in this place.

"Do you know why I fired you?"

"No."

"You were broken up over Zack. I tried to get you to take a leave, but all you wanted to do was work. That would have been okay if your productivity had been at the same level, but it wasn't, and unfortunately, for the first time in our relationship I lost faith. That's why I brought in the consultants. As you know, we had intractable problems that year, and I needed a number two I could count on, but I couldn't rely on you when you were deeply grieving. I don't know if you remember this, but you even came to work drunk a few times that year. Each time, I covered for you, said you were having a bad day, and had someone drive you home. Now, I realize letting you go cost us our friendship, but I didn't know that at the time. I thought we would recover and work through it, like we always did. I wish I had handled it better."

A wave of warmth passes through me. I reach over and take Olivia's hand and turn my head her way. She's trying to hold back tears, but one escapes down her left cheek. In the years I've known her, I've never seen her cry, not even when Zack died. I remember her saying to me at the time, "I'm going to be strong for you, until you regain your strength."

"Thank you for telling me," I say.

"I owed you that a long time ago."

"You were right. My heart wasn't in work. It wasn't in anything but grief. I'm sorry I let you down."

"You were dealing with a lot."

"Still. You were my closest friend. You were family. I should have done better."

"There was so much weight, Dan. From Zack's death and from RR collapsing, we did the best we could. You know, you were family, too."

"I'm glad we had this talk."

"Me, too."

"What will you do next?"

"I'm going to take some time off. I haven't had a proper vacation in years."

"That's a good idea."

"I hope we stay in touch. Maybe we could work on getting back to what we had?" she asks.

Not that long ago, I longed to hear Olivia call me back. I played endless variations of *It was my biggest mistake, Dan. RR needs you, and I need you.* But that time has passed. We could start the friendship over again, maybe we just did, but work will get in the way for both of us soon. That's the thing about Olivia and me. Work spawned our friendship, not the other way around.

"Maybe when we're both done. You're not done yet, Olivia, and neither am I. You'll find another company and go for another round. And that will take all of your emotional capacity. And I'll throw all of mine into CW. We're not the kind of people who have deep friendships outside of work. Deep down, we both know that."

#

Maggie is standing next me, a little nervous. I'm nervous, too. The room looks like all the others—a number of comfortable chairs in a circle with CHalos above them and CSpectacles waiting for us on the chairs. To the trained eye, these halos and spectacles look different, more modern, like the next generations of the technology, which in a way is true. The CHalo is black and both thinner and wider than the current version with extra lens designed to make the image projected in the conversation room more lifelike. On the floor, the circular base is thicker and contains a ton of extra processing power dedicated to creating the alias. The CSpectacles, also black, are smaller than previous versions, and could pass as an oversized pair of Ray-Bans. Of course, with their glasses on, no one in the conversation room will see any of the hardware.

"Can I ask you a question?" Maggie asks.

"Sure."

"Is what we're about to do the only reason you took the hundred million from the NSA?"

"How's the NSA doing?"

Maggie updates me on the government's use of aliases. They're secretive about it, but they appear satisfied with her design. They only reported a few glitches during beta and only asked for a few enhancements: more resolution, more redundancy, a better failsafe algorithm. During my exile, we shipped ten thousand pairs of CSpectacles and ten thousand CHalos to an unmarked, top-security NSA location in Virginia. Because we have the ability to track location of our products, we know these devices didn't stay in Virginia for long and were deployed all over the world. During my absence, Olivia spent no time on the project, told Maggie that it was her gig, and encouraged her to build whatever was needed as long as she stayed within budget.

"Yeah, that's the only reason I took the money," I say.

"After today, we could shut the program down."

"We could, but what's done is done."

Maggie readies the room. She plays with her computer to load the alias and checks the hardware connections to make sure everything is functioning. It's true that I was willing to take the money, to let the NSA do something with our technology I didn't believe in, all for the sake of what we're about to do. We might be able to undo the deal after today, but given the times we live in, alienating the US government is not in CW's best interest. Ethically, the cost was high, but I had to do it.

"Are you sure you want to do this?" Maggie asks.

"You used the audio and video recordings I sent you?"

"Yes, and the photos."

"Then yes."

"I won't know what to say."

"It's okay. Say whatever comes to mind."

We take our spots. Before we slip on our glasses, I nod at Maggie. She nods back with this look—a combination of How-can-I-measure-up and I'm-going-to-wow-you—that reminds me of when I first met her. Glasses on, I rub my palms on the arms of my chair, take a deep breath, and power up my CHalo. A moment later, I materialize in the conversation room.

Sitting across from me is an older teenage version of Zack, about the age he would have been if he had lived. He's wearing jeans, a CW pyramid T-shirt, and sneakers. He's taller, I bet more than six feet. His hair touches his shoulders, and he's experimenting not all that successfully with growing a beard. He has this glow around him, like he knows whatever place he's now in is his playground. I can't take my eyes off him. It smells like the kitchen in our old house.

I start to sob, wail really, and tremble from a wave of cold. How did Maggie? During many of our imaginary conversations these last years, Zack was ten and didn't have the same glow. How did she age him so realistically? As I slowly pull myself together, Zack sits with me, doesn't say a word, and has this kind, compassionate look on his face, as though somewhere along the way he learned the value of being a witness.

"I miss you so much," I say.

"Me too, Dad."

"I built this all for you."

"Tell me everything, Dad."

His voice is deeper, though the way he elongates *Daaad* is the same. His eyes have a maturity, like he knows he can do anything he wants to do. My father passed that gift to me early on; I didn't know I'd passed it to Zack as well. I catch him up on CW, on leaving RR, on my closest friends, on his mom and me, on Willow. As I'm speaking, the shakiness and cold gradually subside. Zack is listening to every word, laughing at parts, and nodding his head in disbelief about his godmother Olivia. He's sad that his mom and me rarely speak, and he's hard to read about Willow.

When I finish, he says, "You love Willow, Dad, as much as you love me."

"I do."

"And you helped so many with CW."

"I'd give it all up to get you back."

"I wouldn't want you to."

That catches me. After Zack died, while I was still at RR, I often played the *What if?* game in my head, a game whose sole goal was to set up the exact conditions in which the universe would allow me to undo the undoable. I always conditioned the same way, without an ounce of doubt. If I had the choice, I would have given up RR, given up my possessions, given up anything to see him again. Wouldn't any father do the same for their son?

"Why not, Zack?"

"Because we had our time together, Dad. The life I lived was exactly the life I was meant to live. And the life you've lived so far was exactly the one you were meant to live. Look at all that you've done since I left. I'm proud of you."

"I bought a big red boat."

"Awesome. Do you go skiing?"

"A little."

"I like skiing."

"I know."

I tell Zack the cool details of the boat, which I've memorized from the spec sheet. The cabin has Brazilwood cabinetry and a 12000 BTU HVAC system. The canvas has a bimini top. The cockpit has a built-in blender, an ice-maker, and a refrigerator. The engine system consists of a five KW generator with a sound shield and a Mercruiser DTS standard engine. The entertainment system controls a DVD player, satellite radio, and two flat screen TVs. The helm has a chartplotter Raymarine C-95, a compass, a digital depth gauge, and a VHF radio with antenna. Zack listens the whole time with great interest, like he's developed that same love of technical detail that I found around his age.

When we're done with the boat, we switch gears and talk about New England sports, spending an equal amount of time on the Patriots, the Red Sox, the Bruins, the Celtics, and the Revolution. I do most of the talking. He's incredibly happy that Brady won his fourth Super Bowl and beams when I tell him about the Red Sox's latest championship. Although he isn't much of a hockey fan, he's glad the Bruins have had their moment. On the Celtics, he agrees with me that they're still a few years away. When we get to the Revolution, he's disappointed, but not surprised, that they continue to live in almost-land.

We go quiet. I'm happy just to be with him and to watch him as he sits across from me. He's breathing slowly now, hardly blinking, and the corners of his lips are barely turned upward. Occasionally, he looks away, sometimes at the floor and sometimes at the ceiling, or he closes his eyes while touching his temple, as if he too is overwhelmed. When Zack was a baby, I came home for lunch one day. From the floor in the corner of his bedroom, as I ate a ham and cheese sandwich, I watched him try to reach up and touch the blue and gray cars on his mobile. He was so full of wonder, of innocence, that this wave of joy washed over me. I remember thinking that if I never experienced another moment like that in my life, that my life would have still been complete. And then, for the next decade, even with all of my mistakes, I experienced so many moments, each one a small, yet infinite miracle. Now, in the middle of another one, I don't want it to end.

"I'm so sorry I didn't pick you up that day," I say.

"It wasn't your fault, Dad. It was an accident."

"I was always so proud of you, Zack. I didn't say that enough when you were here."

"I know you were, Dad. You didn't have to say it."

"Still, I wish I did."

"You are now," he says.

I look away from my technologically recreated, much-more-than-hologram, deep son. I'm so thankful we had this time together, so thankful I could see him and hear his voice, so thankful that I could say what I needed to say. But this will be the last time. After today, we will have no more conversations. After today, he won't appear to me. After today, I'll finally have reached the good-bye return.

The tears come again, this time to both of us. Zack sits on the edge of his chair and reaches his hand out until it's within grasp. I reach out and take it. It's strong and firm, a technological marvel that only Maggie could have pulled off. We hang on like that for a time, eyes locked, full of love and loss, joy and sadness, pride and regret, holding hands not like when he was a little boy, but like two men whose time together has come to an end.

Then I let go.

In the Coming

I stayed at CW for five more years. Pretty much all of the stretch goals we put in place materialized. We continued to grow at a good clip. The conversations and champions paid off tenfold. The culture we built was widely admired and copied. When I left midway through my contract, though many didn't understand my rationale, I did so on my terms. My CW work had come to an end, and the lake was calling me.

At that time, we had more than two billion users, a market cap of three hundred billion, and champions focused on more than a thousand critical issues from aboriginal rights to nuclear proliferation. Furthermore, we had spawned hundreds of millions of meaningful conversations, many of which started movements. Despite all of the naysayers about our subscription service at the start, giving people the opportunity to make real change resulted in them valuing CW like a utility: heat, electricity, Internet, phone, ConversationWorks. During my second tenure, a number of copycat companies surfaced, some new and some retooled, but our customers remained loyal. When I left, I was worth, well, billions and billions.

Zia is the new CW CEO. I strongly recommended her to the board, and they unanimously voted her in. After the announcement, we went on a worldwide tour together to sell it to the media and consumers. My points: we've worked together from the start, Zia's my hand-chosen successor, and she's uniquely qualified. Zia's points: our strategy is in place for the next five years, we expect the transition to be seamless, and Dan will be available to me for advice as needed. Zia, Maggie, and Charles struggled a bit for the top spot, but in the end Maggie and Charles supported Zia, and she did a stellar job of assuring them that the three of them would make all major decisions together. That, and the fact that if the company stays on course in the coming years, they'll all become billionaires, sealed the deal. Since I left, we see each other often.

I kept the same house on Winnipesaukee and moved back. A short time ago, for privacy reasons, I purchased the houses next to mine, knocked them down to create a buffer, and added an elaborate security system to my home. Before that, all kinds of folks were popping in and asking for one thing or another, which I often accommodated. Donate to this charity. Make a connection for an inventor. Join the board of a start-up. But on occasion, it was impossible to help. Once, I had a French Canadian woman make the six-hour drive from Montreal. When she arrived, she promptly asked me to marry her. Though I tend to like strong women who approach me and say what they want, though she was intelligent, kind, and pretty, after we chatted over a cup of coffee, I gently let her know she wasn't the right one for me and sent her on her way. Another time, I had this guy come to the house looking for funding for his robotics start-up. He claimed he'd developed an artificial brain that would allow him to make cognizant robots. He was enthusiastic, eccentric, maybe brilliant, but when I offered to refer him to Jason, he demanded I make the investment myself and said he was going to camp out on my property until I came around. I had to have the police remove him.

These last months I've settled into a new routine. I coach a boys under-12 soccer team. I don't know enough yet to coach the A-team, but the local soccer association was happy to let me coach the C-team. I hold practice twice a week, right after school. At first, some of the soccer moms and dads pushed to talk about CW, but I politely shut them down. "This is about your son and the team. My focus now is soccer." I must have said it countless times. In my practices, I'm big on individual ball skills: dribbling, juggling, passing, receiving, heading. I'm also big on teaming, on helping the kids learn what it means to work together toward a common goal.

And I got another rescue, a puppy named Ronaldo. Ronaldo is a Portuguese Water Dog with a big black mop of hair that makes it hard to see his eyes and a black coat except for his paws, chest, and snout, which are white. Sometimes Messi and Ronaldo fight about who's the true Alpha male, but the bout doesn't last long. Unlike us humans, age wins out with dogs.

I've also taken to rock sculpting in my yard. On age-old stonewalls all around the property, I search for the perfect stones. I still do pyramids, but I've broadened to eggs, squares, and, well, whatevers. When I finish a piece, I let it stand for a day or two before knocking it down. The walls are almost gone now, replaced by mounds of stones all over my ten acres. A few days ago I started two new works, one that turned out to be an igloo large enough to house Messi, Ronaldo, or a small boy and the other a sawed-off tree trunk with an egg-shaped vase on top. They're some of my best.

For an instant, I also tried my hand at poetry. I was beyond awful—terrible rhymes, bland images, no depth. For Willow, poetry was an effortless gift, one that came from a sacred place; for me, poetry was like that aborted season of Pop Warner football, at the end of which I quit and knew it was for the best. A couple of weeks ago, I went back and read many of Willow's poems. "Loss Dances." "Garden of Return." "Faint Beacons." They're all beautiful—

accomplished and emotional—but one I'd forgotten about called "The Lake" got to me: *Let's go down to the big maple by the lake. Carve our names deeply into its bark so we'll never forget this feeling of lost then found.* I had it framed and hung it on the wall over my desk.

Although I'm not an artist like Willow, I did set up this high school in Boston for young poets, artists, musicians, writers, dancers, philosophers, scientists, mathematicians, and spirit seekers. I guess it's a cross between Berklee College of Music, MIT, and a Zen center, but for teenagers. My people wanted me to name it the Underlight School for the Arts, but I vetoed them. The School for an Enlightened Time works better for me, though its name draws its fair share of criticism from people who are, well, where they are. The criticism hasn't deterred my belief that we truly are at the start of a new era—not one based on an industrial, computer, or Internet revolution—but one based on a revolution of heart where those who have studied how to live in kinder and more compassionate ways will guide us forward. For SET, I hired the best teachers I could find, paid them the way teachers all over this country should be paid, and made tuition free. Currently, one thousand students are enrolled from all over the world.

Sometimes I go on the SET website and review student pieces—a poem, a song, a story, a choreographed dance, a science experiment, a theorem proof, a proposal for connecting more people. Seeing young people committed to restoring balance is hopeful, and what's more heartening is that they're committed even though they know it will take generations. Once in a while, I commit to memory a piece a student sends me. This girl who recently graduated, Nadia, wrote a poem for her senior project called "In the Coming."

In sun-soaked morning release the thought-thickets,
the pull people, the tender weapons,

all telling you to come back, as if that truly was a choice,
as if another rubicon hadn't already been crossed.

In translucent fields step with sure-abandon
into uncertain-new and give thanks
that you leapt away
from the zealots
of continue.

In the coming
translucent will color in
with red, blue, orange, and green
and Kadupul flowers will grow abundant.
Resist the urge to let them wither
or the urge to let love
lodge in the past.

In the coming
there will be times
of great doubt, of great falls;
go into them until songs
of reflection and release
guide you forward.

Mostly in the coming
may you see your dreams
through a lucid lens
whose clarity comes from the
mystics and the stuff of rubicons.

I love that poem. Today, Nadia is coming to visit me. She's off to
Columbia in the fall on a full Underlight scholarship. She requested

this meeting, said it was urgent, and said she would drive to the lake anytime it was convenient. During my prep briefing from the SET headmaster, he told me when Nadia was a little girl she witnessed her father brutally murder her mother and then shoot himself in the head. After that, Nadia was in and out of foster homes for years. She went through foster-parent abuse, drugs, sex to cope, and severe depression. For a time, she was convinced she'd die early at her own hand. Then one day she read the Audre Lorde poem "For Each of You," and it deeply moved her. Right then and there she swore she'd become a poet. She was fourteen and since then has written more than a hundred poems. The headmaster didn't know why she wanted to see me. He offered to send me a picture, but I said no thanks, and instead asked for a handful of Nadia's poems and a copy of "For Each of You."

Promptly at noon, Nadia pulls into my driveway in a convertible Volkswagen Beetle with a Zipcar logo on the door. When she gets out, the first thing I notice is her multicolored dreadlocks that are directed off her forehead by a narrow red headband and reach down to her waist. An elaborate purple hoodie with a sun and moon embroidered in red on each side of the front and arms made from orange, red, green, and brown horizontal bands embroidered with different Sanskrit symbols partially covers a red blouse. The blouse is adorned by what must be at least ten gold, silver, and leather necklaces, one with a wooden peace symbol dangling from it. Nadia smiles, walks right up to me, and extends her hand.

"Mr. Underlight, thank you so much for taking the time to meet with me."

"Call me Dan. Would you like to come in for a cup of coffee?"

"I'm a tea drinker, but I don't want to take up much of your time. I just thought it was best to do this in person."

"We can talk on the deck then. You'll like the view."

"Cool. If you don't mind me asking, what's that off in the woods?"

"I sculpt rocks a bit."

"Really? That's cool, too. Would it be okay if I took a closer look?"

We walk into the woods where I show Nadia one of my latest creations. We spend some time discussing the benefits of temporal art, which even though she's never considered it before seems like a valid artistic choice to her. She's drawn to *Tree Stump with Vase*, which she circles multiple times. As she's taking in the piece from every possible angle, I tell her I've read a number of her poems, that I love "In the Coming," and that I'm glad she'll be continuing her studies at Columbia. As we start to talk about Columbia, Nadia notices something off in the corner of the property and says she'll be right back. As she walks away, I can't shake this feeling of familiarity I have toward her, like I've always known her, like I could love her. How is that even possible? There must be something we're meant to do together. But what? A moment later, she returns with two freshly picked amaranth flowers and places them in the vase.

"The reason I'm here, Mr. Underlight, is that I've decided to withdraw from Columbia, so I can't make use of your generous scholarship."

"Oh. How come?"

"Because what I'm going for now isn't something that can be taught, it has to be felt. Thanks to you and SET, I have enough skill now to write what I feel. What I don't have is enough experience."

"You wouldn't get experience at school?"

"I'd get some, but not the kind I'm after."

"I see."

Nadia and I drift toward the igloo, talking about how thankful she is for her experience at SET and that in some fundamental way it changed her to the point where she now knows what she must do. A few times, in a few ways, she says she doesn't want her decision in any way to be misconstrued as lack of gratitude both for SET and the scholarship. When we arrive at the igloo, she gets down on her hands and knees and crawls in. Inside, she uses her phone light to check out the interior wall, which she judges as even more beautiful than the outside one, especially the paintings on the back wall of abstract geometrical figures. A moment later she crawls back out.

"What will you do instead of college?" I ask.

"I'm going to travel. Do you know about pilgrimages?"

"A little."

"I'm sorta going on one of those."

"To where?"

"India. Europe. Japan. Australia. I'll backpack as many countries as I can until my summer job money runs out."

Nadia notices the other rock mounds randomly placed around the property and asks me to describe some of my previous work. There must be thirty of them, so I focus on only a few: a cube with a window in the middle, a pyramid with a three-foot-high pole at the top, pillars in a Stonehenge-like pattern. She likes the idea that my pieces are repeatedly rising up into something new, only to fall back into mounds a short time later.

"And you'll travel alone?" I ask.

"Yes, though there is a boy. He's an artist, too. He wants to come, but I told him these things are best done alone."

"That's wise."

"He loves this version of me, but he doesn't love all the possible mes yet."

"That's also wise."

"Death. Drugs. Sex. Abuse. Almost offing myself. That's the stuff of wise."

"Yes, it is."

Nadia openly talks about many of the details I've already heard from the headmaster. As she's speaking, a level of vulnerability that's rare for anyone, never mind an eighteen-year-old, shines through. Where does that come from? Maybe one of the unforeseen benefits of SET is we're teaching our students to be vulnerable. Wouldn't that be something? Or maybe it's just Nadia.

"I'm glad you made it through," I say.

"Me, too."

"I have an idea if you're up for it. Would you like to sculpt something with me?"

"Sure, but I'm not skilled."

"It's not hard. I'll show you."

We gather rocks. Rather than selecting stones with a particular idea in mind, we let the rocks select us, and during the next two hours we collect maybe two hundred of them in all different shapes and sizes and pile them in a twenty-foot-wide circle in a clearing midproperty. In the center of the circle, we begin. I place a stone; Nadia places one. I've never worked like this before, with someone else and without a blueprint in my head. I don't know where we're going or what will emerge. It's almost as if I've surrendered to something bigger, something that will guide us. In no time, we've built a square base.

"This is like Legos for adults," Nadia says.

"Where every piece is unique."

"It's also like a poem. You don't know what you have until the end."

We build up from the base. Sometimes one of us places a rock that a few stones later needs to be redone. It's like that with this kind of sculpture. The trial and error is what eventually allows the work to come to life. About midway up on what's now on its way to becoming a pyramid, we abandon the traditional design and, instead of making each layer smaller on the way to an apex, we hold each layer at the same width, until we've built a cube-shaped on top of the pyramid's foundation.

"Let's go wider now," I say.

"It will collapse."

"We'll be fine. The rocks will show us the way."

We build out, wedging rocks so each layer extends out into space a few inches more than the previous layer. A few close calls occur during the build-out where the interlocking between certain rocks gives way, and at one point, the entire upper portion of the structure almost topples. When we're done, the work looks like the bottom half of an upside down pyramid resting on top of a cube that is resting on top of the bottom half of a pyramid.

"It's almost done," Nadia says.

"What else?"

"It looks like an empty altar."

On two of the four corners of the altar, we build small urns, big enough to hold more flowers or a small toy. When we're done, Nadia takes off one of her necklaces, a gold one with a gold seahorse, and places it in the urn. Her face holds opposites as she does this, as though she can't and must let go of the necklace. But she levies the emotion back. Part of me wants to ask her about the necklace, but I don't. All I need to know is that it's important to her.

Since Willow died, I've worn two of her Rosewood Mala Bead bracelets on my hand. She loved those bracelets, had received them as a gift many years earlier when in Japan, and wore them for all the years I knew her. I take off one of the bracelets and put it in the other urn. Then Nadia reaches out and takes my hand. We stand there in communion with the land, the rocks, all our loved ones, and each other. This is what we were meant to do together. We are fellow travelers, and this is a guidepost, a not-so-faint beacon.

After a time, I glance over at Nadia, who's barely mouthing something. She notices, smiles, and then starts up again, this time audible. "Today, we give these objects that hold old love, so we may love wider tomorrow." Nadia repeats this chant over and over, and eventually, I join in. These acts—creating a work together in harmony, telling our stories openly, giving up objects we cherish, aspiring to a wider love—are what we all strive for in a good life, and at the same time, what we all fear.

When we're done chanting, Nadia turns toward me and says, "Thank you for this. I'm glad I made the drive and got to meet you."

"Me, too. You're an amazing young woman."

"Thanks."

"I've been thinking more about why you came. I want you to have the scholarship."

"That wouldn't be right, Mr. Underlight. Other students desperately could use that money."

"That's true, but the scholarship is too narrow as written. What you're planning to do is in every important way equivalent to a college education and will give you what you need to do your work. I'm going to change the scope so that more SET students like you can take advantage of alternatives to college."

Nadia smiles and ponders my offer. Maybe what the world needs is not only champions of issues, like CW is doing, but also champions of people? It will take decades, if not a century, to reel in the new era. Between now and then, yes, we need millions of additional conversations, but we also need a new breed of leaders like her. That's why I did SET in the first place. But now, maybe I can go one step further and focus on a few individuals I want to help? Maybe that's something else Nadia and I are meant to do together?

"I have three questions, Mr. Underlight. First, why would you do this? Second, are there strings attached?"

"All you have to do is see the world and write poems about what you experience. I'm doing it because I believe in you. There are no strings. What's your third question?"

"What's your story? If I'm going to accept your offer, I want to start today, start with our sculpture, and start with you."

"That's not necessary."

"I know, but it's what I want to do."

"It's a long story."

"I have time."

"All right, then. It's best told over tea and coffee from a rocking chair on the deck, preferably with Italian pastries."

A short time later, we're sitting on my deck, sipping espresso and Darjeeling tea. Messi and Ronaldo are lying at our feet, looking out at the water. The breeze off the lake is gentle and somehow filled with hints of honeysuckle. At this time of day, the sky, water, and land appear to merge off in the distance. In that spot, words lose their meaning. We name all of these different things and focus on differentiation in business, on individual achievement, on the best this or that in almost every aspect of life. Yet what's underneath the labels, the achievements, the differentiation, is the same stuff as in the spot. That's where I focus as I begin my story.

I tell Nadia everything. Mom. Dad. Hannah. Olivia. RR. CW. Scotch. Nessa. Arrowheading. I especially go into the details about Zack, before and after his death, and about Willow, about the different ways we were together and not together. I don't sugarcoat. I don't revise. Instead, I walk through the whole story, scene by scene, slowly, with joy and sadness for sure, but without anger or fear. Along the way, Nadia mostly listens, occasionally probes a little deeper, and gets up a few times to refill her tea and my coffee. When I'm done, as Nadia holds the story close in a silence only broken by the lake breeze, an openness comes to me, like I've entered the spot, like I am the spot.

"Thank you for telling me."

"Fertile material for a poem or two?"

"Maybe a whole book."

We laugh, loud enough for the dogs to get up, wag their tails, and look at the biscuit jar resting on the table. Nadia asks if she can feed them, and I agree.

"Do you know what a phoropter is?" I ask.

"No."

"I didn't know either until a couple of years ago when I got my reading glasses. It's that mechanical device used when you go to the eye doctor to figure out the prescription for your glasses. It has all these different lenses in it that the doctor adjusts while you're reading an eye chart. He keeps swapping in and out different lens until you can see clearly."

"Oh right. I didn't know what it was called."

"For these different parts of my life, an internal phoropter focused me. The thing is, early on, the phoropter worked narrowly, and I could only see the RR part clearly. Marriage, family, and friendships were blurry at best. When my marriage ended, I focused even more on work. When Zack died, I did the same and added scotch. When I lost the only thing I could see, RR, I was convinced for a time that I was blind. Then with Willow's help, with Nessa's help, and with my close friends' help, not only did I regain my sight, but also something wider came into view. That's when CW took off.

"But it turned out my new wide angle lens was a trickster. Sure, I focused on building a great new company, one that in many ways was a leap forward. But at the same time, I focused on scotch, sex, and self-mutilation. So even though I'd achieved a wider kind of clarity, it was one where ascension and fall were inextricably linked in my mind.

"When Willow was murdered, as horrible as it was, one positive surfaced for me; for the first time, I saw my whole life clearly. And for the first time, I had the strength to shed the pieces I no longer wished to carry forward. I stood my ground and grieved openly. I didn't drink more. I didn't hurt myself more. I didn't return to Katie. And most importantly, I did realize all of my experiences, even the most painful ones, were gifts. Not only that but they had happened exactly as intended. The facts that I divorced, that Zack died, that I lost my dream job twice, that I was capable of beating a man to death, that I sabotaged love, that I drank too much scotch, that I lived duplicitously with a prostitute, that I cut myself, and that Willow died were all teachers. When I had learned their lessons, when I no longer associated a charge with them, when their pull had stopped, I let them go.

"So why am I telling you all this? I guess it's to say that for many folks, wide clarity never comes. Their internal phoropter remains fixed and narrowly focused, and they never see the places that can teach them the most. For you, my one hope is that you see it all, Nadia, especially the stuff that instinctively makes you want to veer away. The road you've chosen will have a lot of twists and turns ahead. Remember that the detours, in particular the ones that take you far off a well-lit path, often are your best teachers."

"Thank you. I will. Do you think you're done with twists and turns now?"

"I don't know for sure. Probably not. But I do know I've been clear about my life ever since I went back to CW, that it's never lasted this long before, and that I'm happy."

"But don't you need love? Don't you need to find someone after Willow?"

"I have plenty of love in my life, but it's not that kind anymore. It's not that I wouldn't welcome it if it came again. I'm just not looking for it. When I think about love now, it's in a wider way, more spread out, like our chant from earlier. I have close friends who I love—Zia, Maggie, Charles—but also a much wider community that I love, for example, the team at SET. vThere's even love here today, don't you think?"

"Yeah . . . things sure didn't go as expected today," she says.

"How so?"

"I figured I'd be in and out of here in five minutes."

"Ah. I had a feeling it would go longer."

"Because of the poems you read?"

"And your story."

"I guess I'll accept the scholarship, Mr. Underlight. Would it be okay if I wrote you on occasion or maybe even called you?"

"Of course."

"It's not too much of a burden?"

"Not at all," I say.

We talk for a little longer before the conversation runs its course. Part of me doesn't want the day to end, but it's time. Messi, Ronaldo, and I walk Nadia to her Zipcar. At the car, she gets down on one knee and gives Messi and Ronaldo big hugs. Before she opens her door, she gives me a hug too and kisses me on each cheek.

"Thank you for everything, Dan."

"Thank you, too. Travel safe."

As I watch her head out of the driveway, out of the corner of my eye I sense some movement by the altar. I turn that way, but no one is there. Willow would have loved Nadia, not just because Nadia is a poet, a pilgrim, and a spirit seeker, but also because she has in her endless songs of possibility. She's going to be something to watch. Willow would have also loved that, after all of these years, after RR, after CW, after Zack, after her, that I'm finally living a simple life.

Acknowledgments

Many friends and family have contributed insight and energy to the making of this book. To my family and first readers, Maribeth Marcello and Matt Marcello, I am deeply indebted. Your regular feedback over the last two years on every aspect of the book—characters, story, book covers, even individual sentences—made all the difference. I love you both.

For their close reading and expert knowledge, huge thanks to authors Mark Spencer, Jessamyn Hope, Rebecca Givens Rolland, Deborah Good, Robert Fernandes, Christine Giraud, Mark Guerin, Winona Winker, and Hollis Shore. You are all gifted writers, and I feel blessed and honored to have worked with each of you on this novel.

For their thoughtful and sincere guidance on an early draft, thanks to Scott Flegal, Tara Levesque-Vogel, Brian Young, Lara Chulack, Myron Rogers, Carl Dubberly, and Mary Ellen Fortier. In different ways, you all helped shape the narrative, and the novel is better as a result.

For her expert knowledge on domestic violence, huge thanks to Dawn Reams. I'm in awe of the work you do each day, and I'm thankful to have captured a small piece of it on these pages.

For her expert knowledge as a therapist, and for being such a great champion of mine for many years, I'm grateful to Amy

Johnson. Without her, this book wouldn't have been realized. I'm especially thankful for her expert knowledge of pipe cleaners, Dove chocolates, chakra mists, and Buddha boards.

To my brilliant daily editor and life-long friend, Donna Anctil, I bow down.